T0039207

UPSHUR'S WAY

OTIS MORPHEW

Order this book online at www.trafford.com
or email orders@trafford.com

Most Trafford titles are also available at major online book retailers.

© Copyright 2014 Otis Morphew.
All rights reserved. No part of this publication may be reproduced, stored in a retrieval
system, or transmitted, in any form or by any means, electronic, mechanical, photocopying,
recording, or otherwise, without the written prior permission of the author.

Printed in the United States of America.

ISBN: 978-1-4907-2315-0 (sc)
ISBN: 978-1-4907-2313-6 (e)

Because of the dynamic nature of the Internet, any web addresses or links contained in
this book may have changed since publication and may no longer be valid. The views
expressed in this work are solely those of the author and do not necessarily reflect the
views of the publisher, and the publisher hereby disclaims any responsibility for them.

Any people depicted in stock imagery provided by Thinkstock are models,
and such images are being used for illustrative purposes only.
Certain stock imagery © Thinkstock.

Trafford rev.   01/07/2014

 www.trafford.com

North America & international
toll-free: 1 888 232 4444 (USA & Canada)
fax: 812 355 4082

PROLOGUE

The mind of a gunfighter was a complicated mind. One that, given time, would have been the project for some future scientist to unravel. But in that era of our history, would only leave questions in the minds of our learned. While those who knew of them, or saw them at their worst, and were afraid of them would only wonder at what might have made them that way? . . . Or what happened that drove them to fight and kill other men with no malice of forethought?

Was it a tragedy in their childhood? A mistake by a fun-loving youth, or an unfortunate accident that led them to that way of life? . . . . Possible, but it could have been that they just had a flare for gun-fighting that made them want to be better than all the rest. The better the reputation. The better! . . . . It was a mystery then, and still is!

William Otis Upshur, however, was very different than any of those, past, present, or future. No doubt he had a natural talent for using his side-arm, but what made him the very best that he was came in the form of a rifle-butt, used in a blow to his forehead at the age of ten, a blow that altered his brain's motor skills, thus giving him a reaction time unlike any other. Had he not been the man that he was, those exceptional skills could have led to a disaster, and a much larger tragedy!

Upshur had a way about him that made some men dislike him, others that wanted to fight him on sight, and even more that respected him! He believed in fair play, and justice for the weak, a man who placed nothing above his love of family and friends. His wife and children were his excuse for living and to wrong them, or his friends, wronged him, . . . and those were wrongs to be set right.

The mind of William Upshur was far different than others in that way of life, evident in the things he does, and the way he does them, . . . and can only be categorized as. "Upshur's Way". The story of Upshur, though

vii

somewhat typical for the times, but totally different because of who he was, and what he became. That story was told in "They called him, Reb, The story of Upshur", A story that was woven around actual events of our past, actual towns in existence then, some of the actual people that were there at the time, . . . and through it all rode William Upshur, on his way to becoming what he is now. If published, this will be number six in my Upshur series and I don't know if there will be a seventh!

This is Upshur's way.

CHAPTER ONE

The spring of 1880 was a stormy one! Heavy rains, hail and a dangerous outbreak of twisters had taken its toll. The Red River had filled to above capacity at least once, and in low-lying areas had flooded farmlands and ranchlands on both sides, . . . rushing inland for a mile in remote places. Loss of life was moderately low due to frantic evacuation of those in proximity of the river. The greatest loss, however, was in livestock, heartbreakingly evident once the water receded. Northern Texas, and the whole of Indian Territory, was left with something not unlike that of a hog-wallow. Nothing could move in the knee-deep muck and mire.

In Texas, rebuilding efforts in the burned-out city of Paris had been at a standstill for weeks. Laborers from surrounding communities such as Cooper, Clarksville, Honey Grove and even a few from as far away as Greenville, had returned home to their families with a promise to return when the weather changed. Many old-timers in the county had predicted the weather pattern for months, but most had paid little attention to them, thinking it only a way for old men to feel needed. However, those same old men were also warning them of the coming winter, that they say would be akin to that of '69 and still, no one was listening, . . . There was just too many immediate problems to think about, the weather being just another part of everyday life.

It had now been two years since the great Paris fire, and almost three months since Upshur, Rodney Taylor and their families had been home for a visit. But until everything dried out again, not even a lone horse and rider could gain much ground on the roads, . . . Let alone a loaded wagon! They had managed to extract another three hundred pounds of gold from the mine before it started to rain, but until the roads dried up, they were all stuck at the mountain.

Even Peter Birdsong, and his force of Light-horsemen had been forced to restrain themselves from their duties, but had made themselves useful by repairing the rain-soaked, and storm damaged thatching atop the buildings, . . . Doing what they could until it became dry enough again to cut the tall prairie grass from the prairie. They had an abundance of mud for the job, but were not able to trek the several hundred yards for the grass.

The small valley in front of the trading post, and Marshal's office, even now, was still standing in almost three feet of water, and the road coming in had almost been obliterated. Fallen trees and branches, toppled by high winds, had covered the landscape, . . . And would take considerable time and work to put things back the way it was. The almost ancient, towering pine trees that surrounded the buildings had given up clumps of needles, cones and smaller branches, and now lay scattered over the entire area of the trading post and living quarters. But still, the mountain loomed as dark and foreboding as ever, and those giant pines and Mountain Fir still obscured the mountains base for miles around, . . . And reaching not even a quarter of the way to the mysterious crest of the large rock.

The great hand-built log wall still protected the bat cave entrance to the lush valley inside, and except for the thatched roofs on the buildings, the very well built dwellings were no worse for wear. Although they were all built on an almost constant down-slope beneath the mountain, their Choctaw builders had used insight and ingenuity to prevent the driving storms from dislodging them their foundations and sliding into the valley's rushing waters below. This was accomplished by driving logs deep into the ground to rest on solid rock, leaving exposed upper portions of them to use as building blocks for their foundations, . . . And as a way to level the buildings. Even the barn and corral was built in this manner. The dozen horses, and as many cows were as yet still in refuge inside the large barn, unable to yet retain their footing in the deep mud and slush.

Upshur, and the rest of them were all still taking their meals in the dining room of the trading post, except for the several days of the storm's most violence, and were forced to stay inside! But the rains had stopped at last, except for the light sprinkling of mist and drizzle, and the low-hanging clouds that still blocked out the sun's healing rays.

During the last part of the winter months, the Choctaw carpenters had been called back to build more split-log steps up to the corral and barn and because of this, Billy, and Willy had been able to feed the animals and milk the cows during the siege. There had been no business, or travel, so the store had been closed off to all but the four Choctaw police and Peter Birdsong, who still slept in the large Marshal's office and jail adjoining it, . . . all was almost as it was at Upshur's Mountain.

CHAPTER TWO

They had worked all morning cleaning the dregs of dripping mud and water from the store's large floor, where the damaged roof had leaked. Connie and lisa finished removing the canvas coverings from the several shelves of foodstuffs and folded them, and as they carried the bundles into the storeroom, Billy wrung out the mop and grunted as he carried the tub of muddy water out onto the porch and dumped it before leaning against a post to scan the flooded areas of land between them and the prairie, three quarters of a mile to the West.

Rodney finished sweeping the long porch and leaned the straw broom against a wall, then sighed and came to stand beside him. "What ya lookin' at?"

"Just lookin'."

"All we need now, is a good freeze!" He grinned, looking down at the deep furrows made by receding waters on the sloping ground. "Put th' icing on th' cake, so to speak!"

"That, it would!" Nodded Billy, and reached to push the eyeglasses up on his nose. "Don't rush it, though, Rod, we could have a hard Winter this year, . . . remember th' Spring a sixty-nine?"

"I remember! . . . That Winter, too!" He reached a thin cigar from his shirt and held it up. "Smoke, Billy?"

Billy looked at it then shook his head. "Can't handle them things anymore, not since th' fire. Still got th' stench in my nose."

"I noticed that." He lit the smoke and flipped the match into the mud. "Been a hell of a month, ain't it? . . . Never seen it like this before . . . . You think it's over with?"

"Worst part is . . . . A few more showers, maybe. Had plans to get that corn planted this week, too! Might be a late crop."

"Can't fight Mama Nature!" Sighed Rodney. "You in th' mood for coffee?"

"Always." He grinned and together, walked back into the store, and about that time was when he heard the voices coming from the Marshal's office, . . . stopping both of them when they recognized Angela's high-pitched voice and curious, walked toward the doorway.

"I'm gonna tell daddy, Willy!" She said as he tied the holstered gun pistol to his leg. "You're not supposed to do that!"

"It'll be all right, if you'll stop yelling, Angie, I'm just tryin' it on!" He looked up then to see Billy standing in the doorway, and the blood seemed to drain from his face. "You mad at me, Daddy?" He asked, sheepishly.

"He may not be, but I am, Young Man!" Snapped Connie as she pushed past Billy and Rodney to step down into the room . . . "You take that gun off, this instant!"

"But I'm just tryin' it on, Mama, I'm old enough!"

"No, you are not old enough, now take it off!"

He reluctantly reached down and untied the leather string. "Daddy wore a gun when he was fifteen, Mama."

She looked up at Billy's expressionless face then. "Aren't you going to say anything about this?"

"Hang it up, son." He said as he stepped down into the room, and was followed closely by Rodney and Melissa.

"Gosh." Said Willy and reluctantly hung the holstered weapon back on the rack. "I was just tryin' it on!"

"Sure you were!" She said angrily, and then took a deep breath in frustration. "Next thing I know, you'll be sneaking off with it somewhere to practice! . . . Well you are not fifteen yet, Young Man, and furthermore, I don't want you to ever wear a gun!" She breathed again before looking at Billy, and then at the silent faces of Rodney, and Melissa before looking back at her son.

"Your father went to war!" She said, a little more calmly. "He was forced to wear a gun! . . . There's no war now, honey!" She sniffed then reached to pull him to her in a hug. "I love you, sweetheart, . . . it scares me to death to think of you with a gun! . . . Now promise me you won't do this again, okay?"

Lisa came to where Cindy and Christopher was sitting silently against the wall watching, and quickly ushered them, and Angela back into the trading post.

"Your mother's right, son." Said Billy, moving across to the desk and turning the chair around. "Sit down a minute, let's talk about it." Once Willy had sat down, he motioned Connie to the desk chair.

"Now!" He sighed as he sat down on a corner of the desk to look at him. "Is this th' first time you done this, son?"

Willy shook his head. "No, sir, . . . once or twice, is all." He stared down at his lap as he spoke. "It don't mean nothin'."

"Anything, William!" Scolded Connie quickly. "It doesn't mean anything!"

"Honey!" He looked at her then. "Ease up a little, okay?" He looked back at Willy then. "Why'd you do it, son?"

Willy shrugged again then looked up at him. "Because I'm almost a man, I guess, . . . and a man wears a gun!"

"You're right, most men do wear guns, but not all of 'em. Grandpa Bailey don't wear one, never did! Storekeepers don't wear 'em, neither . . . . A gun don't make a man, a man, son, remember that!"

"Your father had to wear a gun." Said Connie with a sigh. "If he had not, you, me, Uncle Rodney, none of us would be here now! He saved all our lives. So you see, there was a need for him to wear a gun, there still is. Your, Uncle Rodney, too! Uncle Peter, and the police all wear guns to protect all of us . . . . So, there's just no need what so ever for you to wear one!"

"Who else knows you been tryin' on this gun, son?" Asked Billy.

"Nobody, . . . I always waited 'till they was gone." He looked up at Billy then. "I unloaded it, Daddy!"

"I know, son! . . . How'd it make you feel?"

"Billy! . . . That is not the point!" She said quickly. "I do not want my son becoming a gunman."

"He won't become a gunman, honey, now relax!" He looked back at Willy then. "How'd it make you feel, son?"

He shrugged again. "Scared I was gonna get caught, I guess, . . . but I liked it!" He looked at his lap again. "Sure is heavy though."

Billy nodded and glanced up at Rodney before looking back. "That's right, son, it is heavy, and not only in weight . . . . You have to be responsible when you wear a gun, and that makes it even heavier! You have to know when to use it, and when not to . . . . A handgun is used for only one thing, and you know what that one thing is! It's just no good for anything else. Your mother's right, there'll be plenty a time for a handgun when you're older . . . . It takes a very long time to learn th' rights and wrongs of it, and that's somethin' you weren't born with! . . . Nobody is. When I think it's time, I'll teach you what I know, but right now, I think your rifle is all you need."

You're already pretty much a crack shot with it and come down to it, it's all you'll need if you have to protect th' family, and I depend on that when I'm away! . . . So, leave th' handguns to us for now, okay?"

"Okay, Daddy." He nodded. "I will."

"Good!" He said, getting up from the desk. "By th' way, you are old enough to help with all this clean-up." He looked down at Connie then. "Is that coffee still hot honey?"

"Of course!" She said, still somewhat angry with him. "Come on Junior." She said, getting up and pulling him to his feet. "I have a mop that will just fit your hands."

"Yes, Ma'am!" He replied dejectedly and followed her back up into the store.

"Don't blame, Will too much, Billy." Said Rodney, placing a hand on his shoulder.

"I don't blame him, Rod! . . . Right now, it's somethin' like this that makes me blame myself! . . . I try to explain things, and I don't know how? . . . All I wind up doin' is upsetin' Connie because I didn't say what she wanted to hear!!

"If it means anything, I think you said it all just fine! . . . He's your son, after all."

"That's my point, he's too much like me . . . . Hell, I loved my first gun, I loved bein' able to use it!" He sighed then. "I think he's too much like me."

"That ain't a bad thing, buddy. I've never known you to pick a fight! . . . Never even known you to pull a gun unless you had no choice at all . . . . And for that reason alone, I think he's more like you, in that respect, than you both think!"

"I hope so, Rod . . . . But I wish I'd never let 'im see me use one."

"Come on, man, you had no choice there, neither. Will's a good boy, he'll be an even better man, and don't forget, you got another one comin' up just like 'im!"

Billy looked at him and shook his head. "I can always count on you to make me feel better!"

"I do what I can, you know that!"

"Then let's go get that coffee."

"Amen to that!" They both laughed and went to climb the steps into the store just as Melissa came out of the dining room.

"Rodney, tell Peter and the boys to get ready for lunch in about fifteen minutes."

"Okay, baby." He shrugged at Billy. "You go ahead, I'll tell 'em, . . . they're on my roof."

*   *   *

Connie poured fresh coffee as the meal was finished, and sat back down. After the kids were done, they were sent off to study their lessons for the day.

"How's those roofs lookin', Peter?" Asked Billy, getting the tracker's attention . . . "Had some pretty good leaks at my place."

"Yes, my friend, it had many leaks. But we were very lucky, I think, . . . repair will be easy! We have replaced the missing mud, and saved much of the thatching. If it does not rain again for a week, the winds will dry the mud and we can add more with the fresh grass from the prairie . . . . All is good, my friend."

"Well, we're certainly thankful for all you are doing, Peter." Smiled Connie. "Don't know what we would do without you, and your men around."

"It is nothing, Missus, Upshur." Grinned Peter. "It is our home as well."

"I know, but still, . . ."

"Well, I'm thinkin' that come next spring, we won't have this problem!" Said Rodney as he reached for the mail-order catalog on the counter. "Because," He continued as he thumbed through the pages.

"Because we are going to replace all that mud and grass!" He passed the catalog across to Billy. "With that product right there."

"A tin roof?" Exclaimed Billy as he looked at it.

"Corrugated Tin." Returned Rodney. "It's replacing wood and thatch roofs all over the country. Says right there, it should last for twenty years before it's replaced. Guaranteed never to leak, either! . . . Unless we get trigger-happy and shoot holes in it. Won't blow off, neither, if it's installed right!"

Billy passed it to Peter as Rodney talked. "What do you think, Peter?"

"I think, yes." He nodded. "If it is as the book says?" He gave back to Rodney and shrugged. "But nothing is always as it seems, we will see."

"We sure will!" Nodded Rodney. "I'll order enough to do th' store first, . . . soon's as I can get to th' Fort again!"

"Don't ya think we ought a know a little more about it first?" Asked Billy. "Ask somebody that's used it?"

"Excuse us, my friends." Said Peter, scraping his chair back. "We must get back to work again." They all got up and filed silently back through the store, and out.

"I've never heard of a tin roof before." Commented Connie as she reached for the catalog to look at the lithographed pictures.

"That's because there ain't none in this part a th' country yet." Returned Rodney.

"Anything is better than what we have!" Said Melissa. "I'm sick to death of the leaks, and that awful mildew smell all the time."

"Amen to that!" Agreed Rodney. "My might run a little short on cash, though." He looked at Billy then. "Any plans on th' next Denver trip?"

"Be a couple a months before they'll take anymore, . . . said some bigwigs in Congress are pressin' 'em for th' source a their gold, have been for a while."

"Good thing they don't know!" Nodded Rodney thoughtfully.

"It ain't for th' lack a tryin', I think! Sighed Billy. "I believe somebody tried to tail us last time."

"Yeah, ya told me . . . . Thought anymore about it, who ya thought it was?"

"Not a clue." He drained his cup and put it down. "But they'll keep tryin', if we keep goin'!"

"You could take th' coach again, like th' first time. Or I could go with next time, in case a trouble."

"Takin' a coach might work, . . . once or twice, maybe . . . . But I think we're gonna have to find a new buyer. Sooner or later, they will follow us home! Odds are against us."

"Any ideas?"

"Shreveport!" Said Connie quickly. "There's a Federal Reserve Bank there, it's where Mister Bratcher cashes in the gold we give him."

"I know, honey." Nodded Billy. "Been thinkin' about that myself . . . . I think it might be our best bet, too."

"Then, that's what we'll do!" Nodded Rodney. "We can take th' train out a Paris, or th' stage? . . . Hell, we might all go, be a nice trip!"

"Not so nice, I think." Said Billy with a smile. "It's not a very nice place!"

"It'll be different, then!" Said Melissa. "Anyway, I'd like that, Mama would love to keep Cindy while we are gone, so would Daddy . . . . It's a wonderful idea."

"I guess it's settled then." Grinned Billy. "Okay, we'll try to go, in a month or so. We have to extract more gold first."

"That's no problem!" Grunted Rodney as he got up to grab the coffee pot again. "Right now, I'd just like to get back to work. I'm goin' a little stir-crazy just sittin' around."

"Don't worry, Rod, bad men can't get around in this stuff neither." He held his cup up for him to pour. "They'll wait on ya,"

"I think you're right!" He poured coffee all around and sat down again. "One thing's for sure, it ain't like my job depends on it!"

"That's for sure!" Sighed Melissa. "You'll still have your job, while I still do the worrying!"

"Awww, Lisa." He frowned. "Don't get into that again?"

"Well it's true! . . . I try hard not to upset you when you leave, but it scares me, thinking that one day, you won't come back at all!"

He looked at her for a moment, and then sighed. "I can't argue with that, baby. I think about it, too!"

"Ever thought a quittin', Rod?" Inquired Billy. "We do all right here, ya know, . . . what with th' mine and all."

"Believe it, or not, I have thought of it, . . . I'm still thinkin' about it."

"Oh, Rodney." Sighed Melissa. "Don't do it on my account, . . . I'm sorry I said anything."

"It's got nothin' to do with what you said, baby . . . . When I hang up this badge, it'll be on my account. Why? . . . Because I love you dearly, and I love my daughter!"

"Now that, that's settled!" Said Billy, winking at Connie. "We still got a lot a work to do."

"I would say so!" Agreed Connie. "There's ten bushels of seed corn in the storeroom, not counting the potatoes, and the roof leaked pretty bad in there! . . . It's all going to ruin if we can't get it to a dry place. Lisa already found a large rat in there."

"That's where we'll start then." Nodded Billy. "Rod, what's left a that tent a yours has been stored in your wagon, it ought a be dry. We can cut that up and use it for bags to put th' corn and potatoes in . . . . Hang 'em from th' rafters in here till the sun come out to stay a while."

"Good idea." Said Rodney. "I'll get Will to help me." He got up and went back through the store, while Billy and the women entered the storeroom.

$$* \qquad\qquad * \qquad\qquad *$$

Two weeks of hot, bright sunlight was doing its job, leaving everything living in its muggy embrace. The ground was drying out, and the standing water had completely drained from the prairie and road area to run off down the small valley's muddy floor. One of the Light-horsemen had called on several Choctaw farms and returned with half a dozen carpenters, who were now utilizing their talents by helping to clear acres of the prairie grass, of which mostly still lay flat and covered in dry mud. They spent time digging it out on clumps, cutting or pulling it up, and then hauling cartloads back to properly re-thatch the buildings.

Billy was already plowing the partially cleared ground behind the gatherers, who had a one-day start on him, while Willy followed along behind him planting the seed corn and covering it up with his boot. Billy came to the turn-row and turned the mules to start another, but stopped, as he almost always did, to stare up at the silent, and ever mysterious mountain. He studied the scared face of the tall cliff and remembered what had happened just a short ten years before. Then, just before clucking the animals into motion, would scan the remaining unplowed portion of prairie to think of the hundred or so treasure seekers that were buried there and like always, would shake his head and wonder if his part in the massacre had been the right thing to do?

Rodney and Peter had made the trip to Towson two days ago, leaving the four regular police to watch over the holdings, and since they had yet to return, continued their planting without worrying about the safety of the women and children. Besides, he was sure they had made the trip okay, and expected them back the next day, or that after.

The sun was beginning its descent behind the distant Jack fork Mountain in the west when he called Willy in and together, drove the mules back down to the corral, unharnessed them, fed them and the rest of the stock, and closed the gate behind them when finished.

"Tired, son?"

"Yes, sir." He said finally. "I guess so . . . . I can wring water out a my clothes, can you?"

"Yeah, . . . it was a humid day, makes ya sweat a lot! . . . Come on, we earned our keep today. You get th' wash-tubs down and start carryin' th' water, I'll get th' soap, towels, and clean duds."

"Won't th' crows mess on us out here, Daddy?"

"They might." He said, looking up through the tall Pines at the large, black birds. "Bird shit'll wash off, too, now go ahead, son."

It was almost dark when they pulled on their long-john bottoms and pants, and were sitting on two of the several Pine stumps, to pull on their boots. "Wonder why we ain't seen bigfoot's prints lately, daddy, . . . there's usually a lot of 'em?"

"Don't know, hadn't thought much about it! . . . Could be too hot for 'im, what with all that hair."

"Yeah, I bet that's it! . . . . What are we gonna do about all these limbs and stuff on th' ground? . . . Me, Chris and Angie could start pickin' them up tomorrow . . ."

"Plenty a time for that, after we're done plantin'! . . . Nice try, though . . . . Nope, we'll pick 'em up and burn 'em down there in th' canyon. Get your belt and shirt on, I'm hungry!"

          *   *   *

They were all on the long front porch of the trading post to watch as Rodney and the little tracker rode up to the hitch-rail and dismounted tiredly to come up the steps.

"Good to have ya back, Rod, you, too, Peter. Everything go okay?"

"Yeah." Breathed Rodney. "That road's a mess, though, all th' way to Towson! . . . Saw where a twister came through about ten miles south of us, uprooted trees, th' works, cut about a two mile swath from th' Winding Stair east."

"Three farmhouses were destroyed." Reminded Peter with a sigh.

"That we know of!" Agreed Rodney as he bent to pick up the five year old Cindy, and to pull Melissa into a hug. "How's my two favorite women?"

"We're fine, now!" Beamed Melissa, and kissed him.

Billy also pulled Connie against him, and placed a hand on Peter's shoulder. "When are you gonna get hitched, my friend, you can see what you're missin'?"

"I can see." He nodded. "But I am not yet missing it."

"I understand." He chuckled. "You two get washed up, we been waitin' supper on ya." He turned to Willy then. "Go get th' deputies, son, tell 'em supper's ready."

The meal was eaten in silence, somewhat unusual, and Billy had noticed that Peter had not joined in any of the meager conversation, and so, he pushed his plate away, wiped his mouth, and watched the tracker's preoccupied features for a moment before speaking, thinking he might know what was wrong.

"Did you know any a them folks, Peter?" And when he nodded. "They all right?"

"I do not know, no one was there . . . . One house belonged to Charlie two-crows."

"We saw no bodies, or anything, Billy." Replied Rodney. "Likely at a neighbor's house, or kinfolk."

"Yes, I think, maybe so." Agreed Peter.

"It was th' same at all th destroyed houses." Added Rodney. "We'll hear something in a day or so."

"Maybe you should go find out, Peter, if it bothers you that bad?"

"When I return, maybe." He nodded.

"Return, . . . where ya goin'?"

"We had a couple a wires waitin' for us in Towson." Said Rodney then. "Th' Judge ordered Peter to go help Bass track down some elusive bank robbers up near Oklahoma town . . . . He's leavin' tomorrow."

"Okay, then you and me'll go see about 'em!"

"I got orders, too!" Sighed Rodney, and reached in his vest for the folded papers. "Don't know if it's coincidence, or fate, Billy." He unfolded the wires and passed one to him. "Or, maybe it's a bad omen, . . . we were just talkin' about Shreveport!"

Billy took the wire and read it. "Ben Childers, George Collins and Phillip Long!" He gave Connie the paper. "A mite out a your jurisdiction, ain't it, why you?"

"Some Marshals on assignment elsewhere, others way too far away, like it says . . . . Damn if I know! Wire says they broke jail in Fort Smith this Winter, killed two guards makin' their escape . . . . You should remember when it happened, me and Peter were ordered to search these mountains. Did, too, went all th' way to th' Kansas line! He wants 'em back bad, that's all I know . . . . Must be mean Bastards."

"My God, Rodney!" Exclaimed Melissa after reading it. "How can he expect you to do this alone, anything can happen before you get them all the way to Fort Smith?"

"I don't know, honey, . . . but I'm it! . . . And it's my job to do it!"

"Well, it scares me to death, Rodney, you can't do all that alone!"

"I've done it before, honey, I'll make it!"

"You've always had Peter with you, . . . or Bass, or Billy!"

"He'll have somebody with 'im this time, too!" Said Billy, and drained his cup. "Got an extra badge, Rod?"

"Sure do, I was hopin' you'd say that! . . . Thanks, Billy."

"You could both be killed, too!" Said Connie, getting up to pour more coffee for them. "Bur!" She put the pot back on the stove. "My faith has always been with both of you." She came on to bend down and hug Billy from behind. "I know what Billy can do, both of you, for that matter." She stood and went to sit down again.

"Doesn't something like this scare you, Connie?"

"Every time, Lisa, all the time . . . . But once his mind is made up, he won't change it!"

"I ain't that bad, honey." Grinned Billy. "I always listen to you."

"But then you do it anyway!" She smiled then. "I wouldn't have it any other way."

"When does this have to be done, Rod?"

"Wire said at my convenience. They're in jail, sheriff'll hold 'em for us, I guess. Course, those wires were a month old."

"Okay, we'll give those roads another day or two to dry out, then make the trip to Paris, let th' family visit till we get back."

"For how long?" Asked Melissa.

Rodney shrugged. "I don't know, baby, . . . Could take a month!"

"Peter?" Said Billy. "Think one a your men can find some help to run things here, till we get back?

"Someone will be here, my friend, . . . it will take that long to repair all the storm damage. I will have them bring their families to run the store and prepare the meals."

"Good! . . . They'll be paid, you know that."

"As do they, my friend."

"Then all we have to worry about is th' road." Sighed Rodney. "Lot a debris in places, wash-outs, too! . . . Bridges are all in tact, that's one good thing."

"Don't the army repair roads anymore?"

"Well, . . . that's the last part a th' news, Billy . . . . They had a fire at th' Fort, maybe lightening, they don't know! . . . Pretty much burned th' whole place down. Accordin' to Neville, there might not be a fort there anymore . . . . Him and his men were about to move out when we left."

"Where'll they move to?"

"His troop was goin' to Fort McCullogh. Others went to Fort Gibson . . . . I guess Fort McCullogh will still maintain th' new road, don't know about th' rest!"

"I will have the Light-horsemen do what they can on the road."

"That'll cut their other duties mighty thin, Peter!" Replied Billy.

Peter shrugged. "As you said before, my friend. The bad men will wait for us to catch them."

"Peter," Grinned Billy. "Tou are truly a wise man, and the best friend a man could ask for, . . . thanks."

"What about our plan to sell more gold in Shreveport, Billy, there's no way we can carry that much with us?"

"No, we can't! . . . We'll hold out a couple a bags from Bratcher, won't make that much difference . . . . Just enough to get us by for a month."

"Well!" Said Connie, getting up from the table. "If we're leaving in two days, I have a lot of packing to do!"

"My, God, so do I!" Agreed Melissa, and also got up. "We'll do the dishes later, come on, Connie!" They both left the room and hurried out through the store.

"I've got a couple days a planting left." Said Nilly. "Me and th' boys can finish up by Tuesday . . . . We'll leave on Wednesday, first light, . . . and Peter! . . . You'll be leaving early tomorrow, stay loose, and watch yourself, my friend."

"As do you, and you as well, Marshal . . . Now," He said, as him and the four Light-horsemen got up. "We also have a lot to do, so I will say goodnight." They left to go into the Marshal's office.

"Think we'll have a weight problem with th' wagon, Billy?"

"I ain't got a clue. Shouldn't, with those wider rims, I had put on. Don't think we could carry any more than what we got, though . . . . I ain't worried about it, we'll drive a double team this time. Those mules could pull down a house!"

"Amen to that!"

CHAPTER THREE

Rodney wiped sweat from his face and replaced his hat as Billy did a walk-around on the wagon to check it out.

"How's it look, . . . we ready?" Asked Rodney, replacing the bandana around his neck.

"Wagon seems to be." He looked up over the high sideboards at the women. "All set up there, you comfortable?"

"Of course!" Smiled Connie. "We brought pillows to sit on this time, makes the new benches quite comfortable!"

"How about you, kids?" He grinned at their ready response, and nodded at Rodney. "Guess we're ready." They climbed up to their seat, where Billy looked back at them again. "You sure you brought everything?"

"Anymore, and we wouldn't fit!" Replied Melissa with a laugh.

Still grinning, he picked up the reins, and after they all waved their farewells to the remaining policemen, he slapped the reins on the backs of the four large mules and the wagon lurched into motion.

Rodney leaned out of the seat far enough to watch the wide-rimmed wheels as they made the road, and after a few minutes straightened and leaned back against the seatback. "Looks like we're gonna have five or six inch ruts in the road, . . . ground's still a mite soft."

"Team ain't straining much, we'll be okay . . . . Glad we're double-teamed, though."

*   *   *

Mid-afternoon found them turning West on the Wheelock road, and an hour later were turning South on the new Government road to Paris. The road was almost completed shrouded by ageless Pines, Wild Pecan and several varieties of Oak and Elm which threw the wide lane into almost total shadows. It was very hot, and muggy, allowing for the swarms of flying, biting insects, . . . and was so bad, it forced the women to don their Sunday hats and pull the netting down over their faces, while the children used pillowcases or articles of clothing to cover theirs.

"Jeesus!" Exclaimed Rodney as he slapped at the pests.

"I see some sunlight up ahead." Said Billy, who was also constantly slapping at his face and neck, and urged the mules to a faster pace until they came to the long, wooden bridge, . . . and there were partially out of the cover of trees and into the bright afternoon sun."

"Good Lord, Billy, ya see that?"

"Yeah, I see it!" He exclaimed, looking across the bridge to the west of them, where a hundred yard wide path of total destruction presented them with a view of up-rooted, broken and scattered tree debris for a half mile into the forest. "Look at that, ladies!" He looked back at them and pointed.

"Must a touched down up there and came this way." Said Rodney. "Lifted to cross th' road, and touch back down on th' Wheelock road. "Sure messed up th' landscape! . . . Buzzards are happy though, dozens of 'em over there."

"Dead animals." Said Billy, also looking.

"People, too, maybe . . . . That debris yonder used to be a house last we was through here, with kids and dogs in th' yard!"

"I remember." He said, urging the team up amd onto the bridge, and as they moved over the slightly rounded hump of the creaking timbers, they could see the troop of cavalry as they piled broken limbs in a heap along the road's East side.

"At least, they're busy." Commented Rodney. "Road's looks good, up ahead of us. Day's about gone, too, you up to night travel?"

"Couldn't see th' road, if we did, trees too thick! . . . Naw, we'll go as long as we can, though, . . . maybe stop where th' soldiers made camp."

"The Atoka road?"

"That's th' one . . . . Look there, Rod, ain't that our Major Wilkes comin' at us?" He stopped the wagon as they left the bridge to wait for the officer to stop his horse alongside.

"Major Wilkes." Greeted Billy as the soldier peered at them.

"You have me at a disadvantage here." He said, looking over the tall sideboards at the women and kids. "I feel I know you folks, . . . but your names escapes me."

"Marshal Rodney Taylor, Major." Grinned Rodney. "This is Billy Upshur." He turned and nodded back at the women. "Billy's wife, Connie and their three kids. My wife, Lisa, and my daughter, Cindy."

"Of course." Nodded Wilkes. "Your wife had a wound to her head, I believe . . . . I also remember burying several bodies for you, am I correct?"

"You are." Grinned Billy.

He shifted in the saddle, and then nodded. "Going to Paris again, are ya?"

"Right again, Sir." Said Billy.

"Devastating fire, they had over there." Replied Wilkes. "We had two units of cavalry there for three weeks to help clean up . . . . Terrible thing! Have not been back in a year or so, now."

"Three months for us." Said Rodney. "But they're building back!"

"I know they are. A resilient bunch of folks." He nodded. "Well, the road is clear from here to the river, still quite soft in the flooded areas." He peered at them then. "You're not expecting to provide me with more bodies to bury along the way?"

"That's not our intention, Major." Laughed Rodney.

"I certainly hope not, Sir . . ." He tipped his hat then. "Good day, Gentlemen, you as well, ladies." He reined his horse off the road and rejoined his men.

"Still a stiff-neck, ain't he?" Replied Billy, watching him leave.

"And then some!" Agreed Rodney. He turned around in the seat then. "What you think about th' debris over yonder?"

"We know!" Exclaimed Melissa. "It must have been horrible!"

"Get up there!" Yelled Billy and slapped the teams' backs again. "Gonna be in th' trees again." He warned. "Cover your faces back there."

"Ain't much breeze today, is it?" Asked Rodney, reaching to pull a portion of his clinging shirt away from his neck area. "Shirt's been soaked all day."

"Too much water, ground's saturated, . . . makes it twice as hot . . . . Whoa, mules! He shouted, and hauled back on the reins to stop them, making room for the team of horses to pull the grader past them.

"Gee-up!" He yelled to start them again. "Think you're wet, Rod, take a look at that soldier. Had any sense, he'd be ridin' one a them horses, looks like he just crawled out a th' river."

"I don't feel much better." Replied Rodney. "River'd feel pretty good right now!"

"What's our travel plans for Shreveport?"

"Hell, . . . I don't know, . . . train, I guess. Be faster than a stage coach, and cooler!" He glanced at Billy then. "Why, what do you think?"

"Not up to me, Rod, makes no difference at all! . . . You're th' law, we'll do it your way."

"Train then, . . . I'm all for bein' cooler! . . . We ought to be in Paris by Friday night, want a take that gold in Saturday mornin', before you go to Docs'?"

"Sounds like a plan, . . . but I was thinkin' about from there to Fort Smith?"

"Oh, . . . train all th' way, I think!" He shrugged then. "If it goes all th' way? I ain't even sure th' train goes all th' way to Shreveport, didn't used to?"

"And if it don't?"

"Damn if I know, Billy! . . . Confiscate some horses, there's an Army Post in Shreveport. That or take th' stage . . . . Why, you worried?"

"Be good to know a little more about th' men we're takin' in."

Rodney sighed and reached a semi-soggy cigar from his shirt, uttered a "Damn", and laid the other four on the seat between them to dry out before lighting up. "I'm of that opinion myself! . . . A little worried, to tell ya th' truth. Judge Parker didn't wire any details about the escape, only that they killed tow guards doin' it! . . . I'm thinkin' they had some help, too! Like I told ya, I seen that cellblock, it would take a cannon ball to blast it open."

"I'm with you, Rod, they had help! . . . And that means one thing to me, that same help could try it again!"

"Amen to that! . . . Makes it double hard, not knowin' what to expect?"

"All it means is that we can't trust anybody! We have to keep our eyes open, Rod, be ready for anything."

"We will be . . . . I know you, and I've learned a hell of a lot from you."

"Don't rely too heavy on me, man, a lot a mine is luck! . . . I can't follow a trail worth a damn, and I ain't no detective! . . . Wouldn't know one clue from another."

"Maybe not, my griend, but your instincts far outweigh anybody else's, and ya know what? . . . I trust those instincts a lot more than I would a detective's clues!"

Billy turned to peer at his friend. "I ain't no hero, Rod, so don't make me out one, okay?"

"I haven't done that at all! . . . I'm just sayin', you can read another man and know what he is, just by lookin' at 'im. Hell, I've tried that, and I can't! . . . No, man, all I know Is that you're the fastest man with a gun that I have ever heard of, let alone, seen! You have the ability to feel danger before it ever shows it's self, . . . and you're th' best friend a man could ever have! If that's hero-worship, Billy, then I'm guilty."

"Thanks, Rod, I feel th' same way about you. Just don't think me a brave man, okay, I'm scared to death before every fight, always have been . . . . One day, I'm gonna lose, whether it be another man's luck, or that he's faster, he'll kill me! . . . And it won't have nothin' to do with who's right, or wrong."

"I know the odds, Billy, . . . sorry I brought it up."

"Don't be . . . . You can't bring it up, it's with me all th' time. Only thing I ever worried about was my family, should it happen . . . . But not so much anymore, I know you'll see after 'em."

"With my life, Billy!"

"Anyway," Nodded Billy. "If we use th' train to Fort Smith, it's best we use a boxcar, leaves us room to work in case a trouble, . . . and no strangers to worry about!"

"I think you're right! . . . That's what we'll do."

They fell silent then, each with their own thoughts as the afternoon wore on, and with each of them fighting swarming insects. They were out of the forest of trees by dark, and for the next four hours traveled the road in light from the moon and stars until finally reining the team off the road and onto the one-time camp-site.

*   *   *

The women and children had been asleep for hours, so they left them there and bedded down beneath the wagon, thinking that with the few hours left, they would sleep until they woke up on their own.

Billy opened his gritty eyes and rubbed them before putting on his eyeglasses and pulling his watch, saw that it was after seven in the morning, and reached to jab Rodney.

"What time is it?"

"After seven, let's get everybody up."

"We're awake up here!" Shouted Connie as her and Melissa peered over the sideboards at them. "Here, Billy, take the basket." She gave him the food then turned to wake up the kids.

After a cold breakfast of biscuits, honey and water, Billy, Rodney and Willy hitched up the team to the wagon, and he was rolling up the two bedrolls and getting ready to stow them when Connie took his arm. "What is it, Honey?"

"Lisa and I overheard parts of your conversation yesterday afternoon . . . . Do you think there really might be trouble?"

He looked down at her and sighed. "Takin' those men back? . . . Honey, after all this time you've gone with me to Denver, you know there's always that chance! . . . But we'll handle it, don't you worry about me!"

"You're saying that, after what you said about being killed?"

"You heard that, too. That's all it was, just talk."

"I worry, Billy, I always have . . . . I don't want to lose you."

"I'll do everything in my power to see you don't!" He kissed her then. "Now get aboard, we got a go." He hefted her to the wagon's seat, and once she had crawled over into the bed, he called Lisa over and helped her up before tossing up the bedrolls and climbing up himself to wait for Rodney and Willy, who climbed up first to dive over into the wagon's bed.

"Wheels sank to almost eight inches since midnight, you notice that?"

Billy nodded. "Mud's still wet . . . . Must a flooded in here, it's nothin' but mud."

"Whole area, likely! . . . We're still a good mile from th' bridge, too. Makes me wonder if we'll make it without boggin' down? Be all we need!"

"Won't know till we get there."

"Heee-yaa, get up mules!" He yelled, rattling the reins on their backs. "Pull, you mules!" Failing to move the wagon on their first try, the large mules strained in the harness again, pulling the heavy wagon out of the holes to lurch forward. He slapped the reins again to keep them pulling, and in a few seconds were climbing the small embankment to the road.

"Sky's full a buzzards this mornin'." Said Billy as he studied the terrain in front of them. "Wonder how much stock was lost?"

"More'n enough, I think." Replied Rodney, also looking at the sky. "Lot of 'em are Crows, though, treetops are loaded with 'em! . . . They eat meat, too?"

"Eat anything if they're hungry, Rod."

"Well, I never seen 'em."

"They got a eat, too! . . . But I sure don't like th' smell a rotting flesh, and I can already smell it!"

"Mildew, too." Nodded Rodney. "Just look out across there, Billy, whole ground's covered in mud, can't see no grass at all, and just th' tops a brush . . . . But so far, th' road's in a lot better shape."

"Built on higher ground, . . . I just hope it was high enough!"

"And didn't damage that bridge!"

They spent the next hour looking out across the flat, mud-covered landscape, until finally. "Ain't that supposed to be th' Atoka, Stringtown cut-off, Billy, . . . or what used to be?"

"That's it, ain't been nobody through here since th' storm, I guess." He peered hard up the road's general direction then. "Till now! . . . Your eyes are better'n mine, Rod, . . . is that a rider comin' yonder?"

"It's a rider, all right! White man, too, way he sits his saddle . . . . Horse is high-stepping, too, must be deep up there."

"If he's on th' road at all?"

They could see the floodwater's devastating destruction as they neared the long span of bridge over Red River. Bloated steer carcasses littered the fast-flowing river's brush and timber cluttered banks, and the smell was close to overwhelming as Rodney urged the team up onto the thick, groaning timbers atop the steel girders on the bridge.

"Hold on back there!" Called Billy as he looked back at them. "Don't move around too much, bridge could be weakened."

"My, God, Billy!" Said Connie as she looked out at the tragedy. "All those cows, it's heartbreaking!"

"It's sickening!" Said Melissa. "That horrible stench!"

Rodney grinned at Billy. "At least th' bridge don't seem any worse for wear . . . . Did you know that this is the first bridge in North Texas to use steel trusses and girders?"

"Can't say I did, no."

"It's true, they took iron, added a few more ingredients and came up with steel! . . . It's two or three times harder than regular iron, and stronger. Iron'll break, steel won't!"

"You're a regular encyclopedia, Rod."

"I told you years ago to start reading, Billy. Can't learn, if you don't read."

"Yeah, well, readin' hurts my eyes . . . . Plays no part in livin' that I know of."

"But it could make for a better way of livin'."

"Right now, I just want a get off this bridge, longest two hundred yards I ever traveled!"

"Long bridge, all right! . . . You see our friend back there yet?"

"Ain't made th' road yet. He was a good quarter mile up that road." They finally came off the bridge and onto the eroded roan again, causing the wagon to bump hard as it rolled off into the washed out hole. But then were on more solid ground again.

"Been a few horsemen along here, looks like." Commented Rodney. "But no wagons, . . . dryer, too, guess river banks were higher on this side." He clucked the mules to a little faster walk then as Billy reached over the seat-back for the canteen and took a drink before passing it to Rodney.

They were a mile away from the bridge when Will told them of the rider coming up behind them, causing everyone to turn and watch him.

"What do ya think, Billy?" Asked Rodney, looking back at the road ahead.

"He's no cowhand, . . . gambler, maybe. Keeps lookin' down at th' road, for some reason, wagon tracks, maybe." He turned back around then also. "We'll know soon enough." He looked back at Willy then.

"Watch 'im, son, . . . let me know when he gets here."

"I will, daddy."

"I will, too, Daddy!" Said Christopher loudly.

"Me, too!" Chimed Angela and Cindy in unison.

"All of you can watch, quietly, please!" Scolded Connie.

"Really!" Added Melissa.

Billy looked at the grinning Rodney and shook his head before slowly reaching down to remove the safety-loop from the Colt pistol.

"He's coming up alongside us, daddy." Said Willy.

"Let 'im come, son." He leaned off the seat then to watch him ride up, studying his slightly lean features, narrow, close-set eyes. The mouth was hard to see due to the thick, black mustache. His hair was in need of a good trim beneath the black, sweat-stained hat. His attire consisted of blue shirt, black vest and black trousers. But what activated the tingle in his neck was the wide, bullet-laden gun belt. 'Gunslinger', he thought to himself, and at that moment felt the tell-tale rush of excitement. But in that same instant, shook it off as the man drew abreast of him.

"Pull up, Rod." And when the wagon stopped. "Howdy." He greeted, his eyes never leaving the man's own dark stare.

"And a howdy to you folks." He returned, reaching up to tip his hat at Lisa and Connie. "Ladies." He looked back and extended his hand to Billy.

"Benjamin Thompson's th name!"

"Bill Upshur." Said Billy, shaking his hand. "This is Rodney Taylor."

"Mister Taylor." He nodded his greeting. "Where you folks from?"

"North a McAllester a ways." Replied Rodney. "How about yourself?"

Thompson sighed, and looked at the mules. "Me? . . . Not from anywhere, permanently anymore! . . . Been in Abilene, Kansas, last couple of years, me and my best friend . . . . Opened a business there for a while." He looked at them again and grinned.

"It didn't pan out!" He stared out at the terrain then. "Must a been quite a storm, ya had around here, couldn't believe the dead livestock back there! River must a been out of it's banks."

"It was!" Said Billy.

"How'd it look north a here?" Queried Rodney.

"Not as bad as here, some twister damage on the north side of McAllester, a lot of rain and flooding from there, to the Kansas line . . . . Where you folks headed?"

"Town called Paris, down th' road a ways, . . . got folks there."

"Don't guess you folks had any plans to stop for a noon meal? . . . Lost my sack of supplies crossing the Canadian a few days back. I could do with a bite, maybe some conversation, and hot coffee."

Billy frowned as he looked at Rodney then pulled his watch. "Eleven o'clock, what do ya think?"

"I guess we could do with a bite, stretch our legs a bit., . . . sure, why not? . . . We never turn down a hungry man!"

"I'm awful glad to hear that!" Smiled Thompson.

"Looks pretty dry right out there." Replied Rodney, and reined the team closer to the side of the road, to stop in the shade of a large, spreading Elm to watch Thompson pull in front of them and dismount. He looked at Billy then.

"What's on your mind, Billy?"

"I'm wonderin' what's on his? . . . Better to know now, than when we least expect it! . . . Stay alert." He looked back at Connie then. "Bring out th' food basket, honey. Make some coffee, we're stoppin' for lunch."

"Well. You be careful, Billy." She said in a low voice. "I don't like his looks!"

"We'll see." He said, turning around again. "Help th' girls down, Rod."

Thinking he knew what Billy was thinking, he nodded and climbed down, and after telling Connie and Melissa to exit his side, helped them down while Billy exited on his side and walked to where Thompson stood, watching from the shade.

"What business was you in, Mister Thompson?" He asked, stopping beside him.

Thompson had been staring at the wagon as Billy spoke, and startled, turned to face him. "What?" He asked quickly.

"Your business, in Abilene, . . . what kind?"

"Oh," He stammered. "A saloon, The Bull's Head Saloon!" He chuckled then. "My mind was on something else, sorry about that . . . . Yeah, the town Marshal and me didn't get along well, didn't like the sign I had on the building . . . . I hired a painter to paint a bull on the false-front." He chuckled again. "He did overdo it a mite on the animal's balls and cock! . . . Marshal said the Town Council didn't approve of it, and made me fix it." He shrugged then. "One thing led to another after that, so, to avoid further trouble, I sold out!"

"Must a been quite a sign, at that!" Nodded Billy.

"It was a beautiful sign, covered the entire false front!"

"Coffee fire's bein' lit." Said Rodney as he joined them, and they all watched as Willy placed wood on the ground he had cleared. "We got cold biscuits, honey and some dried beef, Mister Thompson, . . . didn't pack much for a three day trip. But you're welcome to what we got."

"Mighty neighborly of you, thanks."

"You say you hail from Abilene?" Queried Rodney.

"Had a little trouble there with th' Marshal," Replied Billy. "Didn't like th' sign over th' door."

"That why you sold out?" Rodney shook his head. "Why not just change th' sign?"

"My reasons are my own, if you please!" Returned Thompson, his face growing slightly hard. "None of it concerns you, ya know!"

"Didn't mean a thing by it, Ben." Grinned Rodney. "Don't get so riled up, I'm a U. S. Marshal." He took the badge from a shirt pocket and pinned it on. "It's my job to ask questions, comes natural to me."

Thompson blinked a couple of times then let his breath out. "Then I apologize!" He grinned. "Wore a badge myself once, Austin, Texas."

"Oh, yeah? . . . Why'd ya quit, . . . th' lawman's job, I mean?"

"Economics, . . . a man can starve on a lawman's wages. I make a lot more money dealing cards now."

"What about your cousin?" Asked Billy suddenly.

"What?"

"Your cousin, he sell his part, too?"

"Okay, that's enough!" Said Thompson angrily. "What I do is of no concern to either of you, Marshal, or not! . . . And Mister Coe was my friend, not my cousin!"

"Hey, Ben," Said Rodney. "Stoppin' for coffee was your idea. You wanted company and conversation! . . . We're just obligin'."

"I know," He said, almost apologetic. "That whole affair is a sore spot for me. I don't like talking about it!"

"Coffee's ready, Billy!" Called Connie.

"Come on, Ben." Urged Rodney, taking Thompson's arm. "Coffee's done!" They all three walked to the fire as Connie and Melissa filled tin cups with the dark brew and gave each of them one before moving back to join the others.

"Food in th' basket there, Ben." Said Rodney. "Help yourself, man."

They were all silent as each drank their coffee, and when he was done, Thompson placed his cup on the ground.

"Mind if I ask you some questions now, I answered yours?"

"Shoot!" Shrugged Rodney. "We're all friends here."

"All right." He nodded, looking back at the wagon. "About that wagon of yours, . . . I was noticing the ruts it left on the road back there, that, and the extra wide rims on the wheels." He turned to face them again as he spoke.

"Mow, I'm thinking that wagon weighs about eight hundred pounds, empty, give or take a few . . . . and with all of you in it, another eight hundred pounds, give or take. Sixteen hundred pounds ain't enough, even with all your belongings, to sink them ruts any more than six inches deep, the shape that road is in! . . . Yours are a good eight inches deep, maybe seven."

"What's that tell ya?" Queried Billy, his eyes boring into those of Thompson.

"That you are carrying an extra three or four hundred pounds somewhere!" He smiled at them then. "There's gold in the Indian Nations, . . . that what you're carrying?"

"What's on your mind, Ben?" Asked Rodney. "And before you tell me, you say the wrong thing, I'll arrest you for attempted robbery! Because I believe that's your intent, sir."

"Then, I'll cut to the chafe . . . . I had wanted this to end peacefully, I want you all to know that! But first, I'll answer all your questions . . . . After all, you did extend your hospitality! . . . . It weren't only my sign that put us on the outs with Hickok. I took his woman from him, too! . . . And my friend, Phillip Coe, well Hickok killed him one night when I was out a town!"

"As for selling out, it was that, or go up against Hickok and three deputies. I sold out! . . . Money's being sent to a bank in Dallas."

"That wouldn't be Wild Bill Hickok?" Queried Rodney. He's th' Marshal?"

"Bill Hickok is a joke, an ambusher, murderer, and a cowardly son of a bitch, who was afraid to face me on his own, because he knew I'd kill him!" Ge took a deep breath then to compose himself then turned to tip his hat at the ladies.

"I want to thank you dear ladies for the hospitality, and I apologize for all this, but it's something I have to do."

"Gentlemen." He said, looking back at them. "I will tell you that I am good enough with a gun to kill you both! . . . I don't want to, but I will, . . . unless you share what's in that wagon with me?"

"Got a hand it to ya, Ben." Grinned Billy. "Not many men could figure all that out, just by lookin' at wagon ruts! . . . Now, there's a smart man, rod!!"

"That's right!" He snapped. "Weren't hard to figure, neither! . . . Now, if I'm wrong, I'll get on my horse and ride away, nobody gets hurt, . . . but you got to prove me wrong! . . . That being said, you want to unload that wagon?" He glared at Billy's smiling face then.

"You, Sir, are trying my patience! . . . Wipe that grin off your face, this ain't no joke! . . . I know what you are, just like you know what I am, but you ain't fast enough!" He stared at them for a second.

"I won't be so friendly, next time I ask!" He waited again then shook his head. "You play this out, your wife and kids will be orphans, . . . might even get hurt, neither of us wants that . . . . Now unload the God damn wagon!"

Rodney looked at Billy then, and shrugged. "I don't know, Billy, but this guy might be for tral!" He looked back at Thompson then.

"Okay, Mister Ben Thompson, we all like a little joke now and then, but you're takin' it a mite too far. So I think you better drop your gun belt now, I'm placing you under arrest . . . . I won't even charge you for the coffee! But ya see, this badge here ain't for show, I take it real serious!"

"I got a hand it to you both, too." Said Thompson. "You're quite cool under pressure. But out here, that badge don't mean a thing! No amount of gold is worth dying for neither . . . . Now, I ain't even touched my gun yet, but I'm also running out a patience, and if you pull on me, I'll kill you both."

"You do, you'll have to kill our family too!" Said Billy. "Be the only way you could get away with it! . . . I can't allow that to happen, so, I'll give you th' same warnin', pull on us, I'll kill you! . . . Now, do what he said, drop th' gun belt!"

Thompson stared at him. "You're pretty sure of yourself."

"Just statin' fact!" Replied Billy. "It's a simple thing, Ben, you brag too much on what you can do, and us, . . . well, we have a couple a rules we live by. One, we don't allow th' layin' on of hands in anger, . . . two, we won't be threatened and three, . . . nothin' of ours will be taken from us, and what's in that wagon, is ours!"

Thompson's face slowly changed as he glared at them and then, without warning, he went for his gun.

The sudden explosion was tremendously loud in the mid-day stillness, as Billy drew and fired. Thompson's pistol was just clearing the holster as the bullet smashed through his gun-arm just between his wrist and elbow, the impact of which, jerked a yell of surprise and sudden, searing pain from his mouth as he was spun around to stumble and fall to his knees in the tall grass. All this happening before the gunfire completely echoed away.

Clutching his injured arm, he painfully looked up at Billy as he slowly holstered his gun, and came to stand before him.

"You still got one good arm, Mister Thompson, use it to drop that gun belt!"

Thompson did as he was told then pushed to his feet. "You could a killed me, why didn't you?"

"Mostly, because our families was here, which, I'm sorry to say, didn't seem to bother you any! . . . Next, I don't like killin' a man, steals his life from 'im! I didn't figure you much of a threat, neither, you waste too much time tellin' a man how good you are, or how smart!"

"Who the hell are you, anyway, you didn't bat an eye when you drew that thing?"

"He's my deputy." Said Rodney as he came to retrieve the gun and belt. "And just so you'll know, Ben, he could kill you and Bill Hickok both, at th' same time! . . . And let you pull first! . . . Main reason you ain't dead, aside from what Billy said, is because we'd have to bury ya, and it's just too damn hot! Now sit down, I'll have my wife bandage that arm for ya."

"Wait, Marshal!" Said Thompson, as he watched Billy walk to the fire and hug Connie. "It ain't natural for a man to shoot like that, who is he?"

He looked at Billy then and smiled. "He's nobody you ever heard of, Ben . . . . He is what he is, . . . my deputy! . . . Now, sit down, and no sudden moves, okay?" Once Thompson sat down, he went to the fire and hugged Melissa, who was still in tears.

"Lisa, honey, it's okay." He soothed. "Relax, it's over and done." He bent to pick up Cindy, who was also sobbing, freightened by the shooting.

"Lisa, honey, get some bandage, he'll need his arm fixed."

"What? . . . After what he tried to do?"

"I'll do it." Said Connie, pulling away from Billy. "Come along, Angie, you can help me." She went to the wagon for some rags then her and Angela went to the sitting gunman.

"Son," Said Billy. "Take his gun from Rodney, and go with your mother . . . . Watch 'im!"

Nodding, Willy accepted Thompson's pistol, and smiling, turned and left, followed closely by Christopher.

"Everything okay, Rod?"

"Yeah, they're both just scared. And to tell ya th' truth, I was a little worried! . . . I was actually thinkin' he might be th' one, . . . you know?"

"Yeah, I know! . . . Come on, I'm hungry, I want a get to Paris sometime tonight. And, Rod, . . . If you're around when I meet that man, you'll know it!"

"The one?" Sniffed Melissa. "What man, Rodney?"

"Never mind, honey, pour us some coffee, will ya?"

*　　　　　　*　　　　　　*

"I thank you, kindly, Ma'am." Sighed Thompson as Connie tied the knot on the bandage.

"You're not very welcome." She responded, getting to her feet. "You are a vile, evil man, Mister Thompson . . . . I'll never understand people like you! You have no regard for life what so ever!" She backed away then as Billy came up. "My husband could have killed you, you know!"

"Will he live, honey?" He grinned, just catching the last few words of her sermon.

"Oh, yes, he'll live! . . . Through no fault of his own."

"Now, honey, . . . best go get packed up, it's time to go!" He watched her leave with the two kids then turned to Willy and took the pistol from him. "Go bring his horse to the wagon, son."

"Mind telling me how you come to shoot like that?" Asked Thompson when Willy left. "I'd like to know."

"You had a chance to back off, Ben . . . . We both told ya to quit!"

"I know, . . . I was never one to listen too well . . . . Too damn cocky for my own good!"

"Let's move over by th' wagon, Ben." He gestured with the gun as Willy led the horse in beside him, and they followed Thompson to where Rodney and the others were waiting. He took Thompson's holster from Rodney and shoved the gun in it before giving it back to Willy.

"Put it in th' wagon, son, his rifle, too." He nodded at Rodney then. "He's all yours, Marshal."

"Get on your horse, Ben."

Frowning, Thompson turned and pulled himself into the saddle to sit and stare down at them.

"Ben," He said, taking the horse's reins to look up at him. "I don't have th' time to arrest you, nor th' time it would take to convict you for attempted robbery, so I'm letting you go, man! . . . I don't know if you've learned anything here today, but I'm gonna tell ya what you should have learned . . . . Makes not a damn, how fast you are with a gun, and even less, how fast you think you are! Because somewhere, there's a man who'll be faster, there always is . . . . And next time, he could kill you!" He released the horse's reins then and backed away.

"I suggest you leave back th' way you came, because Marshal, Stockwell in Paris won't be so generous, once I report this to him."

"What about my guns, I don't want to be helpless?"

"You won't be." Said Billy. "Use th' one in your boot!"

"You're very observant." He sighed and looked down at Rodney then. "Thanks, Marshal." He started to rein his horse around.

"One more thing!" Said Billy. "Don't ever let me see you again, . . . please!"

He nodded, turned the horse and galloped back toward the bridge.

"Everybody in th' wagon!" Said Rodney. "We still got twenty miles to go." He helped Billy lift the kids up, so they could climb over the sideboards then helped the women up to the seat to climb over. Billy climbed up while Rodney continued to watch the disappearing figure of Thompson, and then he climbed up.

"Think he'll keep goin'?" He asked, reaching down to fetch a thin cigar from beneath the seat.

"Not him, . . . he'll stay out a sight till we leave, that, or cross into Texas somewhere else."

"And if he follows us?" He lit the cigar and studied Billy's face.

"We got his rifle, Rod, he'd have to get real close with that hide-out to do any damage, a lucky shot, at that! . . . He won't bother us again, I think! It'll fester in 'im for a while, and he'll think hard about it . . . . But I don't think we'll see 'im again."

"Well, I don't think you should have let him go!" Said Melissa, from behind Rodney. "What if he follows us to Mom and Dad's place, you'll be gone, what'll we do?"

"It's just one of th' risks we take, baby . . . . It would take Judge Bonner a month to hold court and convict him, and I'd have to be here to testify! . . . . I have to get those men back to Fort Smith! . . . Don't worry, though. I'll ask Jim to station a deputy at th' ranch for a few days, and they'll watch for 'im in town . . . . It'll be okay."

"I hope so, daddy's no gunman, you know!"

He looked around to catch Billy watching him. "She's a worrier, what can I say? . . . Tell me, would you have killed 'im, if we'd been there alone?"

"Damn if I know, Rod . . . . You heard what I told 'im, that's th' truth as I know it!" He sighed then. "I've always hated it when I killed a man, takes a while to get over it! . . . It ain't a good feelin'."

"I know." He nodded. "Me, too." He picked up the reins and slapped the mules. "Heee-yaaa!" He yelled. "Get up, mules."

Nodding, Billy pulled his Samuel Colt pocket watch and checked the time. "It's twelve-thirty, . . . we might make it pretty early."

"I've wanted to ask you about that watch for years, Billy, where'd ya get it?"

"Winter of sixty-five." He grinned, giving it to Rodney. "Not long after I escaped that stockade at Vicksburg."

"For services rendered." He muttered as he read the inscription. "Signed, Colonel Samuel Colt." He looked at Billy and grinned. "This guy give it to ya?"

"Took it from a Bounty-hunter, my brace a guns, too."

"They must a took 'em from this guy, right?"

"Yeah, . . . there was two of 'em, each totin' one a th' new Colts . . . . They wanted that sack a gold and gems, I left with you in Oak Creek."

"Easy to see, they didn't get it! Man, what a story."

"First face to face gunfight I ever had, too. Wondered many times since, how I did it? Me with that heavy old Walker Colt, them both with lighter guns . . . . First time I ever saw guns like them, so I took 'em! . . . And they served me well, I might add!"

"I'd say so." Grinned Rodney then returned the watch.

"Somethin' else about that night, too! . . . I've thought about it over th' years, . . . do you recall th' man who took Willy in sixty-nine?"

"Tiny Sterling, yeah, I remember."

"I didn't think much about it at th' time, but I think I might have killed his brother that night as well! It was before th' gunfight . . . . A mountain of a man, stark naked and mean as hell. He'd just raped th' saloon owner's daughter, and almost killed him when he objected! . . . Took three, forty-four caliber balls to th' chest to put 'im down! Name was Bear Sterling! . . . And there I was, five years later, killin' his brother in Winchester Station. It's a small world, Rod!"

Rodney nodded. "It was th' same with that man, Snake, remember??"

"Yeah, him, too! . . . That's exactly why I never used my real name before I came home."

"Well, it worked, my friend, th' Reb is long dead!"

"In name, yeah . . . . I have been a lucky man, Rod, hell, look at you, when we met, you was a testy, smart aleck of a Sycamore hotel clerk. Look at ya, now, a United States Marshal."

"You regret any of it, Billy?"

"Just th' killin', . . . but what happened then, led up to what is now. I'm still a lucky man, and a very happy one, with what I have!"

"Well, you better be!" Said Connie, from her place behind him. "Glad you revealed the secret about that watch, too, you never did before."

"You never asked before!"

"Well, . . . I'm not one to pry, you know that."

"Not much!" They all four laughed at that.

"Anything else you want to confess?"

"Can't think of a thing, no."

"Okay, I love you anyway." She laughed.

"Thanks, I know that!" He grinned at Rodney then and shrugged. "What can I say, she lost her mind in that desert back then, th' rest was easy."

"I remember that!" Said Melissa, and reached to hug Rodney from behind. "You told me all about it, didn't you? . . . About how the Indians almost killed you all. I wish I had been there!"

"Believe me, baby, you don't! . . . You wouldn't have been very proud a me back then, I was scared to death all the time."

"You came through in th' clutches, Rod, don't forget that."

"I got no regrets, neither, Billy. I have exactly what I want right here."

"Well I, for one, do not want to relive what happened in Sycamore, it was horrible!" Stated Connie. "I almost lost you!

"I thought you had, a time or two. It hadn't been for Ira, I wouldn't be here."

"He was a good man, Billy." Nodded Rodney.

"Th' best." Agreed Billy as he remembered the shoot-out at the sawmill. "Gave his life for me."

"You goin' to th' farm, this trip?" Asked Rodney. "You ain't been there in a while."

"When we get back, maybe . . . . And again, maybe not! We've just about turned it over to Ross as it is, we'll never move back, anyway."

"We could invite them back to the mountain again." Said Connie. "They loved it there."

"Mom and dad, too!" Said Melissa excitedly. "They'd love it, I know they would."

"Maybe they'll go back with us, this time." Returned Rodney. "We'll ask 'em . . . . If we can find somebody to watch th' place."

"That might be a chore." Sighed Billy, and used his bandana to wipe the sweat from his face and eyes. "Got their hands full in town."

"It won't hurt to try." Said Melissa. "You will, won't you?"

"I will try, baby . . . . You goin' on to Doc's tonight, Billy?"

"We can't, Billy." Said Connie quickly. "It would be so late to get them up."

"Then I guess th' Gabbetts will have to put us up for th' night."

"That ain't a problem, you can take th' buckboard when you go."

"As long as they have water and a tub." Moaned Connie. "I'm dying for a bath."

"Me, too." Sighed Melissa. "It's so hot, and I'm so sticky!"

"Maybe you gals ought a take a nap, or somethin'" Said Billy. "Make th' time pass quicker."

"You are so right!" Said Connie. "I think I will." She kissed Billy on the cheek and moved back to lie on the quilt she had spread between the benches. Angela and Cindy moved onto the quilt with her, leaving the two boys against the tailgate watching the circling crows.

Rodney turned around to see Melissa lying back on the bench. "Never tried that approach before!" He said, and looked at the road again. "Worked, too!"

"Wasn't a doubt in my mind." Grinned Billy.

"Amen to that!"

CHAPTER FOUR

Shreveport, Louisiana was established in 1836, and after Caddo Parish was created, was called Shreve Town. Shreve Town consisted of sixty-four city blocks crossed by eight streets running East and West, and another eight running north and South. Incorporated as a city in 1871, the name was changed to Shreveport, Shreveport Landing to many due to it's shipping points, and access to the Red River, as well as the Texas Road.

1880, and it was now a bustling metropolis of a city, and like most of its size and population, had its bad element. Saloons and flophouses were everywhere and produced their share of drunks, muggings and murders, almost on a nightly basis! Prostitution was rampant, as well as almost daily street shootings and public gunfights, an activity that kept local law enforcement on the go from morning to night, . . . to no avail! Perpetrators of these crimes, though arrested, would only be fined, and released by a crooked Judge. Murderers were usually always found innocent due to a ruling of self-defense, or a not guilty verdict by juries of their peers, . . . unless the accused was someone the saloon owners wanted out of the way. Most believed that these jurors were frightened, or forced into their prescribed verdicts

There was, however, an honest element in Shreveport, one being the Mayor. Andrew Currie, a man in his fifties, of medium build and already balding. He sported a thick, black mustache and wire-framed glasses. Never the less, he was also a frustrated man, whose attempts to change the city's image was also to no avail, as the majority of the City's councilmen were either on the take, or too afraid to do the job they were elected for. Currie had only one dependable ally, Sheriff John Lake, a dedicated man, but also frustrated at his job of trying to keep the peace in a large and lawless city. In fact, he had coined the city as lawless many times in open court. He had gone as far as accusing all three of the Judges of being on the take, . . .

though unable to prove it, or find out the actual names of the man, or men who were in control.

John Lake was a family man, with a wife and three daughters. He took his job serious and would arrest and jail any and all lawbreakers, even though he knew they would be released on some technicality. He also knew, that if he was not on the job, Shreveport would likely explode into some sort of outlaw haven. His only help, aside from his deputies, was the Army, . . . there being a cavalry post on the city's East side.

Troops of cavalry patrolled the city at intervals during the daylight hours, no doubt preventing many such muggings and murders. But the nights were wide open, and kept three deputies on their toes. The jail was most always full by morning, and usually quite empty come nightfall, . . . except for three cells. These held the three escaped, and condemned convicts from Fort Smith, Arkansas. Three men that Shreveport courts, or Judges had no control over, because they were Federal prisoners, . . . and late for a hanging!

Lake was not happy they were there, or that he was responsible for keeping them there, and safe, until the U.S. Marshal arrived to take custody. There had already been a dozen attempts by total strangers to set bonds for them to be released, and that led Lake to believe the three had outside influences wanting them free. For that reason, he now had two deputies on jail duty at night. No one had ever been broken out of his jail by force, or otherwise, and he vowed it would not happen now.

Having received the Federal warrants some weeks before, he had been surprised when a deputy came in with news that all three men were in the LePorte' saloon, and having a great time of it! The saloon had been crowded, so it had been easy to come in behind them at the bar, take their guns and make the arrests. Once he did, he became responsible for them, and had been worried ever since that an attempt to free them might be eminent, . . . and if it occurred there, would surely leave dead men when it was over!

The town was full of foreigners, gamblers and gun-hands, so he could not rely on strangers being the suspects, as almost everyone in Shreveport were strangers to him. That being the case, all he could do was guard his prisoners and wait for something to happen, . . . and to hope the Marshal arrived first to take custody.

He had discussed the city's problems with Mayor Currie on a dozen occasions, but their hands were tied. Currie had written to the Government in Washington, requesting a U.S. Marshal, and Federal Judge, be sent to open a permanent office there, . . . but nothing had come of that, either. So, Lake had come up with the idea to write a request to Isaac Parker in Fort Smith, and send it back with the Marshal.

*   *   *

The afternoon passed slowly, and after long since having run out of idle conversation both Billy, and Rodney had resorted to watching the swaying rumps, swishing tails and bobbing heads of the mules until at last, Rodney spotted the cut-off to his one-time ranch.

"See what I see, Billy?" He asked, grinning tiredly at him.

"None too soon for me, my clothes are glued to my skin."

"I know th' feelin', . . . but I also know th' cure for it! Remember that clear-water sump about a quarter mile from th' barn, what say we use it tonight? . . . Thing's got a solid rock bottom, and water that's good and cold, . . . and so clear you can see a coin on th' bottom."

"Rod, . . . I know I've turned that invitation down before, but right now, that's th' best news I've heard in two days! . . . Any snakes in it?"

"Never seen one, . . . but knowin' me and snakes, you better bring your gun anyway." He reached over the seatback and shook Melissa's leg to roust her.

"We're at th' cut-off, baby, wake Connie and th' kids."

"Praise the Lord!" She shouted, and hurriedly woke the others before bringing Cindy forward to lean on the backrest.

"Where's the house, Mommy, I can't see it?"

"We're not there yet, sweetie." Cooed Melissa. "But right there's the road, we'll be there real soon now."

Connie and the other kids soon joined them at front of the wagon as Rodney reined the team onto the old worn road, . . . and a half-hour later were through the gate and pulling up to the long, l-shaped front porch of the, now, Gabbett ranch house.

"Oh, my God!" Shouted Mrs. Gabbett, as she threw open the screen-door and rushed down the steps. Mister Gabbett stopped at the edge of the porch to watch as Rodney climbed down and lifted Cindy into her Grandmother's outstretched arms. He helped Melissa down as his father in law came down the steps to shake his hand.

Billy climbed down and helped Connie to the ground, then Angela, and shook his head as Willy and Christopher both jumped from the driver's seat to the ground. Grinning, he took Connie's arm and ushered her around the wagon where she hugged Mrs. Gabbett and her husband.

"How are you, Mister Gabbett?" He grinned, shaking the older man's hand.

"Never better, William, welcome back! . . . Everyone, come on in the house, it's cooler!" He shouted, to be heard over the excitement.

"Not till we bathe first, Daddy." Said Melissa. "We're all a mess."

"All right!" He nodded. "William, you and Rodney come help with the wash-tubs, the gals can bathe on the back porch. You men can bathe after."

"Th' rock sump got water in it, John?" Asked Rodney as they started around the house. "Me and Billy can bathe there."

"Hardly ever go down there, but it should, we've had some hellacious rains this spring!"

"Good, we'll check it out!"

They had the wooden tubs down and filled with cistern water by the time the women brought their clothes and toiletry. Connie brought his and Willy's clean shirt, jeans and socks, as did Melissa for Rodney, and the two men, and Willy walked out to the barn in the fading light, climbed through the fence and walked across the pasture toward the clear-water sump.

*   *   *

John Gabbett was on the back porch when they came back, and waited while Billy had Willy take the dirty clothes around to the wagon.

"How was the water?" He asked as he held the door open for them.

"Too cold!" Replied Billy with a grin.

"But wonderful, John!" Added Rodney.

"I'll bet! . . . Go on in the kitchen, boys, supper's all set for ya."

"Billy," Said Rodney, as they sat down. "Just look at these gorgeous women." He reached across to squeeze Melissa's hand."

"All five of 'em, Rod." He leaned to kiss Angela on the cheek, and to muss Willy and Christopher's unruly hair as they came to sit down. "Ain't you folks gonna eat, Mrs. Gabbett?"

"Lord, no, we had our supper hours ago . . . . Now, you all go and eat all you want, you hear."

"Have any trouble tis time, boys?" Asked the senior Gabbett.

"Don't we always, John?" Nodded Rodney. "It's th' times we live in, can't avoid it."

"You're right, I think! . . . What was it this time, outlaws again?"

"Just one." Replied Billy as he cut the meat on his plate. "Tried to rob us, nothin' serious."

"Daddy beat him to th' draw!" Voiced Willy. "Shot him in th' arm!"

"Well that doesn't surprise me!" Chuckled Gabbett, and looked at Billy. "Boy holds you in high esteem, William. You should be proud."

"I am."

"William!" Scolded Connie. "Children should be seen, not heard! . . . Now eat your supper."

"Ever heard of a Ben Thompson, John?" Asked Rodney.

"No, . . . can't say I have . . . . What was he after?"

"Th' gold we was bringin' to Horace Bratcher."

"Good, Lord! . . . How did he know you had it?"

"By th' wagon-ruts." Said Billy. "Said we was too heavy."

"He guessed th' truth." Sighed Rodney. "Smart man."

"I still wish you hadn't let him go!" Said Melissa, holding up her cup for her mother to fill it.

"He's too smart to come to Paris, honey, Jim'll watch for 'im."

"Are you going to stay a while this time?" Queried Mrs. Gabbett as she poured coffee all around. "It's so good to have you home, Lisa."

"Lisa, and your granddaughter will, Mama Gabbett." Replied Rodney, pushing his plate away. "Me and Billy's got some business in Shreveport. We'll be headin' that way come Monday, I guess."

"Law business, son?"

"Afraid so, . . . takin' three convicted killers back to Fort Smith . . . . Sheriff's holdin' 'em for us in th' Shreveport jail."

"Take them back? . . . Did they escape?"

Rodney nodded. "Killed a couple a guards doing it."

"Well, you kids be careful!" Said Mrs. Gabbett, replacing the pot on the stove. "Don't know what this world's coming to, all these killings, robberies!"

"That was a fine meal, Mrs. Gabbett." Said Billy as he got up from the table. "Hope you can put us up for th' night, be a mite late by th' time we could get to Docs'?"

"My, Lord, yes!" She said. "Your rooms are all made up for you."

"Then I'd better tend to th' wagon and team, can I put it in th' barn?"

"Not being used for anything else!" Nodded John. "And when you go to Docs, you can use the buckboard."

"Much obliged." He looked at Willy then. "Give me a hand, son?"

"I'll go akong, too." Said Rodney, also getting up.

"I'll get a lantern and go with you." Said John.

*   *   *

They led the team and wagon into the large barn where Billy, and Willy unhitched the mules and relieved them of harness and bridles, then watered and grained them before turning them into the corral. Rodney and John gathered up the clothing and sleeping gear to stack it neatly on the tailgate.

"John?" Said Rodney, as he looked at the surrey. "If you don't mind, we'll need th' surrey tomorrow, we have to take that gold into town."

"Whatever you need, my boy."

"Billy." He said, as him and Willy came back. "If you can wait till tomorrow afternoon to go to Doc's, we could deliver th' gold to Bratcher in th' mornin' . . . . It'll give you more time to visit? . . . Tomorrow's Friday."

"That'll work out great." He nodded. "Better load it up tonight." He climbed into the wagon and pulled open the trap door in the wagon's bed, and began handing down the heavy sacks of nuggets while the three of them carried it to the surrey. When they were done, the gold was covered with a tarp.

"These two, we'll take with us." Said Billy, bending down to put the sacks in Willy's hands. "These go in my satchel, son." And as Willy opened the satchel, he looked down at Rodney. "Guess we're good to go."

"Good!" Said Gabbett. "Now let's go in the house and relax a bit, we got catching up to do."

"Sounds good to me." Said Billy. "And if you don't mind, I'll need to clean my gun while we talk?"

"Don't mind at all, cleaning kit's in the cabinet."

Once in the large sitting room, Billy was at the gun cabinet when he spotted the rifle. "I see you hung onto that Kragg rifle, Rod."

"Weren't mine, Billy, John just loaned it to me."

"Hasn't been fired since!" Grinned Gabbett. "Army didn't adopt it, either. Too much gun for them, I guess."

He went back and placed the kit on the table. "Hadn't been for that gun, we might a been eaten alive! . . . Winchester wasn't doin' a whole lot a damage, as I recall." He sat down and quickly cleaned and reloaded the Colt pistol while Rodney retold the incident with Ben Thompson. When done, he put the kit away and accepted the glass of hard liquor from Gabbett before sitting down again.

"How's th' town lookin', Mister Gabbett?"

"I swear, William, when are you going to start calling me, John, you and yours are as much family now as Rodney is?"

"Thanks, John."

"Okay! . . . Now when the women get in here, we'll want to know what's been going on at that mountain of yours, and I'll tell you all I can about the progress being made in Paris, . . . which, I'm afraid isn't all that much. We don't get to town all that much, just for a few supplies, Sunday Church service and the like."

        *   *   *

They began hearing the sounds of hammers as carpenters drove nails into the town's rebuilding progress within five miles of town, and not long afterward, handsaws cutting into the new lumber. They also began seeing already finished structures, homes that were erected alongside the road. The chug-chug of steam engines from the sawmill was loud in passing, and at that point, the new construction became more numerous as men were seen carrying lumber, others driving nails or cutting timber to length.

There were men atop roofs, on scaffolds and others unloading lumber from wagons and toting it to building sites. Loaded wagons en-route to those sites became constant as they neared the business district, and Rodney had to stop the surrey to take it all in.

New stores and shops had already been built along the street on both sides, while others were still being built, and most were being erected with adobe blocks, or red brick from the kiln factories East of town, . . . and the air was filled with the sounds of progress.

He clucked the horse into motion again, and as they neared the square, they both looked up at the two and three-storied buildings, some still vacant while others had people carrying in furnishings and products to stock the store shelves. The square itself was teeming with activity, men carrying, or unloading lumber, unloading brick or blocks onto wheelbarrows for transportation. Others just jostling each other as they hurried to their chores.

"Still got a long way to go." Sighed Rodney, as he urged the horse across the busy square. "Lookin' good, though."

"Peterson Hotel in business." Nodded Billy. "Sign's up already."

"So's the Courthouse . . . . Rock looks good, don't it?"

"Usin' rock and adobe on all of 'em, looks like."

"Harder to burn, I guess." He stopped the horse at the bank's hitch-rail. "Hope Horace is here."

They got down and climbed the new steps to the porch, turned once more to view the square and then tried the door.

"Locked!" Sighed Rodney. "Must be on th' job-site somewhere."

Billy leaned to peer through the glass. "He's here, Rod." He knocked on the door several times before Horace Bratcher looked up from his books and recognized them. "Here he comes."

"Hello, boys!" He smiled then vigorously shook their hands. "Come in, come in!"

"After we get th' gold in, Horace." Said Billy. "Open th' safe while we bring it in."

Once the gold was secured and locked away, they sat down across from Bratcher at the desk.

"How much this time, boys?"

"Close to three hundred pounds, give or take."

"You two have really come through for this town. No one here will ever be able to thank you enough, especially me!"

"It's our town, too, Horace." Said Billy. "I owe you, and th' people here a lot more than that."

Bratcher cleared his throat "A long, and forgotten chain of events, William, long forgotten!"

"Then why was th' doors locked on a Friday mornin'?"

"What's one thing got to do with the other?" He grinned. "I was way behind on the books, that's why. Sometimes I have to just lock the doors to get it done!"

"We appreciate what you're doin', Horace."

"Well, I'm afraid I have some disheartening news for you." He looked from one, to the other of them for a moment. "A tax agent accompanied the gold proceeds from Shreveport last time. I had to pay taxes on it, and back taxes on all the rest . . . . But it's okay, didn't put much of a dent in it! He also tried to get me to tell him where all that gold came from."

"What did you tell 'im?"

"Donations from various prospectors, and that I didn't ask any questions."

"We been expectin' it, Horace." Nodded Billy. "I'm getting' th' same story at th' mint . . . . So, what do we do?"

"Truthfully, . . . I don't believe you have any choice, but to register your mine."

"You can't begin to imagine th' problems that might incur, Horace." Said Rodney. "Things we don't dare tell you about."

"I don't even want to know, boys! . . . I'm just saying that times are changing. The Government's been levying taxes on more and more of our daily lives. During the war, it was mostly on hard liquor, that and bootleg distilleries. Needed the money to pay for the war, they said! . . . Keeps going, they'll tax the air we breathe! He said he was paid by the Government, and the money had to come from somewhere, and since the Government works for all of us, we have to pay its wages in taxes."

"And by registering th' mine, what?" Asked Billy. "We can pay taxes on what we sell, why register th' mine?"

"I'm afraid it's simple, William. Because now, myself, and every other business owner in Paris will have to pay a business tax! Register your mine, it becomes a business, and the Government can tax it . . . . Of course, it's your decision to make, boys, we can go on like this forever, no problem. But sooner or later, you'll be forced to do it . . . . This is just the beginning!"

"Well." Sighed Billy. For now, I think we'll make it later."

"Works for me, boys. Your secret is safe with me! . . . How long you in town for?"

"We're leavin' for Shreveport on Monday, Horace." Said Rodney. "Got a job to do there."

"Think th' bank there might cash in some gold for us?" Asked Billy. "Couple a pounds, maybe?"

"I think so, but get your story straight. They'll be asking questions."

"We will." Returned Rodney. "Is Jim's office in th' new Courthouse now?"

"Sure is, Judge Bonner's, too. Not holding any court yet."

"What about th' Sheriff's office?"

"Being built, across the square yonder. Right now, he shares the office with Stockwell."

"We have a little business with him, too, Horace." Said Rodney, as they both got up. "So, we'll say good bye."

Bratcher got to his feet and shook their hands again. "It's always a blessing to to see you, boys . . . . Until next time."

"How long do ya think, before things are done here, Horace?" Asked Billy.

"According to the Architechs, another three to five years for all of it. Downtown here, a year, maybe."

"Take care, Horace." Waved Rodney, and followed Billy out to the porch, where they both looked up the street at the Courthouse.

"Ride, or walk?" Asked Billy with a sigh.

"No room to walk, man, let's ride!"

*   *   *

John Lake drew his pistol when he heard the footsteps outside his office door. Still seated behind his desk, gun covering the door, his deputy came in without knocking.

"Damn it, Andy!" He said angrily. "Knock before you bust in here! . . . You can get shot doin' that! . . . How many, . . . never mind!" He said and put the gun away. "What's the big rush?"

"What? . . . Oh, you got another wire from that Judge Parker!" He gave Lake the folded paper then went quickly into the cellblock.

"Did you read this?" He asked when he came back.

"No, sir, I did not!"

"What was you doin' back there?"

"Had to piss, . . . seein' that gun pointed at me, scared me. I had to go!"

"Have you ever wondered if you were in the wrong business, Andy?"

"What?"

"Nothin', Andy." He sighed and held up the wire. "Seems our escapees do have a few friends out there somewhere . . . . Says here they had three visitors while in custody, Same three men, on several occasions. Got their names and descriptions here! . . . Wonder how he did that?"

"It's a prison, Sheriff, . . . they have to sign in when they visit somebody."

"Yeah, guess you're right. Maybe we ought a start doin' th' same! . . . Anyway, one of 'em is, Ed McCreedy, six foot tall, lean face, lanky frame, possible professional gunman, considered dangerous! . . . Next is, Lionel Wallace, five-foot, eight, heavy mustache, paunchy, also considered dangerous . . . Next, is one Morgan Ellis, six foot tall, two hundred pounds, lean face, wears two pistols, possible professional gunman . . . . All three are believed to have abetted in their escape." He put the paper down and leaned back in his chair.

"What do ya think about it, Sheriff?"

"Don't rightly know." He mused. "Unless th' three in there came here to wait for th' other three to show up. . . . Question is, where were they, and why didn't they all come here together? . . . And where are they now?"

"Maybe they're here already."

He nodded. "Maybe they are . . . . may have brought more men with 'em, too! And that raises the possibility of an attempted jailbreak right here!"

"Want us to look for 'em, Sheriff?"

"That would be nice, Andy, I wish you would! . . . But first, go find Grady and Cooter. All three of ya come back here first." He watched him leave then got up to lock the door again, thinking that he had been foolish not to have locked it before. Shaking his head, he came back to the stove, grabbed his cup and poured fresh coffee, and had just sat down again, when someone tried the knob on the door . . . . And then came the knock.

He pulled his gun and went to open the shutter on the window, seeing only one man on the walkway. He went to the door as the knock came again. "Who is it?"

"John Childers." Came the muffled reply.

Puzzled, he leaned closer to the door. "Repeat th' name, please?"

"John Childers, . . . I, . . . I want a see my brother, Ben."

"He cocked the pistol. "Back away from th' door, and I'll unlock it!" He unlocked the door and moved to the side. "Come on in!"

"Hey, ya, Sheriff!" Said the man, holding up both hands.

"Lock th' door, John!" He waited until Childers locked the heavy door. "Now, What's your name again?"

"I done told ya, Sheriff, J, . . . John Childers . . . . I heard you got my brother in jail here, and, and I just wanted to talk with 'im!"

"I guess it'll be okay." He said, and motioned with the gun. "Just put your weapons on th' desk there." He watched as he put pistol and hunting knife on the desk. "Remove your shirt and boots, please."

"What?"

"Mister Childers, I can't take any chances, brother or not! . . . Or would you rather just leave?" He watched Childers reluctantly remove his grimy shirt, then lean against the desk to remove his boots.

"Empty 'em, now!" And when the gun fell out. "What was your plans for that, Mister Childers?"

"Nothin' atoll, Sheriff. I'm so used to it bein' there, I plumb forgot about it, honest Injun!"

"Okay, leave your stuff there and I'll take ya back to your brother." He took the cell keys from the peg and opened the cellblock door. "Go on, lead th' way." And when Childers went inside, followed him down the aisle between the cells to that of Ben Childers, waved John Childers aside and opened the cell door to admit him. He closed and locked the cell door behind him. "Take your time, Mister Wallace, you'll have plenty of it!"

"Wha, . . . my names ain't Wallace, it's John Childers . . . . Ben here's my brother." He turned to Childers then. "Ain't that right, Ben?"

"You're an idiot, Lionel!" Said Childers with passion. "A fuckin' bonehead!"

"Ya, . . . ha, hey, wait, you can't lock me up, Sheriff! . . . I ain't done nothin'!"

"Won't work, Mister Wallace. Judge Parker sent me your description less than ten minutes ago, McCreedy and Ellis, too! . . . Care to tell me where they are?"

"Fuck you!"

Nodding, he left the cellblock and closed the door. That proved one thing, he thought, the other two were already in town. Now, all he had to do was find them before they decided to rush the jail. He sat down and took a swallow of his coffee, thinking it strange Wallace showed up right on the heels of Andy. Could it be, he was watching the office and saw Andy come in? That had to be it, he thought, and got up again to go to the window, opened the heavy shutter and studied the crowded boardwalk across the street, and especially those people entering and leaving the saloon's swinging doors . . . . 'That would be the perfect place to watch from', he thought . . . . 'nothing but the dregs of a rotten barrel in that place, them three would have fit right in'! "Damn it to hell!" He cursed then closed the shutter.

What would they try next, he wondered? . . . Were they still watching to see if Wallace came out? Or did they think he'd be able to smuggle that bootleg gun in to Childers? If they did, they were fools! He thought angrily . . . . Maybe Wallace was only to deliver a message to Childers, their plans to break them out? . . . Maybe they know that a Marshal was coming to take them back, . . . but how? . . . Bert Ables, that's how! . . . That scrawny excuse of a railroad telegrapher! Wouldn't take much to bribe, or scare that weasel into telling them anything!"

If that was it, they'd be planning to take them away from the Marshal when they left . . . . He took another drink of the warm coffee and sat down again. If that was their plan, why send Wallace in with a hideout gun, . . . unless they figured it was worth a try?"

There was still his original question, however. Why hadn't they been with Childers and the other two when he arrested them? Where were they? . . . Recruiting more men? . . . Maybe! . . . Maybe they were planning a job in Shreveport? . . . He drained his cup and slammed it down.

They could have been in that saloon all along, he thought, could have been at that bar right beside them, and he wouldn't have known it. His descriptions, at the time, were only on childers and the other two. If they were there, Shreveport may have been only a stopover for them. Then again, there were two banks in town, and the Federal Reserve. Maybe that was it!"

"This is not going to end right!" He said, slapping his hands on the desktop. He got up then, when he heard the knock at the door, and recognizing Andy's voice, opened it to let them in.

*   *   *

"Well, if this don't beat all!" Said Jim Stockwell, getting up to go shake their hands. "Good to see ya, Marshal, you, too, Billy . . . . Come in, sit down! How about some coffee?"

"How are ya, Kim?" Asked Rodney as they sat down.

"Never better, Rodney." He said, pouring coffee into two tin cups. "Sort a dull around here, in fact . . . . Here ya go." He gave them the cups and sat down himself. "When did ya get in?"

"Last night." He replied, still looking the room over. "Big office, Jim, ground floor, too!" He grinned then. "Beats hell out a three flights up, don't it?"

"Ya got that right!" He chuckled. "Judge Bonner's right next door."

"And th' jail?"

"Third floor, . . . Courtroom's right above us."

"Cool in here, too." Commented Billy. "Must be th' rock."

"Be even cooler when they get th' fan workin'."

"Fan?'

"On th' ceilin' there." Grinned Stockwell. "Called a ceilin' fan, . . . it's electric. Motor's inside th' cover of it."

"I seen them things at a hotel in Denver." Said Billy.

"Well, I read about 'em." Said Rodney. "But we didn't see a power-plant comin' in, where is it?"

"Ain't got one yet, they're gonna build it! . . . That fancy architect says we'll have telephones in a couple a years, too, stringin' wires for 'em all across th' country already. Usin' th' telegraph poles that's already there. Can't imagine that, . . . can't figure how it might work. But if it does, be the end of th' telegraph! . . . Now, . . . what can I do for ya, Marshal?"

"Got a favor to ask, is all, and you can turn me down, no hard feelings."

"That ain't likely, you just name it! . . . Turning you down is out a th' question."

"Well, . . . I have to tell ya, I feel a mite foolish to even ask, Jim/"

"He's tryin' to tell ya, we had a little trouble coming in yesterday." Said Billy. "And his wife's a little anxious about it."

"What kind a trouble?"

"A man name a Ben Thompson tried to rob us."

"Ben Thompson?"

"You heard of 'im?" Asked Rodney. "Said he was Sheriff of Austin, Texas once."

"Ben Thompson, . . . yeah, I think I have heard of 'im, or maybe I read about 'im, I don't know. You say he tried to rob ya, . . . did he?"

"No, Billy shot 'im'."

"Dead?"

"In th' arm . . . . Anyway, Jim, Billy and me have to be in Shreveport come Tuesday, so, we'll be leavin' on Monday. I've got three convicted prisoners we have to take back to Fort Smith."

"Hey, . . . I got that wire a while back. They broke out a jail, right?"

"Yeah, . . . anyway, in lieu of arresting Thompson, and having to spend another month here to testify, . . . I let 'im go! . . . He ain't dangerous, I think, his gun arm's busted. But Lisa's afraid he might a waited and followed us to my ranch, wanting revenge, or somethin'."

"And you want a deputy to watch th' place, right?"

"If you have th' manpower, yes, but only for a few days. He can take his meals at th' ranch."

"How soon ya want 'im?"

"Monday?"

"He'll be there!" . . . And you're right, too . . . . Probably been more'n a month to try 'im, Bonner's sendin' everything to trial in Cooper."

Rodney nodded and reached to shake his hand. "Many thanks, Jim. I'd never of asked ya, except, I promised Lisa."

"You don't need to explain, Rodney . . . . So, what do you think of th' town?"

"It's comin' along just fine, Jim. Gonna be different, that's for sure."

"Won't be able to recognize it when it's done." Added Billy "Won't be th' same! Everything's changin', and I don't know if I like it."

"Like what, Billy?" Asked Jim.

He looked up at the fan. "That, for one, telephones, for another . . . . Next ya know, Government'll try and take our guns from us."

"Naw." Said Stockwell. "I've been readin' th' Declaration of Independence, Judge Bonner has a copy of it . . . . Second amendment states firmly that we will always have the right to own and bear arms."

"Like I said, time changes things!" He got up as he spoke. "I need to be getting' on to Doc's, Rod."

"Yeah, sure, . . . we got a go, Jim, thanks much, ya hear."

"Any time, Marshal. You, too, Billy."

"Thanks, Jim." He shook hands again and they left.

*   *   *

"Come on in, boys." He said, and as they entered, stared hard at the saloon door across the wide street. Seeing nothing he would deem suspicious, he closed the door behind them.

"Andy fill you in?" He asked, coming back to sit at his desk.

"Yes, sir." Said Grady. "It was sketchy at best, but we got it . . . . Think they're in town?"

"There's a good chance, yeah." He picked up the wire and gave it to him. "I want all three of you to memorize the names and descriptions! . . . Yeah, I think they were at that bar when we arrested Childers and the other two, Grady., likely standing elbow to elbow with 'em . . . . We just didn't know it!"

"Sons of Bitches!" Mouthed Cooter.

"If they're here, we'll try like hell to find 'em, Sheriff." Said Grady.

"Oh!" He said, almost grinning. "There won't be but two of 'em, . . . I caught one of 'em already."

"Get out a here!" Exclaimed Grady. "How?"

"Might as well have given his self up! . . . Came in right after Andy left to find you. Said he was Ben Childers' brother, and wanted to see 'im. He fit Lionel Wallace's description, so I had him leave his weapons on th' desk, and strip down to only his jeans, took 'im back and locked 'im up!"

"Was it, Wallace, for sure, Sheriff?" Asked Cooter.

"Childers called him Lionel, and also, an Idiot! . . . It's Wallace!"

"Well," Said Grady. "Be dark in a couple a hours, better start lookin'."

"Yry the saloons first, then rooms to let. You don't find 'em, come on back here, . . . this whole thing could be a ploy to keep all a you away from the office tonight."

"Think they'll try and break 'em out?" Queried Andy.

"Could be, Andy, . . . could be, they've already recruited another man, or men. Maybe they already have men camped outside a town somewhere! . . . Either way, I don't intend to lose these Bastards!"

"When's that Marshal due, Sheriff?"

"Hard to say, Grady. He works the Indian Territory, got his headquarters back in th' hills there somewhere . . . . Anyway," He sighed. "Them storms that came through here, went through there first, except, word is they had twisters! . . . He'll be here when he can swim out, I guess. Federal Judge said he was one a th' best he had, . . . and the only one not on assignment elsewhere." He reached the pot from the stove and emptied it into his cup.

"Our job's over, when he takes custody."

"Well, give us some idea, Sheriff. When do you expect he'll be here?"

"Cooter, . . . rain stopped down there couple a weeks ago, about a few days before it did here! . . . And as anxious as Isaac Parker was to get 'em back, I'd say Tuesday, maybe Wednesday th' outside . . . Today's Friday, we got a hold these bastards another three or four days at most, . . . and I got a know I can depend on you three."

"That goes without sayin', Sheriff." Nodded Grady then looked at the other two. "Right, boys?"

"Thanks, men. We may not have any trouble at all, they may be planning th' break for somewhere between here and Fort Smith . . . . Go ahead now, do what ya can."

He watched them leave then went to lock the door behind them. 'I hope that's the plan', he thought, as he went back to the desk. He pulled the bandana from his neck then and wiped his face and neck, thinking it was too hot to make more coffee, and went, instead, to the water bucket for a long drink before deciding to open the door for a while. He opened it and let it swing inward before going to sit down again and watch the people walk past on the boardwalk.

He hoped that Marshal was tough enough to handle those four men, he thought, but he knew within reason, he would not be able to stop Ed McCreedy and Ellis from taking them away. Was Isaac Parker that desperate, to send one man to do it? He knew what was going to happen, he had to know! Oh well, he thought, it would all be out of his hands when they were gone. The only chance he might have of making it, he knew, was if his deputies could find them in town, and arrest them?

Which would present another problem, he thought, . . . One man, with six prisoners, traveling two hundred and fifty miles. It might work on a train, but the rails didn't go all the way to Fort Smith. Six men wouldn't fit on a stage coach, either, and expect them to be guarded, much too close quartered inside . . . . The only thing left, would be horseback.

He shook his head to clear it. There was just no solution to it, he decided, thinking it best just to be happy they would be gone from his custody. He yawned then, thinking a nap might help things, and went to close the door and lock it, before going into the cellblock, and one of the cells.

CHAPTER FIVE

"Ohhh, myyy, Lorrrd!" Cried Mattie Bailey as her and Doc came out onto the porch, crossed it and came down into the yard, as Willy jumped out of the buckboard to open the gate wide enough for Billy to drive the team through then ran to hug the old couple. At that point, Billy was forced to stop as Chris and Angela literally leaped to the ground to rush into their arms.

Grinning widely, He got down to help Connie out, before getting back in and driving the team on to the barn. By then, Willy had rejoined him and they unharnessed the team and put them in stalls.

"Thanks for th' help, son." He grinned as they went back to the porch, where Doc waited to shake his hand vigorously.

"Good to see you, son!" He beamed. "Good to see you. Come, come into the house . . . . It's only been a few months, but it seems like years since we've seen you all."

"I know, Doc." He smiled, and then noticed the cane. "You weren't usin' a cane, last time I seen ya, what's with that?"

"Old age, I guess, son. Legs are getting weaker, knees are about gone, and Doc Snyder says I may be trying to develop a touch of Gout in my feet . . . . The cane helps a lot!"

They entered the kitchen where Mattie had already placed slabs of chocolate cake, and milk in front of the children and seeing Billy, came around the table with open arms, and tears in her eyes.

"Oh, William." She sniffed. "Welcome home, honey! I love you so very much!"

"I love you, too, Mama." He allowed her to usher him to his chair then watched as she lumbered around the table for the coffee pot.

"Do you want some cake, my love?"

"Just coffee, Mama, thanks." She poured their coffee then quickly placed a cup in front of Will and filled it.

"I did not forget, young man!" She said then looked at each of them. "You three darlings must have grown five inches in the last few months, and even more handsome . . . . All but you, sweet Angela, you are the most beautiful young woman in all of Texas . . . . Just like your mother!"

"Awww, thank you, mama Bailey." Smiled Connie. "We love you, too, now please sit down, you look so tired."

"I am, a little." She sighed and sat down. "I seem to tire out quickly these days."

"Three bouts with Pneumonia didn't help any, old darlin'." Added Doc.

"What's gonna happen when you both can't get around anymore, Mama?"

"Lord, William, I don't know!" She sighed. "We've already outlived our usefulness, I think."

"That's a fact!" Stated Doc. "Government estimated mortality rate is to the age of sixty-five for most folks. We left that behind us fifteen years ago."

"Seems to me, you're thinkin' about dyin' on us." Said Billy. "And I ain't gonna allow you to do that!"

"Now, just how much say, do you think you'll have in it?" Chuckled Doc. "Makes no difference how old you are, if the good Lord sends for you, son."

"I know you're right, Doc." He nodded. "But we don't have to rush it." He looked at Connie then, and nodded. "Seems we only have two options here, too, one of which you have no control over."

"Just what have you got in mind here, William?" Asked Doc. "Because if one of those options is leaving our home, we will not go!"

"That's what we figured, so that leaves the other option . . . . Connie and th' kids will be here for maybe a month while I'm gone."

"While you're gone?" Interrupted Mattie. "Where you going?"

"With Rodney, to deliver some prisoners to Fort Smith, Arkansas."

"Does that take two of you?" Asked Doc.

"There's three of 'em, Doc, condemned killers! . . . They broke out a th' prison at Fort Smith and killed a couple guards doin' it! . . . It's a gut-feelin' I got, but accordin' to Rod, that prison is all but escape-proof, so I'm thinkin' they had a lot a help . . . . If it's true, they might try to free 'em again! . . . Rod won't have a chance alone."

"Then, by all means, you have to go, son!" Agreed Doc. "But do be careful. As good as you are, at what you do, you are not infallible.

"Believe me, I know that, Doc! . . . At any rate, back to th' subject at hand, which leaves you two with one option. Connie will be here, and next week, Her and Willy will bring Doc, Snyder to see you for a complete checkup, and after that, he will find, and hire the best live-in maid, and housekeeper he can, . . . and she will move in here with you, the day I get back, and we leave for home."

"It's only because we love you!" Said Connie quickly. "We want you with us for a long time."

"You and Mama saved my life, Doc." Reminded Billy. "You are my familt . . . . Now, I'm gonna do th' same for you!"

Doc sighed then lay both hands on the table before nodding. "Okay, son, whatever you say. A year ago, I would have said no, I want you to know that!"

"It's settled then." Smiled Mattie. "And you know what? . . . I'm glad, so let's not let it ruin our reunion!"

"I agree." Said Doc, with a smile. "When do you have to leave, son?"

"Monday morning . . . . Rod wants to take th' train to Shreveport, that's where they are."

"No trains go from here to Shreveport yet." Said Doc. "I believe the closest you'll get to Shreveport, is Longview, Texas. I know, I used to correspond with surgeons in New Orleans, and the letters always came by train, by stage from anywhere else."

"Rod'll be thrilled at that!" . . . Oh, well, . . . you see Ross lately, Doc, I won't be able to before I get back?"

"As a matter of fact, Ross brings us fresh garden vegetables every other week or so. We hardly ever go for supplies."

"He's a fine man, and a damn good friend!" Sighed Billy. "He's wonderful." Agreed Connie.

"Well," Said Billy. "Not much daylight left, got anything needs fixin' around here, you now have today, tomorrow and Sunday to use two able-bodied men to do your bidding."

"Correction." Said Connie. "You have today, and tomorrow. Sunday is for Church services, and rest!"

*   *   *

Much of the northeast area of Texas with Louisiana was made up of swampland. A dense bog in a forest of entangled wilderness that was infested with gators, poisonous vipers and hungry insects. Not many, other than the Caddo Indians, had the attitude, or savvy that it required to live and survive there. The few that did choose to build their cabins in the remote areas of the swamp, were without fear of anyone venturing in to find them.

Most of the scant high ground through this wasteland had already been utilized by the Texas and Louisiana railroad, who built their tracks right through the bog, all the way to Texarkana, Texas and on into the Pine wilderness where lumber was being harvested. Lumbermen used it to ship logs and processed lumber to mills all across Louisiana.

The swamp was a dark, dreary place, and among those who chose to live there was a half-breed Choctaw Indian, and his young Caddo wife. Choctaw Joe Haskell had lived most of his life in the Choctaw Nation, had always been a thief who particularly enjoyed aggressive robbery. He feared no one, had no friends, so he preferred to be a loner, who for most of his young adult life, had evaded capture by the U.S. Army, as well as the fabled Choctaw Police Force. Continuing to do so until his twenty-first birthday when, while intoxicated, he raped and killed a very young Cherokee girl.

Everyone suspected, or knew that he had done it, but there was no physical proof, and they couldn't find him. Considering himself to be smarter than the rest, he continued his thievery right up to the time he was finally attacked by the ghosts of ancient Indians. Unsure whether they were ghosts, or flesh and blood Indians, they were after him, and he was sure it was because of what he had done. He knew they would eventually kill him, so he tried to hide out. But wherever he went, he would see them. One moment, an Indian would be there, the next moment, he was gone, . . . and each time, arrows would narrowly miss killing him.

He had grown up hearing stories of the Ancient Ones living inside the Devil Mountain, but no one had ever seen them, only rumors of those who had, . . . and those rumors were that only the wrongdoer would see them, just before they were executed for their sins. He had never believed they actually existed, until he saw them himself.

Believing his only option was to leave the Choctaw Nation, he made his escape into Arkansas, and finally Louisiana where he befriended and lived with an old Caddo Indian and his family. He learned their survival skills needed to live there in the swamp and a few months later, continued the life he had chosen, one of aggravated robbery, thievery, and this time, even murder before disappearing back to the swamp.

Then one day, the young Caddo girl began to grow and blossom into a sexy young woman, and he became obsessed in his desire of her. So one night, he slit the throats of the girl's parents in their sleep and took the girl to a deserted cabin he had found deep in the swamp and there, set up housekeeping.

It was on one of his excursions to Shreveport that he met Ed McCreedy, and was convinced to join him and several other men in a plan to rob the two banks in Shreveport. But first, they had three other members they had to rescue from the law. Why, because a few months before, the six of them had robbed a bank in Tennessee, . . . and one of the men in jail was the only one that knew where the money was hidden . . . . If he would join them, all he had to do was furnish a hideout for him and two other men while he worked out a plan to break their accomplices out of jail. If he agreed, he would not only share and participate in money from the Shreveport robberies, but also in the hidden fifty thousand dollars.

Being greedy himself, Haskell readily accepted and that same night, led them to his cabin where three days later, Lionel Wallace was sent back to town to watch the Sheriff's office, and when a chance arrived, to try and visit Childers, and tell him of their plans.

*   *   *

"It's been three days, Ed!" Said Morgan Ellis from his chair at the small table, then suddenly slapped his hand down on the spider that crawled toward him. "Mildew, spiders, snakes, . . . I'm tired a this shit, too!"

McCreedy turned away from the window where he had been watching the way in from the swamp, and looked from Ellis, to the makeshift bed where Haskell and the Caddo girl sat watching them. "I know how long it's been, Morgan." He replied, looking back at him. "I'm well aware of it!"

"They why do you keep hangin' on to this crazy idea of yours, . . . let's look at what we got, man!" He absently pulled his pistol. "We already know a Marshal is on his way, Right? . . . If we can't break 'em out a jail here, we'll have to do it away from here. We can't rush th' jail, hell, there's people on that street day and night, saloon's right across th' street!"

"Accordin' to you, we can't do th' banks with only three men, and I agree with ya, . . . we need at least four more, and unless we recruit four men, we might not can trust, we need Childers and the other two! . . . . Way I see it, we ain't got a lot, Ed! Only option we got is to break Childers and the others out, and we both know we can't do that!" He looked around at the almost bare shelves on the wall.

"We're out a grub, too." He added with a smile.

McCreedy studied the gunman for a minute then moved away from the window to stand in front of the table. "You're right, Morgan." He nodded. "He should have been back by now, if all went right! . . . . Unless the ignorant Bastard got himself caught, Sheriff could a known who he was."

"Likely knows who we are by now, too!" Said Ellis as he used a dirty rag and began wiping down the pistol. "Wish I hadn't give Childers my other gun! . . . Had a matchin' set . . . . Fuckin' Sheriff's got it now! . . . None of this surprises me, Ed, they caught 'im quick enough! . . . We'd be there with 'im, they knew who we was . . . . Bet your ass, they do, now!" He peered up at McCreedy. "Got any more bright ideas?"

"Let up, Morgan! . . . I never claimed to be more than a genius! . . . I can't make any working plans without all the facts, . . . and we hardly have any at all! . . . Okay, today is Sunday." He mused, moving back to the window. "We'll give Lionel till noon tomorrow. If he ain't back, one of us will go in and find out why? . . . We'll need to bribe that telegrapher again, too. But mainly just to look things over . . . . Maybe we can find out when that Marshal will get here?"

"And if Lionel is in hail?"

"Then we'll do it your way, take 'em somewhere away from here . . . . That hanging Judge knows by now, that Childers had help escaping that prison, even knows who we are, and you're right, Sheriff would know by now as well."

"If he does, you can bet that Marshal will, too! . . . And that bein' th' case, you and me, both, would be takin' a chance by goin' in!"

"True, Morgan." He said, turning to look at Haskell. "But they don't know that Joe's one of us!"

Ellis looked across at Haskell then, his hungry eyes lingering on the slim, young woman.

"What about it, Joe?" Asked McCreedy. "They know you in town?"

"Most everybody knows me, yeah . . . . Law knows I done things they can't prove yet, too. They hassle me when they see me."

"Think you can pull it off? . . . with what we got planned, we'll need to know where Lionel is, and when that Marshal will get here? . . . And when they'll be leaving town with Childers? . . . I'd also like to know how they'll be going, coach, or by horse?"

"Don't forget th' train, Ed." Reminded Ellis. "It goes to Texarkana

"Yeah." He looked back at Haskell then. "Will you do it, Joe, it's possible they know what we look like?"

Haskell thought for a minute before nodding. "I can go, Mister McCreedy."

"Good man! . . . Now, plan on being there all night tomorrow night, ... unless you have the information we need . . . . If you do, then come on back, we'll need to make our plans. If you don't have it, you'll need to watch that jail, . . . if that lawman comes from Texas, it'll be by stage coach. Coach is usually here by three PM. If he's on it, they could be leaving sometime late tomorrow night, that'll give you time to come back and tell us! . . . If he ain't on it, or on that one at midnight, he'll be on that one on Tuesday."

"And don't forget th' grub!" Said Ellis, casting another look at the girl, but quickly looked back at his gun when Haskell caught him.

"I will do this, Mister McCreedy." He said, still looking at Ellis. "But remember this, too! . . . If one of you touch my woman while I'm gone, I will kill you."

"You mean, you'll try." Grinned Ellis. "You'll try."

"All right!" Said McCreedy, glaring at both of them. "Nobody will bother your woman, Joe, you have my word! . . . We can not afford to fight among ourselves, there's a fortune at stake here! . . . Do you understand me, Morgan?"

"Oh, I hear ya, Ed. Just don't threaten me, I wouldn't like that."

"Now, Morgan, . . . in the first place, I don't give a rat's ass what you like, or don't like! . . . I ain't no slouch with a gun myself, remember that! . . . Comes to it, we could both be dead if we fight, so don't go crazy on me."

"Point taken, Ed." He smiled then holstered the gun.

McCreedy stared at him for a moment. "Yeah, point taken! . . . This whole thing is lookin' to fall apart on us already . . . . We spent weeks trying to find a way to get Childers and them out of that lock-up! . . . Childers should a known, Louisiana weren't far enough away!"

"He convinced you, Ed! . . . Can't outrun a telegraph wire!"

"Do ya think?" Sbapped McCreedy. "How could we make so many mistakes? . . . I let Ben Childers get a choke hold on us, by letting him take that money, and what did it force us to do? . . . We had to break them out a prison! . . . And now, now we have to do it all over again, if we ever see a penny of it!"

"Then let's just take one of th' banks, ourselves, leave 'im where he is."

"Fifty thousand reasons, Morgan, know how far that'll go in Mexico?"

"Not far, split seven ways, Ed . . . . Fact is, we both know he never intended to split it with us, anyway. He saw his chance, when that posse was closin' in, and took it!" He watched McCreedy's face as he spoke. "Only hitch in his plan, was them Marshals, he weren't plannin' on bein' caught . . . . Likely surprised when Collins and Long showed up."

McCreedy nodded. "I agree, . . . They must a followed 'im when he left, they knew 'im better than we did! . . . They knew what he was up to, . . . and we should have, just didn't have enough time to think about it."

"If we knew where he was caught, chances are, we'd find that money."

"The answer to that is still in jail!" Sighed McCreedy. "It might not be there, anyway, law could a found it."

"He claims they didn't, Ed . . . . If we can believe anything he says, by now."

McCreedy turned and leaned against the wall. "Guess we all three believed 'im, we got 'im out! . . . What I can't figure, is why he wouldn't take us to the money right away, instead a coming here?"

"Lot a possibilities there, too!" Grinned Ellis.

"I know that now! . . . He either knows it ain't there, or he still has plans for keeping it. Well, if that's his plan, it ain't going to work, Morgan! . . . But to know for sure, we'll have to take 'im away from that Marshal."

"And if we're right?"

"Well, . . . you're so gun-happy, what do you think?"

"All four of 'em, Wallace, too?"

"After what we went through, . . . it's th' price of being stupid! . . . Joe, you'll go to town tomorrow as planned, we find out what we need to know, we'll make our plans."

"You still want more men?" Asked Haskell. "We will need them to rob a bank."

"Been thinking about that! . . . Recalling the bank in Memphis, Shreveport has an Army post as well . . . . We'll get Childers out first! . . . One thing at a time, Joe, . . . one thing at a time."

*   *   *

Rodney, Melissa and Cindy were waiting in the surrey as Billy and his arrived in the buckboard.

"Hey, Billy, Connie." He said, getting out to help Lisa and the girl down. "How's Doc, and Mattie?" He asked, turning as Billy helped Connie down. "They all right?"

"A mite poorly, Rod." He said, reaching to help Angela down. "Connie's gonna find some woman to move in with 'em, take care a things."

"That's a great idea." He reached into the surrey for his bag and rifle. "You look different, Billy, . . . I like that jacket, covers your gun and all."

"Wife's idea, said I should look th' part."

"You're doing important law business." Fussed Connie. "I want you to look important!" She reached to smooth out a wrinkle on the sleeve. "I know it's hot out, you can take it off on the train, just wear it when you get there . . . . See, Rodney's wearing one, too."

"Okay, honey, you sold me. Folks gonna think we're crazy, but ya sold me!" He reached in for his satchel and lifted it out. "We all set, Rod?"

"Far as it goes, yeah. Here's your ticket to Longview, Texas, . . . we'll have to take th' stage from there." He looped his arm in Melissa's and climbed the steps to the platform, with Bill, Connie and the kids behind them.

"Here we are!" Grinned Rodney. "train leaves in a few minutes, . . . this is our car right here." He grabbed Melissa and kissed her, and then Cindy. "We'll be back in no time at all." He kissed her again, and got on the train.

Billy looked down at Connie, and pulled her to him. "Time to go." He kissed her hard, and as he released her. "Been a long time, I went anywhere without ya."

"You know where we are, don't lose your way home!"

"Not a chance!" He lifted Angela enough to hug and kiss her, then pulled Christopher and Willy against him. "You boys watch over things while I'm gone. Take care of your mother and sister . . . . Watch over your Grandpa, and Grandma, too!"

"We will, Daddy." Said Willy.

"I know ya will." He smiled at Connie, nodded at the waiting conductor, and entered the passenger car.

"Pull up a chair!" Grinned Rodney. "Seems to be plenty of 'em, car's almost empty."

Billy placed the satchel on the seat facing Rodney, and sat down at the window as the train began to move with a couple of jerks and rattles. He looked at Rodney then and grinned before leaning out of the window to wave at the family, as did Rodney.

"You bring everything ya need?" Asked Rodney, leaning back to pull a cigar from his shirt and lighting it.

'Spare gun, ammunition, clothes and shavin' gear. Far as I know, that's it!"

"Where's your rifle?"

"You got one." He shrugged, and then removed the light jacket.

"Might wish you had one." He nodded. "What about th' gold?"

"Where Willy put it, in my satchel! . . . Ever been to Longview, Rod?"

"Don't even know anybody from there, . . . you?"

"My folk's family came from around there. Seems a County was named after a great Uncle, or Grandpa a mine . . . . A U. S. Senator, or somethin', accordin' to my daddy."

"I always knew you were royalty."

"That mean you're gonna start bowin' when you see me?"

"You're a little far removed from it all to rate that much formality."

"My first time on a train, too! . . . And it ain't too bad."

"Me, too, and I agree with ya . . . . Seats could use some more cushion, but there's a nice breeze through th' windows. Yeah, I like it . . . . Won't be so nice in winter, I think . . . . Pot-bellied stove won't do much for a car this size."

"That's what coats and blankets are for, Rod, . . . you wire that Sheriff of our comin'?"

"Hour ago, yeah . . . . Ticket agent said we should make Longview in about four hours, five or six, if we're not flagged down for more passengers . . . He had no idea how long th' stage ride would be? . . . Be there sometime around midnight, maybe."

"Still pretty good time." Said Billy. "That's three full days by horseback."

"I'm for rentin' a bed when we get there, myself, . . . do our business tomorrow."

"Sounds good . . . . How'll we restrain th' prisoners for th' trip, Rod, any ideas?"

"Ain't thought about none a that! It's a long trip, though, what do you think?"

"Chain around th' waist, I guess, hands chained to that. It ought a hold 'em! Still won't be easy in a car like this, especially with other passengers."

"That ain't the only problem, Billy. That ticket agent told me th' train from Shreveport only goes as far as Texarkana, Texas!"

"Texarkana? . . . Ain't heard a that one, where is it?"

"On th' border with four states, Louisiana, Indian Territory, Texas and Arkansas. They all come together there, give or take a few miles."

"Looks like another stage ride! . . . That, or where saddle horses could be put to good use! . . . Three chained killers on a stage coach could get touchy."

"Well, I don't think Judge Parker would reimburse us th' price of five saddle horses! . . . Maybe we can arrange for a mail-coach, or somethin'. At least an empty stage coach?"

"Still be crowded! . . . We both know those three didn't escape Fort Smith on their own."

"And whoever helped 'em will most likely try it again, I know! . . . I also know that's your reason for comin' with me! . . . Thanks, Billy."

"You'd do th' same."

"In a heartbeat!"

"Ever been to Shreveport?" He asked, looking out the window.

"Billy, I ain't been much of anywhere since comin' here! . . . But that's where you joined up, you told me that."

"In sixty-one, yeah, . . . and unless it's changed a hell of a lot, it's a wide open, no holds barred river-port. Had nine killings th' day I arrived."

"Like you always said, time changes things. Let's hope it has!" He looked at Billy and sighed. "I'm gonna resign when we get to Fort Smith, Billy!"

"Well, that's out a th' blue, Rod, when did that happen?"

"I don't know, when Lisa let me know how she felt about it, I guess . . . . I had thought about it before though, several times."

"Well, I think it's great, Rod! . . . Way I see it, Marshaling carries about th' same life expectancy as gun-fighting! . . . Both are meant for men with no family, no one to miss 'em . . . . I'm proud of ya."

"It was a hard decision to make, I love bein' a lawman."

"I know ya do . . . . What about Peter, he'll be disappointed?"

"If I have anything to do with it, he'll be wearing my badge!"

"That's a good move, too! . . . He's a damn good man, become quite handy with his hand guns, too. He's already pretty fast on th' draw."

"Almost as fast as me, Billy, but more accurate! . . . Practices all th' time."

"He's a dedicated man, Rod

"Amen to that! . . . In a lot of ways, he's a better man at this job than I could ever be! Gun or knife, I don't know anyone better, reading a trail, there's none better, and when he starts something, he never quits . . . . I wouldn't want 'im after me."

CHAPTER SIX

John Lake was standing by his office window when Grady Sutton came in, and partially closed the shutter again.

"What's happening, Grady?" He asked, turning to watch the deputy.

"Ya know, Sheriff, . . . I don't know!" He gave the paper to Lake. "I went by the telegraph office, since I was close by anyway, and he gave me that . . . . It came in at eight o'clock this mornin', and here it is, almost three o'clock!"

"No harm done, I guess." Said Lake, and opened the paper. Marshal Taylor left Paris, Texas at nine o'clock this mornin', by train. Means he'll he'll be here on th' midnight stage! . . . I want you to be at that stage office to meet 'im, . . . take 'im to Grover's Hotel and get 'im settled then go on home, come in at noon tomorrow." He held the paper up then.

"Moses tell ya why he didn't bring this to me this mornin'?"

"Said he was too busy, then forgot about it. But that ain't what's odd about it! . . . Somebody else asked about that wire, paid Moses five bucks to read it."

"Who?"

"Joe Haskell!"

"Choctaw Joe Haskell? . . . Think he joined up with 'em?"

"We could ask 'im, John! . . . You know, he was in that saloon, day we arrested Childers."

"I saw 'im, could a been there with the other three. Wish I'd taken a better look at th' men along that bar, because I don't recall seeing anybody meetin' McCreedy's description, not even Wallace."

"Want I should look for 'im, bring 'im in for questioning? . . . I seen 'im at that bar a time or two since then, but he'd leave almost as soon as I did . . . . Could be there now."

"No, we'll just watch 'im, see what he does. He ain't there anyway."

"How we gonna watch, . . . What do ya mean, he ain't there?"

"I mean, he's been in plain sight since before noon today, Grady! . . . Ain't you learned nothin' I said about th' power of observation, keepin' your eyes open?"

"I guess not, Sheriff, where is he?"

Lake turned and opened the shutter again. "He's on that bench, right in front a that saloon across th' way."

"Son of a bitch!" Exclaimed Grady. "Bastard's watchin' us!"

"I do believe he is."

"Then he is one of 'em!

"I think it's a strong possibility! . . . They either know, or think they know that Wallace is in jail, too! . . . They only know for sure, that he's missing. If they read this wire, they know that time's runnin' out for 'em to try anything in town here, because that street out there never sleeps, and they don't have enough men to pull it off!"

"That's why they wanted to see that wire." Said Grady. "They're gonna take 'em away from that Marshal!"

"That's my guess . . . . We'll warn th' Marshal, that's all we can do! . . . Did Moses come right out and volunteer this information?"

"About Haskell, well, yeah!"

"You ask 'im why?"

"Said he wasn't paid not to."

"That crooked liittle sack a shit! . . . Don't guess you spotted McCreedy, or Ellis anywhere in town?"

"Not hide nor hair, and I been all th' way to th' river docks and back."

"What about Andy, and Cooter, they still lookin'?"

"Workin' everything East and North a here . . . . I don't think they're here, Sheriff, I really don't!"

"Nor do I . . . . When's th' last time you checked th' saloon over there."

"First stop this mornin', why?"

"No reason, . . . McCreedy and Ellis are likely hold up at old Joe's place, wherever that is?"

"I could follow Haskell when he leaves?"

"We tried that a couple a times!"

"Yeah, that bog's a place, I don't want a get lost in!" He looked through the window at Haskell again. "Cavalry's on patrol."

"Don't get me started on that, Grady." Sighed Lake. "Wouldn't take th' Army twenty-four hours to clean up this town, make it a decent place to live!"

"I never knowed why they don't do it?"

"Reconstruction laws they never changed. They won't interfere with a city's politics unless the Mayor, and the City Council requests it . . . And that, Grady, will never happen, not while th' members of the council are being paid off!"

"Yes, sir, you told us all that before, . . . and it still don't make sense."

"That's why that Marshal's gonna deliver my letter to Fort Smith . . . . Isaac Parker's a well thought of Judge in Washington. Th' President listens to his recommendations . . . . If he'll send us a tough Federal Marshal to take up residence here, and a Federal Judge to back us all up. We'll give that state pen in Baton Rouge a lot a business!" He looked at Grady then, and nodded.

"Best get back to your patrols now, Grady . . . . Don't worry about Haskell,'. But you meet that stage tonight, and watch for old Joe, he could be there, too! . . . If he is, fill th' Marshal in on what to look for."

"You stayin' here tonight, John?"

"That's a good assumption, Grady! . . . I'm thinkin' on a plan that might help th' Marshal out tomorrow, if he'll go along with it?"

"Like what?"

"It involves Colonel Ford, if I can 'im to help us out? . . . I'll go see 'im, soon as Cooter and Andy check in."

*   *   *

"Coming in to Longview, Texas, Marshal." Said the Conductor on entering the car. "Need help with your luggage?"

"We're fine, thanks." Replied Rodney, and looked out at the sprawling, widespread community of Longview. "Good size place!"

"I'd say so." Responded Billy. "Comin' in to down town, looks like . . . . Typical place, two and three storied buildings, mostly of wood structure . . . . I expected to see a lot a brick here! Here's th' depot." He got up, as did Rodney, grabbed their satchels and were standing at the car door when the train shuddered to a stop.

"Stage station is about five hundred yards, straight down that street there." Said The Conductor as he opened the car's door for them. "Lots a luck to ya, Marshals."

"Thanks, Cecil." Nodded Rodney.

"Yeah," Grinned Billy, and then stepped out onto the platform behind Rodney. "Could be our coach down yonder."

"Could be." Said Rodney. "Come on." He led the way down to the dusty street, each wearing their light jackets, and carrying an almost bulky satchel as they made their way to the busy boardwalk, . . . and for the next twenty minutes were jostled constantly, and having to sidestep others as they made their way to the stage station.

The street was just as busy, pedestrians crossing, buckboards and freight wagons, squealing teams of straining horses, the occasional cracking of long, leather whips, and the mouthing's of sweat exhausted teamsters. Groups of mounted cowhands were right in the mix!

"Busy place." Said Billy as they stopped to look it all over.

"In this heat, too!" Rodney shook his head and went inside, with Billy on his heels and after waiting their turn, stepped up to the counter.

"Where to, gents?" Asked an unsmiling ticket agent.

"Two to Shreveport." Replied Rodney.

"Names?" He asked as he wrote out the stubs. "And that'll be four dollars each."

"I'm U. S. Marshal, Rodney Taylor . . . . This is Deputy Marshal, Nilly Upshur."

"Upshur, huh" Repeated the agent as he picked up the money, and then looking up to study him. "Any kin to the Upshur County Upshurs, . . . Commodore Upshur?"

"Appears I am!"

"Commodore was a great man!" He said as he stamped the stubs.

"Is that our coach out front?" Questioned Rodney, nodding at the door.

"Nope! . . . That one goes to Texarkana, with stops at Marshall and Daingerfield. Yours'll be along in half an hour. Be full, too, counting you two . . . . Have a seat against the wall over there, won't be long." He gave them their stubs and turned away.

"Come on, King Upshur, lets sit a spell." Grinned Rodney.

"Rod," He grinned also. "Hope you'll know when I get enough a that!"

"I will!" They laughed and took their seats against the wall.

Guess everybody in town knows your relatives. Maybe one day, you can look 'em up."

"I'd rather leave well enough alone, Rod . . . "I'm quite happy like it is."

"Amen to that!"

*   *   *

"Dad, Mama Bailey." Smiled Connie as her and the kids came in and stood to one side of the door to allow the middle-aged woman to enter in beside her. "I'd like you to meet Mary Beth Rhodes."

"Yes." Said Doc, coming to shake the woman's hand. "I've seen you several times at the Hospital assisting Doctor Snyder . . . . Mary Beth Rhodes? . . . Did I deliver one of your children? . . . I did, didn't I, some twenty-five years ago!"

"You delivered two of my children, Doctor, Billy Joe, and Billy Ray."

"My Lord, yes, I remember now. How are they?"

"Comanche wars." She said. "They're both gone."

"I'm so sorry, my dear."

"We heard about your husband's passing, too, Mary Beth." Interrupted Mattie. "Our condolences, Dear."

"Thank you." She smiled, looking around the room. "You have s lovely home here."

"Mary Beth has been living in an apartment at the hospital since her husband died. To pay her way, she's been keeping the surgical room clean, and assisting Doctor Snyder when the other nurses were occupied. She's well adept at keeping house and cooking for others.

"Are you sure you'd rather live here than at the hospital, my dear?" Asked Mattie, coming to wrap her in a hug. "We're going to be quite set in our ways, you know . . . . Especially this old codger here!"

"Of course." She smiled. "I love you both already."

"Okay then!" Sighed Doc. "Our son and daughter in law says we need you, so I guess we do! . . . Welcome to your new home."

"Thank you so much."

"We'll move her in when Billy gets back!" Smiled Connie. "And you are not to worry about her fee, it's all been arranged. As well as Doctor Snyder's monthly house calls to check on you."

"Well." Said Mattie, straightening her apron. "While I'm still in charge, I still have chocolate cake in the kitchen, some hot coffee and milk, too." She looped a beefy arm through that of Mary Beth's. "So, come on in, honey, we'll sit and visit a while before Connie takes you back."

*   *   *

McCreedy heard Morgan scrape his chair back and looked to see him cross to the old bed where the girl was cowering, her legs drawn up under her chin. "Morgan!" He warned, as the gunman sat down on the bed in front of her.

"Morgan!" He said again, getting his attention this time. "You've shown your restraint till now, leave her alone!"

"God damn it, Ed, look at her! . . . No way in hell, can she be turned on by an animal like him! Bastard stinks of this lousy swamp . . . . Oh, no, this little thing needs a real man, ya can see it in her eyes."

"Well, maybe you can explain all that to, Joe, he's riding in right now!"

"You best not be shitin' me, Ed!" He exclaimed, coming to the window. "Son of a bitch! . . . I ain't had no tail in a month!"

"You'll live, now sit down, he's comin' in." He reached and opened the old door to Admit Haskell.

Haskell stared at him, and then at Ellis before looking at the girl. "They bother you, girl?" And when she shook her head, he placed the potato sack on the table." Brought some jerky and canned beans."

"What did you find out?" Asked McCreedy as Ellis pulled beef jerky from the sack and began eating.

"That Marshal's comin' in tonight, Mister McCreedy, I seen th' telegram."

"How they takin' 'em back?"

"Ain't got no choice, but to take th' train, no stage leavin' for Texarkana till five o'clock tomorrow . . . . They won't wait that long."

"And Wallace?"

"I watched th' Sheriff's office till after three o'clock, he's got a be in jail, he sure ain't in town. I checked all th' saloons."

"Stupid Bastard!" He snapped. "Okay!" He nodded then. "Joe, you know these swamps, there any place along them tracks where we can stop that train?"

"Tracks are laid along th' only high ground for twenty miles, nothin' but Gators, snakes and suckin' mud on both sides. Can't even get on th' tracks."

"Shit!" He cursed. "How about the other side of the swamp, between there and Texarkana? . . . Got solid ground from there on, don't it?"

"I don't know, Mister McCreedy . . . . Jumpin' on a movin' train, wherever it is, is dangerous, and if we did, Engineers, Crew, all of 'em carry sawed-off shotguns."

"Well, it's either that, or ride all th' way to Texarkana and wait for 'em!"

"That's a hundred mile ride, Ed." Reminded Ellis. "They'd likely beat us there."

"Maybe not, if we leave now, we could make half that by mornin', grab some fresh horses somewhere and cover the other half." He looked at Haskell then.

"When's that train leavin'?"

"Ticket agent said noon tomorrow, regular scheduled pick-up."

"That'll give us plenty a time. It'll take that train anotger four or five hours to make th' trip onve it leaves . . . . I tell ya it'll work! . . . We can be there waitin' for 'em, take Childers from 'im as they get off."

"Texarkana would put us closer to that stashed money." Agreed Ellis. "It's your idea, make th' call . . . . Just remember, everything we done this past couple a months has been wrong! . . . Nothin' has turned out right! . . . Been thinkin' about what you said, too, Ed . . . . I'd like to know why he insisted on us comin' here, myself? . . . Son of a bitch must a had somethin' in mind!"

"I'm thinking he did! . . . Getting us as far away from that fifty thousand as he could, that was his idea!"

"He's pretty good at it!" Sighed Ellis. "Had us all believin' it was th' right thing to do. He could a thought, a wide open town would be th' place to hide . . . . Just didn't count on an honest Sheriff."

"Joe," Said McCreedy, turning to look through the window. "How's them tracks work, them running alongside th' depot . . . . I know they run all th' way to th' main line, some ten miles away from town. But th' passenger car's just sittin' there, freight car, too . . . . How's it work?"

"Army laid them tracks durin' th' war." Said Haskell. "They still own it, depot, too! Regular train only runs from New Orleans to Texarkana and back, but it'll pick up them cars in town."

"I know that, Joe, but when do they pick 'em up?"

"When there's enough passengers, or freight to be shipped from here, th' ticket agent telegraphs th' agent in New Orleans, or Texarkana, dependin' on where it's goin', or comin'! . . . They switch th' rails down there when th' train comes, it'll back all th' way into town and hook up to them cars." He shrugged then. "Then it leaves."

"That's it?"

"Far as I know! . . . When the cars come back, they'll back 'em all th' way back, and drop 'em . . . . And I know what you're thinkin', Mister McCreedy, but it won't work! Army may not use it much, but they still got guards posted there day and night . . . . They'd see us."

"What about where it stops to change tracks?"

"It's a freight train, no place to hide, but on top! . . . Trees would sweep us right off it goin' through this swamp."

"Got a backup plan, Ed?" Grinned Ellis.

"Yeah, I do! . . . Pack up, we're gonna beat that train to Texarkana!"

"Guess ya know, we could kill th' horses in all this heat, we'll have to run 'em all th' way."

"Then, we'll get fresh ones, Morgan, like I told ya! . . . There's other towns between here and there, ranches, too! . . . We'll get horses."

"We'll lose time doin' it!"

"Then you come up with a better idea, Morgan! . . . And none a this quit and leave shit, I ain't quitting!"

"You know I can't, Ed."

"Then don't argue with me, and get packed! . . . We leave in fifteen minutes."

*   *   *

'Attractive woman', thought Billy as he sized up the man and his wife in the opposite seat. The man was dressed in dark pants of material, other than jeans. His shirt was pale blue beneath a vest of the same material as the pants. But the coat was also a pale blue, and leaned more to the Continental style. His hair was graying, but the mustache and long sideburns were almost totally gray, a sharp contrast beneath the narrow-brimmed derby hat.

The woman was stylishly dressed in blue and white cotton, ankle length dress, tailored in a way that made her more than ample bosom a prominent feature. The low-cut blouse was just enough to make her assets the main attraction and focal point for him, Rodney, and the other man.

Both him, and Rodney tried several times to keep their attention trained on the view from the coach's large windows, but each time the coach would hit a dip, or a hole in the dusty road, her breasts would a juggling act of sorts and automatically draw their attention. Rodney, being between Billy and the other man, had the harder time of it, having to lean a little forward to see through the windows, and it was either that, or look through those beside the man and his wife, . . . of which Rodney was sure the man would be offended somehow.

The man, beside Rodney, however, seemed never to take his eyes off the woman except when he would open the silver-looking flask and drink from it. He was dressed more in the mode of a gambler than a businessman. Black trousers, store-bought dress-shoes, black coat and vest over a white shirt, . . . and both Billy, and Rodney knew he toted a revolver in a holster inside the coat . . . . And he was not far from being intoxicated! . . . And, the woman's husband had been glaring at him for some time.

Rodney would turn and look at Billy from time to time, and shake his head, both knowing that an encounter between the two men would soon come to a head. Except for the usual introduction formalities when boarding, no one had spoken a word to each other, or to anyone else, . . . all were just enduring the heat and dust being stirred up by the bouncing coach.

"You and your wife bound for Shreveport, are ya?" Asked Billy, thinking to head off an argument, or worse.

The man turned his aggravated stare on him then, and finally nodded before watching the gambler again.

"What kind a business, you in?" He continued, still trying to force a conversation.

The man looked back at him. "None of yours!" He said then looked away again at the gambler. But then, he suddenly leaned forward and slapped the gambler's leg with his opened hand.

"And you, sir!" He growled. "I will ask you to stop staring at my wife like a hungry wolf, you are upsetting her!"

The gambler looked at him then, and grinned. "She don't look upset!"

"Well, she is . . . . Now please avert your eyes somewhere else!"

"Mister," Said the gambler, also leaning forward. "If your wife didn't want to be looked at, she wouldn't a worn that dress, or she would a covered them things up better! . . . There's three of us over here, and when them tits bounce, we're gonna look! . . . So shut th' hell up!"

"You can't talk to me that way, you Bastard!"

"Henry, please?" Begged the woman, grabbing his arm.

"Don't please me!" He said angrily, and jerked away from her.

"All right!" Said Rodney loudly, and moved his coat aside to reveal the badge. "We won't put up with this!" He reached and pulled the gambler back in his seat.

"Me, and this man beside me are Federal Marshals, and I'm pretty damn sure that Sheriff in Shreveport has a couple a spare bunks you two can use tonight! . . . So before this goes too far, I suggest you sit back and think about it! . . . And you, sir." He said, looking at the gambler.

"Hold that flask out the window and empty it."

"This flask, and what's in it, belongs to me!" He returned. "And that badge don't give you the right to take it from me!"

"You're right, it don't!" Said Rodney. "Do what I said, or put it away and leave it there, because if you take another drink, I'll arrest ya!" He looked at the older man then.

"And you, sir, . . . it's no crime to look at a woman, even your wife, . . . ignore him, . . . and us, because we can't help it, either." He tipped his hat to the woman then.

"Forgive us, Ma'am, no disrespect is meant to you, even from this man, I'm sure! . . . Think of it only as admiration, please."

"Thank you, sir." She smiled then and leaned her head back.

He looked at Billy then, and grinned before resting his own head on the seatback and closing his eyes.

It was dark when a large hole in the road caused the coach to careen sideways, jarring them awake again.

"That was some hole." Said Rodney.

"More like a canyon." Nodded Billy.

"Are you going to Shreveport?" Asked the woman suddenly.

"Oh, yes, Ma'am." Said Billy. "Ain't been there since start a th' war."

"Well, it's a pigsty!" She returned. "Henry's a bank auditor, we go there three or four times a year."

"From where?"

"We have a home in Dallas, Henry's office is there, too."

"He works for th' Government, Too?" Asked Rodney.

"Oh, no, . . . they just pay him for his services! . . . He signed a contract with them to regularly audit their books . . . . He's one of the smartest men in the world."

"And just as jealous of you." Reminded Billy.

"I'm afraid that's a fault he can't control. But he's a very loving man."

"I take it, you're not real fond a Shreveport.?" Asked Rodney.

"You take it right!" She said. "Everybody hates everybody else there, gunfire in the streets, and those awful saloons! People are being robbed, or murdered there . . . . Can't even sleep at night for the noise."

"That surprises me." Said Rodney. "From what I've heard, they have a good Sheriff there."

"In my opinion, he's not doing his job very well!"

"Who are you talking to, Annabelle?" Yawned Henry.

"Talking to the Marshals, Henry. They asked me about Shreveport."

"Dregs of humanity, that place." He yawned again. "We stay only as long as we have to!"

"Do you know the Sheriff there, Mister???" Asked Billy, leaving the question open to receive the man's name.

"Forgive me, Sir, . . . I am Henry Westmoreland. This is my wife, Annabelle . . . . And yes, I know John Lake quite well. He's a fine man, whose hands are tied. My worthless opinion is that, the saloon owners have control of Shreveport, and everybody of any importance works for them, or is influenced by them! City Council, Judges, the worthless town Marshal, Buck Owens! . . . It's a rat race, Mister???"

"Marshal Rodney Taylor, my deputy, Billy Upshur."

Westmoreland leaned forward in the dark and shook both their hands. "Seems I've heard the name, Upshur before, . . . from Upshur County?"

"Never been there, never met any of 'em." Said Billy. "We're from Lamar County, town a Paris."

"Oh, yes . . . . You had quite a fire there, I hear . . . . Are they building back?"

"Almost done already." Said Rodney. "Be a while yet."

"Always is! . . . I want to apologize to you both for earlier, guess I'm a little jealous."

"We understand." Said Billy.

"Amen to that!" Nodded Rodney.

*   *   *

An hour after crossing the state line, they began seeing the small adobe dwellings, showing an unmistakable pale yellow in the moon's brightness, and these houses seemed to stretch for a half-mile or more on either side of the wide thoroughfare. Shrill barks of dogs began their nerve rattling songs, with many of them running into the road to bark and nip at the horse's heels in passing.

As they came closer to the city, the coach suddenly lurched up a small grade, and the distinct bumping of wheels across rails caused all of them to look out and down at the straight line of track, in both directions.

"Bringing back any memories yet?" Asked Rodney.

"Not quite . . . . Lot more houses now. Was that th' railroad we'll be taking?"

"Those rails run from New Orleans, to Texarkana, Texas." Said Westmoreland. "It only picks up the passenger car once a week."

"What do ya mean, Pickin' it up?" Asked Rodney.

"Well, these main tracks don't go to Shreveport, there's an alternate track off to the North there that runs into town. There's one passenger car, and one freight car that's always sitting on the tracks in front of the depot . . . . The Army owns it, cars, depot and all! . . . When they're notified, the train will back up all the way in, and couple with the appointed cars, and leave, . . . bringing them back on the return trip. To me, it's a pain in the derriere, but the system seems to work."

"Then I don't know, Billy." Said Rodney. "Let's just hope there's some passengers goin' to Texarkana tomorrow."

"There usually is," Remarked the gambler, who was now awake . . . "But they won't order a pickup unless half the passenger car is filled, that, or a special load of freight that has to go."

"What's your name, friend?" Asked Rodney, peering at his outline in the dark.

"James Bu'dro."

"I'm Rodney Taylor, my deputy here is Billy Upshur . . . . Any hard feelings about earlier?"

"No, sir, . . . I was a little tight, . . . I apologize to one and all."

"Bu'dro, that's a Cajun name, ain't it?"

"Creolle, Cajun . . . . I have Cajun Grandparents. My mother was Cajun, my father a very wealthy plantation owner . . . . They sent me to school in Chicago for an education."

"And here, we took you for a gambler." Said Billy.

"You took me right, I am a gambler . . . . Got hooked on it in college, became good at it and now, I make my living at it!"

"You do know that poker and rot-gut don't add up to a winning night, don't ya?"

"I learned that early, as well! . . . Can I ask what brings a Federal Marshal to a place like Shreveport, . . . surely it's not to gamble?"

"No, Sheriff's holdin' a couple a prisoners for us."

"John Lake!" He said. "One of only a handful of honest people in Shreveport. Handy with a gun, his fists, and his honesty."

"Sounds like you may like th' man?" Commented Billy.

"We've had our run-ins, but we get along. He knows I don't cheat at cards, so he most times lets me be."

They entered the city's bustling main street then, seeing that every other store-front, on both sides of the street were lighted up and open for business, and above each door, and on windows were signs, or painted messages portraying gambling, liquor and women, . . . and every one of them were loud with the out of tune hammering of piano keys that were only drowned out occasionally by a gunshot, or a shrieking woman's laughter.

"Good, God, Billy!" Said Rodney. "You were right! . . . This place is unbelievable, a regular cess-pool."

"That it is!" Said Westmoreland. "This is, by the way, the worst part of town. It's not quite this evident in the area of the stage station, but that's usually because John Lake's deputies patrol the area at night. There are four large saloons in the general area of the Sheriff's office, too . . . . They make arrests, and the courts continue to fine, and release them . . . . A never ending battle!"

"Why don't he quit?" Sighed Rodney. "I might!"

"I'll tell you exactly why?" Said Westmoreland. "John Lake believes that old Reconstruction law of the late sixties, will one day be overturned, and then the Army will step in and clean the place up!"

"Fill us in on that law, sir!" Said Rodney.

"The one that simply says that Government forces can not, and will not interfere with local government, unless requested unanimously by a Mayor, and a vote by the City Council. The one law that continues to be overlooked at every session, that, or purposely omitted! . . . I believe that someone is heavily lobbying congress on the subject, and getting very rich as a result!"

"Nothin' we can do about that, Rod." Said Billy.

"I think you could." Said Westmoreland. "A United States Marshal has free rein to uphold the law in any city, state or county that he deems in need. All he needs is credentials of approval from a Federal Judge, . . . and I believe you already have those credentials."

"Yes, sir, I do! . . . But not for long! This is my last mission as a U. S. Marshal. I'm retiring once it's completed."

"For the life of me, I cannot understand why? . . . The country needs men like you, sir."

"It always will!" Said Rodney. "But I won't make a difference, no one man will! . . . For every man we take down, two more springs up. No, this it for me!"

"You have a family." He said with a sigh. "Well, It is a dangerous profession."

"True on both counts." He replied. "It wouldn't matter anyway, I have an assigned area to cover. We all do. My credentials only cover that area! . . . But, I can see the need for assistance here just by lookin' out th' window."

"Yes, sir!" Returned Westmoreland. "Without a Federal Judge on site, even a Marshal wouldn't be of enough help . . . . Well, gentlemen, here we are." He said, and they all looked out at the lighted boardwalk of the stage office.

"Got a deputy waiting for you, it appears." He added.

The coach came to a stop, and the driver quickly got to his knees on the seat and began lifting the luggage down to the ticket agent as the passengers de-boarded.

"Marshal Taylor?" Asked Grady Sutton as Billy and Rodney stepped down.

"That's me." Replied Rodney, shaking his hand. He put a hand Billy's arm then. "My deputy, Billy Upshur."

"Two of ya." Nodded Grady. "That's good!"

"Where to from here, Grady?"

"Sheriff said to put you up at th' hotel, right over there. Said he'd see you in the mornin', his office is right down th' street here on this side, can't miss it!"

"You will get no argument from us!" Nodded Billy as he looked around at the busy street. "Don't this town ever sleep?"

"Not in th' last fifteen years, I know of." Sighed Grady.

"Marshal?" Said Westmoreland, stopping to shake their hands. "I wish you both good luck! . . . A pleasure to meet you."

"Good luck yourself, sir, . . . Ma'am" They nodded at the woman then watched her walk as they weaved their way across the crowded street to the hotel. "Amen to good luck, sir!" Grinned Rodney.

"That Mrs. Westmoreland's a real looker!" Nodded Grady, and was watching her also.

"And he'll need all th' luck he can get!" Said Billy, turning to look back in time to see James Bu'dro turn the flask up again before picking up his bag, . . . and shook his head before hefting his own and follow Rodney and the deputy across the street.

*   *   *

"Come in, Marshal." Smiled John Lake as they entered. He came to shake their hands. "Didn't know you'd bring help, but I'm damn glad you did! . . . I'm Sheriff, John Lake."

"Rodney Taylor." He nodded at Billy then. "Deputy Marshal, Billy Upshur."

"A pleasure to meet ya both." He moved around his desk then gestured at the chairs. "Sit down and let's talk a minute." He took two more tin cups from a desk drawer then reached behind him for the hot coffee pot. "Just made it an hour ago." He grinned then poured their coffee.

"As you likely noticed last night, this is a very unlawful town."

"That did cross our minds."

"Why don't you fill us in, Sheriff?" Asked Billy curiously. "We rode in with a couple gents that didn't have much good to say about it."

"I'll put it all in one sentence . . . . Crooked Judges, and City Council. Any more, at this point, I'd likely be repeating the story they told! . . . Anyway, I've got four prisoners locked up back there, Marshal, and all four belong to you, once you take custody."

"Three, Sheriff." Reminded Rodney, frowning at Lake. "That's all my warrant calls for."

"That may be true, but it's either, you take all four, or Mister Wallace'll be one more you'll have to fight to keep those three!"

"You saying he's one a th' men that broke 'em out a jail?" Asked Billy, adding to Rodney's frustration.

"That's what I'm saying . . . . I got a wire from Isaac Parker not ten minutes before Mister Wallace came in claimin' to be Ben Childers' brother!" He shrugged then. "Man said he wanted to see 'im, so I let 'im move in." He took the wire from his desk drawer and gave it to Rodney. "Sent names and descriptions of all three."

"Ed McCreedy, Lionel Wallace and Morgan Ellis." Sighed Rodney and gave the wire to Billy.

"I'd got that in time, I'd have all six of 'em for ya."

"Why didn't they try to break 'em out a here?" Asked Billy, giving the paper back to Lake.

"I'm sure that was their plan, till they came up a man short. Couple that with th' fact, there bein' too many people about at any given time, and they were afraid to chance it!"

"That means they'll be waitin' on us somewhere." Said Rodney, and took a swallow of the strong coffee.

"You can depend on it!" Returned Lake. "And they might have already replaced Wallace, we caught a local tough guy watchin' th' jail yesterday! . . .

Man called Choctaw Joe Haskell . . . . So, with Wallace in your custody, you may still be facing three men."

"That makes us feel better." Sighed Rodney.

"I feel for ya, Marshal, but you leave Wallace here, a crooked Judge'll likely let 'im go, and you'll be facin' four!"

"No doubt he would, too" Said Billy . . . "We'd already heard about all that."

"Them on th' stage?"

Billy nodded. "Bank examiner, name a Westmoreland."

"He also says th' town is run by th' saloon owners," Said Rodney. "What about that?"

"He's right! . . . But which one? . . . Hell, all of 'em are greedy, and all of 'em are dangerous, and all of 'em want th' job! . . . None of 'em can agree enough to work together on anything, . . . and I can't find out which one is the most powerful! Because that's th' one paying everyone off to get his way, . . . and that's how he keeps all th' rest in line, too!"

"Well," Said Rodney, reaching to push his hat back a little. "Don't think I'd want your problem, Sheriff, and I don't think you'd want mine! . . . So I guess we'll take all four." He looked at them both then. "I'm sorry, Billy, Sheriff, . . . go ahead."

"We were just discussin' town politics, Rod." Said Billy, and looked back at Lake. "Have you talked with these so-called bosses? . . . Maybe get a notion which one might be callin' th' shots?"

"I've talked to 'em, even threatened 'em, they laughed at me! . . . Even arrested one or two of 'em. But like every other thief and killer I jail, Judge fines 'em and sets 'em free again!" He reached in the top desk drawer then and took out the letter.

"What we need here, is a resident Federal Judge, and a United States Marshal to help make the arrests! . . . If we make every arrest a Federal case, it'll be tried in a Federal court! . . . Then I can put some a these sons a bitches in State prison where they belong . . . . It's all right here!" He said, holding up the letter then passing it to Rodney.

"Took me two days to write that. Even the times the Mayor and myself wrote to Washington for help, and got refused . . . . So, as a last plea for help, I'd like you to give that to Isaac Parker. Just maybe, he can get me some help down here."

"Is it really this bad?" Asked Rodney, giving the letter to Billy.

"It's worse, I just didn't know how to make it sound worse."

"I'll give it to him personally, Sheriff . . . . But right now, we have to figure out how we're gonna transport those four men to Fort Smith? Stage

Coach could work, but it's a little too crowded for six men, they could jump us in tight quarters."

"I've got that covered, Marshal, if you don't mind? . . . I had a talk with Colonel Ford at the Army post, and since they own that utility track, he agreed to furnish a cattle car for you. Now, in all appearances, it'll look empty, we'll lay clean hay down on the floor, and a canvas cover over that to lay on in one end of the car. You can chain th' men down any way you want, but while you're in that car, nobody can see you, but you'll still have a full view of the outside through the slotted walls of th' car . . . . If that's acceptable to you?"

"Sounds good to me." Said Billy. "Plenty a room to work, if we need to."

"Then we'll do it." Said Rodney. "Good thinkin', Sheriff."

"We'll know how good it was when you get there! . . . So, here's what it looks like to me." He took the railroad map of Louisiana and Arkansas from his desk and spread it on the top.

"Here's th' railroad here." He pointed it out. "And here's th' utility tracks running all the way to th' Army post. This area is the depot, where the passenger car, and freight car always sits . . . . Since the cattle car is only used when th' Colonel ships, or buys horses for his troops, it sits on th' track beside the Commissary until it's needed . . . It'll be rigged today, the way I told ya and tonight we'll gag and chain th' prisoners, go out th' back door and use the alleys all the way to the post. That's where you'll take custody"

"Looks simple enough." Nodded Rodney. "What's th' landscape like between here and Texarkana?"

"Well, once you're on th' car, soldiers will move it to the depot and couple it to th' freight car. Train will pick up th' cars at six o'clock in th' morning. There's no way anybody can slip aboard that train before it leaves here, soldiers are on patrol there. Once it leaves, it goes through twenty miles of very rough swamp. So, from here to th' other side a that swamp, no problem at all! . . . But past that, I'm afraid you'll just have to keep your eyes open. You'll have a clear view of the landscape on both sides, though . . . . Besides, they'd have to get on that car to know you're there."

"And it only goes as far as Texarkana?"

"That's it! . . . Stage goes all th' way from there to Fort Smith. Or, you can use horses, I'm sure the Colonel would furnish you with mounts."

"What say, Billy?"

"Like you said, Rod, pretty close quarters on a stage coach."

"We'll go with saddle horses, Sheriff."

"I'll arrange it!" He nodded. "Would you like to see your prisoners now?"

"Be soon enough tonight." Said Billy. "Right now, you could point us toward th' Federal Reserve Bank?"

*   *   *

"I'd say, this is th' safest place in town, right now!" Said Billy, as they climbed the steps. "Six guards at th' front doors."

A soldier stepped in front of them as they made the wide porch, and stopped them."

"Sorry, sir, but you men will need to leave your weapons on the table there . . . part of the bank's security. You can pick them up, when you leave."

"We understand." Nodded Rodney as they placed their guns on the table.

"Mind tellin' me, why so many guards?" Asked Billy. "When two would be enough?"

"Why would you need to know that, Sir?"

"We're Federal Marshals, Private." Said Rodney. "Be no harm in tellin' us."

"This bank was robbed ten years ago, sir, two soldiers, and two civilians killed!"

"Good enough." Grinned Billy. "Thank you, Private."

"Yes, sir!" He said then opened the door for them.

"For an older building, it's quite elegant in here." Commented Rodney as they entered. The dome-shaped ceiling rose nearly twenty feet above their heads, with a dozen molded, wooden ribs running up to to a center point. The long, glass-fronted, teller's counter ran almost the full length against the rear wall, . . . and the walls, themselves, were adorned with colorful tapestry and large paintings of past Presidents, and Union Generals. Along one wall was a row of desks with men in suits working at them, and it was one of those men that got up and came forward to greet them.

"Well, Marshal!" Smiled Westmoreland, as he held out his hand. "Fancy meeting you gentlemen again."

"Not as fancy as this place!" Grinned Billy, looking around again.

"What? . . . Oh, fancy!" He nodded, also looking around. "Just about all the Government owned banks are fairly elegant . . . . This one, however, really stands out in comparison . . . . You have business with the bank, do you?"

"Yes we do!" Said Rodney. "We'd like to see th' head man."

"That will be, Cyrus Greely, come, I'll take you back." He led the way, pushing open a low gate in the patrician and went down a hallway to the bank President's Office, knocked then opened the door.

"United States Marshals to see you, Mister Greely." Said Westmoreland as they entered.

"Thank you, Henry." Smiled the almost short, balding man as he got up to greet them.

"I'll leave you now." Said Westmoreland. "Good to see you again." He left and pulled the door shut.

"Come in, Gentlemen, and have a seat."

"Ahhh, no thanks, Mister Greely." Said Billy. "We won't take much of your time." He took the two sacks of nuggets from his pockets and placed them on the desk. "We need to sell some gold, and thought you was th' man to see."

"Well, of course!" He said, picking up one of the sacks. "About a pound, I'd say." He opened it and poured several reddish-orange nuggets into his hand. "Very nice, some of the best quality I've seen." He looked at them then. "But I have seen it before . . . . Horace Bratcher, in Paris, Texas cashes in quite large sums of this from time to time . . . . Where does it come from?"

"Don't know about his, but that came from creek-beds and streams!" Said Rodney. "I'm a Marshal in Indian Territory, Billy's my deputy, . . . and while we're working, and time allows, we always do a little panning . . . . That is the result of more than a year's worth of panning those creeks!"

"And don't ask us where they are, if you don't mind?" Said Billy. "We'll be goin' back!"

"Of course not! . . . I understand . . . . Horace said he gets his from prospectors out of there . . . . Said they wanted to help with the rebuilding costs! I must say, . . . those hills must be full of gold! . . . Anyway," He said, putting them back into the sack.

"There is now a Federal Tax being levied on most sellable commodities, and I'm afraid gold is one of them. You do understand that, don't you?"

"Well, . . . no, we don't!" Said Rodney. "When did all this come about?"

"Last session of Congress, . . . or the one before! . . . Never the less, it's now a Federal law, even though most of the country still don't abide by it!"

"What are we lookin' at?" Asked Billy.

"Five cents on the dollar, right now, who knows in the months to come?"

"Five cents? . . . That's five dollars for every hundred!" Exclaimed Rodney. "But, if that's th' law, we'll have to live with it!"

"I knew you would, after all, we work for the same Government, don't we?" He got up as he spoke and went to the door, called a Clerk and came back. "Gold is up to twenty-one dollars an ounce." He said as the Clerk came, and gestured at the gold.

"Melvin, take this gold and weigh it, check it for content, and so forth . . . . Bring the money back here, minus the tax, of course."

"Any new taxes comin', we don't know about?" Asked Billy.

"Unfortunately, yes . . . A sales tax, in which you'll pay on the products you buy! A business tax, what you'll pay once a year for owning a business . . . . Well, I've already ruined your day, but the Government has bills to pay and unfortunately, we all have to help pay them."

The Clerk came back with the money, gave it, and the receipt to Greely then left.

"Marshal, you gave me thirty-one ounces of pure gold content, and at twenty-one dollars an ounce, it comes to six hundred and fifty-one dollars, minus thirty-two dollars and fifty-five cents in tax . . . . That leaves you six hundred and eighteen dollars and forty-five cents." He counted out the money to Rodney.

"What else can I do for you?"

"I'd say, you done plenty!" Said Billy.

"Yeah," Said Rodney. "That'll do it, I reckon. Thank you, sir." With a look at Billy, they turned and left the bank.

"Strike one for justice!" Said Rodney as they retrieved their weapons.

"More like legal thievery! . . . And we're payin' 'em to make these laws."

"Well," Sighed Rodney, looking around at the guards. "Guess somebody has to pay their wages, Billy, we just never thought much about it! . . . Whether we like it or not, we all have a boss!" They went down the steps to the street and headed toward the business district.

"Think th' tax was really that much?"

"Don't matter what we think, Rod! . . . But what he charged us, and what he actually sends to th' Government, might be a different thing!"

"True, . . . man has to make a livin', I guess! . . . I'm ready for steak and eggs, myself."

"I'll settle for steak and potatoes." They continued to be jostled on the semi-crowded walkway as they came to the Sheriff's office, and that's when Rodney spotted the café across the wide street, . . . and not liking the idea that it was virtually next door to the saloon, decided on it anyway.

They entered, and almost immediately, the smell of meat frying made their stomachs growl, . . . and finding a table against the wall away from the saloon side, sat down and removed their hats.

"What'll it be, gents?" Asked the tired-looking, middle-aged woman.

"Steak and eggs for me." Said Rodney. "With fried potatoes."

"Just steak and potatoes for me, . . . some good gravy would hit th' spot!"

"Water to drink, or coffee?"

"Water's fine." Nodded Rodney as he cocked his head to listen at the piano next door. "You'd think they could find at least one decent piano player in this world!"

"Don't know what for?" Said the woman. "Nobody listens to it anyway." She turned and went back to the kitchen.

"She's right, ya know." Said Billy. "It's just noise . . . . Want a hear good piano, go to Church, Rod, or a good ho-down somewhere. Barn dance'd be th' best, though."

"What th' hell are you talkin' about, Billy?"

"Good piano music, ain't that what you was talkin' about?"

"I was talkin' about a saloon's piano player, none I ever seen has one, not a good one!"

"Not much point in it, nobody listens!"

"She just said that!"

"I just agreed with her!"

"So ya did, . . . How long till our party starts?"

Billy pulled his watch then closed it and put it away. "Sheriff said ten o'clock . . . It's two o'clock now, we're lookin at eight hours."

"It don't get dark till nine." Sighed Rodney. "Guess I'm getting' a little anxious."

"Yeah, me, too! . . . Ain't got a good feelin' about this at all."

"Well, you keep those feelings, cause I've learned to trust them, and your instincts!"

"Might be your downfall one day, too."

"I'll chance it!"

"Yeah, well you're a mite gullible, too."

"I don't know about that, we both agreed on that cattle car, when Lake suggested it . . . . It is th' best way to go, but that smell, for four or five hours!"

"Beats a bullet from ambush!"

"I know, that's why we did it! . . . What do ya think about Lake?"

"A likable man, Rod, . . . and he uses his head, which is not always common in a lawman. I like 'im for that! . . . I hope Parker gives 'im some help, too."

"Makes two of us . . . . He's a stickler for th' law, though. It could go either way."

"Here ya go, gents." Said the woman, placing the large, steaming platters in front of them. "Eat hearty, . . . I'll bring your water."

The meal was finished, and after Rodney lit his thin cigar, they both sat to watch the wide variety of customers in the café. Most of the men looked as if they had not bathes, or shaved in a month, and smelled that way, . . . and the one or two scantily dressed women left no question as to where they came from.

"Place depends on that saloon for business, don't it?"

"Speaking of which?' Said Rodney. "I've got a sudden urge for a beer, ain't had one since I don't know when! . . . How about it, we got eight hours to kill?"

Billy dropped four silver dollars on the table and they got up, walked out onto the boardwalk, and to the saloon's swinging doors where they pushed inside, stood for a moment to look the semi-crowded room over then went to the end of the bar.

"What'll it be, gents?" Inquired the bartender as he sized them up.

"Couple a beers'd work." Returned Billy as he met the man's hard stare.

"Beer's only a little cool." He said. "Closer to warm."

"Still cooler than rot-gut!" Said Rodney. "We'll take th' beer." And when the man shrugged and left, he looked at Billy. "You see our friend back there?"

"Mister Bu'dro? . . . Yeah, I see 'im. Appears to me, he ain't makin' any friends neither." They watched the gambler as he argued with one of the players at the table, and though they were almost in the rear of the room, they could tell it was not going well.

"That'll be a buck-fifty." Said the bartender, placing the mugs of beer in front of them.

Rodney paid him, and they continued to watch the argument, which by now had drawn the attention of everyone in the room. The piano player stopped his feeble attempts at the ivories and had also turned to watch.

Finally, the obvious loser in the game got to his feet, leaned on the table and said something before taking his hand and sweeping money, cards, drinks and all off the table and onto the grimy floor. He then turned and threaded his way through the tables to the bar before turning down along the bar toward them, and the door.

Billy, however, was still watching Bu'dro, who had gotten up to brush off his pants and vest before quickly moving through the tables behind him to stop at the bar, watched the retreating loser's back for a second then yelled loudly and went for his gun.

The sudden burst of thunderous noise rocked the smoke-filled room as Billy drew and fired, the slug wrenching a scream from Bu'dro as the bullet struck the shoulder of his gun arm as he was clearing leather. The numbing, unexpected impact caused the pistol to fly from his hand as he was spun around then thrown sidewise into the table next to him, overturning it, and the two men sitting there.

Billy watched the room for several seconds before holstering the gun then looked into the face of the intended victim, who was still looking from him, to glare back at the fallen Bu'dro, and those helping him to a chair at a table.

"Son of a Bitch was going to shoot me in th' back!" He gasped. "I don't believe it! . . . Cheatin' son of a Bitch!"

Billy gripped the man's arm then and turned him toward him. "You're still alive, Mister, go home!"

The man stared at him then. "Who the hell are you, man? . . . I was looking right at you and didn't see you draw that gun, I never seen anything like it!" He shook his head then. "But, thank you very much, whoever you are."

"You almost went to where every loser goes eventually." Said Rodney. "Now go on home."

Nodding, the man left, leaving everyone else in the room staring at Billy7, and talking excitedly among themselves.

Billy called the bartender over again at that point.

"Yes, sir, . . . what can I do for ya?"

"You can get that man a Doctor before he bleeds to death!"

"Law'll handle that!" He said, nodding at the door. "Deputies are here."

"All right, folks." Yelled Cooter Brown. "Quieten it down! . . . Who fired that shot?" Several men pointed at Billy, and when Brown came toward him, Both of them moved their jackets aside enough to reveal their badge, thus stopping him and Deputy Bridger in their tracks to gawk at them.

"Wh, . . . what happened here, Marshal?"

"Wounded man down there tried to shoot a man in th' back, I stopped 'im!"

Nodding, brown turned to Bridger. "Go check on that wounded man, Andy, get statements from them that seen it!" When he left, Brown leaned against the bar.

"Sheriff said you was here, I'm Deputy Cooter Brown, that one's Andy Bridger . . . . I'm sure glad to meet ya."

"Name's Bill Upshur, man beside me is Marshal Taylor."

"Like I said, damn glad to meet ya . . . . Sheriff's down at the blacksmith's getting th' chains cut and rigged for th' prisoners tonight . . . . Also, last I heard, soldiers already got that cattle car ready." He nodded then. "Guess we'll see ya tonight, I got an arrest to make! . . . Little good it'll do." He left and made his way to the fallen man.

"How'd you know Bu'dro was gonna do that, Billy?"

"Gut feelin'." He shrugged.

"I rest my case!" He grinned. "Bottom's up, my friend."

    *   *   *

"Come in, gentlemen." Smiled John Lake, stepping aside to let them in. "Heard you had an altercation at out fine saloon over there?"

"Part of the job, Sheriff." Said Rodney, sitting down to smile up at him. "Man was about to commit a murder."

"James Bu'dro, I got th' report." He looked at Billy then. "You're quite a celebrity over there right now, Marshal."

"I was just lucky I saw it comin'."

"Well, Mister Bu'dro's had it comin' for a long time now! . . . . He's been in Dallas, or so he says, for the last three months. Before that, I don't know, . . . but he's been involved in several shootings here, and needless to say, never convicted!"

"You arrest 'im?" Asked Billy, also sitting down.

"No, . . . if I jail 'im, he'll be released again. Besides, you stopped 'im from committing murder, no crime! . . . I confined 'im to his hotel room till his wound heels enough to travel. Then I'll put 'im on a stage back to Dallas! He won't be back, Doc said your bullet tore up the tendons in his shoulder. He won't pull a trigger with that arm again, not without a lot a pain, and he knows he's a dead man if he stays here . . . . That's how popular he is!"

"Man's got a know his limits." Nodded Billy.

"So true." Sighed Lake, coming to his desk to sit down. "Be dark in an hour or so, and we can get this show on th' road."

"Where's your help?" Queried Rodney. "They gonna be around to help?"

"They're all here, in back, introducing our guests to their travel gear."

"Sure quiet about it." Commented Billy.

"No man's mean enough to argue with a sawed-off!"

"I believe you're right." Chuckled Rodney. "Sheriff, . . . that saloon we was in, . . . is that owned by one a th' bosses you spoke of?"

"Rockford Prince, yeah . . . . His office and livin' quarters takes up the whole second floor."

"I was wondering because, if he has gunmen workin' for 'im, why didn't they try to step in today?"

"They were there, at least some of 'em, . . . th' flunkies! They don't lift a hand without orders from Prince, or his bodyguards. Besides, they all saw how fast your Deputy is."

"He own anything else?"

"Only a dozen pigsty bars, and brothels scattered across the West side. Jacob Green owns the House of Cards, two streets over from here, he has another dozen establishments along th' River Front. There's four of 'em, but only one of 'em is rich enough, or smart enough to keep the others in line . . . . I've tried to get one of them to give the boss man up several times, but as ruthless and greedy as he is, he's not brave enough to commit suicide."

"Which one was that?"

"Marvin Cruise, he's pretty well got th' North side to his self."

"Maybe he's th' man his self?" Said Billy. "And smart enough to make you believe he ain't."

"I thought a that, too! . . . Anyway, if I find 'im, I couldn't take 'im down . . . . Probably wind up dead myself, me and my deputies! . . . Nothing would ever come of it! I wish you two would stay around for a while, we might make a few changes."

"This is my last job as a Marshal, John . . . . I wish we could help ya, but we can't . . . . But if Judge Parker dows help you, you can bet he'll assign one of his best men to do it!"

"As good as Mister Upshur is with a gun?"

"Sheriff, there ain't a U. S. Marshal in this country that is not handy with a gun, me included . . . . Billy is just the exception! Actually, Billy and me are best friends, business partners in a large trading post. This job keeps me away from my family and business, and Billy here, . . . well, he only volunteered to help me out on this one."

"Guess I might do th' same, if I had somethin' to fall back on?"

"I doubt it!" Said Billy. "Crime would be three times what it is, you weren't here . . . . Nope, . . . I know we just met and all, and I don't actually know you, . . . but I've seen enough to believe you love your job. Tougher th' situation, the better!"

"Yeah, you're right about that, too! . . . I do like my job, I like this city and what it could become, and will, . . . if I can get some help in here!"

"There's a good chance, Judge Parker will help ya." Said Rodney.

"Damn, I hope so! . . . Dallas had our same problem some years ago. They were also hogtied by th' Reconstruction laws, until Federal Judge Emmitt Castle, and a U. S. Marshal took matters into their own hands . . . . It'll work here, too!" They all looked up then as the three deputies came un from the cellblock and closed the door.

"You've met my deputies." Said Lake as Andy Bridgers replaced the shotgun on the rack.

They both nodded their assent.

"You done back there, Grady?"

"Oh, yeah!" He grinned. "They look real cute in their new getups."

"They'll het used to 'em! . . . Give you any trouble?"

"Th' new tenant, Wallace tried to, said he was gonna fuck you up real good for th' way you done 'im. Rest never said a word."

"I was sure Childers would have a few choice words."

"He did!" Voiced Cooter. "Wanted to know if th' Marshal would have th' key to his chains?"

"Guess he ain't plannin' to stay for th' party." He looked at Rodney then, and gave him the key. "Don't let your guard down for a minute,

Marshal, Ben Childers is a mean one. Most of his men, too! . . . I talk with 'im some when I take their meals in, man's got no heart at all."

"I ain't lost a prisoner yet, Sheriff." Grinned Rodney as he looked up at Brown. "Barring any chance at offending you, Mister Brown, . . . how'd you get a name like Cooter?"

"It's an old joke, Marshal. My daddy used to go drinkin' with my uncle Jake on Saturday night, and well, uncle Jake couldn't hold his liquor, so daddy had to help 'im home . . . . He'd put 'im to bed, and when he'd come back, he'd say, "Bastard's drunker'n old Cooter Brown", say it ever time! . . . I got stuck with th' name, cause my name is actually, Elmo scooter Brown, so they started callin' me Cooter."

"Well, Cooter, you worked that shooting like a professional today, . . . you, too, Andy! . . . Sheriff's lucky to have ya."

"I appreciate that, comin' from you, Marshal."

"In fact, I have to hand it to all of ya." Continued Rodney. "Having th' guts and determination to do a job, in spite of such adversity."

"It's our town, too!" Voiced Andy Bridger.

"Yes it is." Nodded Rodney. "And if I can, I'm gonna see that letter gets read by Judge Parker personally!"

"We do appreciate that!" Said Lake.

"I think it's time we took a gander at our mean prisoners, Sheriff." Said Billy.

"You got it!" Said Lake, and they all got to their feet. "Grady." He said as he went to the cellblock door. "You boys go get your supper, it's almost nine, . . . be back here in an hour." He opened the door and led the way down between the cells to that of Ben Childers.

"This, Marshal, is Mister Ben Childers, shaggy beard and all."

Childers had a chain around his waist with a keyed lock to hold it. His wrists were adorned with wide, metal bracelets that were also anchored with a chain to the one around his waist, severely limiting his arm movements . . . . He stared at the three of them for a minute before getting off his bunk and walking to the bars.

"That hangin' Judge must think we're pretty dangerous characters. Sent two brave men to take us back!" He lifted his hands up as far as he could. "Which one a you has keys to these things?"

"We'll leave that Judge Parker." Said Rodney.

"Okay." Grinned Childers, and looked at Billy. "You a Marshal, too, . . . teacher, lawyer, or what? . . . Never seen a lawman wearin' specks before . . . . Well, which is it?"

"Yeah." He grinned, still meeting the killer's stare.

Lake grinned also, and moved to the next cell. "This one is Lionel Wallace, alias Ben Childers' brother."

"Fuck you, Sheriff!" He growled. "When I get out, I'm comin' back to see you!"

"That's right neighborly of ya."

"That's right, I'm gonna be real neighborly! . . . And what's all these fuckin' chains for, how am I gonna take a piss, or scratch my nose?"

"Wouldn't have to scratch, you'd shave that shit off your face! . . . You'll manage." He turned to the cell opposite Wallace's then. "This hard-eyed cuss is George Collins, man in th' next cell is Phillip Long . . . . All but Wallace there was picked up by Marshals in Arkansas for murder. They were tried and sentenced to hang for it . . . . But before sentence could be carried out, Mister Wallace, Ed McCreedy and Morgan Ellis broke 'em out!" He turned to look back at Childers then.

"Old Ben there thinks they're gonna do it again!" He looked at Rodney and grinned. "Pretty sure of his self, too!" He looked back at Childers then.

"What are you holdin' over them old boys, Ben? . . . Must be somethin' big, to make them risk their own lives to spring ya."

"You can stop fishin' any time, Sheriff, you won't catch anything."

"You're right, Ben, and it don't matter to me anyway, because it was all for nothing! . . . . Seen enough, Marshal?"

"Quite!" Replied Rodney.

"See you in an hour, Ben, . . . you boys be ready to go, ya hear!"

"Fuck you, Sheriff!" Yelled Wallace. "And th' horse you rode in on!"

"Man's got an outhouse for a mouth!" He sighed as they re-entered the office. "Come to think on it, so does every other man in town."

*   *   *

A dozen armed soldiers stood guard at the double gates of Post Parade grounds as Lake. Rodney and Billy, and the three deputies ushered the four gagged and chained prisoners past them and entered through the gates, where they were met by another six guards who led them past the commissary to the dark bulk of the cattle car.

Colonel Ford, and two other officers were waiting in front of the heavy, wooden ramp leading up to the dark, wide entrance to the car.

"Colonel Ford!" Said Lake as they arrived. "Is everything ready?"

"Yes, and you're right on time, John."

"Thank you, sir . . . . I'd like you to meet Marshal's, Taylor and Upshur."

"Gentlemen." He said, shaking their hands. "Six horses, with saddles are tethered in the rear of the car. They have fresh hay to eat, to keep them busy. You, and your prisoners are in front of the car. A large tarp was laid on the floor, fresh hay on top of that for comfort, and another tarp on top of that to keep you free of straw." He turned to the man beside him then.

"Lieutenant, have the prisoners escorted aboard, please, and secure them to the front end wall of the car in a seated position."

"Yes, sir." He said, and called the Sergeant over, gave the order then all of them watched the orders being carried out.

"Now," Said Ford, taking a paper and small, flat board from the Lieutenant. "All I need is your signature, Marshal."

"My signature?"

"On this requisition, . . . for the horses and gear." He placed the paper on the board and held it while Rodney signed.

"What if we're not able to bring 'em back, Colonel?"

"They'll be replaced, sir . . . . Now, this car will remain at the rail yard in Texarkana for two weeks. Since there are currently no rails laid to Fort Smith, I assume you will see that they are returned to the car at that point . . . . If not, the car will return without them, and I will collect from Isaac Parker . . . . You may board now, Gentlemen, . . . and good luck!"

Nodding, Rodney turned to Lake. "Sheriff, I'd like you to wire the Sheriff in Texarkana, ask 'im to meet th' train . . . . They could try and take Childers there."

"First thing in the mornin'." He shook their hands, as did the deputies before they all turned and walked back the way they had come.

"My men will move the car down to the depot once you're aboard." Said Ford. "You will be picked up when the train arrives from New Orleans, it is already en-route." He, and his lieutenants abruptly turned and walked away.

"Well," Breathed Rodney. "Let's do it!" They walked up the ramp, passing the soldiers as they exited, and stood in the darkness to watch as the ramp was raised and locked into place.

Dropping their satchels, almost simultaneously, they worked their way forward in the dark car until contacting the tarp-covered bedding, and sat down to lean back against the side of the car.

"How many a them sandwiches did ya get, Rod?"

"Couple a dozen, biscuits and ham . . . . Wonder if they thought to put canteens a water on board, be up th' creek without water."

"Don't think he'd forget that! . . . They're movin' th' car now, anyway."

They watched the dark shapes of men and animals as the team was hitched to the cattle-car. Two soldiers removed the wheel-chucks and the car began its slow progress along the tracks toward the depot, and waiting freight car.

The walls of the car was made up of dozens of what looked to be two by six by twelve rough-cut timbers, all laid horizontally, with four inch gaps left open between them. Each one was bolted securely to as many vertical ribs every two feet apart all around. The car's top was solid, decked with one by twelve rough lumber, with a skin of corrugated tin. Both ends of the car were also solid.

"Guess that's it!" Said Billy, once the cars were buckled up, and they were both watching as the soldiers led the team of horses away. "Got a long wait now . . . . Sure hope this was a good idea."

"Me, too, . . . couldn't be sure their friends weren't in town, though. I just hope we can avoid any trouble."

"This day and time, Rod, . . . that ain't likely."

"How true! . . . Put five men in jail, ten takes their place, a no-win situation."

"Well." Grunted Billy as he lay down. "One thing you can be sure of, Rod . . . . If it makes you feel any better?"

"And what's that?"

"It'll never be any different!"

"Thanks! . . . Know what else? . . . We are sitting ducks if they find out we're in this thing. No cover what so ever, . . . and we can't get out!"

"Yeah, I noticed that! . . . . It's a trap all right! But still better than a stage, I think. If those men are still in town, they'll be watchin' to see if we board that passenger car in th' mornin' . . . . If they don't, maybe they'll think we're waitin' for th' stage?"

"Stage don't leave till five o'clock tomorrow afternoon."

"They'll have a long wait then, we'll be in Texarkana by then."

"Yeah, but in th' meantime, we still got four assholes tied to th' front wall there. How do we all take a piss, hang it out a these holes in th' walls?"

"Ya piss on th' floor, Rod, . . . floor's nothin' but iron grates. Stock has to piss, too, and it's got a go somewhere!"

"How would I notice th' grates, I never been this close to a cattle car before? Anyway, . . . it's still gonna stink to high heaven when that sun comes up! . . . Ain't nothin' worse that smellin' horse shit!"

"No argument there, but it's well ventilated."

"Like we'll be, if they open fire on us!"

"Be th' same on a stage coach, thin walls don't stop bullets! . . . But I don't think they will, might hit Childers. They wouldn't chance that."

"Wonder why? . . . Was th' Sheriff right, ya think, and he is holding something over their heads, somethin' they want, maybe?"

"I deo believe that's it, yeah, . . . and money's the only thing that motivates men like them. Could be loot from a robbery, and he knows where it is."

"must be a lot of it, cause they sure took a risk in Fort Smith. Had to have keys to several doors to leave that place, then cross fifty yards of open space to even get to th' wall. There's two gun-parapets with armed guards on that wall! . . . Don't make sense."

"You need to rethink that, too! . . . Guards have keys to th' doors, and they killed at least two to get away . . . . Don't that make sense? . . . Anyway, that wire didn't explain anything, so we don't know."

"That would make sense, though . . . . The only way it could a happened!" He grunted then as he, too, laid down. "Shouldn't to us anyway, I guess. My job's to bring 'em back!"

"There ya go! . . . Can't be any tougher than takin' down a lunatic, like Loughmiller!"

"Amen to that!"

CHAPTER SEVEN

It was dark in the large barn, the only light coming from the open double doors and the moon's yellow glow. The two men worked quickly as they changed saddles and bridles to fresh mounts."

"You want to saddle th' horse for Ellis, Mister McCreedy?" Asked Haskell as he dropped the stirrup in place.

"Yeah, go ahead!" He growled, looking toward the open doors. "Sure is takin' a while to tie up two people, . . . should a done it myself!"

Haskell had the gunman's horse saddled by the time he made his appearance.

"Does it take that long to tie up somebody?" Asked McCreedy as Ellis mounted.

"They put up a fuss, Ed, had to lecture 'em a little."

"Son of a bitch! . . . You raped that woman, didn't ya?"

"Let's just say, I made her happy, Ed, and leave it at that!"

"You're an idiot, Morgan. Once them cowhands find 'em, they'll bring everybody after our ass!"

"No, they won't, Ed!" He said, and reined his horse around. "Won't know who to look for?"

"You killed 'em? . . . For th' love a God, Morgan, why?"

"They knew what we looked like, relax! . . . We'll be ten miles away when that cook rings th' breakfast bell."

"Well, we better be! . . . Brands on these horses can get us hung! . . . You're one heartless son of a bitch, Morgan!"

"That, I am, Ed!" He walked his horse toward the open doors as McCreedy and Haskell mounted and followed him.

Twenty minutes later, they were through the property gates and on the road back to the main road,

"How far ya think we come, Ed?" Asked Ellis, turning in the saddle to study the surrounding trees before looking at McCreedy. "Come on, Ed, you're not still upset about that, are ya? . . . That woman was a looker, for her age, you seen her, . . . made my dick hard, come on! . . . How far?"

"No idea, . . . we've been riding pretty hard! . . . Discount the times we had to rest th' horses, maybe forty, forty-five miles. Got that far to go, yet."

"You still plannin' to wait, and hit th' stage in Arkansas?"

"It's the only way, . . . be a posse waitin' on 'em at that depot."

"What if they don't take th' stage?"

"Then they'll be takin' horses, Morgan, Jesus Christ, man, no plan is ever perfect! . . . Not anymore . . . . We might have to work a little harder, but we'll find 'em, and we'll take Childers away from 'em, now let's go!" He spurred his horse past them and they quickly followed, and were settling the stolen horses into a mile-eating gallop along the old wagon road.

*   *   *

"What th' hell?" Gasped Rodney as they were jarred awake.

"Must a ordered th' train in a little early." Said Billy, checking his watch in the dim light. "Ait six o'clock yet."

"I ain't complaining . . . . Must a took some doin', ordering it in this early. Ain't supposed to leave till noon."

"Might not, when Th' Army does it!"

"Yeah, well I got a try out them grates, anybody lookin' this way out there?"

"Ticket agent on th' platform, but he ain't lookin . . . . Three or four passengers waitin' to get on, go ahead."

"You got a go, come on."

"Already went! . . . Appears like our guests got a piss though, guess I better ask 'em." Still watching the ticket agent, he walked across the bedding to squat in front of the prisoners, who were all glaring wickedly at him.

"How about it, you got a piss?" And when they quickly nodded.

"Soon's we clear th' depot, we'll let you up, you'll have to hold it till then." Rodney came to squat beside him then.

"Once we're away from town, we'll take th' gags off, too, . . . now just stay quiet! Wouldn't want your friends to know you're here, would ya?" Asked Rodney, elbowing Billy jokingly on the arm, and at that moment the train lurched forward, causing them both to fall backward.

Once the cattle car cleared the platform, Rodney got to his feet and untied the rope securing Childers to the front of the car. "One at a time, boys." He said, reaching down to help Childers to his feet. "Use th' grating there, middle of th' car, Mister Childers, . . . and don't get funny on us, we got a long ride ahead of us! . . . I'll take those gags out, and feed ya soon as we make th' regular tracks."

Once all four had relieved themselves, Rodney sat them against the side wall of the car while he opened his satchel, and unwrapped the cold biscuits and ham.

"It ain't much, boys, but it's better'n goin' hungry . . . . and don't touch them gags! . . . Can't have you givin' us away when they switch them rails."

Him and Billy ate while the train made the last mile and turned onto the main rails, and after the conductor had finished the junction and returned to the passenger car, Rodney nodded at the bound men, as the train lurched forward again. They all lowered their heads, and used their hands to pull the gags from their dry mouth. He then tossed them the canteen before taking sandwiches from the bag and moving to give each of them a couple . . .

"Ain't there laws against tyin' us up like animals?" Growled Wallace.

"There's laws against what you did, too! . . . You broke 'em! . . . So, I guess I did, too! . . . Ya see, I'm just a little like you, Mister Wallace, I don't pay much heed to laws."

"Fuck th' law, and you, too!" He said, filling his mouth with food.

"Pay him no mind, Marshal," Smiled Childers. "He's an idiot!"

"And fuck you, too, Childers!"

"See what I mean?" Said Childers, turning to cast a sidelong look to watch as Billy stood peering out at the dark, thick, maze of trees and swamp in passing.

"Is he really a Marshal? . . . He don't look like one?"

"What's he supposed to look like?"

"Damn if I know!" He mused. "Like you, maybe. Way he holds his self, gun tied down and all, looks like a gunslinger! . . . But I never heard of no gunslinger that wore specks before . . . . And I can tell, by lookin', he ain't no fighter, so who is he?"

"My deputy." Said Rodney, also looking at Billy. "And he's the very best there is!"

"Then tell me this, . . . what would he do, if, . . . and I say, IF, all four of us were to jump you right now?"

"He'd shoot ya! . . . Everything you said was almost on the money, Childers, he has never had a fist fight in his life, neither have I . . . . We never had to!"

"Then what good is he?"

"Better hope you never have to find out!" He got to his feet and stared down at him. "He'd be mad as hell, if he heard me say this . . . . but there ain't a man alive, that can outshoot 'im! . . . Now, believe that, or not, it don't matter where you're goin'." He turned to move away.

"Marshal?"

"Yeah?"

"We ain't there yet!"

"We ain't lost a man yet, Childers."

"There's always a first time!" He nodded at Billy again. "Gonna tell me who he is?"

"I just did, now eat your breakfast, . . . won't eat again till we leave th' train."

"Seein' as how we got horses aboard, I take it, we're gonna be ridin' tp Fort Smith."

"You objecting to that?"

"On the contrary, you two'll be better targets on a horse."

"So will you! . . . Now eat your food and shut up!" He walked to where Billy was standing and looked out.

"Have a nice talk, did ya?"

"Man's got a pretty good head on his shoulders . . . . Damn if I know why a man like him would live this way."

"Each to his own liking, Rod . . . . Look out there, swamp's alive with gators, crawlin' all over each other."

"They're fightin' over food, Billy. That's another gator, they're eating . . . . Likely why they're here like that, one of 'em crawls up on th' tracks to sleep, train comes along and carves it up then slings it off th' tracks! . . . Train probably sounds like a dinner bell to 'em."

"That's a gross story, Rod. You're right about it, but I don't need to hear it . . . . That's about as bad as hearin' about people who eat people!"

"That happens, too!" He grinned. "Tribe a natives in Africa somewhere that call themselves cannibals . . . . They eat their enemies. I tell ya, you need to read more!"

"You read enough for both of us! . . . If I need to know somethin', I'll ask ya."

Rodney slapped him on the shoulder. "I hear ya, Billy . . . . Our Mister Childers is pretty confident, we'll never get 'im to Fort Smith."

"Anything can happen, Rod." He said, looking along the sides of the car. "You're right about this thing, too! A good rifle shot could take us both out, if they find out we're here . . . . Once we clear this swamp, we need to stay alert."

"Amen to that! He looked back at the prisoners then. "Think I'll secure our baggage to that side wall there . . . . They might just decide to try and jump us when we ain't lookin', . . . want a give me a hand?"

*   *   *

They were clear of the bog, and the suffocating smell in a little more than an hour, and were both seated against opposite sides of the car watching the vista of thick trees and rolling pastureland, . . . and when seen, would stare hard at any riders, or farmers plowing their fields. But there was nothing as yet to spark any suspicion.

As the minutes turned into a couple of hours, and with his head and eyes aching, Billy removed the eyeglasses, and rubbing at his eyes lay back on the pallet of hay.

"You okay, Billy?"

"My eyes hurt, give me a minute."

"Sun's too bright for 'im, Marshal!" Said Childers. "Maybe he needs stronger specks."

"Maybe you need that gag back in your mouth!" Returned Rodney. "Now button it!"

"All I'm sayin' is that you won't see them old boys, no matter how hard ya look! . . . They're ex-military, all of 'em . . . . Some a the best snipers in Grant's Army."

Billy replaced the glasses and sat up again to look at Rodney. "Don't let 'im spook ya, Rod, he's playin' a mind game! . . . He don't know where they are!"

"Oh, I know all that, it's his talkin', I don't like!"

"Then gag his ass, if ya want, he don't bother me."

"Well, he bothers me . . . . What time ya got, anyway?"

He pulled his watch. "Ten-thirty-five, about an hour out a Texarkana, if this train ain't too slow. Seems to be a lot slower than th' we was on, comin' in."

"We got a be doin' twenty miles an hour." Said Rodney. "No less than fifteen, anyway."

"Then give or take another two hours, we'll be there. Way I see it, they've had plenty of opportunities to board us, or even stop th' train, if they was goin' to, . . . and they ain't done it!"

"What's that tell ya, Specks?" Asked Childers.

He looked at Rodney and grinned. "They'll hit us somewhere between Texarkana and Fort Smith, Rod . . . . He just confirmed it!"

"Hey, I didn't confirm anything!" Returned Childers. "Them old boys could be anywhere."

Rodney got up and went to work the gag back into Childer's mouth then took the loose ends and tied his head back against the two by six vertical rib on the wall. "I warned ya, man." He said, and backed away.

"Ha!" Voiced Wallace. "Who's th' fuckin' idiot now, . . . huh?"

"Shut up, all of ya!" Snapped Rodney, and then went back to look through the stiles at the landscape.

"Feel better now?" Asked Billy, getting up to stand beside him.

"Yes, . . . but that ain't what's been buggin' me . . . . It's been thirteen years since I deliberately road a horse into the face of sudden death! . . . That's what's buggin' me."

"When was that?"

"In th' desert, with Comanche all around us! . . . You have no idea how scared I was, because I knew they were there, and I knew they were trying to kill me!" He grinned at Billy then. "Know how I got through it? . . . I could see you all bent over your horse's neck and fighting back, even with that wound in your side, you didn't quit! . . . I knew that as long as we were with you, we'd make it."

"I never knew that." He placed a hand on Rodney's shoulder then. "Rod, . . . You was a number one tenderfoot back then, never held a gun before then. Hell I was scared, too, we all was! . . . But it took all of us to make it, and that was part a what made you the man you are now! . . . So, what brought all a this on, th' decision you made to quit?"

"Don't know for sure, maybe it was! . . . Maybe it's what my job was doin' to Lisa, maybe it's because I'm liable to be a moving target again tomorrow, I don't know! It just hit me, that I might not be comin' back with you." He looked at Billy again. "That feelin' I had in th' desert just suddenly flared up on me . . . . It was like I could already feel the bullets hit me! . . . I'm okay, Billy."

"I know you are, man, you're the bravest man I ever met, best lawman, too . . . . And you know I don't lie!"

"No, . . . you don't! . . . I'm fine, Billy."

"Good . . . . Because this job is a far cry from being the most dangerous we've ever been in!"

"You're right about that! . . . We've faced some bad ones."

"We're gonna face this one, too! . . . Now, keep your eyes open."

*   *   *

"These nags have about had it, Ed." Commented Ellis as they walked the animals to cool them down. "Lathered up pretty good."

"I know that, Morgan!" He growled. "Jesus, don't you ever quit complaining?"

"Sure, now and then . . . . I'm just wonderin' about your next bright idea, cause these horses ain't gonna make it to Texarkana, let alone th' other side! . . . Bout out a Jerky and water, too!"

"One a you got any wire cutters?" Asked Haskell.

"Always." Returned McCreedy. "What's that got to do with it?"

"A lot, if you can still swing a loop? . . . I count about a dozen horses about a hundred yards off in them trees yonder."

Both McCreedy, and Ellis followed his stare, and McCreedy quickly reached the cutters from his saddle bags and reined the tired horse off the road to the vine-covered barbed wire fence, dismounted and hastily snipped the wires and moved them aside.

"Watch th' road for traffic, Morgan, give joe your rope. We'll catch up th' horses . . . . We get 'em, come runnin, we'll have to work fast . . . . Come on, Joe." He mounted and spurred the horse across the pasture of tall grass, with Haskell close behind, each shaking out their ropes as the loose horses broke from the trees at a run.

They quickly caught up three of the best looking horses and led them back into the trees as Ellis was already galloping his spent animal toward them. He dismounted and took his fresh one from Haskell, and five minutes later, all three were mounted and spurring fresh mounts back to the road.

"Let's go!" Said McCreedy, and they were once again at a fast-paced gallop along the rutted and dusty trail to Texarkana.

"Any idea where we are?" Yelled Ellis as he pulled alongside McCreedy.

"Arkansas!" He yelled back. "Twenty miles to go . . . . Stage Coach comin' yonder, too, best let it pass." They slowed the animals to a walk as the coach approached then stopped completely as the driver slowed and then stopped beside them.

"You boys was kickin' up quite a cloud a dust back yonder, anything wrong?"

"Not particularly!" Said McCreedy as he eyed the passengers through the open windows. "In a bit of a hurry, is all."

"Little hot to be runnin' horses that hard!"

"Ours to run!" Yelled Ellis.

"You're right about that!" He flicked the lines and sent the four horse team to a walk, and as the coach began moving again, urged them to a steady trot.

"Can't you keep your mouth shut, Morgam?"

"Weren't none a th' old fart's business how we treat horses."

McCreedy cursed and spurred his horse to a gallop again.

*   *   *

Texarkana, Texas, a thriving town, split right down the middle by the Louisiana, Arkansas road, which ran along the border with Texas, and

Arkansas. The downtown business district occupied both sides of the long stretch of dusty street, each side with the same name, Texarkana.

At one time, this site was home to Caddo Indians living along the banks of Red River, and along the much used Southwest Trail, which for many years was the line of travel between Indian villages of the Mississippi Valley, and of those in the West, and southwest. Those Caddo along the river harvested great fields of maize, beans, pumpkins and melons, which they traded with the trail's many travelers.

In 1840, rudiments of a permanent settlement began, and shortly after came the stamp of approval, awarded in the form of a post office, located at Lost Prairie, 15 miles from the present site of Texarkana.

In the 1850's, builders of the Cairo and Fulton railroad were pushing rails across Arkansas and by '74, had crossed the border with Texas where passengers and freight were ferried across the river to Fulton, to continue by rail to their destinations. The Red River Bridge was opened then, and from that date, trains have run directly from Texarkana, in a round about way, all the way to St. Louis, Missouri.

The Texas and Louisiana line, however, crossed into Texas just South, and West of Texarkana and continued on North only as far as the mills, and logging camps of northwest, Texas, and extreme southeastern part of the Indian Nations. Alternate tracks were laid in Texarkana where the idle train cars were stored until their use.

Stores, shops and business places of all kinds lined the wide street on both sides for most of a mile. Smoke from adobe, and brick kilns could be seen rising in the sky both day and night west of the city. Wagon yards, stables and blacksmith shops on either side of them. Adobe and frame housing stretched for a half-mile in any direction from town, on both sides of the border.

The Sheriff's Office was located along the street, on the Texas side, but utilized an alternate office on the Arkansas side, and was manned by two alternating deputies, as agreed on by the Mayors of both.

"Buford F. Hargett, Texarkana, Bowie and Miller County Sheriff was newly elected to that position, with all the headaches that go with the job and today, he was sitting at his desk with two of his six deputies over a cup of coffee, and rereading first, the wire from Fort Smith requesting the recapture of Benjamin Childers, George Collins and Phillip Long, should they come to Texarkana, . . . and then read the other one from Shreveport requesting he meet and assist U. S. Marshals at the train depot with their prisoners of the same names.

He looked up then as another deputy came through the open door. "Everything okay, Walt?"

"Yes, sir, station attendant said th' train was en-route, left Shreveport a mite after six this morning."

Hargett pulled his watch and looked at it. "It's eleven o'clock, train's due anytime now."

"It's a freight train, Sheriff." Reminded Walt. "Station man said it would be slower than th' regular train."

"Be another, . . . what? . . . Thirty minutes, or an hour?"

"He just said it was slower."

"Okay, . . . take Pete and Ruford with ya. Check th' buildings around that depot, anywhere men might hide with rifles. Only those people inside th' depot it's self is allowed to stay there, anybody else, no closer than fifty yards away till th' Marshal leaves with his prisoners . . . . I'll be along as soon as soon as George and Luke gets here, now go!"

*   *   *

Rodney chewed the bite of sandwich and swallowed while watching Childers and the other men eat. "What's th' time now, Billy?" He asked, looking back at him.

Billy corked the canteen and pulled his watch. "Eleven o'clock."

"Guess we ain't makin' no twenty miles an hour." He sighed then.

"Any time we get there'd suit hell out a me! . . . Hotter'n hell in this car!"

"Smell's gonna make me sick!" Said Rodney, drinking from the canteen. "Hot water ain't helpin' none, . . . makes me think we should a took that coach!"

"We been hot before, Rod, . . . you sure you're okay?"

Rodney shook his head. "Got a bad feelin' is all, . . . but I'm good!"

"Rod, . . . I got a tell ya . . . . Whatever's come over you has got me buffaloed. I can't recall ever seein' you like that! . . . But I do know, you're gonna have to put it behind ya. You don't, you'll get careless, and that's what'll hurt ya!"

"I know that! . . . I'll work it out, too . . . . I'm okay, Billy."

"Then I'll go water th' horses . . . . Try layin' down and closin' your eyes."

"What's wrong, Marshal?" Asked Childers. "Nerves getting to ya?"

"Billy walked over to squat in front of him . . . "That mouth a yours is just about to become hazardous to your health, so do yourself a big favor, and don't open it again this side a Texarkana . . . . Do not fuck with me!" He got up and went to water the animals then.

"What's wrong, Ben?" Chided Wallace. "Find somebody, ain't afeared of ya? . . . Huh?"

"Shut up. Lionel!"

"Now, that's somethin' you ain't able to do, too . . . . Make me shut up, you fuck!"

"No, but I can!" Snapped Rodney. "Else I'll gag th' lot of ya again."

"Yes, sir, Mister Marshal!"

*   *   *

McCreedy and the two men were walking the horses again, when he suddenly held up his hand and stopped.

"What is it, Ed?"

"Shut up, Morgan, I heard something!"

They all cocked their heads to listen, and then Ellis looked at him and shook his head. "Ed, all you're hearin' are locusts singin' in th' fuckin' trees!"

"I hear them, too, God damn it! . . . I heard something else." And then they all heard it. "Train whistle! . . . Fuckin' train must have left early!"

"How far to Texarkana now?"

"Shit-fire, Morgan, I don't know! . . . Five, . . . could be ten miles . . . . How far, you reckon that train was?"

"Hell, I don't know, weren't all that loud! . . . Mile, maybe?"

"We'll have to get off this road before we get to town." Said McCreedy. "If that engine ain't no more'n a mile away, it'll be in town before we are, but it could be more than a mile, maybe two, or three miles . . . . Either way, we can't take Childers in town, and this road is th' main street of town. We'll skirt the town, we get close enough, hit th' road again on th' other side . . . . We'll start watchin' our chance once we see 'em."

"This is gettin' more and more complicated all th' time, Ed!" Said Ellis.

"Shut up, Morgan, and come on!" They once again spurred the animals to a full gallop, their flying hooves kicking up clouds of hot, dry dirt.

"Why don't we just stop th' train out here?" Yelled Ellis, from beside him. "Pile dead wood on th' tracks, it'll stop!"

"I ain't in no mood to face a shotgun, Morgan, there's five or six of 'em on that train! . . . We get our ass killed, that money's gone! . . . We got a chance, my way!"

"Yeah." Yelled Ellis. "A fat one, you ask me!"

"Better'n none at all, Morgan! . . . Now shut up, and ride!"

*   *   *

Billy put the watch away as the whistle blew again. "Eleven-forty-four, Rod, . . . must be getting' close."

"None too soon for me . . . . What about th' horses, Billy, they good ones?"

"Couple of 'em better'n th' rest, we'll take those! . . . . Once we leave th' train and get 'em mounted, we'll tie their feet under th' horses' bellies, tether th' horses together, side by side, two in front, two behind . . . . You'll ride in front with the tow rope around your saddle horn, I'll take th' rear, and Rod, . . . if we're shot at, lean over your horse's neck and head for the woods!"

"You got that right!" Nodded Rodney. "If I'm able."

"You got a shake that feelin', Rod, and do it right now! Cause this ain't Rodney Taylor I'm talkin' to . . . . With this attitude, you're just some wet-nosed kid in that desert thirteen years ago! You're not him anymore, Rod, you're a United States Marshal, a proven law man, so forget it, okay? . . . Resigning from your job, makes you no less the man you always was."

"Okay, Billy!" He frowned. "I'll be okay! . . . Don't think I ever heard you give a speech before! . . . I'm okay, I'm fine, I agree with everything you said!"

*   *   *

They could see the train's black trailing smoke as McCreedy stopped them again. "Five miles to town!" He said, reading the sign on the post. "We'll leave th' road here and head North. Be slow going at times, but th' horses'll be cooled down, and fresher by th' time we stop." He reined the horse down the embankment and then up into the trees, with the other two close behind.

*   *   *

Buford Hargett, and all six deputies were waiting as the train pulled to a slow stop at the depot's raised platform, and after assigning a deputy to wait until the few passengers could de-board, and usher them into the depot, him and the other five left the platform as two attendants began to unlatch the cattle car's heavy ramp.

"Go help 'em, Walt, you, too, Pete." And while the four men eased the ramp to the ground, they were in front to watch as Billy stood in the opening, satchel in hand to allow the four, heavily chained convicts to walk down. "Watch 'em, boys." He said, and moved to shake Rodney's hand as he came down.

"Sheriff Buford Hargett, Marshal!"

"Marshal Rodney Taylor." He shook his hand then turned as Billy came down. "My deputy, Billy Upshur."

"Sheriff?" He said, shaking his hand.

"Sheriff, we are soaked clean through." Said Rodney. "Think one a your men could bring our horses down, while you show us a place to wash up and change?"

"Walt, you and George get the horses out a there, rest of ya confine these old boys till we get back! . . . Sit 'em down in th' shade somewhere, give 'em some water. And keep an eye on these buildings, we don't want any trouble! . . . This way, Marshal."

A half hour later, they were tying the horses in front of the Sheriff's Office to watch, as the deputies took the prisoners inside and locked them up.

"Well, . . . nothing happened back there." Said Hargett. "Are you sure they were supposed to hit you here?"

"No, sir." Said Rodney. "We just know they will hit us. One a th' men back there is part of the three that broke 'em out a prison, so we know the other two, or maybe three more will try to do it again . . . . We just wanted to be sure they didn't do it here!"

"And we'll need to head out pretty quick, Sheriff." Said Billy as they entered the office.

"And you will, soon's you get a hot meal under your belts." He nodded at Walt then. "Tell Rosemary, we need three lunches sent over right away, . . . and a pot a stew for th' prisoners." When the other five men came in from the cellblock, he looked at them.

"Pete, you all go with Walt, get your lunch."

"Now then," He said, once they were gone. "Why th' cattle car, and why th' horses, for a two hundred mile ride to Fort Smith? . . . It'll take you a week to get there with prisoners to slow ya down."

"About th' same on a coach." Said Billy. "And twice as dangerous."

"Maybe so." He sighed. "Never been that far North."

"Cattle car was Sheriff Lake's idea." Said Rodney. "There was evidence part a th' gang would try to free 'em again, he just didn't know when, or where . . . . Anyway, a cattle car was inconspicuous to anybody lookin' to find us, especially with nothin' inside but horses . . . . We were pretty well hidden."

"You're talking about this McCreedy fellow, right?"

"One and th' same." Nodded Billy.

"What was Lake's evidence?"

"He's locked up back there, Lionel Wallace."

"Oh, yeah, . . . that's evidence enough!" Nodded Hargett. "That means the danger is still ahead of ya, and that's all th' more reason to take th' stage, you'll be easy targets on horseback."

"Six men in a coach don't make for easy goin', Sheriff." Said Billy. "Shootin' starts, they'd likely jump us to help out . . . . Horseback gives us room to fight!"

"I see your logic!" He nodded again. "In that case, all I can offer you, is good luck wishes . . . . What I will do, is have my deputies escort you as far as Ashdown, a town about twenty miles North on th' main road. After that, you're on your own. You'll be going into a heavily forested landscape once you leave there, too . . . . A bushwhacker's paradise!"

"We'll have to chance it!" Said Rodney. "Besides, it can't be much worse than where we work already."

"Where's this?"

"Indian Nations . . . . Isaac Parker assigned it."

"Judge Parker. I was surprised when I saw his name on th' wire, . . . course I've heard rumors about him for years! . . . Why don't you wire him to send some help this way?"

"I'm afraid we're it!" Shrugged Rodney.

"Then I have used up my advice, and options!"

"You've helped enough, Sheriff . . . Town this size keeps you busy enough, without goin' out a your way, to help us."

"You're right about that! . . . I've been in office three months now, one before I found out how big two counties were. Half of it's in Arkansas!" State line is that street out there."

"How's that workin' out?" Asked Billy.

"Except for havin' two totally different Mayors, and mailing addresses, quite normal. I have an office, and two deputies across the street there. Other than that, it's workin' fine." They looked up then as the woman entered with three steaming platters of food. "Ahhh, Rosemary, . . . thank you, my dear."

She placed the large plates in front of them, along with cloth lap-napkins, knives and forks. "Steak, potatoes and meat gravy." She smiled. "Enjoy." She left just as Walt and Pete came back with a crock-pot of stew, bowls and utensils for the prisoners.

*   *   *

Two hours of riding through a forest of trees and brush thickets to avoid a growing residential section of Texarkana, brought McCreedy, Ellis and Haskell in view of Fulton's distant railroad depot and rail yard, across the wide river, . . . and climbing up to an old wagon road, they crossed an almost worn out bridge over a swift moving, and quite deep creek to continue on into the trees.

At last, they were forced to stop their horses beside the wide, deeply rutted and very busy, Texas, Arkansas main road leading to the town of Fulton and points beyond. Having to sit as several freight wagons lumbered by, as well as three buckboards, a Doctor's carriage and a group of no less than nine cowboys passed before they could cross the thoroughfare.

Crossing quickly, they entered the trees again, where McCreedy stopped to look back.

"Busy road." He said, taking the bandana from his neck and wiping his face. "Must of opened the new bridge already."

"We're wastin' time, Ed." Said Ellis. "Which way is th' road they'll be takin'?"

"Straight South from here, let's go."

*   *   *

"That," Said Billy, pushing back from the desk. "Made that miserable ride in a cattle car worth while."

"Amen to that!" Agreed Rodney. "You eat like that all th' time?"

"Of course, Rosemary's my sister in law . . . . Cooks about as good as my wife does!"

"Well, . . . thanks for th' hospitality, Sheriff." Said Rodney, with a chuckle. "But we got a go!" He moved his chair back, and looked up to see Hargett's six deputies coming back as he got up.

"A couple of you bring the prisoners out, and get 'em mounted." Said Hargett, as him, Billy and Rodney walked out onto the covered boardwalk, followed by the other four deputies.

"Pete," Said Hargett, turning to face them. "You, ruford, George, you, too, Luke, . . . where's your horses?"

"The lean-to." Nodded Ruford.

"Go get 'em, . . . you four will ride as far as Ashdown with th' Marshal. There are men out there somewhere waitin' to take their prisoners from them! You'll be of help should they strike between here and there . . . . Any farther than Ashdown will be out of our jurisdiction, so head on back!"

The deputies came out with Childers and the other three, and helped them to their saddles as Rodney and Billy, each took rope from their saddle and proceeded to bind their feet together beneath the animals' bellies. When they were done, they took more rope and looped a section over the heads of Childers', and Wallace's horse, then did the same to those of Collins and Long.

When they were done, Rodney came to look up at Childers. "Rope too tight for ya, Mister Childers?"

"We ain't to Fort Smith yet!" He grinned. "Anything can happen in a week. When it does, it'll be so sudden, you won't know it."

"Could be, but if that happens, Billy there will blow your damn head off! . . . Now, you chew on that bit a knowledge for a while."

The deputies rode around from the alley then, and both, Billy and Rodney shook Hargett's hand again before motioning the four lawmen to lead the way. They mounted, and once Rodney had the lead rope secured, he reined his horse in behind them, with the four horses in tow behind him.

Billy nodded at Hargett, and the remaining deputies before following them, all walking the animals along the very wide street, . . . and it seemed to both of them, that everyone in the crowded roadway, and on the boardwalks were watching them. He took it all in, even those peering at them through the plate-glass windows in the storefronts and still, no tingle at the back of his neck. He was sure that Childers' men were not in Texarkana, . . . but almost wished they were!

He looked past the four outlaws to watch Rodney's straight-backed stature in the saddle, and wondered what had come over him so quickly back on the train? It had been totally out of character for the man he had come to admire and trust with his life. He was also his brother, as well as the only true friend he ever had. He knew he might never understand, and neither would he, but he hoped sincerely that he was over it, whatever it was. Sighing, he scrutinized the busy street and boardwalks again then pulled his pistol, checking its action and loads before putting it away again.

They were finally out of the business district and on the long winding road to Ashdown, . . . and an hour later were past the last of the occupied dwellings along the road. It was at that point that he began to intently watch the trees on either side of them for movement, although, the landscape West of the road was only sparsely decorated with any trees to speak of. One thing he knew for sure, was that unless he could see it coming first, the shots would come suddenly, and from ambush. But, he thought it not real likely to happen this side of Ashdown, because of their four man escort, . . . but when it did, he hoped like hell that Rodney would be ready for it!

If McCreedy was an ex-sniper, he would surely have a large caliber rifle, one with a scope on it, and if that was the case, six or eight hundred yards wouldn't be a hard shot to make, . . . and only those, who were not his target, would even hear the shot, hardly enough time to duck and run!

He had never before doubted Rodney's reaction time, but he was worried about him now, . . . and a man in that state of mind, would let confusion cloud his thinking . . . He knew, also, that what he went through on that train appeared to be temporary, and was also something that he would have to work out on his own, . . . mainly because he had no idea what so ever, how to help him?

Sighing heavily, he pushed the thoughts from his mind and concentrated on the partial wilderness on the road's East side, particularly the trees six to eight hundred yards away. Almost the entire landscape was dotted with small groups of cattle, and horses, and even one or two cowboys working the stock, but nothing that would cause him to become suspicious. But he was sure that if he saw the right movement beneath those trees, he would know it was them.

*   *   *

"Is it them?" Asked Ellis as all three of them watched the riders.

"It's got a be!" Said McCreedy, and got to his feet, being careful to stay behind the heavy growth of brush. "If it is, they got some help from that Sheriff down there . . . . Too far to recognize Childers, though."

"Hell, you got a scope on that fuckin' rifle, Ed, use it!"

"Can't chance it, Morgan . . . . Scope glass, even a rifle barrel has a way to warn someone we're here, especially on a sunlit day."

"Yeah, I guess, so what now?"

McCreedy turned to scan the flat pastureland behind them. "We wait, . . . we follow them, and we wait." He looked back through the trees at the distant procession. The four in front, maybe the one in back are likely deputies . . . . If they are, they'll be turning back. Maybe at that town we came through before, what was it . . . ?"

"Hell, I don't know, Ed, . . . Ash, something, I think."

"Ashdown, that's it! . . . It's th' county line, they'll turn back right there. Jurisdiction, Morgan . . . . Come on, we'll get there ahead of 'em! We can pick our spot after that." They made their way to the horses and mounted and, keeping the timber between them and the riders on the road, continued northward toward the community of Ashdown.

*   *   *

Although he had been watching the heavily foliaged landscape intently since leaving town, he had seen no movement at all, save the grazing livestock in the open areas. But having see the sudden flight of blackbirds from a group of distant trees to the East of them, coupled with the slight chill on his neck, he was reasonably sure they were being watched, . . . and most likely by the men in question.

It was doubtful they would have tried anything so close to town anyway, he thought, even without the presence of the four lawmen. But he couldn't be sure of it, because foolish men did foolish things. However, he trusted his instincts when it came to things he couldn't see, . . . and those instincts were telling him they were being watched!

He was also sure that three of those men in chains were of no consequence to the men out there, and would only be, what was considered, collateral damage if they were killed! . . . He was just as sure, that Childers was the man they were after, boss of the outfit, so to speak! . . . But, he thought then, . . . there had to be something very important to induce three men to chance breaking Childers out of a security prison, . . . and to be willing to do it again now, . . . and it had to be that he knew something they didn't, or had something they wanted bad enough to risk dying for. There just would be no other reason for that sort of persistence. None, that he could think of.

He could see that Rodney was intent on watching that area East of them as well, and grinned when he saw him reach foe, and light his thin cigar. A good sign that he was becoming his old self again, alert, and ready! It was also more than he could say for their four escorts. They were busy in conversation among themselves, and laughing at some obvious attempt at joke telling. Obviously, they were in no way concerned with the seriousness of the situation, and would likely abandon their duties at first sign of trouble. But there was some safety in numbers, at least till they got to Ashdown.

He noticed the large hand-painted sign then, barely visible in the tall grass and weeds, and stopped for a few seconds to read it. 'Future planned right of way for the Texas, and Louisiana railroad'! . . . 'We could use it now', he thought wryly, then scanned the timber line to the East of them before urging the horse to a trot to catch up. The area to the West of them, he remembered when leaving town, was quite sparsely inhabited by any solid growth of trees, or farmland, being mostly wide areas of grassland, dotted with small groups of cattle, but with no inhabited dwellings, which was odd. But for now, still ignored it as having any cover for the attackers to work with and so, turned his attention back to the wooded areas to the East, and the occasional farmer behind his plow and team.

*   *   *

Believing they were a safe distance in front of the lawmen, and Childers, McCreedy stopped to look through the trees at the empty road.

"What now?" Asked Ellis irritably.

"I think, now we can use the road . . . . We ought a be a half mile in front of 'em now! . . . Besides, I don't feel up to swimming that river."

"I'm all for usin' that Bridge myself, Ed."

Grinning, McCreedy reined his horse through the trees again

*   *   *

It was another two hours before they saw any traffic on the rutted road, and most was in the form of farm wagons, one or two with farm equipment, or loaded with hay, . . . and still some with their families in the tired-looking wagon beds, all eying them with curiosity in passing . . . . But there still was no sign of their would-be attackers!

It was getting on well into the late afternoon, when he urged his horse up past the prisoners and alongside Rodney.

"You see somethin', Billy?"

"I don't think we will, long as we got our escort . . . . But I think we ought a speed it up a bit, it's getting' late fast."

"I think you're right!" He nodded as he once again turned to scan the trees. "I don't look forward to makin' camp, with them out there somewhere."

"You see anything at all before now?"

"Nothin', expectations, I guess . . . . You?"

"I can feel 'em, Rod . . . . I know we were being watched a while back."

"That's good enough for me . . . . We should be in that Ashdown by dark."

"I'd like to be on the other side, by dark. We can pick our own spot to make camp, without them four jokes for lawmen!"

"They ain't very serious minded, that's for sure! . . . I'll tell 'em to go at a trot from here to town."

Billy dropped back to his position as Rodney called to the deputies, and they were soon moving at a faster pace.

The pace, and movements of the horse made it harder to distinguish any movement in the tree-lines, but he was fairly confident by now that the attackers were well ahead of them, . . . and most likely in, or soon would be in Ashdown waiting for them to lose their escort. He was already making plans for their first night out, too, and that, he thought, would be best served just at the outskirts of town! Being that close to a populated area might stave off trouble until tomorrow, . . . he hoped! Maybe they'd have time to plan out the rest of the trip, that way. Those men out there, he knew, were smart enough to know they couldn't afford to get careless, not with only three, or four men . . . . Not near enough to attack in force, and hope to free Childers.

An hour later, they were crossing the long bridge across a fast-moving Red River, a bridge they had to climb a steep grade to reach, putting them at most, fifty feet above the swift waters. Half way across, they were all watching the hard-working crew maneuver a long, very wide, freight-loaded flatboat as it passed under them, and continued to watch as they exited the creaking timbers.

They were walking the animals as they finally came to Ashdown town limit marker, and Billy pulled his watch to check the time before riding up beside Rodney again.

"We best pick up a few supplies here, Rod . . . . Beef jerky, can beans, food for a few cold camps."

"Amen to that!" He nodded at the deputies. "They'll know a place to stop." He called out to them, causing the lawmen to stop and wait for them.

Billy dropped back in place, and as they continued on into the one-sided business district, was surprised that the road it's self, like Texarkana, was the main street of town. The entire business section was on the East side of the road, while nothing at all, save a lone shed, or two adorned the road's west side. He could see several streets running from the road, eastward, and several places of business could be seen from the road on passing. They were almost through town when the deputies pointed toward a hitch-rail in front of an open market, and pulled in to stop.

Billy dismounted, as did the deputies, to walk around a bit while Rodney went inside.

"Guess this is where we leave ya, Marshal." Said Pete, coming to shake his hand. "Our jurisdiction ends here."

"We appreciate th' escort." He nodded. "Give our thanks to th' Sheriff."

"You serious about those men waitin' for ya?"

"Oh, no, . . . They're waitin' for you to leave, they know we're comin'."

"Man, I hate that! . . . Would it help, if we stayed till mornin' before goin' back?"

"It would just prolong it, Pete, but thanks for the offer."

"Well, I don't feel right about it!"

"I like your attitude, Pete." Said Billy, shaking his hand again. "But we're paid for this, no jurisdictions . . . . Go on home, and don't feel bad about it, you did hour jobs."

"Yes, sir."

Rodney came back with a cloth bag of supplies and tied it to his saddle before saying his goodbyes then watched the lawmen mount up and ride away.

"Alone at last!" He said then grinned at Billy before looking up at Childers. "You all right up there?"

"I could do with a piss, it's been five hours on this fuckin' horse!"

"You need to go, Billy? . . . I went a minute ago."

"Wouldn't hurt none."

"Outhouse around back . . . . I'll bring th' boys around."

The old store owner was closing and padlocking the heavy doors to the market when they came back around to the street, so they stopped there for a minute to wait until he looked up at them.

"Closin' up already?" Asked Rodney, leaning his arms across the saddle horn.

"Always do before it get's dark!" He gestured an arm at the road then. "All kinds a riff-raff on that road at night . . . . I'm too old to worry with 'em! . . . You boys forget something, did ya?"

"No," Said Billy also looking at the road. "Just wonderin' what th' country's like to th' North?"

"Ain't so bad, ya stay on th' road, but once ye leave here, it's mostly solid Pines, course there's a few other varieties mixed in, ye understand . . . . Few hole in th' wall shacks along th' way, callin' themselves a town. But DeQueen's th' next real town, got a crossroad there in th' middle a town, one way goes North, other'n, all th' way to Towson, in Injun Territory . . . . Why, where ye bound for?"

"Fort Smith." Said Rodney.

"Oh, well, . . . never been that far North. I do know, once ye leave DeQueen, you're gonna start seein' some downright real trees, mountains, too, tall Mother-r!oos! . . . Never been that far North myself, . . . went to Little Rock once, maybe fifty years ago. Not much of a town then . . . . Even took me a bath in th' Hot mineral Springs. Cherokees was there then, cost me a sack a tobacco to bathe. Place got so famous, they built a town around it."

"Well, much obliged, old timer." Said Billy.

"Lot a very bad men on that road, Marshal, thieves and killers, some of 'em, so watch yourself! . . . Was me, I'd hop th' stage, tie them fellers down on top with th' luggage."

"You're talkin' out your ass, you old Fuck!" Said Wallace.

"Shut up, you!" Snapped Rodney. "At least he ain't in chains, like a young Fuck!"

"Fuck you, Marshal!"

Rodney grinned, as did Billy, then both leaned down and shook the old man's hand. "Thanks for the information, sir."

"Any time, boys." He waved as they rode off toward the road.

"Billy." Said Rodney as they rode together. "We're in for a hell of a ride, I think! . . . And that old timer's right, th' Judge calls this road, the outlaw trail. Another thing, accordin' to that territorial map on his wall, we could still more than two hundred miles away from Fort Smith, right here!"

"Two weeks away, at this rate." Nodded Billy. "Well, that's a bridge to cross when we get to it! . . . Right now, we need a place to stop for th' night, . . . and I suggest we get off this road to do it!"

Once they were clear of the few last remaining structures, they rode another hundred yards along the wide lane where they stopped to look both ways, and not seeing any traffic, turned off into the darkening trees on the road's East side. Billy led the way into the dense maze of Pines and briar thickets for another fifty-odd yards before finding a suitable spot for them, and the animals.

"I don't relish sleepin' with snakes, Billy, you know they hate me." Said Rodney, dismounting to lift his satchel up, and remove the bedroll from behind the mantle.

"Billy loosed the ropes binding the prisoners' feet beneath their horse, and ordered them to dismount and sit against a tree, while he removed their bedding and tossed them at their feet. "You can spread your own blankets." He said evenly. "Just make sure that's all ya do."

"You're sounding awful tough, all of a sudden, Specks." Said Childers as he got to his knees and managed to spread out his bedding.

"Naw, . . . I ain't tough at all, Childers!" He loosened the animals' cinches as he spoke, and finished turned to watch the other three spread their beds and sit down on them before walking over to squat in front of them.

"In lieu of sounding tough again, . . . I was wonderin' if any of you want a tell us why them old boys want a take you away from us?"

"They're my boys." Smiled Childers, with a shrug.

"Your boys? . . . That mean yours, as their father, or yours, as their Boss?"

"I'll tell you something, Specks . . . . The only way in hell you two are gonna live through this, is to let us go and head on back to that town out there! . . . You don't, you can both expect to be shot from your saddles, . . . if not tomorrow, then the day after, or th' day after that! . . . Think about it, it's a long way back to Fort Smith!"

"A hell of a speech, man!" Said Billy, turning his head to see Rodney watching, and nodded at him. "You hearin' this, Rod?"

"I'm listening."

"You just might be right, Mister Childers." He said, looking back at him. "But you, sir, will never be rid a them chains . . . . Why? . . . Because the moment that bullet shoots me from the saddle, my reflexes will kill you! . . . You, . . . all of you think about that! . . . Before that Marshal and me die, we'll take you all with us!"

"No way in hell, you're fast enough to do that!" Sneered Wallace.

"That's th' very same mistake made by other men!" Said Rodney, as he opened the sack of supplies. "Truth is, ain't a man alive faster than he is." He brought the sack of food over and gave each of them a stick of jerky, and dropped the canteen where they could reach it. "That ain't no brag, Childers, just a fact!"

"Well, I think you're both full a shit!" Said Childers.

"Way to know for sure, is to wait and see." Said Rodney. "Or be stupid enough to try somethin' tonight! . . . Now eat, and no more talking th' rest a th' night, you do, I'll gag ya for th' rest a th' trip!" Billy got to his feet, and they went to spread their own blankets and sat down.

He gave Billy a stick of jerky, and with a canteen between them, ate their cold meal.

"You know he's right, don't ya?"

"I know that, Billy . . . . But now, he ain't so sure of himself. Every one of 'em will if they'll live when th' shootin' starts."

"Childers won't, I promise ya that!"

"Yeah, I know . . . . What's th' plan here, Billy, I know ya got one?"

"What would you do, Rod?"

"I wouldn't get back on that road out there, I'll tell ya that! . . . Hell. I don't know, . . . I just hate th' thought of failing to do my job, especially my last one! We know they're out there somewhere, Billy, and we know they'll be able to see th' road from where they are! . . . They could be a half-mile ahead of us, or ten!" He sighed and breathed deeply of the stale air. "So, I'll ask you again, what's th' plan here?"

"You're right about not usin' that road again, Rod. I'm thinkin' we'll break camp well before full light, and get th' crew back in th' saddle . . . . Only this time, we're gonna tie their hands to th' saddle horn, and gag 'em, . . . then we'll head out through them trees right there!" He looked across at the four men, who were busy eating their jerky, and being sure they couldn't quite hear what was being said, leaned closer to Rodney.

"We'll tie their horses in single file, with you holding the lead rope as usual . . . . You'll lead off and go another, say, thirty tards or so to the East, and then turn North! . . . Rod, if we're lucky, we'll go right past 'em, and they won't even know it!"

"If we don't come down that road, they'll know it!"

"We'll be half a mile ahead of 'em, by then . . . . No, what they'll do first, is send somebody back to Ashdown to see if we stayed in town, . . . or just wait for us. Either way will give time . . . . Second, it's possible they'll think we waited for th' stage to come through. At any rate, they'll be forced to hunt for us . . . . And when they do, I'll be waitin' for 'em!"

"How?"

"I'll be somewhere behind you in th' woods, out a sight . . . . I'll see them before they find you. But who knows, they might just hightail it on up th' road, tryin' to catch us there . . . . Whatever they do, they'll be blind, they won't know where we are!"

"We'll do it, Billy." He said, and reached for the canteen. "It's crazy, but it could work!"

"I'll take first watch, Rod, wake you around midnight."

Rodney shook Billy awake, and once he got to his feet they both knelt to quietly roll up their bedding, got up and tied them in place again. While Billy tightened the animals' cinches, he woke up the prisoners and bade them roll up their blankets and tie them in place on their saddles.

"All right!" He said, in almost a whisper. "No talking, not a grunt from any of ya . . . . I want you to bend your heads and put those gags in your mouth, and do it now!" Once they grumpily complied. "You first, Childers, turn around while Billy tightens your gag."

After Billy was done. "Okay, You got a piss, do it now and get mounted . . . . Don't cough, don't fart, don't even grunt. You do, I'll plant this rifle butt on your skull! . . . Now, do your business."

While he was getting them mounted and lashed to the saddles, Billy anchored the horses together, one behind the other.

"That ought a do it." He breathed, as Billy came to look up at Childers and the other three in the coming light. "They can't use their hands, mouth or feet."

"Better hold your hats in your hand." He nodded at Rodney then. "Guess we're ready!" He said, taking Rodney by the arm and moving him away. "I'll move out right behind you, as usual, and remember, none a this is any different than them trees back home, you know how to get through 'em! . . . Don't look back at me, you won't know when I drop back. Keep th' rifle in your boot, too, can't use it anyway in this . . . . Let's go, Partner, . . . and take that hat off." He mounted, and watched as Rodney mounted and secured the lead-rope. They nodded at each other, and Rodney reined his horse into the trees.

He waited until the small caravan moved into the thicket then removed his own hat and urged his horse in behind that of Long's.

CHAPTER EIGHT

The three men considered themselves well hidden in the heavy growth of brush and trees alongside the road, having had ample time before dark the night before to position themselves comfortably in the underbrush, rifles in hand, to wait for their intended victims . . . . And with Haskell taking the first watch, and Ellis the next, they closed their eyes to wait.

It was almost light enough to see for several hundred yards in any direction along the road when Ellis threw sticks at McCreedy and Haskell to wake them.

"Sleep well, Ed?" Asked Ellis, with sarcasm.

"Matter a fact, I did, Morgan . . . . See anything yet?"

"I'd a woke ya! . . . Naww, nothin' but two wagons, and four men with rifles ridin' behind 'em . . . . That was two hours ago."

"Which way?"

"Why would that matter, they went to town! . . . Now get your ass up and watch th' fuckin' road for a while, I'm bushed!"

"Well, I was right." Grunted McCreedy as he got to his knees to see the road. "They made camp back there close to town somewhere . . . . They'll be along."

"Not if they know we're here!" Said Ellis.

"How could they?"

"Wallace, that's how!" Spouted Ellis angrily. "Mother's son don't know when to shut up!"

"You're right about that." He agreed. "But if they expected anything, it would a been before that train got to town. What is possible, though, . . . that Fort Smith stage would a left Texarkana sometime last night, . . . could be. They're waitin' in Ashdown to catch it!"

"That don't make sense, Mister McCreedy." Said Haskell. "Why ride horses this far to catch a stage, they could a caught it there?"

"He's right, Ed, . . . they know we're here!"

"Horse shit! . . . They wouldn't expect us to ride all this way, just to hit 'em here . . . . That's close to a hundred and twenty, maybe thirty miles! . . . I think they'd expect us to still be behind 'em somewhere . . . . We'll wait and see."

"And if they don't show?"

"Okay, we'll wait an hour, they don't show, we'll go to town and see about it . . . . Guess they could a locked th' boys up for th' night, they did, they'll be along."

Ellis looked at Haskell then. "You're an Indian, Joe, you was them, what would you do?"

"I wouldn't use th' road."

"Then what?"

Haskell shrugged. "I'd go across country . . . . If, I thought we was waitin' for me."

"I tell you, they don't expect any trouble this far from Shreveport!" Argued McCreedy. "No way they could, . . . and I don't think Lionel talked, he knows our plans."

"Maybe they're just cautious." Said Haskell. "I would be."

"Yeah, . . . they're just cautious." Said McCreedy, looking back through the trees behind them. "Nothin' but a coyote could get through that jungle a trees anyway, we'd a heard a horse squeal or somethin' . . . . You hear anything like that?"

"Didn't hear a thing." Said Ellis. "Did hear your coyote a time or two, wolves, too!"

"Then we wait!"

*   *   *

For the next two hours, after Rodney had turned the procession northward in the tangled forest, Billy had followed close behind Phillip Long's horse, and spending most of that time laying flat on the animal's neck, as were they all, to avoid the wild growth of low-hanging Pine limbs with their thick, sharp needles and that, mixed with equally sharp, and gouging branches of dead, fallen timber that brought blood while raking the skin of men and horseflesh, was nothing short of agony. But still, Rodney kept them moving, having to use a zigzag pattern at times to avoid heavy growths of deadly briar patches . . . . And at that point, somewhere, he felt, rather than knew that Billy was no longer in line behind them.

Though the snapping of dry twigs and brush was heard beneath the horses' hoofs, and the occasional snort, or whinny from the animals, they were fairly quiet in their slow progress, thought Rodney, and although he expected to be startled at times by wild animals, his heart about stopped a time or two by deer, as they were rousted from their beds. But even at that, he was too busy finding a way through the maze of tangled forest to let any of it unnerve him . . . . Not even the muffled grumbling from gagged and helpless convicts.

He had not once bothered to look behind them, because he knew that Billy was there somewhere watching their backs. He was also confident, that if they were being followed, he would stop them from coming any closer . . . . And every time he thought about him, or wondered where he might be, he would wish, as he had so many time, that he possessed Billy's instincts and savvy of outlaws . . . . And especially his speed with a gun! No other man would have volunteered to come with him like this, he thought, as he ducked more low branches. Especially not just another friend, . . . nobody, but Billy Upshur. But there was no other friend like Billy Upshur!

He reined the horse around another outgrowth of briars then, and thought of home, and of what Melissa had said about waiting, and not knowing if he was coming home? . . . He had never before stopped to think of what his job was doing to her, after all, it was a dangerous job . . . . But it was a job he had always taken with a grain of salt, it went with the territory. He sighed then, almost coughing from the steaming smell of decomposing underbrush.

He thought about the night she told him about her feelings, and it was the same night, his first thoughts of resigning his post had crossed his mind. As much as he loved being a peace officer, he loved his family much more, and he knew it wouldn't be easy telling Judge Parker of his decision . . . . He was a very persuasive man!

"Shit!" He cursed when he was suddenly gouged again by a dead branch, and catching himself, quickly searched the surrounding trees and brush . . . . This, he thought, was not the time to be daydreaming.

He looked up through the treetops at the sun's position, thinking that it must be close to noon, but he couldn't be sure, however, it seemed like many hours since leaving the campsite. 'I'm going to get me another watch', he thought, as he concentrated on the task at hand again. But he couldn't help wondering how far they might have come since leaving the camp, and if they had already passed the waiting McCreedy, and his bunch? . . . He wished he knew where Billy was, too?"

*   *   *

McCreedy, Ellis and Haskell watched the DeQQueen stage go by in silence, from their place of concealment.

"Nobody but a man and his bitch in that thing, Ed." Snapped Ellis. "Anymore bright, fuckin' ideas?"

"Yeah," He said, looking at Haskell. "Get th' horses, Joe, we're going to town! . . . They got a be there."

They led the animals out on the road, mounted and spurred them hard toward Ashdown. Ten minutes later, they dismounted at the first hitch-rail they came to, and stood looking at the sparse pedestrian traffic along the boardwalk, and the five or six droop-headed horses at the hitch-rails along the street.

"Morgan, get back on your horse and find th' jail, they could be ther . . . . Tell that Constable you're from Texarkana with a message for that Marshal, anything, nobody knows us here!" He watched Ellis mount and ride by them to turn down the first side street.

"Joe, let's start askin' these storekeepers along here, somebody had to a seen 'em." He watched Haskell go inside, and went to the next building with no success. He met Haskell coming out and sent him to the next establishment while he went on to enter the market.

"What can I do ye for, Mister?" Grinned the old man.

"You can do a lot for me with th' right information, Pop . . . . Sheriff over in DeQueen sent me, and a couple men this way to meet a United States Marshal, supposed to be bringin' in some prisoners . . . . They weren't on that road anywhere, . . . would you a seen 'em, maybe sometime late yesterday?"

"Sure 'nough did, bought jerky and beans from me."

"They still in town?"

"Nope, rode out afore dark, watched 'em ride off down that road out there. Don't know how you missed 'em?"

"Jesus Christ!" He cursed then abruptly left just as Haskell passed, "Get th' horses, Joe, go, go, go, I got a find Morgan!" He ran to the side street as Haskell ran for the horses, and had just turned the corner when he saw Ellis walking his horse toward him, and waved wildly at him. Ellis spurred his horse to a run only to slide to a stop in front of him. "You find 'em, Ed, . . . they ain't in jail?"

"We missed 'em, Morgan, . . . and stop with, I told ya so, okay? Come on, Joe was right!" He ran back toward the corner, and as Ellis passed him, Haskell arrived with his horse. He mounted quickly, and all three spurred back to the road where McCreedy stopped them.

"You were right, Joe, . . . They're not on th' road anymore! Question now is, can you read sign?"

"Am I an Indian?"

"Good man, you lead the way . . . . They left th' road somewhere between here and where we was." He pulled his watch again, and cursed at the time. "After nine o'clock, God damn it! . . . Sons a bitches could be five or six hours ahead of us now . . . . You was right, too, Morgan!" He said, as they followed Haskell along the road.

"How's that, Ed?"

"They know we're here! . . . Had to be Wallace."

"Remind me to shoot th' Bastard!"

"A little late for that, . . . we're dealing with a very smart law man here, he's proving that." He looked into the trees then. "How fast could five horses move in woods like that?"

"I ain't never been in woods that thick, I don't know . . . . But it'll be damn slow!" He pointed then. "Joe dismounted, he found somethin'!" They galloped up to dismount beside Haskell.

"They left the road here!" Said Haskell, looking down at the tracks. "Six horses, four side by side."

"Six? . . . Two Marshals? . . . Th' man in th' rear!" Nodded McCreedy. "Well, lets go in after 'em." He mounted again and waited for them. "Lead off, Joe, it's up to you now." They followed Haskell into the thicket for four-dozen, well-earned yards before he stopped again.

"They slept here." He said, then led off into the trees again.

*   *   *

Continuing to reference the sun's track across the sky, Rodney determined his northerly direction, and having to stop several times to look for ways in and out of a half-dozen shallow ravines, he suddenly found himself on the bank of a quite large pool of water.

He dismounted there and moved the horses into positions to drink and when done, mounted and skirted the pond, looking up at the sun's position again before entering the trees.

Assuming the time to be around mid-day again, he thought about it, thinking that's what he thought it to be two hours ago. He shook his head then, and concentrated on a route through the forest of trees again, thinking that time didn't matter anyway as long as they were moving north! His only fear was that Billy would not be able to read their trail enough to follow them . . . . He was not a tracker, had said so a hundred times! He had also toyed with the idea that he should stop and wait for him, but each time had decided against it.

An hour after leaving the pond, he heard what sounded like the dry squeak of a wagon's wheel, and was more cautious as he approached the very old, and grass-covered road. He stopped just inside the trees to watch the wagonload of hay being pulled by a team of large mules. Deciding to chance it, he urged the horse out onto the road in front of the mules and stopped.

"Whoa there, you miles!" Shouted the teamster as he peered at Rodney then at the bound and gagged men behind him.

"I'm a U. S. Marshal," He said, moving up beside the wagon to show his badge.

"What can I do fer ya, Marshal, . . . and if ye don't mind me askin', . . . why are you travelin' in all that mess, you boys are scratched up purty good?"

"Some men don't want me to bring my prisoners in."

"Lookin' fer ya, huh?"

"That's a good guess." He looked down the road then. "What's down that way?"

"Little town a Wilton, . . . saloon, if ye can call it that. General store and a dozen houses, folks are livin' in."

He nodded. "North still that way?' He asked, pointing at the trees. "Sort a hard to tell in all that timber."

"Yep, that'll be North, all right! . . . Why not go back to th' road, ain't but ten mile or so?"

"They'd run me down on th' road. Thanks for your time."

"Don't mention it, Marshal. But I'd be careful, you gonna travel in there. Folks livin' in there be cookin' whiskey, most of 'em'll shoot strangers on sight, 'specially them with a badge! . . . Oh, you come across a field filled with cultivated weeds, best go around it real quiet like, it's mari-wani."

"Mari, . . . wani, . . . what's that?"

"It's dope, man . . . . They sell that stuff for a lot a money! . . . They see ya, they'll kill ya quick, and I ain't jokin'!"

"Ahhh, . . . Marijuana, . . . I've heard of that. Thank you. I'll be careful."

"Best ye do, . . . HEEE-yaaa, get up, you mules."

He watched the wagon leave then dismounted and relieved himself, before going to untie Childers feet and hands. "You can remove th' gag now, Ben . . . . If ya got a piss, get on down." He looked up at the others then. "One at a time, gents, you know th' procedure."

*   *   *

"Son of a bitch!" Cursed Ellis loudly as he was gouged by another dead limb. "We ain't never gonna catch them Bastards in this shit, Ed!"

"We'll catch up to 'em . . . . Pay attention, you won't get stabbed so much."

"Fuck you, Ed, . . . this is bullshit!"

"Ain't giving up, are ya? . . . Thought you was tougher than this."

"I'm as tough as you are, don't forget that!"

"Then shut up, and come on! . . . If that Marshal can get through here, we can, too! Just follow old Joe there . . . . And be quiet, don't want 'em to know we're comin'."

*   *   *

It was mid-afternoon when Rodney found the small clearing and decided to stop and wait for Billy to catch up. He dismounted tiredly and tied the reins to a branch before stopping to relieve himself.

He stood for a minute to peer into the surrounding timber, while smelling something sweet on the warm breeze. 'Sour mesh', he thought as he went to untie Childers' feet and hands, allowing him freedom to pull the gag from his mouth.

"Don't say a word, Mister Childers." He warned then looked up at Wallace and the others. "None of ya! . . . Childers, you got a piss, get to it, . . . then find you a tree and sit down! Got somethin' to say, keep your voice low."

"Nothin'!" He said, he dismounted and proceeded to relieve himself. "You know there's a still somewhere around here."

"I can smell it!" He waited until Childers sat down before releasing Wallace, who quickly pulled the gag down and donned his hat. "I meant what I said, . . . shut up! You got a pee, get down and do it then sit down over there."

In a matter of minutes, all four men were sitting against a tree, and he was giving them their ration of jerky and water.

"You said you could smell it." Said Childers calmly. "If you can, you know this ain't a good place to hold up!"

"I know that, too! . . . but this is th' best place I've found to stop . . . . Maybe they'll leave after dark."

"They find us here, they'll kill us all, do you know that? . . . . You think we're bad men, them old boys are worse! . . . Probably already know we're here!"

"Be quiet, Childers, eat your supper."

"Where th' hell is Specks, Marshal?" Asked Wallace, with a grin. "Run off and leave ya?"

"If he's smart, he did!" Smiled Rodney. "Now shut up! . . . Be a little more like Collins, and Long there, they ain't said nothin' this whole trip."

"That's cause they're both pussies." Said Wallace.

"Fuck yourself, Wallace!" Said Long. "We talk when there's somethin' to say."

"There ya go!" Said Rodney, sitting down with crossed legs, and rifle across his lap to chew on the jerky. He watched as Childers ate, seeing him cast somewhat nervous glances at the surrounding trees around the clearing. He was sure Childers had been serious about the danger of being caught by bootleggers, and that alone made him more wary of the surroundings. He pushed to his feet, and with rifle in hand went to stand next to a tree for a better view through the woods, and remained there for the better part of an hour before sighing tiredly and starting back toward the horses.

"Jes' stop rat theah, Pilgrum!" Came a high-pitched voice from the trees behind him. "An' ye can drop that theah gun on th' groun'."

The man's verbal attempt at the English language was hard to decipher, but he got the meaning, and dropped the rifle at his feet, . . . and at the same time, felt as if his heart would jump from his chest, as a fear for their lives suddenly clutched at him.

"Now, yer' pistol, belt an' all." And once he complied. "Come on in, Amos!' He yelled. "You, too, Chigger!" . . . Now, you move back from 'em guns, ye heah?"

Rodney turned to look at the man as he moved back, unable to believe the ragged, filthy over-alls, the man's shaggy, shoulder-length, and very matted hair that mostly covered his eyes. The beard was most as shaggy, and almost to his waist in length . . . . But the long-barreled Greener shotgun in his greasy hands was not to be argued with. He watched the man come toward him then bend to pick up the rifle, and then his belted pistol.

"Rat nice shootin' iren, ye got 'heah." He nodded his head, and at that moment, Amos and Chigger entered the clearing.

"Wooo-Hoooo!" Shouted Chigger as he bent to look at the men in chains. "See whut we got cheer, brother Luke, . . . Convics, Yesireee, Convics!" He looked at Luke then. "Ain't got no guns 'oh, . . . I wanted a new gun, can I have me one a your'en, brother Luke, ye gots two?"

"Nope, all mine! . . . Ye can 'ave th' boots, you, too Amos."

"Get away from me, you hillbilly, Fuck!" Yelled Wallace as he kicked Amos in the belly when he reached down for his feet. "You smell like horse shit!"

"Ye shutn't ought a done 'at!" Yelled Amos, while Chigger slapped his knees with laughter. "I'm a gonna blow yer haid off now!"

"No ye ain't!" Shouted Luke, stopping him from pulling the trigger. "I tell ye when to do any killin' 'roun' heah." He looked at Rodney then. "Chuck me 'at shiny badge on yer shirt theah, Pilgrum, . . . won't tell ye twicet."

He removed the badge and tossed it on the ground then watched Luke pick it up and pin it to his over-alls. "You men should let us go, and get back to your still." Said Rodney. "I ain't no revenuer, but I am th' law . . . . I'm takin' these men to jail."

"Not now, ye ain't! . . . Ye mite nevah leave 'eah, ye think about 'at?"

"What ya got in mind?"

Luke looked at him with a glint in his eye. "Mite d'cide ta poke ye in th' ass, 'ow bout 'at? . . . Ol' Chigger theah's tard a pokin' pigs anyways . . . . Ain'y ye, Chigger?"

"At's right, Luke, I shore am! . . . Hope they's better'n th' last 'uns."

"You fuckin' people are insane!" Said Rodney.

"Don' ye say 'at!" Said Luke, raising the shotgun's barrel. "We ain't, . . . yer on our lan', wheah ye ain't wanted, 'at gives us th' rite!"

"Hey, Luke!" Said Billy, stepping from behind a tree, and causing Luke, Amos, and Chigger to stare at him with open mouths. "Drop th' Shotguns!" He said, and waved the pistol to cover them all.

Rodney quickly moved to take the shotgun and rifle from Luke's hands then took his gun and holster from around the bootlegger's neck and buckled it on as Chigger and Amos reluctantly dropped their weapons.

Wallace raised his foot then, and kicked Amos in the ass, sending him face-first onto the rough ground. "How's a boot up your own greasy ass feel, shit for brains?"

"Whut ye want heah?" Asked Luke, his eyes still on Billy's pistol. "This be our lan', not your'en!"

"Appears to me, you ain't got much to say about it! . . . Appears to me, folks'd be better off, if I shot all three of ya."

"Ye got no call doin' 'at!"

"He might not!" Said Rodney, and when Luke turned toward him, he hit him in the jaw with his fist, sending him sprawling. "You," Said Rodney stooping to take his badge from Luke's over-all front, and pinning it back on his shirt. "You are th' first man I ever hit with my fist! . . . And I use th' word, Man, loosely! . . . Felt good, too."

"Way to go, Marshal!" Said Wallace. "Now, shoot th' pig-fuckers!"

Billy holstered his gun and came forward to look down at Luke. "You ever been to a town?"

"'Ey don't like us in a town!"

"You took a bath, they might." Said Rodney. "Maybe cut that garbage off your face!"

"Unload th' shotgun, Rod." And as he did, Billy walked to where Amos and Chigger had dropped theirs and did the same. "You!" He said to Chigger. "Empty your pockets on th' ground there, . . . You, too!" He said, looking at Amos. When they did, he bent to pick the several shotgun shells, pocketknives and hunting knives.

"Make old Luke do th' same, Rod."

"Never thought I'd be glad to see you again, Specks." Said Childers. "I never knew you was on th' place."

"Didn't hear them comin', neither, did ya?" He turned and told Amos and Chigger to go stand by Luke, and followed them.

"Sure was glad to see you, Billy." Said Rodney. "Had me worried."

"Why'd you stop in a place like this, Rod, didn't you smell that sour-mesh?"

"I smelled it. Didn't think th' still was that close, smell weren't all that strong! Besides, . . . this is th' only place I found, all day long, that was fit to stop in."

Billy nodded as he looked around the clearing. "I hadn't heard one of 'em give a holler, I might a missed ya . . . . What do ya want a do with 'em?"

"Let 'em go, I guess, . . . they're their own worst enemy."

"You, Luke!" Said Billy. "How many good men you killed out here?" He kicked the downed man. "I'm talkin' to you, man . . . . You lie, and I'll kill ya!"

"I don' know 'at, I can't count!" He shouted shrilly. "Non' a us can."

"More than this many?" Asked Rodney, holding up five fingers.

"More'm 'at!" He shrilled, and looked from him, to Billy.

Rodney held up both hands. "This many?"

"Maybe, yeah." He nodded.

"You poke 'em all like pigs?" And when he nodded. "Kill 'im, Billy, I'm already sick to my stomach."

"Ye ain' gonna kill us, 'er ye?"

"If I was like them men over there, Yeah, I would! . . . And I still might, unless you pay me not to."

"We ain' got no money!"

"Listen to me, Luke . . . . In about four, maybe five hours from now, three men are gonna come in here lookin' for us. They'll have guns and horses, enough for all of ya . . . . You stop 'em, and I won't come back and kill ya."

"We can do 'at!" Said Chigger. "Can't we, Luke?"

"You better, you don't, I'll hear about it, Luke . . . . You won't even know I'm here, when I come, I'll just shoot all three of ya!"

"We'll do it, we'll do it!" Nodded Luke.

"Get th' men back in th' saddle, Rod."

"All right, Childers, th' rest of ya, too!" Ordered Rodney. "Get mounted, it's time to go!"

"Jesus Christ!" Growled Wallace as they got to their feet and came forward. "You ain't even gonna shoot th' fuckers?"

"Get on your horse, Wallace." Grinned Rodney. "All of ya, get aboard." Once they were mounted, he retied their hands and feet.

"You gonna gag us again?" Asked Childers.

"Keep your mouth shut, I won't have to." He came to stand with Billy then. "Guess we're ready . . . . Reason I stopped, I was afraid you'd get lost, you said yourself, you can't follow a trail!"

"I was lost a time or two, used th' sun to come North . . . . Hey, Luke, there any roads north a here?"

"Shoa is, . . . out 'at way, mile'r two." He waved his hand northward.

"Where's it go?"

"Lockes burg, ova yonder way." He waved his arm southward.

"Is this Locksburg on th' road to DeQueen?"

"DeeQueen, yeah." He waved northward again. "Road ova theah take ye to Lockesburg . . . . 'at ol' road be long an' crooked 'oh, goes a long ways."

He looked at Rodney and shrugged, when he saw him grinning. "All right!" He said, and looked back at Luke. "Listen to me, we're leavin' now, and we're gonna take your weapons with us."

"Noooo! . . . Don't take our guns away, we needs 'em."

"Shut up, Luke, and listen! . . . We're goin' North, . . . I'll leave your guns and shells on th' ground about fifty yards out there, you'll find 'em! . . . But, you're gonna stay right here for one hour after we go, before you go for your weapons, understand that! . . . And Luke, . . . I'll know if you don't!"

Rodney was still grinning as he listened, and then went to where the other two shotguns were dropped, and picked them up before coming back to mount his horse.

Billy was still holding the handful of shells and knives, so he reached and pulled the wet bandana from his neck, wrapped the stuff in it and held it like a bag as he walked back into the trees out of sight. The three of them stood motionless, their eyes on the spot where he disappeared until he came back with his horse, mounted and rode up beside Rodney

"Them old boys are about four hours behind us, Rod, and one of 'em must be a tracker, likely th' Choctaw . . . . They're makin' fairly good time."

"You see 'em?

"Heard one of 'em cussin'! . . . I hung back about an hour behind ya, so I figure they must be about a mile back, th' voice was faint, could barely hear 'im . . . . But they're there, and they're comin' after us."

"We knew they would!" Nodded Rodney. "Hope they're havin' as good a time of it!" . . . "So what's this thing about a road?" . . . "You got a change a plans?"

"If it works, I do! . . . We're gonna take that road back to th' stage route, air out these horses a bit . . . . Maybe get us a few more miles ahead of 'em, before we take to th' woods again . . . . What do ya think?"

"I had th' same idea when crossin' that first road back there . . . . I like it! . . . We'd best go, though, this mess'll kill us in th' dark."

"Lead out!" He watched as Rodney rode into the trees with the four horses in tow before looking down at Luke again. "You boys lucked out today, Luke, you do know that, don't ya?"

"Yeah, yeah." He nodded. "We knows 'at!"

"Then you best remember what I said, . . . you still owe me! Stay here for one hour, then go fifty yards to find your guns . . . . Watch out for those men tailin' us." He reined his horse in pursuit of Rodney then.

*   *   *

"God damn it, Ed!" Shouted Ellis. "Hold up a minute, I'm bein' cut to pieces here."

McCreedy called to Haskell to stop then turned in the saddle. "Morgan, we are all being cut to fuckin' pieces by this shit, now quit bellyaching, will ya?" . . . They went through here, and we can, too!"

"Well, let's go back to that fuckin' road, get ahead of 'em again, we know where they're goin'!"

"Yeah, we know where they're going, but we don't know how they'll get there. We go back to that road, now, we could miss 'em for sure. They could get there, while we're still on th' road lookin' for 'em! . . . This is th' way they went, Morgan, we know they're in front of us right here, and we are gonna stay on their ass till they make a mistake! . . . They will, too! . . . Let's go, Joe."

"Well, I'm startin' to think none a this shit's worth while, Ed!" He shouted then leaned over the saddle horn to avoid a low limb and started after them. "I still say, let th' Bastards go! . . . Couple a stage coach jobs would make us that much money, let Childers take his to th' fuckin' grave with 'Im!"

"Morgan, if you want a quit, leave! . . . Otherwise, shut up! . . . Quit complaining."

"Awww, fuck you, Ed!"

"That's th' spirit, boy, . . . come on!" Said McCreedy, ducking another limb. "They got a stop sometime, when they do, we'll catch up."

"You're full a shit, too!" He said under his breath then grunted from another sharp branch. "One a them law men could be waitin' on us out there somewhere." He mumbled. "We'd never know till too damn late . . . But, okay, Ed, we'll go after 'em . . . . But you'll see, man, you'll see."

*   *   *

It took them almost three hours to finally find the road, and Rodney stopped in the middle of it to look both ways along the narrow, overgrown trail as he waited for Billy.

"We made it!" He said as Billy stopped beside him. "Looks like th' road might turn North down there."

"Well, he said it was crooked."

"They ain't gonna stop McCreedy, ya know." Said Rodney, looking back into the trees.

"You're right about that, Marshal!" Said Childers. "Them heathens'll be laying out to rot by dark. Nothin' but worms'll touch 'em, neither."

"You're givin' your friends too much credit, Childers." Said Billy. "Be well after dark before they get there, they was a good five hours behind us, . . . might not get there till mornin'!"

"I'll gag you again, you don't keep quiet!" Saud Rodney.

"Anything you say, Marshal."

"We ready, Billy?'

"Not yet . . . . I want you to take this bunch back in th' woods, just like we was still goin' north, go in about thirty yards, turn left for another thirty then back on th' road . . . . If them boys happen to make it this far tonight, that tracker'll see where we went in and think we're still usin' th' woods."

"They can't follow a trail in there at night."

"I know, I'm hopin' they'll camp on th' road here, go in tomorrow."

Nodding, Rodney reined the horse across the road and into the trees again, and once back on the road, led off again, only this time, holding the animals to a mile consuming fast trot along the old wagon road, with Billy bringing up the rear.

They kept up that pace for, what Billy thought to be two hours, and checking his watch in the starlight, could barely see the hands. But being right in his estimation urged his horse to a gallop and pulled alongside Rodney.

"Let's walk 'em for ten minutes, Rod." And nodding, Rodney slowed the animals to a walk.

"Wouldn't want a throw a shoe out here." Said Billy. "Best look 'em over, first stop we make."

"When'll that be?"

"When we get to that Locksburg town! . . . That Sheriff Hargett had a map on th' wall, looked to me like Locksburg was close to forty miles from Ashdown, with a smaller place in between."

"Wilton, . . . I met a farmer on that first road we crossed. Said it went to a place called Wilton."

"I figure we're still some twenty miles from Locksburg, way this road twists and turns . . . . Could be mornin' getting' there . . . . It's eight o'clock now!"

"How far ya think we've come?"

"Ten, twelve miles, maybe. Good trotting horse can make six to eight miles an hour, up to twenty at a slow gallop, all before havin' to cool down! . . . That's what we'll be doin' once we leave Locksburg!"

"You said somethin' about takin' to th' woods again." "I thought we'd leave th' road again after leavin' DeQueen, be in th' mountains after that."

"Couple a rivers that way, too, we'll need th road for that!"

"Ain't been easy yet, what do you expect?"

"True!" Nodded Rodney. "Ain't got but two hundred miles to go yet, what are we worried about?"

"Pick up th' pace again, Rod!"

"You bet." He urged the animals back to a fast trot again as Billy dropped back into position.

Billy had studied the horses when he slowed Rodney, and even with the heat, had noticed they were hardly breathing hard at all. Maybe they could make twenty miles in the next four, if they didn't stop . . . . They couldn't chance a full gallop, not knowing what might lay beneath the belly-high grass.

$$*\qquad\qquad *\qquad\qquad *$$

"We'll have to stop here, Mister McCreedy." Said Haskell in the darkness ahead of them. "We don't, us, or these horses gonna lose an eye."

"I told ya, we should a made camp on that fuckin' road back there."

"All right, Morgan, I should a listened to ya . . . . What do you suggest, Joe?"

"Can't track in th' dark, Mister McCreedy, can't see th' stars to guide us, neither . . . . But I think I can see some kind a clearin' up ahead a ways . . . . We can stay th' night there."

"Lead th' way."

There was just enough starlight through the trees to bring the small clearing into a dim focus, and once there, Haskell rode out into the middle of it and dismounted.

"This'll do, Joe." Said McCreedy as him and Ellis dismounted tiredly to stretch their battered and bleeding legs. "Yeah, th . . . ." He stopped when he heard the stick break. "Heads up, Morgan."

"'at's okie-dokie, boys!" Came a high-pitched voice from the trees, and caused all three of them to draw their pistols.

"Got three shotguns on ye, fellers!" Came a voice from yet another area of the dark trees.

"Throw 'em guns down, ye heah." Came yet another squeaky voice.

"Well, who th' hell are you?" Queried McCreedy loudly.

"We's th' ones wit shotguns, and ye best drop your'en afore we start shootin . . . . You on our lan'."

"What do ya think. Ed?" Said Ellis in a low voice. "We open up on, we can make a run for it while they're duckin."

"You know what a shotgun can do, Morgan? . . . One or two of us might make it, but th' horses won't if they open up with them things."

"Whut say, Fellers?" Came the first voice. "We's getting' tard a waitin."

"All right!" Said McCreedy. "We'll put 'em down. But you old boys need to come on out here so we can talk . . . . You hearin' me out there?"

"We's hearin' ya, . . . we's ain't seein' 'em guns drop yet."

"Morgan." He said in almost a whisper. "You still got that hide out?"

"In my belt."

"Okay, we're droppin our guns, come on out!" . . . Let's talk . . . Drop th' guns, boys." They dropped their pistols on the ground. "Guns on th' ground, . . . show yourselves and lets talk."

They watched as Luke, Amos and Chigger came out of the trees, each appearing as dark, moving blobs coming toward them.

"Move on away frum 'em guns now, ye heah? . . . Off at th' side theah, . . . go!"

The three of them slowly moved aside to watch as Amos came to pick up the pistols.

"Hoooo-weee, Brother Luke, a short gun fer each of us."

"Where's th' rest of ya?" Asked McCreedy.

"Ain' nobody else." Said Luke. "We don' need nobody else."

"Then who's that behind ya there?" And as they all three turned around to look. "Now, Morgan!"

Reaching behind his back, Ellis snaked the pistol from his belt and shot Luke, filling the night's stillness with ear-splitting noise as the bullet's impact sent the unsuspecting bootlegger flying forward, falling on his face in the dead mesh of rotting needles and cones. Ellis fanned the hammer twice more before the first explosion could dissipate, leaving all three of them dead before the thunderous noise could roll away.

"Good shooting, Morgan!" Said McCreedy as he went to retrieve the weapons. "Marshal knows we're here now, for damn sure!" He gave them their guns then looked at the lifeless blobs on the ground. "Dumb Sons a bitches!"

"Hey, Ed, . . . You smell that?" Asked Ellis.

"Sour-mesh! . . . Them shit for brains was bootleggers, . . . where's it comin' from?"

"Why, you thirsty?"

"Fuck no! . . . But that thing could blow, left unattended, set this whole country on fire, dry as it is! . . . Where's it comin from?"

"What do you care, Ed." Laughed Ellis. "Let it blow."

"It's comin' from there." Said Haskell, pointing westward.

"Find it, Joe, shut it down . . . . We'll drag these bodies out and make camp . . ." He watched him leave then went to take Luke by the feet and drag him into the trees.

"Whewww! . . . Shit! . . . Bastard stinks to high heaven!"

"This one, too!" Said Ellis. "God damn!" They had them all three far enough away not to smell them by the time Haskell returned.

"Find it, Joe?"

"I found it, fire's out . . . . Ten gallons a whiskey in crock jugs down there, too, . . . right good tastin' stuff!"

"You drank it?"

"I'm an Indian, can't help myself!" He went past them and untied his bedroll, draping it across his shoulder while loosening the horse's cinches. Once done, he took his bedding and spread it on the ground.

CHAPTER NINE

Billy checked his watch in the moon's pale light then reached down to feel his horse's neck area, and finding it a little wet, urged the animal past the four prisoners to ride up beside Rodney again.

"Best cool 'em down, Rod."

Nodding, Rodney slowed the animals to a walk again. "We're headin' a little more northward now, Billy . . . . This is one crooked-ass road! How far do ya think we've come?"

"In all, thirty miles, or better. It's midnight already."

"Midnight?" He chuckled then. "Wonder if old Luke put out th' welcome mat yet?"

"I think old Luke, and his buds are history . . . . I think I heard the faint remnants of gunfire a few hours ago."

"Can't say I'm sorry about it! . . . Think they made it to th' road?"

"Not likely, . . . Surprised me, they made it to that clearing in th' dark . . . . They'll make th' road in th' mornin' around eight o'clock, spend another hour before realizing we took th' road! . . . Be nine-thirty by then, and we'll be well on our way to DeQueen at a gallop."

"They'll kill their horses tryin' to catch us!" Laughed Rodney, turning in the saddle to look back at Childers. "You hearing all this back there, . . . your friends are fifty miles behind us now."

"We ain't to Fort Smith yet." Said Childers.

"I got a piss, Marshal!" Called out Wallace.

"Wouldn't hurt me none, Rod."

"I hear ya!" He stopped the horses in the road. "You first, Billy. You can watch 'em while I untie 'em."

Once Billy was ready, he dismounted and did his own business before untying Childers. "Get down and piss, then mount up!" He moved aside to wait for Childers to finish and remount.

"Marshal?" Moaned Wallace.

"One at a time, man." Said Rodney as he secured Childers again.

They were at a fast trot again in, under twenty minutes, with Billy once again bringing up the rear. Within reason, he knew they had to be fairly close to Locksburg, another ten miles, he thought, . . . maybe! He also hoped he was right about their pursuers. If they followed logic, he was right about it. But not all men were logical, or as persistent as McCreedy seemed to be, he was not following logic! They were mad at having missed their chance at Ashdown, and they have to believe that we now know they're coming, he thought, because of the gunfire.

Rodney was right, he decided, once they learn they had been tricked, they would ride those poor horses into the ground. But he also knew it would be good for them, if that were the case . . . . He had not forgotten that Choctaw Indian with them either. He surely had enough horse savvy to keep McCreedy on the up and up, if a man of his supposed mentality would listen to the logic?

He shook the thoughts away as he saw the house in the trees, and the large barn behind it. 'Civilization', he thought, as the two barking dogs left the yard and ran onto the road in front of Rodney's horse to nip at it's heels The second dog had stopped short of the road, and after a minute, the first dog rejoined it to head home again.

But what worried him was the half-dozen horses in the pasture alongside the road, and he knew he was looking at fresh mounts for the killers behind them. He was sorry, too, for what he knew would happen to the people there, if they tried to stop them . . . . And there would be nothing anyone could do about it!

He looked at the house again, thinking that he could stay behind and wait for them again, but another look ahead at Rodney, he knew he couldn't chance it! Things had a tendency to go wrong, and in their case, very wrong! A fight would come, he was sure of that! But he wanted to postpone it as long as possible. He wanted to fight on his terms, if that were possible? At any rate, he would not allow Rodney to fail in his last mission . . . . He would see him safely back home to Lisa.

They were passing more occupied houses now, and the road was becoming void of the tall grass., when he checked his watch again. It was close to four o'clock in the morning, he thought, and looked up at the moon, that was still almost overhead . . . . And then they were there, seeing several dark buildings on both sides as they stopped the horses at the road's intersection. They turned onto the street and rode North as they all scanned the dark buildings.

They saw the lights then, and were soon passing the saloon, open and doing business at four a.m. A half dozen horses were standing, drop-headed at the hitch-rails in front, and a few insomniacs occupied chairs along the boardwalk. He rode up beside Rodney then and pointed at the Livery stables, and they stopped at the closed double doors. Both of them dismounted at the weather-beaten, slightly warped doors to look the building over.

"Hostler usually lives in his business." Said Rodney. "Want a wake 'im up?"

"No, we can handle it, give me a match, Rod." He reached, and tool the lantern from its hook and raised the globe for Rodney to light the wick then gave him the light to hold while he lifted each hoof on all six horses to check for loose shoes, or stone bruises.

"I don't know why." He said, releasing the leg on Long's horse. "But all th' shoes are on tight, no stone bruises anywhere." Rodney mounted as Billy blew out, and re-hung the lantern. "Let's put some distance behind us now. Stay on th' road's shoulder, no ruts there, okay?" He mounted. "Keep 'em at a slow gallop, not all out!

Rodney nodded and left, and they were soon away from town and urging the animals to a mile consuming gallop along the wide, dusty DeQueen road.

*   *   *

It was coming light when McCreedy, Haskell and Ellis rolled up their blankets and stowed them. They tightened cinches and watered the animals from the canteens.

"Want one a them shotguns, Ed, they're still layin' there?"

"Got no use for 'em, . . . no place to tote 'em anyway . . . . Leave 'em lay."

"We lost a lot a time last night." Said Ellis, removing his hat and mounting his horse.

"Maybe not, . . . if we couldn't get through that shit in th' dark, they couldn't either . . . . They made camp somewhere."

Haskell led his horse past them to check the trees at the clearing's North side. "They were here, too, Mister McCreedy." He said. "Trail leads north."

"How in hell did they miss bein' seen by that welcoming committee?" Queried Ellis.

"Maybe they got th' drop on them." Said McCreedy, and with hat in hand, mounted his horse. "Could a got through without bein' seen. Too! . . . Okay, Joe, lead out, it's close to seven o'clock."

It was a good three hours before Haskell led them out on the weed-covered wagon road, and as McCreedy and Ellis, both waited to peer up and down the unused lane, he followed the tracks across it to where they re-entered.

"They stopped on th' road to rest the horses, Mister McCreedy." He said, still looking at the ground. "They went back in right there." He said, pointing at the tall Pines.

"We got a road here, Ed!" Said Ellis. "Not a fuckin' tree on it! . . . Let's forget th' whole thing, get th' hell out a here!"

McCreedy looked down the road again then leaned on the saddle horn before looking at Ellis. "It's gone beyond that with me, Morgan . . . . Them fuckin' Marshals must be laughing out their ass at us, putting one over us that way! . . . No, . . . I'm gonna catch up to th' bastards, at least close enough to put a rifle-slug in 'em . . . . They'll know then, that it didn't work! . . . You want a go, hit th' road, man, I won't hold it against you."

Ellis shook his head, and peered back down the road. "Naww, . . . I'm a better rifle shot than you, you might miss! . . . Guess I'll stick! . . . But I'm still gonna bitch and complain!" He looked back at him and grinned.

"Good man, Morgan! . . . But, tell me, how'd you ever beat me at shooting anything?"

"Ain't happened yet, Ed, . . . but it will!"

"Well, that's good to know! . . . Then I'm glad you're with me, Morgan . . . . Lead out, Joe!" They followed Haskell into the thicket again, but ten minutes later, saw him stop and look around at the ground.

"What is it, Joe?"

"I don't know, . . . but they turned back West here."

"Follow 'em, see where they're goin'." They followed the tracker closely for another twenty or thirty yards where he stopped again.

"Now what?"

"I know what they did." He said, pointing back toward the road.

"They're on th' fuckin' road." He yelled. "Son of a Bitch! . . . Lead on, Joe, let's run them Sons a bitches down!" They made the road again, and quickly spurred the horses to a hard run in the waving grass.

Ellis immediately spurred his horse alongside that of McCreedy's "Better think about these horses, Ed!" He yelled. "We're pushin' 'em too gard."

"We'll rest 'em in a mile or two!" He yelled back. "Come on, let's cover some ground!"

"What if they're trickin' us again?" He yelled. "What if they got off again already?

"Naww, naww!" He yelled, shaking his head. "They're tryin' to put distance between us!"

Shaking his head, Ellis let him take the lead, knowing it was no use trying to get through to him. But he also knew, that the horses they had, were not built for stamina, they were range-horses. He dropped back beside Haskell then.

"How long can we keep up this pace, Hoe? . . . He won't listen to me!"

"Twenty, thirty minutes, no more!" He returned.

"Then, you're gonna have to to tell 'im when to slow down! . . . He'll listen to you."

*   *   *

They had been in progressively more and more traffic on the wide road since just before daylight. At first, it was incoming cowboys on their way to town in groups of three and four, all trying to ride abreast of each other. Then it was spring wagons, or farm wagons, all taking it slow and easy on the somewhat rutted lane. But all of it significantly slowed Billy's intended rate of speed.

They were now moving at a steady lope as they passed a wagon loaded with Pine logs that extended off the rear of the wagon to drag the ground behind it. They passed the straining eight-horse team and moved over in front, as Billy came up beside Rodney again.

"It's close to mid-mornin', ain't it, Billy?" He shouted, reaching up to hold his hat.

"Ten-thirty!" Shouted Billy. "Better walk th' horses for a while."

Nodding, he slowed the animals to a fast walk. "Think they're after us already?"

"They been poundin' that old road for thirty, forty minutes now." He nodded. "I figure we've come about twenty, twenty-five miles from Locksburg, and there was a marker back there, said DeQueen was another twenty-three!"

"We're gonna be in bad shape for sleep before long!"

"I'm already feelin' it, Rod!"

"That puts McCreedy one up on us, they slept last night."

"We'll take a rest in DeQueen!"

"How?"

"Jail!" He nodded. "You can enlist help from th' local Sheriff . . . . We can sleep for three or four hours in a cell."

"Amen to that! . . . Gonna bring us back to about a four hour lead on that bunch, . . . maybe only twenty miles."

"We can live with a twenty mile lead!" Said Billy. "But right now, we have to get to DeQueen . . . . Road's clearin' out a bit, now, too . . . . Keep 'em at an easy gallop, Rod."

Nodding, Rodney urged the animals to a faster pace again, as Billy fell back into place behind them.

Rodney was right, he thought tiredly, they couldn't go much longer without sleep. Childers and crew were already leaning forward over their horses' necks trying to close their eyes. Lucky they're secured to the saddles, he thought again, . . . then shook his head and reached down to pat the galloping horse on the neck in reassurance.

They had no choice but to ask that Sheriff for professional help. Four hours sleep would go a long way toward keeping them alive. But, he thought then, they'd have to decide at that point, whether to stay on the road, and try to stay ahead of them, or trick them again and take to the wilderness. Rodney was also right about there being waterways they would need a bridge to cross, and McCreedy would know that as well!

If they did leave the road again, not only would they not know where the men behind them were, they would be slowing their pace to a crawl like before. It would give McCreedy ample time to pass them, and wait at one of those bridges for them to cross. He was fast coming back to his original idea of dropping back to head them off. He was sure that he could stop them, and that would end any resistance they would have to finish the job at hand . . . . However, he thought then, that would put Rodney in jeopardy of being jumped by the prisoners, if they were forced to stop for some reason, . . . and he couldn't chance not being there! As remote as that possibility might be, with Rodney's experience and abilities, he had been around enough to know that if the unlikely was possible, it could happen, . . . and most times did, and especially with men this desperate to avoid the hangman's noose!

McCreedy would have no idea how far behind them they were, and he hoped they believed they would also have stopped for the night. Because, by his calculations, since leaving that wilderness, they were between fifty, and seventy miles in front of them, . . . between six and eight hours, possibly more, depending on the durability if their horses. But they would get more, he thought, remembering those in the pasture. He pulled the wet bandana up over his nose then as the dust of riding drag, was beginning to take affect on his sleepless eyes, as well as his breathing. He tried rubbing at his eyes with a finger behind his glasses, but the grit was there to stay, and anyway, it was time to cool down the animals again and spurred forward.

"Slow 'em down, Rod!" And once they were at a walk. "How's th' horse holdin' up?"

"Sweatin' some." He said, reaching to rub the animal's neck. "How about th' others?"

"About like yours. Let's walk 'em a bit, then stretch our legs, give 'em some water."

"Sounds good, should be another ten miles closer to DwQueen, right?"

"There about!" He said, removing the bandana to wipe the caked dirt and sweat from his face and eyes. "A nice wind would help." He put the eyeglasses on again and replaced the bandana around his neck.

"Gonna be a bitch of a summer." Nodded Rodney. "Way too hot for th' month a May . . . . Weather moves from one extreme to another!"

"There's a good place, Rod." He pointed, and Rodney reined his horse off the road, across a shallow ditch, and in under a large Elm Tree where they both dismounted to relieve themselves.

"What about us, you fuck!" yelled Wallace. "I'm about to piss on myself, I could use a dump, too!"

"Might as well take th' time, Rod."

"All right, Wallace!" Said Rodney, going back to his horse. "You first this time." He released his feet and hands to let him dismount.

"Drop your pants behind th' bush over there, Wallace, . . . but remember this! . . . You make one bad decision over there, you won't get three feet before Billy shoots ya . . . . Go ahead.!" He went to Childers then and released him.

"You got a go, get down and do it, you got a shit, wait your turn!" He watched Childers dismount and relieve himself, and when he was done. "Use your canteen and water your horse, Ben."

"Yes, sir, Marshal!" He angrily did as he was told, and after watering the horse, he drank from it and hung it back on the saddle. "Now what, Marshal?"

"Now, you can untie Mister Collins, so he can do th' same." He watched Childers release, then waved him back while Collins dismounted.

"Stay by your horse, Ben, you face th' same warning as Wallace, remember that! . . . Go ahead, Collins."

"Thanks, Marshal." He nodded, and quickly opened his jeans.

Rodney looked back then to see Wallace coming back. "You okay, Wallace?"

"Fuck, no! . . . You ever use a handful a leaves to wipe your chapped ass?"

"Not yet." He grinned. "Come on, water your horse, you, too, Collins, and when you're done, release Mister Long."

They were done in a while, and all sitting beside their horse while eating their jerky.

"Didn't I see you with can-beans, or somethin'?" Asked Childers tiredly . . . . Jerky ain't cuttin' it!"

"Wallace there ain't complaining." Grinned Billy, and all looked to see him curled up and sound asleep on the ground.

"Childers." Said Rodney as he swallowed his jerky. "You can thank those good friends a yours back there for that jerky, and no sleep! . . . Besides, you're eatin' th' last of it, beans'll be your next meal."

"He'll catch up, ya know." Said Childers.

"We know his name, Ben, you can use it!"

"You may know his name, but ya don't know him! . . . Ed McCreedy's like a hound-dog, never gives up th' hunt."

"Is that why he's seventy miles behind us now?"

"Don't let that bother ya, Marshal, he's ex-military, aside from being a sniper. He's a brilliant tactician, and planner . . . . He'll find us in time!"

"Well, your time's up!" Said Rodney. "Back in th' saddle, boys, come on. Wake up Wallace, Collins, and get mounted."

With Billy's help, they had them all secured again to their saddles. "How much time did we lose?" He asked as they walked to their horses.

"Half-hour! . . . We'll make it up." They mounted and led the the horses back to the road again, just in front of the slow-moving log-wagon, . . . and Rodney, once again spurred them to a gallop.

*　　　　　*　　　　　*

"I told ya, Ed! . . . So did Haskell!" Said Ellis, angrily raking a handful of foamy sweat from his horse's neck. "We're damn lucky all of 'em ain't wheezin'! . . . We're in th' fuckin' middle a nowhere out here!"

"All right, Morgan, All right!" He said, dismounting to stand and stare down the road ahead of them.

Ellis went to his saddlebags and took out his dirty shirt, and following Haskell's lead, loosened his horse's cinches and began wiping it free of the sweat and foam.

McCreedy watched for a minute then cursed and followed suit.

Haskell poured water on his rag and used it to wipe down the animal's legs, and then its neck.

"How's that help?" Queried Ellis.

"Blood moves from the legs up through the body, cools 'em down quicker. We can give 'em some water in five minutes."

"How do you know all this stuff?"

"I'm an Indian!" He said, and tightened the cinch again before turning to look at him. "I could follow a rabbit through the woods to his lair when I was six, at eight, I could ride a horse at full gallop, without a saddle . . . . I grew up being taught that a horse meant the difference between life and death, and had to be tended to like a friend . . . . Because that's what he is!" He turned and took the canteen, opened it and poured water in his hand to let the horse drink from it several times. Hanging it back on his saddle, he mounted, and walked his horse past them to continue on down the road.

"Son of a bitch!" Said Ellis, and quickly watered his own horse, as did McCreedy. They tightened their cinches, mounted and followed the Indian.

"All right." Nodded McCreedy as they caught up to Haskell. "From here on out, Joe, you tell us when to stop and go . . . . I ain't much on horseflesh, Joe, as you know already. We'll cool 'em down when you do, . . . you know what we need to do, and how fast we need to do it, so keep that in mind."

"How far behind, do ya think we are, Ed?" Queried Ellis as they continued to cool the animals.

"No tellin', we came out a them woods at about ten o'clock, it's goin' on noon now . . . . If they left their camp at say, seven, or even six, they're not more than four hours ahead."

"They didn't sleep last night, Mister McCreedy." Replied Haskell.

"What?"

"Tracks on th' road back there, was between twelve and fifteen hours old . . . . There was no sign of any campsite."

"Son of a Bitch!" Exclaimed McCreedy, and shook his head. "You sure, Joe?"

"Tracks don't lie, Mister McCreedy . . . . They are still on a road, and moving fast."

"Damn it all to hell!"

"We still got time to give it up, Ed."

"I ain't never quit on anything in my life, Morgan!" He peered at Haskell then. "Can we catch 'em, Joe?"

"If we get lucky, maybe . . . . Without our horses, no chance! . . . One of these lawmen is a smart man, thinks like an Indian, this one!"

"Well, fuck that, Joe! . . . We got a catch these Bastards!"

"Let's go then." He spurred his horse to a gallop as he spoke.

$$* \qquad * \qquad *$$

Billy spurred his horse past the prisoners again to join Rodney, who immediately slowed the animals to a walk again.

"I'm about to drop, Billy! . . . And by that marker back there, we're still three miles away."

"We'll be there in less than an hour." Said Billy, removing the bandana and eyeglasses again to wipe his face. "Animals are wet, but no foam as yet . . . They're holdin' up pretty good."

"Didn't know you had so much horse savvy, Billy?"

"After thirteen years, Rod?" He grinned and put his glasses on. "Thought you knew me too well."

"Me, too! . . . Guess I'm still learning. Right now, I'm too tired to think."

"Well. Let's trot th' horses on into town, . . . sooner I'm behind bars, th' better."

"Amen to that!" He urged the animals to a fast trot, with Billy falling in beside Long's horse.

They began seeing a lot of traffic again, most of it leaving town, only to turn off on one of the side roads, and most consisting of farm-wagons with feed and supplies in their beds, . . . and they were met with smiles and waves from all of them. They began passing frame houses on both sides of the road, each with not more than twenty feet of space between each one. But almost all sported whitewashed picket fences, with some sort of flower garden visible.

They were entering the business district then, seeing single, and two storied shops, clothiers, dry-good stores, hardware stores, . . . and each of them seemed quite busy, as did the covered boardwalks in front, while the main street and side streets were almost void of traffic.

Rodney led the way at a walk along the road until coming to a crossroad, their road giving way to a cross street, . . . and directly in front of them, across the wide expanse was the Sheriff's office . . . . And that's where they headed to dismount at the hitch-rail in front.

"I'll stay out here, Rod." Said Billy.

Nodding, He sidestepped a man and woman, and entered the open doorway to see a tall man get up from his desk.

"Can I help you sir?" He asked, coming to stand in front of him.

"I'm U. S. Marshal Rodney Taylor, Sheriff."

"Steve Williams, Marshal, Sheriff of this berg!" They shook hands. "Good to meet ya."

"Same here, man . . . . Sheriff, my deputy and me are transporting four prisoners back to Fort Smith, we picked 'em up in Shreveport nearly four days ago."

"That would Childers, Collins and Long." He nodded. "I got th' wire from Judge Parker . . . . But you said four, who's that?"

"One of th' men that helped break 'em out a prison, name's Lionel Wallace."

"Lionel Wallace, . . . got that wire, too . . . . What can I do to help?"

"You can put us up for four hours, . . . we ain't slept in two days. The other men are behind us somewhere, wanting to take these men away from us."

"McCreedy and Ellis." He nodded.

"And a third man, one Choctaw Joe Haskell, accordin' to Sheriff Lake in Shreveport . . . . Ya got room for us?"

"Matter a fact, I do. Got two cots in each cell, will that work?"

"Like a dream."

"I'll give you a hand." They walked out, and Rodney stopped in front of Billy. "My Deputy, Billy Upshur, Sheriff."

"Billy?" They shook hands then all went to free the prisoners and walk them inside. The Sheriff grabbed the cellblock keys, and they all followed him down the row of cells where he opened one and ushered Childers and Long inside before locking the door. "Keg of water, soap and towel in th' corner, drinkin' water in a bucket with a dipper."

He opened the next cell for Wallace and Collins before turning to them. "When's th' last time they had a shave, and a bath, they stink?"

"A month, I'd say." Replied Rodney. "Lake said they refused the conveniences."

"You sure you don't want th' hotel, got hot water and a bath tub there?"

"This is th' hotel!" Grinned Billy. "And we will use th' conveniences." He whirled then as another man walked into the cellblock, but stopped when he saw the badge on his vest.

"What's going on, Sheriff?"

Williams told the deputy what was happening before introducing him. "Marshals, This is my deputy, Todd Royce." And after they shook hands.

"There's six horses out front, Todd, take 'em to the stables, have Elmo rub 'em down good, doctor their cuts and scratches, and give 'em a good feed, and Todd, . . . they'll need to be saddled and back out front in four hours, four hours! . . . Got it?"

"I'll see to it, Sheriff."

Grinning, Williams led them back toward one of the front cells, and unlocked one close to the cellblock door. "Your suite, gents."

"Thank ya kindly, Sheriff."

"I'll have hot coffee ready for you, and them when you're up!"

Rodney reached money from his pocket. "Could you get Todd to get a sack a supplies from th' local eatery for us, . . . maybe three dozen sandwiches, whatever they've got? We're down to a few cans a beans."

He took the money and placed it in his shirt pocket. "It'll be waitin', too . . . . I'll wake you in four hours."

"Got a razor, Sheriff, ours are still in our satchels?"

$$* \qquad\qquad * \qquad\qquad *$$

"You stoppin' again already?" Exclaimed McCreedy. "We just stopped less than a half hour ago!"

"Horses are tired." Returned Haskell. "Already sweatin'." He continued to keep his horse at a fast walk and ignoring McCreedy.

"Shit!" He yelled loudly then shook his head. "I guess they'd have to do th' same thing, Right?"

"Yes." Nodded Haskell.

"Well, can you tell me if they stayed on this road? . . . Maybe they're in th' woods again!"

"Look at th' grass, Mister McCreedy, . . . see how it leans forward, . . . they held their horses at a trot th' whole way! . . . If not, th' grass would be broken, and scattered by the running hooves . . . . It ain't broken, only bent! . . . A horse can trot for hours without tiring, cover twenty or thirty miles sometimes without stopping."

"Fucks know what they're doin' all right! . . . God Damn it!"

"I think we'll be closer soon, Mister McCreedy."

"How do ya know that?"

"They've been without sleep since early yesterday morning . . . . They'll have to stop soon."

"How much closer will that put us?"

"At least four hours, not more than five . . . . But they can't go much farther without sleep."

"Four hours, that ought a bring us within thirty miles of 'em."

"No way, we can go fifty miles in four hours, Ed!" Said Ellis. "Not in this heat, man . . . . We're ridin' wore out cow ponies."

"Joe's watchin' out for th' horses, Morgan . . . . Can we do it, Joe?"

"If they don't stumble, break a leg, or throw a shoe, me might do sixty miles. But Mister Ellis is also right, ours was a poor choice of horses, they won't take much abuse."

"What else can go wrong? . . . Outsmarted by a fuckin' law-dog! . . . Well, twice, but not three times, by God!"

"Time to go!" Said Haskell, and spurred his horse to full gallop, with McCreedy and Ellis close behind.

CHAPTER TEN

Billy's eyes popped open with the sound of a key turning in the cellblock door, . . . and was sitting on the bunk pulling on his boots when Williams stopped at the cell.

"Already up? . . . What woke ya?"

"Key in th' door." He said, and pulled on the eyeglasses. "It's th' way I'm put together, Sheriff, slightest noise can wake me."

Williams came inside and shook Rodney awake.

"Wha, . . . What is it? . . . Oh, Sheriff, I just went to sleep, what is it?"

"That was four hours ago, Rod, it's time to go!" Said Billy, getting up to buckle on his gun-belt then bending to tie it to his leg. Both him, and Williams watched as Rodney got dressed and stood before them.

"How do ya feel, Rod?"

"Got a hangover! . . . You promised us coffee, Sheriff."

"Waiting on you in th' office, couple a sandwiches, too . . . . Come on in."

"Uh, here's your razor back." Said Rodney, reaching to give it to him. They followed him back in the office and sat down while he poured their coffee and placed the cups in front of them.

"Three days without coffee, Sheriff, thanks." Said Billy, sipping at the hot brew. "Sausage sandwiches, just my style."

"Amen!" Said Rodney, biting into the bread and meat. "I'm damn sick a jerky."

"What about th' prisoners, want me to roust 'em?"

"Just take 'em coffee and sandwiches, Sheriff." Said Rodney. "Leave 'em there till we're ready to go . . . . Oh, wait, Sheriff, forgive me, man . . . . That's my job, not yours!" He got up as he spoke.

"Sit down, Marshal." Said Todd. "I'll take care a that for ya, my pleasure."

"Thanks, Todd, I appreciate that!" He watched him gather poit, cups and sandwiches and leave before sitting down again. "That's a good man."

"He your only deputy?' Asked Billy, also watching him leave.

"One's all I need right now, it's a pretty quiet town . . . . He's a mite young, and fancies himself a fast draw, but he'll mellow out, long as I can keep 'im in tow . . . . But tell me, . . . how far you figure these men are, behind ya now?"

"Thirty miles, I'd say." Said Billy, swallowing a mouthful of coffee. "Leastwise, I hope they are."

"You gonna be able to stay ahead of 'em?"

"We have to." Said Rodney. "Judge wants 'em back real bad!" He looked up then as Todd came back with the pot and put it on the stove.

"They get up?" He asked.

"Up and cussing a blue streak." He grinned.

"Horses'll work that out of 'em."

"Sheriff," Said Billy, looking at the map on th' wall. "That a map showin' from here to Fort Smith?"

"Yes, sir, . . . and it's close to a hundred and fifty miles from here."

"How far are we from Texarkana?"

"Maybe ninety miles, a bit more."

"Ninety miles." Mused Billy. "In nearly three days, thirty of 'em in that wilderness . . . . Pretty good time."

"Wilderness?"

"McCreedy was waitin' on us at Ashdown, we took to th' woods to keep 'em guessing . . . . They'll eventually overtake us, we stay on th' main road long enough . . . . How's cross-country travel north a here?"

"Rougher than hell, and that can't describe it! . . . The Cossato River is up at Vandervoort, and there must be a dozen bridges between here and there."

"Don't sound too promising, Billy."

"No, it don't. We'll stay on th' road, at least till we cross that river, Rod . . . We'll decide what to do then."

"You could take th' stage, I could requisition an empty coach from th' stage line?"

"We'd be puttin' a civilian driver in jeopardy, Sheriff, maybe a guard, too . . . . We can't chance I, thanks anyway."

"We best get our guests now, Billy."

*   *   *

Place ain't changed any!" Said Ellis as they entered Locksburg's main street.

"Ain't been a month, Morgan!" Growled McCreedy, as he stopped his horse to painfully rub his left shoulder and arm.

"Want a see if they got a Doctor, Ed, that shoulder might be broke?"

"It ain't broke!" He looked the busy road over again. "We need to know if they came through here, they could a took to th' woods again."

"They didn't leave the road, Mister McCreedy." Assured Haskell.

"I want a be sure, Joe, . . . I got a be sure!"

"Hell, ask somebody!" said Ellis. "Town's full a people."

"Okay, . . . we'll try th' Livery." He urged the horse into the road and led the way to finally stop at the weather-beaten double doors.

"Light down, Gents." Said a muscular middle-aged man in a leather apron. "Horse need shoeing?"

"Naw, . . . horses are fine! Lookin' for some friends of ours, don't know if they stopped here, or went on through . . . . Be six of 'em, you notice anybody like that?"

"I'd a seen 'em, I would, but I'm usually busy in back there . . . . Man to ask would be old Gus yonder, he sits in that chair day and night."

"Where?"

"Front a th' saloon there."

"I'll go ask 'im." Said Ellis, and weaved his horse across the street.

"If I can't help you gents, I got work to do!" He turned and went back inside.

"What did he say?" Asked McCreedy when Ellis came back.

"They was here all right, . . . At four o'clock this mornin'!" . . . Said they stopped right here to check the horses' shoes."

"Four o' fuckin' clock this mornin'!" He fumed, and then pulled his watch to look at it. "Five o'clock, . . . seven fuckin' hours to get here!"

"Whose fault is that, Ed, it was your horse that stumbled?"

"It was my arm nearly got broke!"

"It couldn't be helped, Ed . . . . Took me an hour to go back and steal that horse for ya, remember? . . . I nearly got shot for it! . . . Fuckin' rifle slugs flyin' all around me!"

"All right, I owe ya one, Morgan . . . . Now go over there and get me a bottle, will ya, my shoulder hurts real bad? . . . You can catch up to us, . . . come on, Joe."

They were loping their horses along the wide DeQueen road when Ellis finally galloped in beside McCreedy and gave him the bottle.

"A pint?' He grabbed the bottle, pulled the cork with his teeth and drank some of the fiery liquid before re-corking it and putting it away. "Didn't they have anything bigger'n a pint?"

"Not for a dollar, it's all I had!"

McCreedy angrily spurred his horse to a gallop again, only looking around when Ellis and Haskell pulled even with him again.

"Better use your head with this one, Ed!" Shouted Ellis. "Kill this one, you'll find th' next one yourself!"

He reluctantly slowed the pace to a fast trot, . . . and then looked at Ellis. "Ten years in th' fuckin' Cavalry, Morgan." He said loudly. "Ten years, . . . and I was never this frustrated, always knew what I was doing, . . . planned everything out to th' letter and then made it work! That prison in Fort Smith, th' bank in Memphis, right under th' garrison's noses, all of it! . . . Till this! . . . All I want in this world right now, is to cut those law men's guts out! . . . Ben Childers, too, for startin' it all!"

"We get that fifty thousand, I'll hold 'em for ya!"

"You know what the worst part is, Morgan? . . . I think I could feel it! The very minute we hit Shreveport, I felt it . . . . Felt it again when we watched th' three of them get arrested. For the first time ever, I was not sure what to do about it? . . . Watched 'em march right out a that saloon, and all I felt was confusion!"

"Four deputies and a Sheriff, Ed, what could we do?"

"Maybe nothin'." He shouted. "I don't know! . . . That's th' problem, I still don't know! . . . I do know we got a go faster." He motioned Haskell up beside him.

"Set th' pace, Joe."

*   *   *

Billy checked his watch again when they finished securing Childers and crew to their horses. "Almost six o'clock." He said when Rodney looked at him. They both went shake the two lawmen's hands again.

"I can't thank you enough, Sheriff." Said Rodney. "You, too, Todd."

"Glad to be of service." Replied Williams, taking Billy's hand in a firm grip. "We'll keep an eye out for th' men behind ya, do our best to detain 'em."

"Desperate men are dangerous, Sheriff." Said Billy, pulling himself into the saddle. "And these are desperate, don't take any chances."

"Likely by-pass th' town anyway." Said Rodney. "They'll figure we alerted ya . . . . But," He said as he mounted. "Won't hurt to try, if you're a mind to . . . . Thanks again." They reined the horses around, but Billy stopped again.

"We ran out a road comin' in, where does it pick up again?"

"West, for three streets, and turn North."

Billy tipped his hat, and grinning, waited for Rodney to lead out then fell in behind them as his thoughts turned to their pursuers. He knew they were en-route to DeQueen by now, and he also knew that the lost five hours could not be made up again . . . . Still, he thought, as he studied the curious faces of men and women along the boardwalks. Thirty miles was a fair lead . . . . If they could maintain it?"

He brought his attention back to the boardwalks again where people were now stopping to point them out, and realized that they must present an oddity at best, six men in a line, four of them in chains, and looking like unwashed heathens, . . . shaggy hair and beards, filthy clothing! That thought began to spark the beginning of an idea that could come in handy later on.

They were around the corner now and heading for the edge of town, as his thoughts once again turned to the pursuing McCreedy. What was the motivation behind this aggressive attempt to free Childers? It has to be money, he thought, and a lot of it! . . . Money that Childers has, . . . or has hidden somewhere. Bank money, he thought with a grin. It has to be, and they were all in on it! . . . Must have promised that Indian tracker part of it to help them. He remembered what Childers had said then, about McCreedy's abilities. But if it was true, why did they follow them through that tangle of wilderness, they knew the destination was Fort Smith? A Tactical response would have been to use the road, get far enough in front of us, and wait! . . . That, he thought then, was not very tactical of a man reputed to be that smart! But it was a smart move in our favor! All they had to do now, he knew, was keep it that way

He also thought he knew why Childers, and the rest refused to clean themselves up, or shave off the beards. They were almost unrecognizable, and if they did make their escape, their appearance would be the perfect disguise. That, he thought, was a little farfetched, but farfetched sometimes was in the family of Logic.

Rodney spurred the horses to a fast lope then, . . . an energy conserving pace designed to cover the miles quickly with less exertion on the animals.

Rodney was learning fast, he thought, take care of the horses, and take care of our-selves. He knew within reason, that McCreedy might not be as conserving, and hoped he was not! But with an Indian tracker, they might have the same ideas, . . . If a tactical McCreedy could put his ego aside long enough to listen to an underling? . . . Surely, he was that smart! He hoped he was not, however, because his gut told him they were still there, and riding hard.

It was close to ab hour, and a half-dozen lumbering freight wagons later when Rodney slowed the horses to a fast walk and turned to see Billy coming alongside.

"How far have we come?"

"Since leavin' town? . . . Seven or eight miles . . . . Ought a be twenty miles away come full dark! . . . Can't chance runnin' th' horses after dark, too many ruts. Keep 'em at a lope along the road's shoulder, hardly any ruts there, and watch for holes and washouts . . . . You be th' judge, Rod, think we can lope th' horses, go for it!"

"Let's hope McCreedy does th' same, Billy, don't want 'im to catch us napping."

"They got an Indian with 'em, Rod, if they'll listen to 'im?"

"Lot a creeks and gullys out there, Billy, totally different landscape than before, a bridge every two or three miles."

"I noticed! . . . That Cossato River must be a big one, accordin' that map, it's close to a place called Vandervoort, . . . and that's where we start seeing some real mountains."

"Quachita Mountains." Nodded Rodney. Pine covered, and a thousand square miles of it."

"You saw th' map, too." He chuckled.

"And taking convicts through 'em wouldn't be easy!"

"We ain't convicts yet!" Said Childers. "We ain't in jail yet."

He turned in the saddle to look at him. "Th' word is short for convicted, Ben, . . . and you was damn sure convicted!" He turned back to grin at Billy.

"Well, we ain't hung yet, remember that!"

"A matter a time, Ben, . . . now stuff it!"

"Sure thing, Marshal."

"Lead out again, Rod." He reined aside as Rodney urged the horses to a lope again, and fell in behind them.

*   *   *

Haskell slowed them to a walk again, and McCreedy reached for, and took another pull at the bottle before looking at his watch in the fading light.

"Seven o'clock! . . . be dark in another hour, or so . . . . How far have we come, Joe?"

"Twenty miles, maybe."

"Well, how far to DeQueen?"

"Never been there, Mister McCreedy, I don't know!"

"Marker back there said thirty-five miles, Ed." Voiced Ellis.

"How far back?"

"Two, three miles."

"We're gonna need a lot a luck to carch these fuckers!"

"Yeah." Said Haskell. "But we're gaining on 'em. Leadin' four horses slows 'em down, horse'll naturally balk at bein forced to run with a lead-rope."

"He's right, Ed." Said Ellis. "You ought a know that much."

"I do know that, just didn't think of it . . . . It's your show, Joe, catch 'em for us."

Nodding, Haskell spurred them to a gallop again.

*   *   *

Think they'll come through town, Steve?" Queried Todd, as he carved his steak.

"Lower your voice some." Replied Williams, looking around at the patrons closest to them. "Loud, idle talk can spread rumors, rumors have been known a riot, and riots mo . . ."

"Most always mean trouble." Interrupted Todd. "I know that."

Williams nodded, and forked potatoes into his mouth before answering' "Okay, . . . yeah, I think they might come through town." He looked up at him then. "But if they do, they won't come in together, it'll be one at a time, and we might not even notice 'em, once they mingle . . . . And they might go around, too!"

"Well, if I see 'em, I'll know 'em, Steve. I memorized their descriptions from that wire."

"Those descriptions were given by dying guards, Todd, and vague, at most! . . . Now listen, Todd, . . . you're eighteen years old, you have no real experience at this sort of thing . . . . You're fast on the draw, I've seen you draw and plug cans. But tin cans don't shoot back, and until you've actually stood in front of a killer with a gun, and kill him, . . . you've got less than half a chance to turn nineteen."

"I can take care of myself, Sheriff! . . . I ain't afraid to face any man."

"That ain't what I said, not at all! . . . I know you ain't afraid, and that's why you're my deputy, you've got guts! You're a damn good law man, and one day, you'll be a great one, likely replacing me! . . . But none of ir will happen by being careless . . . . That's what you have to learn before you go facing down a seasoned killer."

"When have I been careless?"

"You haven't been careless, I haven't let you . . . . Something else, too. It don't make a thimble full a difference how fast you are with that gun, or even how fast you might think you are. Somewhere, there's somebody that's gonna be faster, no ifs, ands, or buts about it! . . . The odds are against you ever meeting him, but he'll be out there. That's something I'd like you to memorize, and keep at the top of your list."

"You're making me out, like I;m a kid, or something, Sheriff, . . . Well, I ain't!"

"You're acting like one right now, Todd . . . . Never get mad at a little criticism, you're supposed to learn from it. Besides, I ain't telling you a thing, I wouldn't tell my own kid, . . . if I had one! I want you to learn things now, that it took me thirty years to learn, and I've got th' scars to prove it! . . . Now, if you're mad, get glad fast, and finish your supper, mine's getting cold arguing with ya."

Todd grinned then. "Thanks, Sheriff." And began eating again before once again looking up. "What time you figure they'll be here, I mean, if they come?"

"Between ten, and midnight sometime."

"We're gonna try and stop em, . . . I mean, if we recognize 'em?"

"Yeah, yeah." He said, looking up. "It's our job to stop 'em, they're wanted men! . . . But if you do recognize one of 'em, call me over, I'll be close by. Do not take 'em on yourself! . . . Unless you have to, . . . okay, boy?"

"Okay, Steve, I promise!" He began eating again. "Eat your supper, Sheriff, it's gonna be a long night!"

*   *   *

It was coming onto full dark when Rodney slowed the horses again, and Billy moved up beside him.

"Saw some clouds building off to th' West, yonder, Billy, lightening f;ashes, too! . . . Sure hot enough for it!"

"Right now, I wouldn't mind a good rain . . . . It's tryin' to ride in mud, I don't like!"

"Amen to that! . . . Wou;dn't mind not seein' any for a while . . . . Was that a town, I saw back there a ways?"

"Couple a buildings, three or four small houses . . . . Bigger one on th' road ahed, maybe a couple of 'em, if I remember that map right . . . . Harton was one of 'em, another called Wickes."

"What do ya think, . . . we come about twenty miles from DeQueen?"

"Every bit a that!" He pulled his watch, holding it up close in the darkness. "Twenty past eight o'clock! . . . We could a come farther than twenty miles, we're makin' good time!"

"Think McCreedy's in DeQueen?"

"No, . . . be another three hours yet, . . . we'll be fifty miles away."

"I hope you're right!" He turned in the saddle then. "Anything you want a add, Ben?"

"Well, I sure as hell do!" Yelled Wallace. "I got a piss!"

"How about you, Ben?"

"Wouldn't hurt none."

"Now that, Billy, is a mild-mannered reply."

"What are you tellin' Specks for, he wouldn' know?"

"Now, that's more like it!" He looked at Billy in the dark, and they both chuckled.

"Tell ya th' truth, Marshal, . . . he ain't gonna do ya much good when McCreedy does catch up." Added Childers.

"Now, Ben . . . . be careful, you'll let your gutter-mouth overload your chicken-shit ass, you keep mouthin'!" Returned Rodney. "Cause I ain't got a piss at all, we could probably go, what, Billy . . . . Another two hours?"

"Fuck, no!" Said Wallace. "Shut your fuckin' mouth, Childers, I gotta piss!"

"Don't be an idiot, Lionel!"

"Fuck you!"

"I apologize, Marshal. Yes, I do need to piss."

"Then shut your face . . . . What say, Billy, here okay?"

"No traffic in sight, why not?" They stopped in the road and did their own business first, before releasing Wallace and the others, one at a time. Ten minutes later, they were walking back to their horses when Rodney stopped him.

"You ain't lettin' him get under your skin, are ya?"

"Rod, I've been called specks a hundred times, and everything else from sschool marm, to son of a bitch! . . . No, I've been cussed by meaner men than him, and I never introduce myself unless I have no choice, you know that!"

"I know that! . . . Guess you're more tolerant than me."

"It's just talk, Rod, it's the only weapon they got . . . . And you're right about that tolerant thing!" He jabbed Rodney's arm playfully, and mounted his horse, . . . and once Rodney was mounted.

"Too dark now to lope th' animals, Rod. Keep 'em at a fast trot, and along th' side a th' road, away from th' ruts . . . . Shouldn't need to cool down again for a couple hours."

"Let's do it!" He reined the horse around and left at the given pace, leaving Billy to take his place behind them, and to let his thoughts return to the men behind them.

They would have to have a plan of some kind by daylight tomorrow, because if McCreedy and men were reckless enough to gallop their horses in nothing but moonlight, and if the horses survived the abuse, they could be a little too close for much comfort by then, . . . if they weren't delayed in DeQueen? He had the feeling that the Sheriff there would be waiting for them . . . . If he was, he hoped he would know that they wouldn't be coming through town as a group, but one at a time. Yeah, he thought, he would know that! 'Whatever you do, Mister Williams'. He thought, 'don't get yourself killed on our account!

*   *   *

Knowing the wide road's extra rutted condition, Haskell insisted that the two men stay in single file behind him, as he kept his horse at just under a full gallop along the road's outer, less traveled shoulder. The moon's pale light was just enough to keep the animals from straying onto the more dangerous areas of the old trail.

Stopping only once during the next two hours, Haskell finally yelled for them to hold up again, and slowed once again to walk the horses.

"We should be getting' close to DeQueed now!" Said McCreedy. "Anybody seen a marker?"

"Coming up on one, Mister McCreedy."

"Ten miles!" He said angrily, and pulled his watch to hold it up in the moonlight. "Ten minutes past trn o'clock! . . . Be eleven-thirty wher we get there."

"Wonder where they are now?" Queried Ellis.

"Fifty miles the other side! . . . Now listen, both of ya. We get there, we go in one at a time, maybe thirty seconds apart! . . . It's safe to say, our Marshals confided in th' Sheriff there, so they'll be on the street lookin' for us. I don't need to tell ya we can't afford to waste any time in that town . . . . Th' town, however, can always elect a new Sheriff, it comes to that?"

"Nobody will know we're there, if we don't go into town." Said Haskell.

McCreedy took the bottle from his pocket and drained it before throwing it into the tall weeds alongside. "We'd lose an hour or more goin' around, Joe. We can't afford it!"

"If you say so."

"You fall off your horse in that street, or get shot, you're on your own, remember that!"

With that, Haskell spurred his horse to a gallop again.

*   *   *

Sheriff Williams looked up at the chime-clock on the opposite wall, and got up to put his hat on before nodding at Todd, who had been watching the road across the wide street from them.

He moved away from the window as Williams nodded again. "Now?"

"Yeah, . . . I'm gonna be on th' corner across the street, I'll be able to get a look at 'em in th' light from that lamp-post . . . . I want you on the boardwalk, right here in front, with that Winchester. You see me pull my gun on somebody, you take aim on 'im, and watch 'im, . . . I'll handle it."

"Why aim, if you're gonna handle it?"

"Because, if I recognize one, there'll be another one right behind him, you'll have to keep th' first one from getting' away."

"Shoot 'im?"

"If you have to! . . . No, just point your rifle and yell for him to raise his hands, he don't, then shoot, but not to kill!"

"He won't get away, Steve." He said, picking up the rifle.

"There's still gonna be civilians out and about, so watch what you shoot at." He walked out across the boardwalk then crossed the street at a jog.

*   *   *

"All right!" Said McCreedy as they stopped the horses. "That street's lit up pretty good on th' corner there, got another lamp in front a th' Sheriff's office, two or three more along th' street . . . . So, I'm gonna change th' plan a bit here."

"Like how, Ed, ain't hardly nobody on th' street?"

"That Sheriff is! . . . That's why we're cuttin' West in that alley, come out down there somewhere across from thy' road we want . . . . Come on, let's go." He led the way down the overgrown alleyway behind the dark buildings. He had failed to see Williams' dark shape at the corner, who was also watching for movement up the dark road, and Williams could not see them for the darkness.

However, thinking he actually saw something, but equally not sure he saw anything at all, he remained hidden rather than take a chance at being seen. He could see Todd's dark shape just out of the lamp's light and satisfied, was just turning away when he heard the faint nickering of a horse coming from farther West of his position.

"The alley!" He said loudly. "Damn it!" He leaped from the walkway to the road, waving his arms wildly at Todd as he crossed the road, and seeing him leave the other boardwalk and start down the street. He leaped to the other walkway and ran, his boots making loud clopping sounds on the weathered planks as he tried to keep step with Todd in the street.

They were still some fifty yards away when McCreedy sent his horse darting from between two buildings at a run, the horse and rider appearing as ghostly images as they crossed the wide street to disappear behind the corner building. That's when the second rider darted out to cross, and that's also when Todd suddenly stopped to yell and raise the rifle.

Seeing the deputy, Haskell pulled his pistol just as Todd fired, the sudden tremendous explosion of noise piercing DeQueen's serenity as Haskell was almost knocked from his saddle, the bullet creasing his upper arm and gouging his flesh as it narrowly missed killing him. He held on and was soon around the corner as well.

The explosion of gunfire literally shattered the late night stillness, and as Todd levered the rifle again, Ellis spurred his horse into the street, pistol in hand, and arm extended to fire. Williams saw him and quickly fired his own pistol just as Ellis fired at Todd, his bullet coming close enough to cause the gunman to duck, and drop his aim as he fired, the slug striking Todd in the leg, and the rifle discharging harmlessly in the air as he yelled in pain and fell to the street.

Still in a panic, Williams fired again, missing the second time as well, and as Ellis disappeared, he cursed and ran to see about the downed deputy. Fearing the worst, he dropped to his knees and raised Todd in his arms.

"Where ya hit, son?" He asked as he quickly opened his shirt.

"It's my leg, Steve!" He groaned. "Not my chest! . . . Did ya get 'im?"

"Missed 'im twice!" He breathed. "Too dark, and happened too damn quick!"

"I hit one of 'em! . . . Did ya see it?"

Williams looked up as a half-dozen people came running. "One of you go get Doc. Richards, will ya, . . . couple of ya help me get Todd back to th' office, and be careful, he's shot in th' leg!" He quickly pulled the bandana and tied it around Todd's leg to slow the bleeding as two men came forward to lift and carry him toward the office.

By now, the local saloon had emptied and men were running toward them, all yelling, and wanting to know what happened?

Getting to his feet, Williams stared at the dark corner, where they had disappeared, and knew how close he had come to losing Todd. He heard the approach of horses then and turned as a dozen riders slid to a stop in front of him.

"Where'd they go, Sheriff?" He pointed at the road, and they spurred their horses to the corner and rounded it. "You won't catch 'em in th' dark!" He said aloud then dejectedly turned and followed the crowd back to his office.

*   *   *

McCteedy ran his horse hard along the rutted street until he cleared town then stopped, having heard the gunfire behind him, . . . and waited until Haskell pulled to a stop beside him.

"Anybody get shot?"

"Why hell. Yeah!" He groaned. "Took a chunk out a my arm!"

"Where's Ellis?"

"Don't know, I heard more shootin'!"

"There he comes, let's get out a here!" He spurred his horse to a gallop again, all three racing at a reckless pace over the dangerously deep-rutted road for another mile before stopping the hard-breathing animals again.

"What happened back there, Morgam?"

"I nearly got my ass shot off, Ed, that's what happened!"

"They was waitin', just like you said, Mister McCreedy." Said Haskell, still gripping his wounded arm. "If we'd gone into town, we'd be dead now!"

"We still might be!" Said Ellis. "I hear a posse comin'!"

"They'll turn back in th' dark!" Said McCreedy. "Lead out, Joe, set th' pace!"

*   *   *

Williams moved the well-wishers aside enough to squeeze into the office, and on into the cellblock where the two men had placed Todd on a bunk in the closest cell. Two men outside the cell were holding lanterns to give them a pale, inadequate light as the first two were holding the struggling deputy down.

"Let me through, here!" Shouted Doctor Richards as he pushed inside and hurried into the cellblock. "More light!" He said loudly. "Get me some light!" Several men left to quickly return with coal-oil lamps, and lanterns, handing them off to others in the cell, who held them high as Roberts opened his bag, took out scissors and cut Todd's pant-leg up to his hip. He then poured chloroform on a rag and covered the deputy's nose and mouth to put him out as he worked.

"How is he, Doc?" Asked Williams, as Richards closed his bag and came out.

"Very lucky, Steve, that's how he is! . . . Bullet missed the Femoral Artery by an inch. If it had not, he'd have bled to death within minutes . . . . He's young, he'll be okay, the bullet went clean through his leg."

"Thanks, Doc, . . . thank you very much!"

"What's this all about, Steve?"

"Wanted outlaws, Doc, . . . I'll explain later."

"I think you should do that now . . . . Me, and about thirty people out there in the street, would like to know! . . . We all know, and like that boy in there."

"Okay, Doc." He nodded then went to his desk for the two wires from Isaac Parker before going to the door.

"Friends?' He said loudly, to get their attention. "Thanks for your support, concern, and patience. Todd is okay, he was shot in th' leg."

"Who shot 'im?" Came a voice from outside.

"I'll explain that in a minute, I know how you all feel about Todd. But first, I want a read two wires, I received from Judge Isaac Parker in Fort Smith." He read the two wires slowly, to let the words sink in then put them away.

"The three that escaped were arrested in Louisiana, and th' Judge sent two U. S. Marshals to bring them back to Fort Smith . . . . The three men that broke them out were waiting in Ashdown to try and free them again. The Marshals eluded them."

"Earlier today, the two Marshals arrived here, needing rest and food. They all slept here for four hours before leaving . . . . Anyway, the three men were still coming, about five hours behind them . . . . Todd and me were waiting for them, hoping to arrest them . . . . We failed, and Todd was shot!"

"We could a helped, you'd a told us!" Came another voice.

"And you could a been killed!" He said. "Folks, . . . it was our job to uphold th' law in DeQueen, not yours. You elected me for that reason. This is my town, you all are my friends, and I don't want you hurt tryin' to do th' job you hired me to do . . . . That boy in there is like my own son, he was shot doin' th' job I hired him to do. He stood his ground like a professional, too! . . . Even wounded one of them before going down. I'm so proud of him, I could bust, too!"

"I'm sorry for th' fuss, we was tricked, thinkin' they would come in on th' Locksburg road, but they used the alley instead, came out across from th' North road . . . . Don't be upset, Folks, please? Not everything turns out as planned."

"You done your best, Steve." Came yet another. "We thank ya for that." They all began to disperse then, all nodding their heads and talking among themselves.

Taking a deep breath, he turned back to face Richards as those in the cellblock began to filter back into the office, each saying goodnight as they left.

"You did good, Steve." Said Richards. "They deserved an explanation. But tell me, did I hear a posse was giving chase?"

"Dozen or so cowboys from th' saloon." Sighed Williams. "They don't kill themselves, or their horses, they'll give up in a while." He went to his desk then for pencil and paper. "You goin' past th' telegraph office on th' way, Doc?"

"Yes, I am, why?"

"I need to inform Judge Parker of what happened here. Maybe he'll send th' Marshals some help, they'll need it!"

*   *   *

Billy rode up beside Rodney as they walked the animals.

"What do ya think," Asked Rodney. "Close to midnight?"

"There about . . . . Town back there was Hatfield, so said th' marker. If I read that map right, it should put us fifty miles or more from DeQueen. We already crossed that Cosotta River, and if my memory serves me right, that map showed this road turnin' more to th' northeast there ahead of us somewhere . . . . We stay on it, maybe fifty miles out a th' way before it turns back toward Fort Smith again."

"And that means what?"

"We got a make a decision . . . . Th' long way, or as th' crow flies."

"Well, we ain't crows, and it's dark, Billy . . . . And that rain is slowly getting' closer to us! . . . I don't relish goin' cross-country in a flash-flood, . . . Do you?"

"No, . . . we'll stay on th' road then, as long as we have to."

"Think McCreedy made it past DeQueen?"

"If he's the tactician he's made out to be, yeah."

"You can count on it, Specks!" Said Childers.

"And you can stick that up your asses!" Yelled Wallace.

"You two don't want that gag in your mouth, you'll shut up!" Said Rodney angrily. "Whether you know it or not, the four of you are actually expendable."

"What th' hell does that mean?" Voiced Wallace.

"It means, according to law, we're dead already." Snapped Childers. "You figure it out, Idiot!"

"Fuck you, man!"

"Shut th' hell up!" Yelled Rodney again.

"I can't wait to quit this job." He said, in a much lower voice.

"We got a get there first." Said Billy, looking up at the approaching clouds, and lightening flashes that were becoming bright enough to light up the road ahead. "We got maybe an hour before it rains, Rod, let's take advantage of it."

Nodding, Rodney spurred the horses back to a mile-eating fast lope along the road's unused shoulder again, as Billy waited to fall in behind them.

*   *   *

Haskell slowed the horses to a walk again, and grabbed his shoulder. "I got a stop this bleedin', Mister McCreedy, my whole arm's wet!"

"Okay, Joe." He rasped. "We'll stop here, I'll bandage it for ya, if you got any?"

"I got an old shirt in my saddlebags. We can tear up th one I'm wearing." They stopped the horses in the road while Haskell removed his shirt.

"Got a storm comin' in." Said Ellis. "Might put a crimp in things?"

"They'll have the same problem." Returned McCreedy, taking the soiled shirt and tearing the dirty tail of it into a long strip. "What's that, Joe?" He asked as Haskell took a leather pouch from his saddlebags.

"It's called Lizard's tail . . . We use it as a poultice for wounds."

"Well, what is it?"

"Wild roots, mashed up and boiled . . . . It's a drug used to stop pain and bleeding, . . . makes it heal!" He placed the thick salve into the cut made by the bullet then put the rest away. "It's ready now."

McCreedy wrapped his arm and knotted the bandage then waited while Haskell pulled on the spare shirt. "Ready when you are, Joe. We got a ways to go before that weather hits." He turned to Ellis then.

"That posse, go back, Morgan?"

"They didn't last long."

"Let's go, Joe!"

Haskell led off at a gallop again, with them in hot pursuit.

*   *   *

They had been holding the animals to a fast, steady lope along the road's shoulder when the wind began to pick up in gusts of cool, almost cold air, and that's when Rodney slowed the animals to a walk, and then to a stop as Billy came forward.

"Best get our slickers on, Billy, won't be long now!" They both opened their satchel and took out the gray slickers. Rodney dismounted to button it up down the front then to look up at the clouds as thunder boomed overhead.

Billy dismounted also to button his. "Might be some ice in them clouds, Rod, wind feels like it!"

Rodney walked back to look up at childers, unable to see his face except between flashes of lightening. "You boys don't have a slicker, we can't help that! . . . But what I can do," He said, reaching up to release his hands from the saddle horn. "Is let you be able to keep your hats on . . . . Be a mite awkward for ya, but it's th' best I can do."

Billy went to untie Collins and Long's hands, allowing them room to hold their hats on, by leaning forward enough.

"Wonder where we are?" Queried Rodney as the went back to their horses. "Saw a marker back there a ways, but couldn't read it."

"I did, . . . place called Mena . . . . Good sized town, accordin' to Williams."

"How far?"

"Don't know . . . . I figure we've come about fifteen miles this go-round, shouldn't be more'n a couple, three miles."

"Then let's go, I don't cotton to hail stones!" They mounted and quickly urged the horses to a gallop, chancing the animals' own sure-footedness to stay out of the dangerous ruts on the road's shoulder. With the cooler wind blowing, the horses were not tiring as fast, and had gone about a mile when Billy saw Rodney turn in the saddle and point westward.

Waving back, he watched the curtain of rain approaching and lowered his head, turning it to let his hat take the first impact of water that immediately drenched his exposed pants and legs.

The road quickly turned to a muddy nightmare and still, Rodney kept the horses at an easier lope, the flying hooves of each showering those behind with mud and grime.

Billy felt the sting from a small hailstone then, and braced himself for more. He didn't have long to wait, and could see Childers and crew laying flat over their horses' necks and holding on to their hats . . . . While the cursing and yelling from Wallace was all but drowned out by the storm's icy fury.

Lightening flashes were constant, illuminating the hailstones, and also the standing water in the roadway. The flashes allowed Rodney to keep them all out of the rising water alongside the road, as the ditch began to overflow back onto the already deepening mud.

Having endured the almost blinding rain for another hour, the on again, off again hail storm finally subsided enough for him to see the illuminated buildings of town, and on crossing yet another bridge, were on the wide, churned-up street of Mena, Arkansas, . . . where he immediately saw the open, and swinging double-doors of the Livery Stable and reined the horses through them to stop in the dry hay of the large barn.

He quickly dismounted and removed his hat, and was slapping water from it against his leg when Billy dismounted just inside the double doors. In the lightening flashes, Billy saw the lantern on the wall and brought it to Rodney to light, while he went back to pull the doors shut, and lock them.

With the hay-littered barn's floor in the lantern's flickering light, Rodney located two more, and lit them as well, throwing the barn into an even brighter light.

"Any time, Marshal!" Grunted Childers. "Feels like I been hit by a rockslide here!"

"For once, Ben, I know how you feel." He unbuttoned the slicker and took it off before going to untie their feet, allowing all four of them to all but fall from their saddles to lay prone on the floor of stale hay.

"Not fit for man, or beast out there, Rod." Grinned Billy as he shucked the rain-gear. "Found a grain-bin back there, we can grain th' horses."

"Too bad we can't eat it." Sighed Rodney, lifting the water-logged cloth sack from his saddle,. "This thing was filled with sausage-biscuit sandwiches!" He tossed the bag across the large room in disgust.

"This is Mena, I guess," Said Billy, looking around at the old weathered walls of the stable. "A good sized town, from what I seen in th' lightening flashes, . . . so it's got a have a Sheriff, and an eatery. We can get more food!" Thunder rocked the barn then, and rain began coming down harder than ever. "If this storm ever gives out!"

He cocked his head then and peered up at the rafters as the sounds of a downpour on a sheet-iron roof, was suddenly drowned out by a much louder noise.

"Take Cover, Rod!" He shouted suddenly. "It's a twister!" He dove into a pile of hay as the barn began to shake.

The horses were spooked, and in a frenzy began squealing and rearing, even nipping at each other in their efforts to free themselves of the binding ropes. And then it was over, the roar replaced by the sounds of heavy rain again.

"Everybody okay?" Yelled Rodney, as he got to his feet and looked around. "Hey, Billy!" He yelled, but then breathed a sigh of relief as he crawled from beneath the hay.

"That one came close!" Said Billy as he went to the double-doors and opened them wide enough to see out, . . . and in the lightening flashes, was able to see the twister's devastating path along Mena's outskirts. Posts and lumber, from the livery's corral lay scattered across the width of the street, only missing the stables by a few yards. A barn, across the way was in shambles, and a windmill was down.

The rain continued to fall, however, and he closed the doors to go directly to the feed-bins, and carried two buckets of grain to a long feed-trough in front of the several stalls and dumped them, . . . making two more trips while Rodney untied the towropes to allow them to eat.

"First good meal they've had since leaving Shreveport!" Said Rodney as he took a bucket to the water barrel and brought water back. He looked at Billy then.

"How close was it?"

"Th' corral's gone."

"Close enough!" He breathed.

"Took out a barn across th' street, and a windmill, that's all I could see . . . . Better get some sleep, Rod, I'll wake you in a couple a hours . . . . Don't see this ending before mornin'."

"I can use some sleep." He walked in front of Childers then to look down at all of them. "You got time to sleep some, boys, better use it!" He went on to the haystack and lay down to look up at Billy. "Couple a hours, right?"

"Couple a hours." He nodded then watched him close his eyes, to fall instantly asleep.

*   *   *

Having taken refuge beneath the overhang of an abandoned gristmill, McCreedy stood against a wall to watch the heavy rain, hail mix as it pounded the street of Wickes, Arkansas. The town was dark, the buildings eerie-looking in the lightening flashes. The ground was wet where they stood, and all they could do was wait it out.

Finally, He cursed his bad luck again and sat down, grunting from the pain in his swollen shoulder as he adjusted the tail of the long rain-gear beneath him, . . . and then leaned back against the rain-soaked wall. Seeing it, Ellis and Haskell did the same, and were soon fast asleep.

He watched them as he tried, unsuccessfully, to position his back against the wall to ease his pain and so, allowed himself to think back to the bank job in Memphis, Tennessee. He had spent three days planning that job, he remembered, but he had needed six men to pull it off. Thinking back, the worst day in his life was when he met Ben Childers, Collins, and Long and recruited them. However, the job was pulled off without a flaw and they were almost out of town when the Cavalry gave chase. That should not have happened, but it did! . . . First sign of impending bad luck, and he still didn't recognize it as such!

The cavalry gave chase across eastern Arkansas, only turning back in the hills north of Little Rock, . . . good luck, he had thought then. But an hour later, they spotted a posse from Little Rock, consisting of more than twenty men following their trail . . . . Second sign of impending bad luck, and he still did not see it as such!

Having several skirmishes with the large posse, he recalled, they slipped away again into the Ozarks, near the mountain community of Saint Jo, thinking they were finally in the clear. They were almost caught napping by that posse, barely escaping up the south side of Wakefield Mountain, swapping lead with that unrelenting militia all the way to the top, and across . . . . Third sign of impending bad luck, he thought. But he still failed to see it as such!

They had been running for almost six days to that point, he recalled, and still, a persistent posse pushed them. It was then, he remembered that Childers, having spent half his life in the Ozarks, so he said, convinced them all to take the road to Clarksville, saying they could outdistance the posse there, they did not! . . . Fourth sign of impending bad luck, and he still believed Childers' main concern was for everyone's safe escape!

He reached to rub his throbbing shoulder again as he remembered the convincing way Childers had of making him, Ellis and Wallace agree to split up, and each go separate ways, . . . even that he should keep the money until they could meet up again in Van Buren and divide it. It worked to the point of their getting away. Even when he met up with Ellis and Wallace again, all three had agreed the plan worked.

It was only when reaching Van Buren, they learned that Childers, Collins and Long were in the prison at Fort Smith, awaiting execution! . . . Fifth sign of impending bad luck, of which he had recognized at the time, as being only a set-back! . . . He failed to recognize it as such!

'How could I have been so fucking gullible'? He wondered, still watching the water cascading off the tops of silent buildings with every lightening flash . . . . 'I was better than that, God damn it'! He thought begrudgingly. 'Was'! . . . It had not dawned in his mind that Childers had been the core of it all, had been his plan all along to keep the entire fifty thousand dollars for himself, and his cohorts! . . . Ben Childers was the cause of his frustration!

'I was stupid', he thought, to finally realize it that day in a Shreveport saloon. At that point, he had become mad enough at himself to vow that he would take that money back from Childers. He would break him free again, and he would lead him to that money! . . . And that, he thought, would be the tool to regaining his self-respect . . . . He closed his eyes then.

CHAPTER ELEVEN

It was still raining, although nothing that even started to compare with the overnight deluge. Rodney opened the double doors enough to look out at the river of mud and water that was once the main street of Mena, Arkansas. Traces of the coming dawn could be seen in the thinning clouds as he scanned the twister's debris for a few seconds. He started to look up the dark, wide street at the buildings of town, but changed his mind and closed the door, . . . deciding it best that he wake Billy and get started again.

He walked over and kicked Billy's foot, and he quickly sat upright in the hay, looked at the sleeping prisoners for a minute, and got to his feet to brush the hay from his clothing, when the double doors suddenly burst open . . . . And before the two men could enter, his gun was out and covering them.

"Hey, . . . hey!" Yelled the man, his eyes glued on the bore of the pistol. "I'm th' law here!" He stammered, put that thing away."

Billy holstered the pistol and nodded. "It's a good idea to knock before bustin' in on a man, Sheriff . . . . I came close to shootin' ya."

"I'll say you did!" He blurted. "I was lookin' right at you, and I swear, I never even saw your hand move! . . . Who are you people?"

"I'm U. S. Marshal, Taylor, Sheriff." He said then jerked a thumb at Billy. "This is my deputy, Billy Upshur."

"Well," He chuckled. "I didn't mean to intrude on ya, Marshal." He looked back at the older man with him then. "This is Oscar Willis, he owns th' Livery . . . . He saw you folks come in here last night from his window, storm woke 'im up! . . . Anyway, he didn't come tell me about it till this mornin'."

"No harm done, Sheriff." Grinned Rodney.

"Constable." He said quickly. "Constable, Jerry Cole's th' name."

"Constable, . . . Okay, Jerry, we're transporting four convicted killers back to Fort Smith." He nodded at the sitting men. "Storm caught us about three miles out last night. The doors were open here, and we came in. Wind must a sucked 'em open!"

"He's right, Jerry." Said Willis quickly. "They was open."

"No harm done then." He looked back at the street then. "You ain't plannin' on leavin' in all this mud, are ya?"

"That's what we were just about to do, yeah!"

"Course, I can't stop ya, but that road out there is knee-deep in Arkansas blue clay, be a week before anything can travel on it, and that's no joke!"

"Nobody, but us, Jerry, . . . three friends a theirs are behind us somewhere, and they're pretty determined to stop us."

"I'll be damned!"

"You the only lawman in Mena?" Queried Billy.

"No, we got a Sheriff, name's Wade Gilbert. Probably still asleep in his office down there."

"How about a café, one that's open about now?"

"Yeah, Nellie's, she's open now, . . . if she didn't frown gettin' here."

"Okay then." Said Rodney. "Constable Jerry Cole, if you'll wait while we get these old boys loaded up, you can show us th' way to Nellie's café."

*　　　　　*　　　　　*

The rain had all but stopped when one of the horses snorted, waking McCreedy from a hard sleep. His eyes popped open, and grunting loudly from the pain of a badly bruised, and swollen shoulder, pushed to his feet to wake the other two men.

"Get up, Morgan, Joe, th' rain's stopped . . . . You got hard-tack or jerky left, best eat it, we got a go!"

"Goin' ain't gonna be easy in all that shit!" Exclaimed Ellis, getting up to tighten his horse's cinches then watched Haskell do the same, as he took jerky from his saddlebags. "Ain't that arm even sore, Joe?" He bit off a bite and chewed it vigorously.

"No!" Replied Haskell, and flexed his arm a couple of times before reaching jerky from his own saddlebags. "Tingles enough to know it's there, is all . . . . But it ain't sore."

"Potent stuff." He mused. "What was it, Lizard???"

"Choctaw calls it, Lizard's Tail! . . . You couldn't say it in Choctaw."

"I understand . . . . Maybe you ought a smear some a that stuff on your shoulder, Ed, might not be hurtin' at all, you had?"

McCreedy dropped the stirrup and took jerky from his saddle. "I want it to hurt, Morgan, reminds me of how mad, I am, and of what I'm gonna do . . . . Now, mount up!" He walked his horse out from beneath the overhang to look down the muddy street of Wickes.

"Come on, Joe!" He said as he mounted. "This one-horse berg is waking up, and we don't need another lawman on our tail." He reined the into the deep mud, and with a last look at the town, spurred the animal back up the slick, muddy incline having to use the reins to control the horse until he made the road again.

"Come on, Morgan." He said angrily. "It ain't that slick!"

"Up your ass, Ed!" He shot back, finally urging his horse up beside him. "I didn't make it rain, neither did, Joe!"

"All right, Morgan . . . . I'm a mite testy today, so what? . . . My shoulder all swollen, can't use my arm, and it hurts like hell, so cut me some slack!"

"Well, it's sure keepin' you mad, all right! . . . Just don't take it out on us, okay?"

"Yeah, yeah!" He looked back then. "Come on, Joe!" He said, as Haskell's horse finally found it's footing enough to join them. "Be light in another hour." He said, looking at them both in the pre-sawn. "Lead out, Joe."

"Lead out?" Laughed Ellis as he stared into the semi-darkness at the road ahead. "On what, ya can't even see th' fuckin' road. I can't even tell where it is!"

"What about it, Joe?" Queried McCreedy. "It gonna be a problem?"

"Yeah, some." He replied with a sigh. "I'll keep us on th' road, Mister McCreedy, but at a walk, no trottin', no runnin' . . . . Land up here is mostly clay, travel too fast in that mud, it could suck a horse's shoes off, even trip it . . . . We walk!"

"All right, we walk, Joe! . . . Shit!" He shook his head then. "We'll never catch up this way, . . . fucking weather! . . . Lead out, Joe, at a walk."

Haskell urged his horse past them in the deep water and mud, the animal's hoofs making sucking noises each time it lifted a leg to walk.

*   *   *

Rodney didn't bother binding their legs for the ride up the street, and as Billy watched them, he mounted up to wait for him.

Billy turned to Willis, reached in his pocket for two silver dollars and gave them to him. "For th' grain we used."

"Well, I thank ye kindly!"

Billy nodded and mounted his horse.

"Lead th' way to that café, Constable." Said Rodney, and followed him through the double doors into the mud of the street. The horses quickly sank to almost knee-deep in the sucking mire. Seeming to take an extra long time in following the slow-moving Constable across to the opposite boardwalk then waiting for him to stomp and scrape the mud from his tall boots before continuing on down the walkway, he was relieved when he saw the sign on Nellie's café.

Dismounting, Rodney ushered them all inside to a wall table and seated them before sitting down with Billy.

"What'll it be, boys?" Smiled the slender, quite homely woman. "I'm Nellie, at your service."

"A large pot of coffee to start, Nellie." Grinned Rodney.

"And for them?" She asked, staring at the prisoners' wrist chains.

"With six cups." Added Billy.

"And to eat?"

"Steak and eggs, all around." Said Rodney.

"With biscuits and gravy." Added Billy then looked at Rodney. "Mister moneybags today!"

"Expenses, . . . I'll get it back in Fort Smith."

"Positive attitude, I like that!"

"Why not, we got some time? You saw that bridge we came across."

"Th' one with th' Cottonwood layin' across it? . . . I saw that."

"Where ya figure McCreedy stopped at last night?" He asked as Nellie served coffee all around.

"Can't be sure, but if they made it through DeQueen without a hitch, they likely made twenty, twenty-five miles before it hit . . . . Wickes'd be my guess. It'll take 'em most all day long to get here in all that mud."

"And half th' night, if that bridge ain't cleared!"

"Can't count on that, Rod, . . . it's a stage route, they'll have to keep it open."

"No stage gonna run in that stuff, Billy, not for a week or more!"

"McCreedy will, but he won't gain any ground on us, horses can't do better than a walk in it, could lose a shoe, even break a leg any faster."

"And we could be back on dry land again by dark." Said Rodney.

"That, we could." Nodded Billy. "And I'm countin' on it!"

"Here you are, boys." Said Nellie, placing the large, steaming plates in front of them. "Will they, . . . your prisoners, I mean . . . . Will they be able to cut up their own meat, or would you prefer I didn't give them knives?"

"No knives." Said Rodney.

"I'll cut it up for them in the kitchen."

"A brilliant idea, Nellie!" Said Rodney. "Thank you very much!"

Nodding, she went to Childers' table and told them their food would be right out then hurried back to the kitchen.

"I'm surprised Nellie would even want a wait on 'em, th' way they look! . . . Probably wouldn't, that rain hadn't washed 'em down . . . . Look like four grizzly bears, with all that facial hair." He looked up at Billy then. "Why wouldn't a man want to at least shave while in jail, can ya figure that one?"

"Old Nellie there's a fine woman, Rod, a mite plain, but a good woman! . . . As for that last question, . . . leave me out of it!"

"Amen to that!" He shook his head and forked eggs into his mouth. "I'll tell ya one thing, our Mister McCreedy is a persistent son of a bitch! . . . Pardon th' language."

Billy put meat in his mouth and nodded as he chewed. "Good Steak, Rod."

"Been a while, too!" They looked up then as Nellie brought food to the other four, and then refilled their cups with fresh coffee.

"You're a peach, Nellie." Grinned Billy.

"Amen to that!" Agreed Rodney.

"It's always good to hear the truth now and then." She smiled. "Thank you."

"It's got a be money, Rod." He said, watching her leave.

"What's got a be money?"

"The reason McCreedy's so persistent. You asked th' question!"

"I did? . . . Guess I did . . . . I think so, too! . . . Bank money, ya think?"

"Got a be, . . . Childers likely got it hid somewhere."

"But they was convicted for somethin' else, and McCreedy wasn't with 'em. What do ya make a that?"

Billy shrugged. "Had to have happened before they met up with McCreedy. Might a happened a year ago, even two."

"Well, if all six of 'em pulled a job together, what made 'em split up and leave him with all th' money?"

"Good question, . . . a posse, maybe?"

"Works for me!" He said, filling his mouth with eggs and chewing. "Reasonable, too!" He swallowed and pointed his fork at Billy.

"We might never know, neither!"

*   *   *

For a wide thoroughfare, that for many years of almost constant use, and the fact that for all those years of travel, was one that should be as hard as a rock by now . . . . The sucking clay, reddish dirt-mixture was still almost a foot deep, and between the hoof and knee on a tall horse. Blended with the high humidity after a heavy rain, and the heat of a premature summer day, both men were sweating profusely.

The fact that each animal was forced to lift it's legs very high with each step, gave the appearance of something akin to that of the strutting march of a circus horse on parade, they were tiring twice as fast! Rodney noticed the flecks of white, sweaty foam trying to form on his horse's neck and made the decision to stop and rest.

He removed his bandana, and was wiping sweat from his face and neck, as Billy worked his horse up to join him, and as Billy removed his own neck-piece to follow suit, retied his around his neck.

"Horses are doin' their best, Billy, it's just rough going."

"Almost like home, ain't it?"

"Worse! . . . What time's it getting to be?"

Billy pulled his watch. "Ten o'clock in the a.m.!" He sighed looking out at what should heavily foliaged, broken land, that now appeared as a very flat and level swampland with brush and a forest of trees growing out of it. "Some flood, huh, Rod?"

"Yeah, and you know what lies in th' direction it came from, don't ya?"

"Home!" He nodded. "Already thought a that . . . . Hope Peter got th' roof fixed in time."

"Knowin' him, he did! . . . I sure ain't lookin' forward to summer, Billy . . . . Not if it's anything like this!" He turned in the saddle for a look back at the crooked road.

"Hope McCreedy's havin' th' same problem, we are."

"He is! . . . Good news is, I can see clearing skies other side a them mountains to th' North, west of us, too! . . . We ain't seen hot, yet!"

"How localized, you figure that storm was?"

"Hard to say, Rod, . . . maybe thirty miles wide, could a reached as far as DeQueen . . . . But I also think we're about out of it, clouds are real thin here already."

"Hope you're right!"

"Hey, Marshal!" Said Wallace. "I got a piss again!"

Shaking his head, he grinned at Billy. "Come to think about it, me, too!" He urged his horse around in the sticking mud, as did Billy.

"How about th' rest of ya?" He asked, pulling up beside Childers, and once they all nodded, he reached over to untie Childers' chains from the saddlehorn. He looked at Billy then.

"You'll have to do th' rest, Billy, this two-rope ain't long enough." Billy went about the task of freeing the others.

"Now listen, men . . . . You got a piss, you'll have to do it standing in th' stirrups, because we are not going to wade knee-deep in mud to untie you!"

*   *   *

"Why are you stoppin', Joe, hell, it ain't been two hours yet?"

"It's been closer to three hours, Mister McCreedy, . . . and th' horses are about played out, . . . they're foamin' up!" Haskell turned in the saddle to look at them. "It's real hard for a horse to walk in this stuff, it's like quicksand!"

"All right! . . . How far have we come, anyway?"

"A mile, maybe more . . . . But I don't worry too much, they're in this mud, too!"

"But for how long? . . . A storm is usually very localized. It could a been very wide spread, or maybe not rained at all where they are, we don't know!"

"Ain't doin' any good to bitch about it, Ed!" Commented Ellis.

"Morgan," Catching himself, he released the air in his lungs, and became much calmer. "At this point, it ain't just the money, Childers stole from us, it's the idea that he might get away with cheating us! . . . Ain't you ever heard that old saying, honor among thieves?"

"Can't say that I have, Ed, no! . . . There ain't no honor among thieves, least none, I know of."

"No, I guess you wouldn't, . . . it ain't written down anywhere. It's an unwritten code that thieves do not steal from each other."

"Don't reckon Childers ever heard of it, neither."

"Well, I intend to inform him of it! . . . He's gonna take us to that money, and then I'm gonna kill 'im!"

"Well, now you're makin' sense, Ed, that's what I want a do, too!"

"Then stop arguing with me, Morgan . . . . If I can do this, I will have regained my self-esteem. Right now, confusion is all I'm feeling, . . . all I have felt since Childers got arrested."

"Man!" Breathed Ellis. "I can't say I know about none a that, Ed . . . . Maybe cause I never had none a that self-esteem stuff! . . . I do know you're talkin' about revenge, though, and that, I do know about! . . . No more arguments from me, man . . . . I'll even do th' killin' for ya!"

"We got a catch 'em first, Morgan!" He looked back at Haskell then. "Right, Joe?"

"Yes, sir, Mister McCreedy." He gigged his horse back to the laborious task of walking in the knee-deep, muddy clay again.

*　　　　　*　　　　　*

They were still moving at a slow time-consuming, and very tiring pace in the clinging mud and yet, Billy found himself close to laughing every time he watched Wallace stand in his stirrups, in his attempt to keep his wet pants off of his already raw backside . . . . And each time, he would mentally recall the picture of him standing in his stirrups with pants open, trying to relieve himself off the side of his horse, and then wound up wetting his pants anyway!

He shook his head and still grinning, turned his eyes on the surrounding, very tall and tree-shrouded Quachita Mountains, thinking that they must be riding in a very large, long and wooded valley . . . . One large enough to support the many small towns and communities they'd seen along the way. But what concerned him, aside from the very high water under every rickety bridge they had to cross, was the crooked road they were now forced to follow.

Each time the road turned a little more eastward, he could imagine them going even farther away from Fort Smith. But then, Sheriff Williams' wall map came to mind, and it had shown the road eventually turning back to Fort Smith. That was a good thing, he thought, except for one, . . . it made their trip some fifty miles longer than, as the crow flies!

His first plan, of taking to the woods again at DeQueen, would not have worked. Williams and Rodney were right, he thought, they had already crossed two dozen bridges, and every one was over an almost impassable gulley, or creek! Even if they had managed it all, they could not have survived that storm. He remembered seeing, what was believed to be Belle Starr and her bunch, a few years back, as they crossed in view of the small valley at the mountain. But they were so far away, no one was sure it was her . . . . 'Wonder if she had a problem in these mountains', he thought. She would have been used to it, he decided . . . . It was a wild and untamed wilderness, even with the many small towns and dozens of cross-roads crisscrossing it! . . . But all in all, he loved what it represented, . . . freedom!

'Well, we ain't free yet', he thought, and turned to look back at the reflecting water covering the road behind them. There was no sign of them ever having traversed it. Sighing, he faced forward again, and though he had tried not to, thought of his wife and children being alone with the only mother and father he had known since he was ten . . . . And though he hated to think about it, one day, he was going to lose those parents as well!

He should have wired Jim Stockwell from DeQueen, and had him tell them he was okay. He shook his head to clear it then, and watched Wallace stand up again, and that's when Rodney decided to stop. He urged his horse up past those of Long, and Collins to stop beside Wallace, and although he had not planned to, was unable not to rib him a bit.

"Should a hung it out a mite farther, man."

Wallace's face turned red with anger. "Shut up, you Fuck!"

"He did, Specks." Smiled Childers. "Didn't have anymore!"

"You shut up, too, man!" He growled.

"It'll dry when that sun comes out, Wallace." Nodded Billy.

"I ever get my hands on a gun, I'm gonna introduce you to all six bullets, Specks! Said Wallace angrily. "You, too, Mister Marshal!"

"Personally, I think your gun-totin' days are over, Mister Wallace." Replied Billy. "Besides, . . . I don't take to bein' introduced to strangers much." He looked at Rodney then, who had turned his horse enough to lean with crossed arms on the saddle-horn to grin, and listen.

He looked back at Wallace for a second before starting to move up beside Rodney, but stopped again to peer at Childers. "You got somethin' to say, Mister Childers?"

"I don't know what to say about you, Specks, don't know your name, cause you won't tell me who you are . . . . You carry yourself like you know your way around a gun, but with them specks on, you appear more like some weak-kneed school teacher with more brain than gun-savvy . . . . I don't know what to say?"

"Mister, Childers." Said Rodney. "Sometimes, it's best not to ponder too hard on a mystery, messes up a man's brain! . . . Terrible thing when that happens . . . . But what th' hell, I'll clear it up for ya! His name is Billy, he's a sworn deputy, United States Marshal. And he's takin' you back to hang! . . . But you already knew all that, you been listening to us talking all this way! . . . So, what is th' mystery?"

"Okay, Marshal." Nodded Childers. "I meant no disrespect, I just never met a man that didn't want to say who he was?"

"Name's Bill Upshur, Mister Childers." Nodded Billy. "You know me now?"

"Your name, . . . not who you are?"

"You're an irritating man, Childers!" Said Rodney. "You talk too damn much! But I'll tell ya this, . . . Men who did find out who he is, wish they'd never met 'im! . . . Now, much more will earn you that gag again."

"Point taken, Marshal."

Billy rode on up beside Rodney then, and in a low voice. "You need to stop defendin' me like that!"

"Why not, if it saves a man a hard lesson? . . . Anyway, I'm sort a proud a who you are!"

"Thanks, Rod." He said, staring up the road ahead. "But if you want a be proud a somethin', look up th' road yonder, a couple hundred yards."

Rodney turned to look. "Why, what are you seeing?"

"It's what I don't see! . . . Ain't no water standin' in th' road ahead."

"Shit, man, you're right! . . . Come on, Billy, I'm sick a this crap!" He turned the horse and jerked the towrope, moving them all forward again.

The horses were sinking less and less in the clinging mud with every few yards of progress, and a half hour later, were completely on a dry, and just as rutted stage route again. Once out of the mud, he stopped them again and dismounted.

"What's up, Rod?" He asked then watched as Rodney squatted at his horse's legs, and saw the thick blobs of mud clinging to them.

"Good thinkin', Rod!" He said as Rodney began cleaning the animal's legs, and dismounted to do the same. It took them a full half-hour to completely clean all six horses' legs and hoofs, and after washing their hands in the run-off water of a roadside ditch, mounted their horses again.

"We'll pull ahead of 'em again now." Breathed Rodney, looking back the way they came.

"Yeah," Agreed Billy. "But we'll be goin' more east again, instead a north!"

"It'll still be faster."

"And fifty miles further!" Said Billy, also looking back. "Let's go, Rod, . . . at a fast lope, okay, . . . I'd rather not stop again for a while. Just keep an eye on your horse's sweating."

"Amen to that!"

*   *   *

Haskell urged his horse up on the shaky bridge, and stopped to look at the rushing water as it tried to lap up onto the timbers, then dismounted as McCreedy and Ellis half jumped their tired animals onto the bridge.

"We rest the horses here." He said, and turned to relieve himself into the swirling current.

The other two quickly followed his lead and once done, McCreedy looked up the water-covered road ahead of them. "How long are we gonna have to put up with this stuff?" He asked angrily. "How much fuckin' bad luck can a man have!"

"You know what they say, Ed." Remarked Ellis as he buttoned his pants and adjusted his gun-belt. "Weren't for bad luck, wouldn't be none at all."

"Well, "They" were idiots!"

"You're prob'ly right!" He grinned, also looking up the road ahead. "What time is it, Ed?"

"Why, you takin' medicine or something?" He pulled the watch and looked at it. "It's after one o'clock in the afternoon, Morgan, and we're not more than four or five miles from that mud-hole of a town, we stopped at! . . . if that many . . . . We keep stoppin' like this, they'll have Childers hung before we can get there!"

"If that be th' case, I don't want a get there!" Said Ellis with a grin.

"You need to get serious about this, Morgan!"

"It's hard to do, Ed, when ya got no choice in th' matter."

"Yeah!" He breathed then turned to look at Haskell, who was still watching the rushing water. "Any idea when we'll get out of all this, Joe?"

"Tomorrow, Mister McCreedy, . . . maybe! . . . Storm was a big one, stretched a long way."

"Could be a lost cause, Ed."

"We'll see, Morgan, . . . their luck can't last forever."

"Well, I'm givin' you notice, man, . . . we ain't caught up with 'em in five miles a Fort Smith, I'm cuttin' my losses."

"If that's th' case, We'll go with ya."

"Not me, Mister McCreedy." Said Haskell. "I ain't cut out for robbin' banks and stuff . . . . Safer to mug drunks."

"Time comes, that's your choice, Joe." He mounted his horse then. "Come on, Joe, let's go!"

*   *   *

Rodney slowed them to a walk when he saw the buildings ahead of them, and looked around as Billy trotted his horse up beside him. "Funny name for a town." He said, as Billy came abreast.

"Sign there says, welcome to Acorn, population one hundred and one."

"Must be an Oak Tree in th' road ahead." He grinned, as they began passing the few stores and shops on one side of the road, and on the other, a café, saloon, and a stable.

"Got all they need, looks like." They began nodding at the few pedestrians that acknowledged a return greeting in passing, even the handful of men and barroom girls that filed out of the saloon onto the boardwalk to stare at them.

"We must be a sight." Said Rodney, reaching up to rub the two-day stubble on his face. "Nope!" He grinned. "Can't be us." He looked back at Childers and the other three, whose full facial hair was hanging down from chin, to almost the first button on their shirts, all accented by their sweat-drenched clothing.

"Yeah," Nodded Billy. "Gor a be them!"

"Ever seen a bridge in th' middle a town before?"

"Appears I just did." He said, as they crossed over the deep, wide creek. "Got water in it, too." He commented, and then they were off the old bridge and clearing the last few buildings of Acorn where Billy pulled aside, when Rodney spurred the horses to a fast lope again.

Billy pulled back in behind them again and worked the bandana up over his nose and mouth in an effort to block most of the dust being kicked up by the horses. If they could just gain a few extra miles on McCreedy, he thought, they just might beat them to Fort Smith without having to fight . . . . That would be his first hope, his second would be, not to be overtaken in a wide-open space. McCreedy's persistence still had him buffaloed as well. What could it be, if not money? . . . No, he decided, it was money! Nothing else would, or does motivate a man to take chances that would put him at risk.

One thing was sure, he thought, and that was that he wanted this last job over with, so they could go home. He knew Connie and the kids were all right, it was the thought of leaving them behind, and them not knowing if he was all right? . . . 'She knows the odds, I face when I'm gone', he thought, 'and so do I'! . . . After all, his old wanted posters were still out there, the one in Denver had been fourteen years old, or would have been had not Sheriff McCoy allowed Connie to burn it! . . . Chances are, even Isaac Parker would still have one, and him being the stickler for law, that he was, he would not hesitate to try and enforce it!

That was one chance he did not want to take . . . . He also knew that a man's past was never truly dead, there was always a part that would come back to haunt him. Snake Mallory proved that ten years ago when he attacked the mountain. There would be others, too, he was also sure of that!

An hour had passed before Rodney stopped the horses again and to watch, as Billy came forward, . . . and was curious when Billy stopped to peer at Childers once again.

"Something on your mind, Specks, . . . I mean, Bill Upshur?"

"Yeah, as a matter a fact!"

"Well, spit it out, man, I don't read minds." Returned Childers, with a sigh.

"No, sir, you don't!" Said Billy thoughtfully. "But you try awful hard to! . . . I was just wonderin', back there, if you might want a tell me what you got, that McCreedy wants bad enough to risk his neck for? . . . Care to tell me?"

Childers shifted his sore backside in the saddle as he studied Billy's face. "We are pards, man, that's all." He grinned then, showing his badly unbrushed teeth. "Pards stick together, we're all pards." He turned in the saddle to look back at Wallace. "Even old Lionel there! . . . I might rib 'im a lot, but he knows it's in fun, because we're Pards! . . . Right, Lionel?"

"Yeah, we're Pards! . . . And I got a piss again!"

"There, you have it, Bill Upshur." He said with a grin. "All of it!"

"You're lying through your teeth, Ben, and Billy knows it!" Said Rodney. "McCreedy likely wants to kill your sorry ass! . . . He must hate you real bad, . . . and I wonder why?"

"Marshal, you got no call to run me that way, and me defenseless like this! . . . It ain't lawful!"

"Real smart man, Rod." Said Billy, moving up beside him.

"No, he ain't, Billy . . . . Hell, he likely hopes McCreedy will kill 'im, save 'im from th' hangman!" When Billy got closer, he leaned toward him.

"He won't tell us, ya know, not as long as there's a chance!"

"Like I said, he's a smart man! . . . Ya know, Rod," He said, leaning on the saddle-horn with crossed arms. "I sure hate goin' a hundred miles out a th' way just to go fifty, this road's still goin' northeast."

"I know, Billy, . . . but we both know, we wouldn't gain any time cuttin' across country."

"Yeah, I know, . . . it's just the idea of it, I guess."

"I think it's more than that, Billy . . . . You've always been a patient man, what's wrong?"

"Ain't got a clue! . . . I don't know, maybe what you said on th' train."

"Like what?"

"You know, about somethin' happening to you."

"A moment of weakness, Billy, . . . forget about it!"

"It's hard to do, Rod, when you're reminded a somethin' like that!"

"Like what?"

"You was speakin' from th' gut on that train . . . . You say you always trust my gut-feelings, Rod, . . . well, everybody has 'em, even you, but not everybody trusts 'em, . . . I do! . . . That was your gut-feeling, and you have to pay attention to it, . . . it's warning you of something that could happen, you ain't careful. We both know that if it can, it most-times will! . . . I just want a get this trip over with, and get you home with a whole skin."

"Man!" He said, turning to stare at the road. "I didn't think of it that way, Billy." He nodded and looked back at him. "Thanks, . . . really hits a man hard, don't it?"

"Not really, . . . what'll hit ya hard, is when somethin' does happen, and you know you should a listened to th' warnin'!"

"How do ya know it's a warnin'?"

That, I don't know! . . . You're on your own with that!"

"Thanks again!"

"Any time." He grinned. "Now let's see what we can do about getting' there."

"Amen to that, but we got a let th' rat pack empty their bladders first." He sighed, and they both dismounted to release the prisoners' feet and hands.

Back in the saddle, Rodney stared up the empty road again. "Late afternoon already, . . . wonder why we ain't seen any traffic, Billy, . . . hasn't been a soul on this road since that storm hit, and it's the only road to points south?"

"Maybe that's why, . . . they know this country better than we do. There was several wagons along th' street there in Acorn, one was a freight, maybe they're havin' to lay over and wait."

"Guess so." He nodded then turned the horse around and spurred it back to a lope, leaving Billy to once again fall in behind.

*   *   *

Mid-afternoon found Haskell stopping them on yet another bridge. They all dismounted again to quickly relieve themselves. McCreedy adjusted his gun-belt and reached inside his vest for a silver case, opened it and retrieved a tight-rolled, fairly large cigar from it, along with a match before putting it away again. He rolled it around with his fingers, smelled it then bit off the end before putting it in his mouth. Striking the match on his pistol-butt, he lit up to blow the bluish smoke skyward . . . . Then looked to see them both watching him.

"Settles the nerves, . . . helps with the pain." He said, with a shrug. "What's wrong with that?"

"Not a damn thing, Ed!" Replied Ellis. "Ain't seen you smoke one a them things in a week, hell, I thought you'd quit."

"Morgan, . . . this is a genuine imported, four-bit cigar! . . . Man don't smoke one a these every day, you want to anticipate it as long as you can! Because once they're gone, they're gone."

"Why not buy some more?" Queried Haskell.

"At four-bits each, forget it! . . . I lifted these from a fat-cat in Memphis."

"Where do ya think we are, Ed?"

"Damn if I know! . . . A fuckin' long way behind Childers, I know that!"

"Sure you ain't ready to give up?"

"Not by a long shot! . . . We're gonna be in that Mena town by dark tonight, and I'm thinkin' we'll sack out in that livery stable for three or four hours."

"Aint that th' place with that two-gun sheriff, Ed, one that made you so nervoud comin' through?"

"Speakin' of two guns, Morgan, why ain't you wearing yours?"

"Left one kept hangin' up on branches back in th' woods, so I took it off . . . . It's in my saddlebags . . . . Don't take but one to kill a man!"

"Yeah, I reckon . . . . Anyway, that Sheriff is only a problem if we let 'im, Morgan. Besides, that Livery's on this end a town."

"Well, I'm all for eatin' a good meal before I sleep!" Said Haskell.

"Guess we could do that, too!" Nodded McCreedy.

"And chance meetin', Mister Two-gun?"

"He's a fancy-pants, Morgan, . . . he ain't nothin'."

"Guess that cee-gar is a good one!"

"It is, Morgan, but you'll never know!" He said, then saw Haskell squat down by his horse. "What's wrong, Joe, what are ya doin'?"

"What you best be doin', Mister McCreedy, . . . cleanin' the mud from my horse's legs . . . . Mud adds up, adds another twenty pounds to each leg! Mud dries, more gets on and dries. Can't fall of when we're ridin' in mud. Horse gets tired faster."

Both McCreedy and Ellis reached for their gloves and quickly followed suite, working for a good quarter hour before washing the gloves off in the rushing water.

"Time to go yet, Joe?" He asked, placing the gloves back in his belt.

"Time to go!" Nodded Haskell, and mounted his horse again to lead the way off the bridge into the clinging mud again, . . . and the drudgery of urging the animals through the sucking muck . . .

"Sun's comin' out!" Said Ellis. "Or tryin' to, clouds are breaking up!"

"Just gonna get hotter, that's all!"

"Hotter? . . . Come on, Ed, we're soaked already!"

"You'll know what hot is, when th' steam starts rising from this mud."

They fell silent then while the animals labored at their task, and for the next two long hours, no one uttered a sound, but did raise their eyes to the sky now and then, to watch the large crow-like blackbirds flocking in and out of the water-logged trees and brush protruding from the flood-waters, . . . their loud cawing becoming an irritating nuisance, and as their droppings began to randomly strike them and their horses, Ellis pulled his pistol and fired it twice in the air in an effort to disperse them.

"Don't waste your lead, Morgan." Said McCreedy. "Won't do any good."

"Well, I don't like bein' shit on!"

"Then you ought a hate Ben Childers as much as me, he shit on all of us!"

"And I'll kill 'im for it!" He replied. "Hard as hell to kill birds, they're all feathers."

"Well, put it away, We're comin' up on Mena."

"Jesus." Spouted Ellis. "Look at that path of destruction, Ed, . . . had a fuckin' twister through here! . . . Touched down a quarter-mile southwest there, and came right through here! . . . Looks like a bunch a loggers been at work."

"Missed th' town, Morgan, . . . save for th' corral there at th' Livery, barn and windmill on th' right there."

"Got some bridge damage up ahead, Mister McCreedy." Said Haskell. "Railing's gone, holes in th' timbers, . . . cross it careful!"

They crossed the damaged bridge, each staring at the huge, downed Cottonwood Tree that had been pulled to the side, the splintered stump of the giant tree could be seen in the area of the Liver's corral, which was also gone.

"Must a come down on th' bridge!" Commented Ellis, as he viewed the deep drag marks.

"Appears so," Returned McCreedy. "Damn glad they got it off." They passed the fallen tree and continued on up the muddy street to Annie's café, having to urge the animals to step over the two by twelve planks someone had laid across the wide street end to end to walk on.

"Town's full a geniuses, thinkin' up that idea." Chuckled Ellis.

"Probably some kid!" Said McCreedy, stopping at the hitch-rail and dismounting, . . . and tossing the very short cigar-butt onto the street, turned and stepped up to the boardwalk and went inside. He found a table and sat down as Haskell and Ellis came in to join him.

"What'll it be gents," She smiled. "Besides a good bath, and a shave?"

"Mind your business, Missie!" Growled McCreedy. "We are tired."

"Well, excuse me, Sir! . . . What'll it be?"

"No offense, ma'am." Grinned McCreedy. "We been fighting knee-deep mud for two days."

"I was only funnin' ya." She said, and smiled. "What can I get ya?"

"Three cups, and a poy a coffee, and th' biggest steak in th' house!" Said Ellis. "I think that just might save my life."

"Make that two." Added McCreedy.

"Three!" Said Haskell.

"Coming up, coffee first!" She left and went back to the kitchen.

"Thought there'd be more people about." Commented Ellis. "Hardly anybody on th' boardwalks . . . . Not like it was when we came through before."

"Weren't this muddy out when we came through." Sighed McCreedy. "Smell them steaks, boys?"

She brought the coffee then, and poured it for them. "Steaks will be ready soon." She turned to leave.

"Uh, Ma'am." Said McCreedy, stopping her. "We was hopin' to catch up with a U. S. Marshal, actually two of 'em, takin' four prisoners to Fort Smith . . . . We was waitin' for 'em at Wickes when that storm hit, must a missed 'em . . . . They been through here?"

"You missed them all right! . . . I fed them, about five o'clock this morning, prisoners, too!"

"Wonder why they passed us up?" He mused, his eyes flicking from Annie, to Ellis, and back again. "Judge Parker said they'd know we was there."

"Maybe they didn't see th' town." Said Ellis. "Couldn't see nothin' in that downpour!"

"Yeah, that had to be it!" Nodded McCreedy.

"That's too bad." Nodded Annie. "They got to be forty miles away by now." She turned and went to the kitchen again.

"Well," Sighed McCreedy. "They were here, twelve hours ago! . . . Likely out a th' mud by now, too! . . . Boys, I know I said we'd get some sleep here, but them being that far ahead of us, that's exactly what they'll figure we did . . . . Why? . . . Because that's exactly what they'll do, stop for th' night! . . . . You boys up to ridin' all night?"

*   *   *

"Where's all th' traffic at?" Queried Rodney, looking up the empty stretch of road ahead of them. "I know, you said it was because a th' storm, and I agree . . . . But I ain't seen as much as a cottontail on this thing! . . . You'd think there'd be one or two people traveling between towns?"

"Rod, that twister took th' telegraph wires down in Mena, we saw th' pole, with no wires on it! Don't you think somebody there would a wired ahead to every town this side a Fort Smith? . . . Wouldn't be surprised to see traffic backed up in one a th' towns ahead of us somewhere, all waitin' for th' road to dry up."

"Yeah, you're right." He sighed. "It's just strange, is all."

"Can't fight mama Nature, she'll win every time! . . . Gonna be dark in a couple hours, what say we pitch us a camp right here, get an early start in th' mornin'?"

"In th' middle a th' road?"

"Why not, nobody on it? . . . We'll build a fire, and take turns sleepin'."

"Are we far enough ahead of McCreedy?"

"We're forty, fifty miles ahead of 'im . . . . I think he'll stop, too, likely in Mena."

"Well, I'm all for it! . . . . Four hours sleep last night didn't last long."

Nodding, Billy dismounted and loosened his horse's cinches, as did Rodney before they tied them to a low-hanging branch.

"We stopping here th' night, Marshal?" Queried Childers, looking around at the thick mass of timber on either side of them. "Middle of th' road?"

"No better hotel than this, Ben." Smiled Rodney. "Plenty a room, sky for a roof!" He went to untie childer's hands then. "Any complaints?"

"You'll get none from me, Marshal."

"Good!" He untied his feet and stepped back. "Come on down, bring your bedroll, and loosen your horse's cinches."

Billy had the fire going in the middle of th' road, and once they were all seated on blankets, and while Rodney bound their feet, he went for the bag containing the half dozen cans of beans and what jerky that was left, and brought them to the fire. Using his knife, he opened the cans and placed each next to the flames to heat.

"You must be awful sure of yourselves." Commented Childers. "Not knowin' where McCreedy is . . . . Knowin' him, like I do, he'll be pounding leather all night, while you're here sleeping."

"Maybe you don't know 'im as well as you think, Ben." Replied Rodney. "He ain't had any more sleep than we have, . . . he'll stay th' night somewhere."

"Have it your way, Marshal."

"I generally do."

Billy used his gloves to carry the hot tins to the four men, "You'll have to use your hands to eat with, . . . or drink it." He said, putting the cans down in front of them. "Not like you ain't done it before."

He came back to the fire and sat down by Rodney.

"You sure about this, Billy?"

"Nobody can ever be sure a somethin' like this, Rod . . . . But logic says he'll stop tonight!" He picked up the can and used his knife to eat with.

"We're about five miles from a town called Y-City." He said as he swallowed. "Saw a marker back there a ways, . . . if it has a Sheriff, we'll get 'im to watch for 'em, maybe buy us some time."

"And hope we don't need it!"

"We'll still be ahead of 'em, Rod . . . . If he does ride all night, they'll still be fightin' that mud to Acorn, that'll take up half th' night, maybe as much as ten hours . . . . That be th' case, we'll still be a couple hours ahead of 'em."

"Hope that's enough!"

"It will be, . . . we'll be in th' saddle again by four o'clock."

"Another four hours sleep . . . . But that's better'n none at all."

"Stop worrying, Rod! . . . Comes down to it, I'll drop back and stop 'em."

"I never really worry, when you're with me, Billy."

"That's because I do all of it."

"I doubt you worry all that much!" He looked across at Childers then. "Think he'll take that money to the grave with 'im?"

"He wouldn't be th' first!"

"Wonder how much it is?"

"Between twenty, and fifty thousand, no doubt."

"Motivation enough!" He began eating his beans then, by using his hunting knife like a spoon.

CHAPTER TWELVE

Billy was standing beside one of the horses and staring back down the road, when he decided to check the time. "Twelve-fifteen', he thought, and turning to look toward the fire, had just put the watch away when movement caused him to quickly look at Rodney's sleeping form as he was restlessly turning over beneath the blanket. He didn't see the large snake until the blanket's movement caused it to coil.

Without thinking, and on reflex alone, he drew the pistol and fired as the reptile struck. The snake's head was severed from it's body as the ear-shattering explosion suddenly broke the night's serenity.

Rodney was on his feet in a split second, his mouth still open in a yell that he couldn't quite get out, . . . and with gun in hand, wildly searched the darkness of trees. His eyes fell on Billy then as he holstered the gun, . . . and at that instant, he knew what had happened and quickly searched the ground until he saw the writhing length of reptile near his bedding.

"How th' hell did you see that thing?"

"It coiled!" He said, coming to the fire to watch it.

Childers, and the other three men were on their knees, and also watching the snake's death-throes in silence.

"What is it with me, and rattlesnakes, Billy?" He shook his head and holstered his own weapon. "Shit, man, that's th' fifth time you saved my bacon. Thank you, My friend, thank you!"

"Any time, Rod, you know that! . . . It's just luck, that I saw it in time."

"No, I'm lucky you saw it in time!"

"You saying you shot that thing from thirty feet away, . . . in this light?"

"No, he ain't, Ben, I'm sayin' it!"

"As it was striking?"

"Drew and fired, yes! . . . Now shut up, and lay down, I ain't in th' mood!" He turned back to watch, as Billy gutted the snake then peeled the thin hide from it's meaty length before slicing off the rattles and tossing them to him.

"Twenty one rattles, Rod!" He got to his feet, and holding the reptile off the ground, bent to retrieve a length of stick from the road and brought both to the fire, . . . where he squatted and cut the meat into shorter pieces before skewering them and placing them over the flames to cook.

"You ain't gonna eat that thing?"

He looked up and grinned. "A piece of it, yeah, . . . tastes a lot like chicken!"

"Well, I draw th' line at rattlesnake, man!" Still shook up, he went to his horse for the canteen and drank from it, and was still there to watch as Billy slid a piece off the stick and ate it.

Billy grinned at him then got to his feet and took the rest to Childers and crew, . . . all four, of which readily accepted.

"Still got some, Rod, try it, ya might like it! . . . See it as payback for tryin' to bite ya."

"I'll pass, Billy."

Shrugging, he gave the rest to Childers and went back to lie down on Rodney's bedding, but then sat up again. "I was just gonna wake ya, Rod, it's past midnight, . . . wake me at four." He covered with the blanket, and left the watch open on his stomach before covering his face with his hat.

Rodney fished a cigar from his vest and lit it with a twig from the fire before sitting down in the road to smoke.

"Is he really that good with a gun, Marshal?" Queried Childers, causing Rodney to frown at him. "I mean no disrespect, Marshal, I'd just like to know."

"He's better, Ben, . . . a lot better! . . . You would not want to test 'im."

"Who is he, Marshal?"

"He's a farmer . . . . Well, he used to be a farmer! . . . We're partners in a trading post, back in th' Nations. He's th' best man, I ever knew, best friend I could ever have . . . . He's God-father to my daughter."

"How long have you known 'im?"

"Thirteen years now, Ben." He looked at Childers then. "And why am I tellin' you all this, I don't even know who you are, . . . don't want to!"

"Come on, Marshal." He chuckled. "No harm bein' done here. Who am I gonna tell, anyway . . . And what good's it gonna do me, I'm gonna hang?"

"You're right about that!" He nodded.

"You really think you're gonna get me there, don't ya?" Asked Childers then.

"Like I said from th' start, Ben, . . . any false moves, Billy will shoot ya."

"Yeah, well, I believe that now, . . . after what just happened. But you know what, Marshal? . . . It would appears to me, a man that fast would have a known reputation, . . . except, I've never heard of a gunslinger anywhere, who wore specks."

"He ain't known anywhere, Ben." He grinned then. "Except to those who forced him to fight, . . . course they never told anybody! . . . Nope, he's not known anywhere, Ben, that's th' way we both want it . . . . Now, want a tell me who you are?"

"I'm a thirty-six year old convicyed killer, Marshal. When I was eighteen, my name was Ben Calico . . . . I was a gunslinger, too, back then . . . . Still am, and I think, a mite better than old Billy there! . . . Tell me, Marshal, who were some of th' men he shot, maybe I heard of 'em?"

"I only recall a couple, Ben, . . . Lance Ashley was one, Joe Christmas was another."

"Kiowa Joe Christmas? . . . That one had th' devil in his gunhand, one crazy Indian, totally insane . . . . And that, Marshal, is hard to believe, that anybody could have beat him . . . . Ashly, too, for that matter! . . . Sort a makes old, Bill Upshur there, a man to reckon with, . . . but I can still beat 'im! . . . Anybody else?"

"None with any importance . . . . Except, they all thought they could beat 'im, too!"

"I bet they did!"

"Where did you hide that money, Ben?"

"What money?"

"Th' money, McCreedy wants, where is it?"

"You're fishin' again, Marshal, and like I told ya, you won't catch anything, . . . not in my pond!"

"Go your ass to sleep, Ben, conversation over!"

"Sure thing, Marshal, and thanks for sharing . . . . And if you're kickin' yourself in th' ass for opening up to me, don't, . . . no harm's been done."

"I'm not, Ben, . . . He happens to be my favorite subject!" He looked across at Billy then, and wondered why he had let himself be drawn into a conversation like that? If Billy had wanted him to know, he would have told him himself! . . . He knew then, that Billy was right about Ben Childers, the man had a knack for getting into a man's mind . . . . Got the information, he wanted, too, he thought, . . . and without giving much in return.

Well, he thought, it wouldn't do him any good where he was going! The only thing he hated about telling him about Billy, was telling him about Billy. He was pretty sure of himself, and his ability with a gun, he thought, then wondered if Ben Calico Childers might be the one Billy was afraid he would meet someday? . . . Of course not! . . . Not a man alive could beat

Billy Upshur, he knew that with all his heart. He was the fastest gun alive, and he always would be! He looked back at the sleeping Childers then, or was he asleep? . . . He was a strange man, asleep or not, he decided, . . . but was too sure of himself, if he thought he was going to fool the hangman!

He put the cigar in his mouth and stared back down the dark road. Right now, he thought, Ed McCreedy and friends were their only threat, and they were wanted men now, as well. Isaac Parker would be very pleased if him and Billy were to bring all six of them back! But, what a chore that might turn out to be, especially if McCreedy was the great planner he was made out to be? . . . And they were coming, he thought, getting closer all the time.

He looked back at Billy then, and wondered how he could sleep like nothing had happened? He shuddered then, thinking about the size of the snake, and how close he had come to being bitten . . . . Five times, he thought, and if not for Billy, he would have died all five times!

His thoughts turned to Melissa then, and his baby girl. What would happen to them, if for some reason, he couldn't make it home? . . . No, they would be fine, he thought, . . . they were home! He shook his head then to clear it, and pushed to his feet to walk to the edge of the firelight to stare down the moonlit road as he smoked, and thinking it strange there being no traffic at all on the only road to Fort Smith, . . . not even between towns? He shook those thoughts away as well, and turned back to watch the prisoners.

*   *   *

"This is the fourth time, you've stopped us, Joe!" Said McCreedy. "We'll never catch 'em at this rate!"

"We won't catch 'em without horses, neither, Mister McCreedy."

"Yeah, yeah! . . . I know that." With a look at the clearing skies, he pulled his watch in the moon's pale light. "One-thirty, . . . shit! . . . Where is the end of that fuckin' storm, anyway?"

"A walkin' horse gets ya nowhere fast, Ed." Reminded Ellis. "And we damn sure been walkin'!"

"Yeah." Growled, McCreedy, turning to look at the road ahead.

"Another four, five miles, we'll be on a dry road again, Mister McCreedy."

"You sure a that, Joe?"

"Maybe so, yes." He said. "Horses don't seem to be sinking in th' mud so much here!"

"Some good news at last, . . . can we get on with it, now?"

"We can go now." He led the way again, to painstakingly urge his reluctant horse forward in the sucking mud, . . . and for the next two hours, sat their saddles in boring silence, save an occasional snort, or grunt from the tiring animals.

"A town is here." Said Haskell as they neared the buildings. "The horses need rest."

"This is Acorn." Said McCreedy. "Another one-horse, shot in th' dark!"

"We rest the horses here?"

"Yeah, sure, . . . bridge ahead, in th' middle a town, we'll stop on that! . . . I got a get off and piss anyway." He looked at his watch again in the patchy moonlight as they trudged past the dark buildings. Another two hours gone, he thought, as they finally reached the bridge and stopped the heavily breathing horses.

"Three-thirty, boys!" He grunted, quickly dismounting to open his pants.

"Place looks better in th' dark." Commented Ellis as he dismounted.

"Well, Joe." Said McCreedy as he buttoned his trousers. "How much farther?"

"Real soon now, Mister McCreedy, . . . mud's not near as deep."

"Good, . . . they'll be up and about before long, now, and when they do, I'd like to be ridin' up their asses!"

"Get real, Ed." Chuckled Ellis. "We don't even know they stopped for th' night."

"They did, Morgan, . . . and they think we did! . . . They'll be on their way again in another hour."

"We won't be ridin' up their asses, neither!" Returned Ellis.

"No, . . . but we'll be within range of 'em! . . . How about it, Joe?"

                    *   *   *

They had Childers, and the others mounted and roped to their horses when Billy checked his watch again.

"Four-thirty, Rod! . . . Lead out, I'll catch up." Rodney mounted and spurred the horses to a gallop along the moonlit shoulder of the wide road.

He watched them leave then kicked out the fire's dying embers before looking back down the road. He knew there was a good chance, McCreedy didn't stop at all last night, and if he didn't, they would be awfully close to the dry roadway by now, . . . and tired as hell! He pulled his pistol and replaced the spent cartridge before mounting and urging the animal in pursuit of Rodney.

Rodney had slowed the horses back to a mile consuming lope as he caught up to fall in behind Long again, and for the next hour, allowed his body to adjust to the horse's gait and relaxed to the swaying motion of the loping animal.

It was coming daylight when he saw Rodney hold up his hand, and spurred his horse forward to walk beside him.

"It appears we got a decision to make, Rod." He said as they watched the half-dozen men at work on the badly damaged bridge. "That should answer your questions from last night, too."

"I'd say so." He sighed heavily as they walked the horses in, and then stopped when one of the men saw them and came forward to look up at them.

"What happened here?" He asked, still looking at the bridge.

"Heavy rains in the Quachitas," He said. "Runoff brought a couple a trees downstream, took out th' bridge!" He pointed back behind him then. "Pulled 'em out on th' bank there late yesterday . . . . Be a week before we get a new one built, got timbers comin' from Waldren already, . . . But we can't use 'em till we get this one tore out. You're out a luck till then!" He stepped aside then to peer at the prisoners.

"You th' Marshal in these parts?"

Rodney showed him the badge on his vest. "No, sir, . . . we do work for Judge Parker, though. We're taking prisoners back to Fort Smith, they're late for a hangin'."

"I heard about that already. We relayed a wire to th' Judge from DeQueen, a couple days back, . . . knew you were coming! . . . I'm real sorry about all this, happened yesterday! Must be ten freight wagons stranded in town, not countin' th' DeQueen stage, and a dozen or so drifters . . . . Heard you was bein' dogged, too, they still comin'?"

"Still comin'!" Nodded Rodney

"How's th' country west of us there?" Asked Billy. "Is it passable?"

"Yes, sir, it is. Not easy, mind ya, but passable!" He turned to look west of them. "That hill yonder is about the last one of any size between here and Fort Smith. I been huntin' over that way for th' last ten years or so, and the only problem you might have, is a couple dozen ravines and creeks to cross . . . . This one right here narrows about a mile off yonder, at a shallow ford, that's where I cross at. There's a worn deer-trail out there a quarter mile or so in, goes up and across th' mountain, that's what I use."

"There's a dozen trails crisscrossin' each other on that mountain, just stay north, and you'll be okay."

"What about th' timber?"

"Thicker'n hell about sums that up . . . . You in that big a hurry, are ya? . . . Be able to ford this one right here, come nightfall, you can use th' road again."

"Can't wait that long." Breathed Rodney. "Men behind us are too close."

"How far is Fort Smith that way?" Queried Billy.

"Over th' mountain? . . . Thirty, forty miles, I'd say . . . . Maybe closer to fifty, never been there, that way."

"And by th' road?"

"Seventy, eighty miles, maybe."

"Well," Said Rodney, looking at Billy. "Back to th' wilderness!"

"Is that Y-city up ahead there?" Asked Billy.

"That, it is!"

"Got a Sheriff there?"

"You're talkin' to 'im!" He said, taking the badge from his shirt. "Wilford Penny, at your service."

"Don't take any chances when those men get here, Sheriff." Said Billy. "They're dangerous, and desperate, and you got civilians here that could get hurt, if you try to interfere."

"He's right, Sheriff." Added Rodney. "You decide to keep workin' here, keep your badge in your pocket, these men are gunmen!"

"Who are they?"

"Ed McCreedy. Morgan Ellis, and a man called Haskell . . . . You should a got word about all this."

"I did, about a month back."

"I was you, Sheriff," Said Billy. "I'd take myself, and these men here back to town till those men come, and go . . . . They can't cross here, so they'll follow us."

"I'll consider it, . . . thanks for th' warning."

"Yes, sir!" Rodney nodded and led the way off the road, and into the trees where once again they were forced to find a way through a heavily foliaged wilderness.

*   *   *

It was more than an hour since leaving Acorn, when Haskell stopped them again, and McCreedy pulled his watch to check the time.

"It's four-thirty, Joe, why are you stopping?"

"To rest the horses, Mister McCreedy." He dismounted and squatted to remove the mud from his horse's legs.

"Now what?"

"There's no more mud here, I'm c;leaning my horse's legs . . . . Come on up and join me."

"Son of a bitch!" He exclaimed. "At fuckin' last! Come on, Morgan." They rode up out of the shallow mud and dismounted to clean their animals' legs. "I've been in Arkansas rain before, . . . but it was nothing like this damn road!" He said as he worked, laboriously with his one good arm.

"I'll do that, Mister McCreedy." Said Haskell, as he finished, and once McCreedy stood and moved back, proceeded to clean his animal's legs.

"You're a good man, Joe." He said, and grunted as he reached to rub at his still swollen shoulder, . . . and to look up the road ahead of them.

"We'll make up some time now, boys!"2

"After we rest the horses." Reminded Haskell.

"That's what I meant, Joe." He grinned then. "We're close now, I can feel it, they likely just broke camp about now . . . . How far ahead of us, you think they are, Joe?"

"Hard to say, Mister McCreedy, . . . ten miles, maybe less."

"That far?"

"Yes, sir." He got to his feet then. "Think about it, they must a been fifty miles ahead of us when we left DeQueen. That town we stayed when th' storm hit was maybe twenty-five miles from DeQueen. By that time, I put them in th' town that twister hit . . . We been in mud ever since."

"Yeah, but we traveled all night, they didn't!"

"We might a gained twenty miles on 'em, Mister McCreedy, too dark to see."

"Okay, Joe." He nodded. "I'll settle for ten."

"Then again, they might a traveled all night, too." Reminded Ellis.

"They didn't! . . . Horses ready yet, Joe?"

"We can go now, yes." They mounted and spurred the horses to a fast gallop along the road's shoulder. Haskell held his horse at that pace for most of an hour before slowing to a walk again to cool them, and then for another half-hour before the remnants of a fire made him stop in the road.

"You were right, Mister McCreedy, they stayed here last night."

"I knew it!" Laughed McCreedy. "See that, Morgan? . . . How old is it, Joe?"

"One and a half, maybe two hours."

"Now that's more like it, . . . let's go."

"Hold it, Ed!" Said Ellis, sismounting to pick up the reptile's skin and hold it up. "See this?"

"Snake skin, Morgan, what of it?"

"What of it? . . . Th' head was shot off, Ed, but th' rattles was cut off . . . . What's that tell ya?"

"You tell me, Morgan."

"One a them Marshals is damn good with a sidearm, Ed, . . . he's a gunslinger! . . . No powder-burns here, neither, means he weren't close when he shot it!"

"Get mounted, Morgan, . . . let's go, Joe!"

                     *   *   *

The maze of trees and undergrowth was becoming thicker with every several yards of progress into the deep forest, prompting Rodney to stop and remove his hat.

"Best take your hats off back there, ya want a keep 'em!" He said loudly, and saw them lean forward to take theirs in hand. "Be ready to bleed some from here on, too!" He turned and led off again, ducking the low-hanging limbs, and grunting when raked by the thorny briars.

It was almost noon when he found the narrow, worn animal trail, and rode out onto it until the other horses filed in behind him then stopped to see that Billy had emerged from the trees before leading off again . . .

The well-used trail continued ever upward toward the large hill's tree-covered crest, and with hundreds of other pathways intersecting, or crossing theirs, he stayed with the one they were on, as it suddenly veered downward into what appeared to be a narrow valley. He followed it for several dozen yards down the mountain before coming to the shallow waters of the creek, the Sheriff had spoke of, . . . and stopping there, dismounted and allowed the animals to drink.

He took his canteen and poured the old water out before kneeling down to refill it, and nodded at Billy when he knelt down beside him with his.

"Pretty place, ain't it?" He asked, getting to his feet to drink from it, before hanging it in place on his saddle.

"Except when it rains." He grinned, and frank from his canteen before getting up to replace it then both of them refilled the other canteens before standeing to peer across the creek.

"This th' ford, Sheriff told us about?"

"Got a be." Said Rodney, nodding.

"Guess it runs clear through. Valley likely peters out somewhere up there."

"Yeah, . . . guess we better let th' men empty their bladders before we start climbing again . . . . And I hope these horses can climb." He said, still looking up the narrow trail on the other side.

"Guess we'll find out." Said Billy, going to untie Childers' hands and feet.

"Guess so." He went to untie the ropes on Wallace as he spoke.

*   *   *

"Now what?" Said McCreedy, when they stopped again to look at the almost totally damaged bridge, and the fast moving stream of water, some ten feet below them. "What th' hell happened here, . . . and why ain't nobody tryin' to fix th' damn thing?"

"Water from th' mountains washed it away." Said Haskell. "Trees over there, must a washed down and hit it!"

"Then why in hell ain't they fixin' it, there's a town up there? . . . Any way across it, Joe?"

"Too deep!" He said, shaking his head. "Horses would never make it up th' far side. Could be more timber under th' water, too."

"Well, they got across, God damn it!"

"Maybe not." Said Haskell, and dismounted to walk into the tall grass alongside the road's shoulder. "Over here, Mister McCreedy."

Him and Ellis dismounted and joined Haskell at the side of the wide road.

"They left the road here." Said Haskell, and pointed at the trees. "Tracks lead into them trees yonder."

"How long ago?"

"Two, maybe three hours."

McCreedy stared at the trees for a moment then nodded "Guess it'e up to you again, Joe, . . . what do you think? . . . If we follow 'em, we're not gonna gain on 'em, not in that mess, and we don't know what's on the other side a that mountain!"

Nodding, Haskell studied the tall mountain again before looking at them. "Was me, I'd try and find a way across this creek somewhere between here and that mountain . . . . An Indian would try and get ahead of them, circle around to the other side, . . . maybe head 'em off."

"We could lose 'em, too, Joe."

"How, Mister McCreedy, they are goin' North to this, ah, Fort Smith?"

"We could still miss 'em, we could pass each other in twenty yards, and not know it!"

"Mister McCreedy, what I'm telling you, is th' Indian way. Figure the time it takes to go through woods like this, and we'll know where they might be, . . . and we watch for them!"

"Okay, Joe, how so we watch for 'em, just look at that mess!"

"We watch from some high point, with the scope from your rifle."

"Who's th' smart one now, Ed?" Chuckled Ellis.

"I'll have to bow to the professor on this one, Morgan." He nodded. "Show us th' way, Joe, . . . we'll do this thing Indian style!"

*   *   *

Although the animal path was fairly steep in places, and very narrow as it lead them through tight gaps between the large Pines, the horses did manage to keep their footing and continue upward toward the mountain's crest. There were places where they were forced to lay almost flat on their horses' necks to avoid low-hanging limbs, and were even raked by random, protruding dead branches from time to time, . . . but were still to move faster on the trail, than otherwise.

Mid afternoon found them on the rim of a very deep crevice, that stretched for fifty or more yards, appearing to Rodney as being akin to a huge, eroded sink-hole, perhaps caused by flooding, or a quake sometime in the past. He was somewhat mesmerized by the whole thing, and to the extent that he had not noticed the fairly large, broken limb that had snapped off at one time, and now lay suspended, and balanced atop other smaller limbs, . . . and almost directly over the deer-trail. He also did not see the lower branches as they sagged beneath the much heavier limb, . . . until he heard the sharp crack of breaking branches.

Billy, however, did see the possible danger, and was watching it intently when he saw the movement a split second before he heard the cracking.

"Rod, look out!" He yelled, but the warning was lost in the loud cracking of broken limbs. He heard Rodney yell as the suspended limb fell, seeing it strike him on the shoulder on the way down. The large limb struck Rodney a glancing blow, knocking him out of the saddle to disappear over the side of the crevice.

"Rod!" He yelled shrilly, and leaped from the saddle to run past the four horses, and quiet Rodney's, noticing the long, bleeding scrape on the animal's left hip as he took the reins and tied them securely to the fallen limb. He dropped to his knees and looked over the side of the crevice.

"Rod!" He yelled again, and still couldn't see him in the darker shadows below. He yelled his name several times before getting an answer, and was flooded with relief when he finally did. Leaning further out over the lip of the hole, he saw him, he lay sprawled across the trunk of a Pine Sapling that had grown out of the crevice wall.

"You okay, Rod, anything broke?"

"Don't know, Billy, I . . . hurt all over! . . . Get me out a here, will ya?"

"Can you fit a loop over your head?"

"I, . . . think so, maybe!"

"Hold od, it's comin' dow to ya!" He pushed to his feet to quickly take the rope from Rodney's saddle then looked up at Childers.

"You four try anything stupid, I'll blow your heads off!" He shook out the rope and formrf the loop then went to his knees again at the crevice. 'It's comin' down, Rod, catch it!" He dropped the noose over Rodney's upraised arm.

"You know where to put it, Rod . . . . Work it over your head and shoulders." His heart was beating wildly, his eyes burning from the sweat on his forehead, but he kept watching as Rodney struggled to get the noose over his head and around his shoulders . . . . and unable to move his left arm at all, he yelled out in pain as he used his right to lift the arm through.

"Pull me up!" He yelled.

Billy went to Rodney's horse and untied the tow-rope to retie it to the fallen limb. He looked back at Childers as he took up the slack in the rope. "Remember what I said!"

He mounted the horse, looped the taut rope around the horn and reined the animal into the trees, and hearing Rodney's yell of pain as he was lifted from the sapling. He urged the animal into the trees an estimated ten to twelve feet before dismounting and tying the reins to a branch. Moving back to the crevice, he could see Rodney's good arm above the lip as he tried to find something to grab.

"I got ya, Rod!" He said, taking his hand and arm in his and pulling him back onto the deer-path where he sat down on the ground and looked at him.

"You don't look so good." He commented. "That arm broke?"

"I don't think so, . . . it's just numb, can't feel a thing, . . . and I can't move it!"

"What about th' rest of ya, legs okay, back, neck?"

"I'm okay, Billy . . . . Back's bruised some where I hit that tree, but I can move my legs okay . . . . Help me up, will ya?"

With Billy's help, he grunted in pain, but got to his feet to let Billy remove the rope. "Shit, Billy!" He gasped then reached to hold his arm up.

"You okay, not weak or nothing?"

"Legs are wobbly, but I'm okay! . . . Thanks, Billy."

"I'll get your horse." He coiled the rope as he went to retrieve the horse, and tied it in place before grabbing the reins. He turned the animal around in the thick trees and retraced his steps, . . . and once there, moved the animal back in place and retied the tow-rope to the horn before helping Rodney back in the saddle.

"How's that, Rod?"

"Hurts like hell!"

"Teach ya to watch where you're goin', won't it?"

'Not gonna let me live this down, are, ya?'

"Nope, . . . want me to tie ya to your horse?"

"No!" He grunted. "I'm fine."

"Well, I'm gonna take th' lead for a while, find a place for you to rest." He went back to retrieve his horse and led it into the trees until he could work his way back to the trail. He took the dangling reins of Rodney's horse and mounted his own before urging it on up the beaten trail, with all five horses in tow behind him.

He turned hi the saddle to see Rodney slightly slumping forward. "You okay, Rod, need to stop?"

"No, don't stop . . . . Don't hurt as bad when I lean over, I'm okay."

Nodding, he went back to watching the trail again, keeping the horses at a very slow walk so as not to jar Rodney's shoulder and arm, . . . and it was then that he noticed the weakness in his own arms, and held his hand up in front of him. It was shaking. He had not, or could not recall ever having been more afraid for anyone's safety before. If not for that sapling, he thought, he would have surely lost Rodney. But it was not over yet, he knew, his pain was nothing compared to what it would be when the feeling came back! . . . There will be chills tonight, maybe fever, and if the lungs were bruised enough, . . . possibly pneumonia! He had nothing what so ever to treat pneumonia with, . . . He would just have to keep the fever down, should it occur.

He had to find someplace to safely build a fire, heat a blanket and wrap him in it, . . . and keep doing it until the chills passed, and if he had a fever, wet rags to the head and neck! He couldn't remember anything else to do? It'll have to be enough, he decided, and looked up at the sky.

"If you really do exist up there, we could use a little help down here." He muttered.

It was late afternoon when they made the mountain's crest, and that's when he spied the rocky shelf of solid rock through the trees. He reined the horse into the trees to finally exit into the clearing, and onto the polished surface of protruding rock. The perfect place, he thought as he rode along the tree-lined edge of the clearing and stopped to relish the cool breeze that seemed to be a constant thing.

He dismounted, dropping the reins to the ground, and quickly went to help Rodney down and walk him to a tree to sit him down near the edge of the rock to lean against a tree.

"That okay, Rod?"

"Yeah." He grunted. "Thanks."

"I'll be back, just take it easy." He walked back across the clearing and untied Childers hands and feet then watched him dismount. "Sit it down against a tree, and don't move!"

"Can I piss first?"

"You can piss, then sit down . . . . You try anything, I'll plug ya before you take a step."

"I believe ya, man!" He said, and walked to his designated tree as Billy released Wallace.

"Pick a tree, Wallace." He untied Collins and Long then watched until they were all seated against a tree then loosened the cinches on all six horses before quickly gathering wood and building a fire, keeping it as far away from the windy ledge as possible and then, with a look back at Rodney, he untied his bedroll and removed the top blanket as he carried the bedding back.

"Here's your bedroll, Rod, roll over some, and I'll spread it for ya." He helped Rodney to his knees then spread the blanket and helped him down again, . . . and could already feel his body trembling as he did. "You cold, man?"

"Yeah, it's freezin' up here!"

"Hold on, I'll fix that for ya." He took the blanket to the fire and held it close to the flames for a time before taking it back to wrap him up in it.

"How's that, Rod?"

"Oh yeah, . . . feels good!" He nodded then dropped his chin to his chest and closed his eyes.

Still worried, he went back to the horses and removed all the bedrolls and canteens then carried them back to drop them at the feet of the escapees.

"If you boys never do anything else, do not give me cause to shoot ya, . . . because I will shoot ya!" He turned away, and went back to take Rodney's canteen from his saddle then went to sit down beside him.

"Still cold, Rod?" He asked, reaching to close the blanket around his neck.

"No, . . . not so much now, . . . shoulder and arm hurts like hell!"

"I can't help ya there, Bud."

"Bud? . . . Been thirteen years since you called me that."

"Slipped out! . . . Don't fan th' blankets., I'll heat it up again in a minute."

"Pa, . . . prisoners secure?"

"Secured, Rod . . . . Don't talk, I'll heat another blanket." He got up and retrieved his bedroll, removing the top blanket as he carried it back then went to hold to the flames. All four men were watching him, and he stared back at them with something akin to hatred in his heart. If not for them, they wouldn't be here, he thought. But he knew they were not at fault. He remembered Murphy's law then, if it can happen, it will! He took the hot blanket back to remove the first, and wrapped him again in the warm one.

"Th, thanks, Billy, feels good."

"You're welcome, now don't talk so much . . . . You get ready to sleep, let me know."

"Arm hurts too bad to sleep! . . . Heat helps."

"You'll get plenty a that! . . . Ya still cold?"

"Does freezin' count?"

"I'll reheat th' blanket."

"It's still warm, Billy."

"Okay, . . . then take a deep breath, tell me if it hurts."

"Yeah, Billy, . . . a little . . . . But my back's bruised."

"Yeah, well, Doc gave me some Sulfa tablets. I'm gonna heat up that other blanket, and then give ya one, just in case!" He took the blanket and got up to go to his horse, opened his satchel and took out the bottle before going to heat the blanket.

"Hey, Marshal?" Said Childers, from his place against the tree, and when Billy looked at him. "Can I offer you a suggestion?"

"I'm listenin'."

"He's chilled, right? . . . Why not heat up some rocks, plenty of 'em around? . . . Put 'em under th' blanket along both sides of 'im. Course, he'll need to lay down for it to work."

Billy looked around the clearing at the random sized rocks strewn about. "Where'd you learn about that?"

"Grandmother was a full blooded Cheyenne."

"Thanks, man, I'll try that!"

*   *   *

"Mister McCreedy?" Said Haskell, turning in the saddle to look back at him. "Creek bank's not too steep here, water's pretty shallow, I think we can make it across."

"You think, huh? . . . What about getting' out again?"

"Be easier than goin' down, it's slanted over there . . . . We might not find another spot."

"Let's do it, then!"

Nodding, Haskell spurred his horse to send it down the four-foot embankment and into the water, which turned out to be only belly-deep on the animals. He reined it across the current, and after several attempts, finally urged it out and up the grade on the far side of the stream where he waited for them.

"Okay, Joe, we're across." Growled McCreedy as he came up behind him. "What now?"

"We go around th' mountain." He urged his horse through the brush and into the trees again, with a cursing McCreedy fighting Pine branches behind him.

*   *   *

Using the blanket, Billy carried the hot stones and placed them on the ground beneath the blanket Rodney was laying on, making sure they were snug against him along both sides.

"That warm enough for ya, Rod?"

"Feels good, Billy, thanks."

Moving back to sit, he crossed his arms atop his drawn-up knees and looked out at the vista of treetops below them. The tops of the Pines no more than a stone's throw away from the rock ledge. Be dark soon, he thought, and he was bone tired from constantly heating blankets and rocks to fight Rodney's chills.

Where did the day go, he wondered? . . . He looked back at Childers and the others then. They were all laying on their blankets with hats over their faces. He heard Rodney snore then, and knew he was finally asleep. Gonna be a long night, he decided, looking at the prisoners again. He would need to secure them to the trees tonight, he thought as he watched them, and his eyes came to rest on Childers.

He was a strange one, he thought, calm, collected, and sure of himself . . . . Why had he offered to help Rodney? With the threat of hanging on his head, he'd have thought he would want Rodney to suffer, . . . or die? Still buying time, he guessed. He grunted to his feet, and after looking out over the trees again, sighed, and went to place more wood on the fire, and more stones to heat.

He went to his horse then and took down the rope before going to stand at Childers' feet to nudge him with his boot. Childers sat up and leaned forward enough to remove his hat.

"Why'd you tell me about th' rocks, Ben?" He asked, still watching his face.

"Wondered that myself, Bill, damned if I know."

"Well, ya best all get up and piss if ya want, . . . I'm gonna have to tie ya to these trees for th' night!"

"Do what ya have to do, Bill." He grunted to his feet and turned to relieve himself while Billy woke the others.

"Some more advise, though." Said Childers, watching Wallace, and the other two get up while he buttoned his pants. "Marshal's gonna need food in 'im, . . . won't fight off pneumonia without some energy."

"Got none left." He said, uncoiling the long rope. "Lay back down now."

"Plenty a deer up here." He added as he lay down again.

"Rifle shot would be a good way to tell your "Pard" where we are, too! . . . That what you're thinkin'?"

"You're a very untrusting man, Bill Upshur, . . . that never crossed my mind!"

"I know." He looked up them. "Mister Long, you boys get on your blankets." He tied Childers' feet together, then threaded the rope through his cuffed hands, and arounf the the tree-trunk a couple of times before moving over to Long and doing the same thing, . . . and almost out of rope, moved to tie the feet of Collins'. "Stay put." He said, and went for the other rope.

Done, he tied the end of that rope around a nearby Pine trunk. Satisfied they couldn't free themselves, he went and began the task of swapping hot rocks for cold ones under Rodney's blanket. That done, he sat down again to look around the clearing. It was already dark enough for the trees to show the firelight's reflected flames. The night was closing in fast, he thought, as he watched the darkening treetops, and then closed his eyes while wondering where McCreedy was?

It was a fitful sleep, filled with images of Rodney being knocked from his horse, and falling into a bottomless crater. He was calling for him to help him, but his voice was far away, . . . and all the ropes tied end to end couldn't reach down far enough the help him out . . . He was jerked awake with Melissa's screams in his ears, and quickly looked down at Rodney's sleeping form then shuddered, and reached to feel the blanket he was laying on. The rocks were still fairly warm to the touch, . . . and with a look at the fire, and the rocks he had placed there before dozing off, and knew they must be plenty hot by now. He got to his feet, and spent the next ten minutes swapping out the colder rocks for the hot ones . . . . Childers and crew were all snoring in their sleep, and confident they would not slip away on him, sat back down again.

CHAPTER THIRTEEN

"It's darker than hell in these woods, Joe!" Growled McCreedy. "Near as I can tell, we're around th' mountain, too! . . . So, where do we stop?"

Haskell stopped his horse to look up the side of the tall mountain behind them, and then he looked up the side of the smaller hill beside them, and nodded.

"All right, Mister, McCreedy, . . . maybe this is where we'll see them."

Where, got this fuckin' hill in th' way?"

"From on top of the hill." He replied. "They will stop up there somewhere tonight, start down tomorrow."

"No place up there to camp, that I see!" He said, looking up the brush and tree-covered hill.

"We camp here, climb up in the mornin'."

"Good enough! . . . But right now, I ain't so sure about seein' anything through all those trees, barely can see th' top up there!"

"That's where they are, on top! . . . We can see better in the daylight. From up there, you can see all along the north face. Through the trees, yes, but you can see."

"All right!" He turned to look back at Ellis's dark shape behind them. "We make camp here, Morgan."

"Right here? . . . Place is prob'ly crawlin' with fuckin' snakes!" He complained as he dismounted in the brush.

"Use your feet to tramp down a spot!" Advised Haskell. "Piss a circle around it, . . . messes up a snale's sense of smell, . . . they won't cross it!"

"Never heard a that before."

"You ain't an Indian, neither!"

*　　　　　　*　　　　　　*

Rodney's yelp of pain caused Billy's eyes to pop open in half-panic, and when he saw him sitting up on his blanket and holding his arm, he noticed the cocked pistol in his own hand and puzzled, quickly released the hammer and holstered it before reaching to grab Rodney's good arm. "You okay, Rod?"

"Feeling just came back with a rush, Billy. Hurts like a son of a bitch!"

"I can't help ya with that! . . . How's th' chills, you still cold?"

"Oh, naw, I'm sweatin' now! . . . Shirt's soaked."

He reached to touch Rodney's forehead and found it sweaty, and warm, but not hot to the touch.

"I'm okay, Billy, . . . that cool breeze up here feels damn good!"

"Well, you ain't got a fever . . . . How's th' breathin', hurt when ya breathe deep?"

"No, a little soreness is all. It's my shoulder that's comin' off!"

He took his hunting knife and cut a long strip from one of the blankets then tied the ends together for length, and looped it over Rodney's head and right arm. "Lift your arm and it in th' sling, Rod, it'll help th' pain a little."

Rodney did as he was told and nodded. "Yeah, that's some better, Billy, thanks." He looked across the clearing then and saw the bound prisoners. "It's under control, I see . . . . How long was I out of it?"

"Since a little after mid-day." He pulled his watch then. "It can't be five o'clock in th' afternoon!" He looked up at the star-studded sky then, and shook his head. "Make that, since mid-day yesterday! . . . It's five in th' mornin'!"

"Well, it worked!" Said Rodney, and yelped in pain again when he tried to push himself up. "Jesus!" He moaned as he eased back down.

"What hurts, Rod?"

"Me! . . . I hurt! . . . My back, hips, ass, everything."

"Okay, let's move ya over, you can lean against th' tree." He got to his knees and half-lifted him into position. "How's that?"

"Better." He nodded, and leaned back against the pine trunk. "What hit me back there, Billy, . . . all I remember is th' pain from hittin' that pine sapling?"

"Large tree limb, smaller branches must a been holdin' it up for some time, just picked that time to let go!"

"Layin' in wait for me . . . . Guess that's the answer to my gut feeling."

"Could be."

"What'll we do, Billy, no way I can get on my horse, let alone ride it?"

"We'll keep applyin' th' hot blankets to your back and shoulder today, and again tonight! . . . We'll try to leave at first light tomorrow."

"Any sign a McCreedy?"

"Nothin', . . . they had to of found our tracks when we left th' road. But I ain't heard nothin' that would tell me they was comin' in behind us . . . .

If they was, one a th' horses would a snorted, or all of 'em! . . . I don't know what to make of it yet."

"No gut feeling about it?"

"Nothin' yet . . . . Maybe that Sheriff took our advise, he did, they don't know about th' deer trails."

"Speaking of deer, Billy, . . . we need food!"

"Been thinkin' on that, too! . . . Can't very well hunt somethin', Shot would tell McCreedy where we are . . . . They was followin' us, they'd a been here by now."

"Then where do you think they are?"

"They got an Indian with 'em, Rod . . . . I'd say, they're on the other side a this mountain waitin' for us! . . . Or soon will ne."

"You ain't makin' me feel any better."

"Weren't meant to. But from here on out, I'm gonna be out front!"

"You won't see 'em, Billy, they'll snipe shoot us."

"Yeah, well, . . . that's why, once we get close to th' bottom, we ride side by side with them old boys there, put them between us and McCreedy, . . . and we hit th' bottom at full gallop. Might have a better chance at makin' 'im miss with that sniper gun, and give us a chance to take cover!"

"Amen to that!"

"Well, that's tomorrow, Rod, today, we take care a that back, maybe tomorrow, you'll feel a little more like ridin'"

"We still need food, Billy."

"What do you suggest, Rod, it's out a season for rabbit or squirrel, meat's bad! . . . Got a have bait to trap coon or opossum . . . . Want a kill a horse?"

"Don't tempt me! . . . We're screwed, ain't we?"

"Nope, . . . I saw some berry vines back a ways, ought a be some wild onions around, too . . . . Soon as it gets light, I'll take that empty sack, and maybe, Mister Long there to hold it open, and go lookin'! . . . Who knows, might even get close enough to some game to use my knife, I throw one pretty good, ya know."

"You still practicing?"

"Now and then, . . . it's not really somethin' I need to do well . . . . Sky's gettin' lighter, Rod, I better heat that blanket for ya."

"While I'm enjoying this cool breeze?"

"It's all I know to treat ya with, Rod. It's one a th' times I wish Peter was here, he'd know more about what to do for a bruised back or spine . . . . We got a keep that swelling from goin' down your back, if it does, be a week before you can ride a horse!"

"Better heat that blanket!"

*   *   *

McCreedy opened his eyes and used his finger to rub them briskly. Yawning Mightily, he looked to see the predawn outline of Haskell leaning against a tree. "You get any sleep, Joe, . . . you got a be as tired as we was?"

"Not too much, no."

"Then, what was you thinkin' about, that kept you awake?"

"I'm thinkin' this is a mistake, Mister McCreedy."

"What are you talkin' about, . . . you calling fifty thousand dollars a mistake? . . . That's near-bout seventeen thousand dollars, your part, . . . how's that a mistake?"

"Killin' United States Marshals, Mister McCreedy, that's a mistake! . . . And that money, split four ways only comes to twelve and a half thousand dollars . . . But seven ways, well that comes to almost nothing!"

"You have it all wrong, Joe, that money will be split only three ways."

"That means we'll have to kill all six people, Marshals and all . . . . That's th' mistake, Mister McCreedy, we'll be hunted down like dogs."

"That's th' way it has to be, Joe! . . . You said yes to my proposition in Shreveport, remember? You knew there could be killing . . . . I can't allow you to back out now, we've come too far!"

"I ain't backin' out, Mister McCreedy, I gave my word! . . . I'm just sayon' it's a mistake."

"Well, don't worry about it, we'll bury the evidence." He removed his hat and hit Ellis with it. "Get up, Morgan, we got some climbing to do." He looked back at Haskell then. "You got a spot in mind, Joe?"

"On top, in th' trees . . . . We can see a long way from there."

"Good, . . . how far is that mountaintop, from this one?"

"Three, maybe four hundred yards, but it'll be uphill from us."

"Will that Buffalo Gun shoot that far, Ed?" Queried Ellis.

"A lot farther! . . . I get 'em in them crosshairs, they're dead meat!"

"We best go now, Mister McCreedy, . . . we'll leave th' horses here." He got up and moved through the brush to start up the slanting, tree-covered hill with Ellis on his heels. McCreedy pulled the long-barreled, scoped rifle from the boot and followed them, . . . and by full light, were all seated snugly behind the towering trunks of giant Pines.

"You're right, Joe." Said McCreedy as he stared westward. "Good vantage point from here. They ought a be coming down that north face about eight hundred yards out." He picked up the old Sharps and removed the long scope from it then used it to scan the mountain-top, and the only possible way down the north face of the mountain.

"Fuckin' lawmen won't know what hit 'em!" he exclaimed, laying it across his lap.

"You sure, Ed, . . . that thing's a single-shot?"

"Shee-it!! . . . I'll have two rounds on th' way before they ever hear th' first shot, at eight hundred yards." He picked up the scope and affixed it to the rifle then raised the gun to look again. "Took this gun off a dead buffalo hunter, Joe." He said as he pulled it down and ran his hand along the barrel.

"That was after he shot th' fella, Joe." Added Ellis.

"He was dead, was he not!" He raised the gun again to peer through the scope at the mountain, but brought it down before long. "Gun gets heavy real quick, . . . Joe, drag that dead limb over here." He waited while the limb was put in place, and tried it again, by laying the long gun across it.

"Not perfect, but it'll work! . . . I see an open area off yonder, about thirty yards up from th' bottom, . . . that's where I'll nail 'em! . . . Now, if I can just catch some movement up there, tellin' me they're on th' move."

"What if they're down already, and long gone, Ed?" Queried Ellis.

"Morgan, if we couldn't get through that mess in th' dark, . . . neither could they!"

"Think they could, Joe?" He asked, reaching to touch Haskell's arm.

"If they found a deer-trail, maybe."

"But not likely." Replied McCreedy, his eyes still glued to the scope. "Right, Joe?"

"Maybe, yes."

"Okay, Ed." Breathed Ellis. "But I'm tellin' you right now, this, right here, is as close as I'm gonna get to Fort Smith ever again."

"Thought you said, within five miles, Morgan?"

"I changed my mind."

"You gonna leave, Morgan?"

"I'm of a mind to, we ain't seen 'em by tomorrow mornin'. Damn straight!"

"Gonna miss ya, if ya go, man." He took his eye from the scope and looked at him. "But I would hope you wouldn't . . . . We're a burr under each other's saddle at times, but we been together a long time, . . . we need each other." He grinned and went back to watching the mountain.

*   *   *

Rodney was sitting against the tree with his pistol on his lap when Billy and Long entered the clearing, and watched as Billy told Long to sit down again before coming across the clearing with the bulging, red-stained flour-sack.

"Half a sack of th' biggest, juiciest berries I ever saw, Rod! . . . Cup your hand." He dumped his hand full with the fat blackberries and watched him eat a mouthful. "Sweet, huh?" He went back across the clearing then to fill the waiting hands of all four prisoners before coming back to sit down and dip more into Rodney's hand.

"Eat up, Rod, it'll help get your strength back." He grinned and ate a mouthful himself. "Got half-dozen small wild onions, too, a bit spicy, but good!" He ate more of the berries, and filled Rodney's hand again. "You try to get up yet?"

"Not yet."

"You get done, I'll help ya up to walk around a bit . . . . How's th' arm feel?"

"A constant, throbbing pain, Billy . . . . Shoulder's trying to swell up, I think."

"That's expected, we'll put more heat on it in a while, after you walk."

"Billy, . . . if I'd hit that sapling any way, but what I did, I'd a broke my back!"

"You was lucky it was there at all, Rod . . . . I couldn't even see th' bottom a that gorge . . . . Want a Leek?"

"What?"

"Want a onion?"

"No, . . . not into spicy today, not on top of all these berries." He accepted more of the fat berries and continued to eat. "Berries are damn good, though." He looked back across the clearing then.

"Don't guess you seen anything of McCreedy?"

"He knows we're up here somewhere, Rod. That Indian read our trail at th' road, . . . if he's any good, he convinced McCreedy to circle around to th' north and wait for us."

"And that don't worry ya none?"

"Sure it does, but it ain't gonna rule my life. They ain't gonna shoot us till we come off this hill, and even then, they'll have to shoot through those boys to hit one of us." He got up then and carried the rest of the berries to Childers, giving him the sack.

"Pass 'em along, Ben." Nodding, he went back to stand in front of Rodney. "You ready?"

"As I'll ever be!" He reached up with his good arm to grip Billy's hand, and when Billy gripped his upper arm, he pulled his legs under him and pushed up as Billy pulled. "Ahhhhh, Christ!" He gasped as he gained his feet, and leaned back against the tree to get his breath. He took Billy's hand again and slowly walked across the polished rock to the horses, and back again.

"Legs are a little weak, Billy, but it don't hurt to walk."

"That's a good start, . . . want a sit down again?"

"Oh, no! . . . Let go of me, I'm gonna walk around a bit.

Nodding, he let go and stepped back for a minute before moving back to the prisoners.

"Say, Bill?" Voiced Childers then. "Think you might untie my feet, my bladder's runnin' over?"

"Yeah, sure!" He freed them and coiled the ropes as he watched them all get up to frantically loosen their pants and relieve themselves. He replaced the ropes on the saddles and turned back as they buttoned up.

"Stretch your legs a bit, if ya want . . . . Just remember what I told ya."

"Are you really that good, Bill?" Queried Childers with a curious grin.

"Would you bet your life on it, Ben?" Asked Rodney as he walked.

Billy went to stand beside the horses to watch Rodney, and the other men walk the stiffness in their legs away, . . . and especially Ben Childers. As he did, he wondered what would make a man with his obvious self-esteem turn to robbery and murder for a living? The man was a gunslinger, or had been, he could tell by the way he held himself, and walked. Yes, he thought, Mister Ben Childers was a thinking man, a convincing man . . . . And dangerous, if given the chance! . . . He remembered the tingle in his neck at the jail in Shreveport. He knew then what he was, could feel the unspoken challenge that passed between them.

Ben Childers was a man capable of manipulating other men's minds, and their way of thinking, . . . had even tried to work it on him! He even knew that McCreedy wouldn't quit until he was free again, for whatever reason that might be.

He pushed the thoughts aside then and watched Rodney's efforts to walk away the pain in his hips, and legs, and grinned at his determination. He had become a hell of a man, a damn good one, he thought, and there was no better lawman anywhere. He frowned then, thinking, that at times, he was able to detect a little of Ben Lang in the way he worked. He thought of Lang then, and still couldn't find a way to really hate him . . . . He looked up then, and grinned when Rodney approached.

"How's th' legs, Rod?"

"It ain't th' legs so much, Billy. It's th' hips . . . . Pains me some when I walk . . . . But nothing's broke, they work! . . . I'll be ready to go by mornin', you can count on that!" He became serious then.

"I remember it now, Billy . . . . I saw that limb falling, and couldn't react to it, . . . if I had, me, horse and all might a gone over that cliff, and pulled them right in on top of me! All I could do, was take my foot from th' stirrup and go over. Scared hell out a me! . . . Thought I was a goner."

"You are a lucky man."

"In more ways than one!" He looked across at Childers then. "I saw you watchin' Childers, Billy . . . . He's a gunman, ya know."

"I know."

"He was a gun for hire, I think, called himself Ben Calico . . . . Asked me a lot a questions about you, that night on th' road . . . . He thinks he can beat ya."

"Maybe he can, or could!" Nodded Billy, and also watched him. "But without a gun, he's just a braggart."

"Wish I had your attitude, Billy . . . . I know he's gonna hang, but he still worries me."

"Don't let 'im get in your head, Rod, . . . it appears that's what he did, too! But, if you're worried about yourself, don't, . . . I've seen you in action."

"You're right, I think he did, . . . guess I was a little vulnerable, after that snake thing. Next I knew, I was givin' 'im names of men you killed . . . . Didn't realize what he was doin' till after, . . . and that's enough to worry me!"

"He has a talent, that's for sure."

"He ain't got to you, yet, how's that?"

"I won't let 'im!"

"And you say, I shopuldn't worry!" He turned to continue his walking then, leaving Billy to watch the prisoners . . . . And thinking it enough time, he walked toward them.

"Okay, gents, that ought a do it! . . . Sit down against your tree, and stay put." He watched them grudgingly comply.

"Don't give me any trouble, I won't tie ya down till tonight." He started to turn, but stopped and looked back. "I'm about to go shave now, and those of you who want a shave that crap off your face, I'll loan ya my razor?" All of them reached up to feel their heavy beards.

"It has been a while." Nodded Childers. "Lake wouldn't give us a razor, knife, or bath water . . . . I'd appreciate that, Bill."

"Why you so suddenly bein' so fuckin' nice?" Growled Wallace.

"Ain't had an outburst from you in a while, Wallace, had me worried! . . . But, if don't want a shave, it's fine with me?"

"Fuck you, lawman! . . . Asshole."

"Shut up, Lionel!" Snapped Childers.

"Fuck you, too, Ben Childers, you God damn chizzler!"

"He must like you a lot!" Grinned Billy.

"Who, Lionel, he's my Pard, . . . he just don't like anybody!" He grinned then. "I'd appreciate that razor, Bill."

"Soon as we shave, it's your turn." He went to his satchel for shaving mug and razor, took out the strop and went across to Rodney's blankets. Sitting down, he poured water into the soapy mug, and lathered his face.

"Good idea." Said Rodney as he came back to lean against the tree and watch.

"You want a go first, Rod?"

"No, . . . I'll wait my turn, too. In fact, I'll just walk over and get my own razor." He pushed away from the tree and left again, leaving Billy to his duty.

Giving Rodney the mug to lather his face, he then took it, razor and all across the clearing to Childers. When he was done, Rodney came to stand beside him, as Childers used the razor to, first, cut the beard to a short-stubble, then used the strop to re-sharpen it, and shaved his face clean . . . . Nodding his thanks, he accepted the small towel, wet it from the canteen and cleaned his face before passing it all over to a waiting Collins.

"Many thanks, Bill." He said, running his hand over his face. "I almost feel human again."

"I doubt you been human for a while now." Replied Billy, and saw the smile fade from Childers' face, and his eyes harden.

"What about you, gunfighter?" He smiled then. "Yeah, I know what you are, just not sure who you are?"

"There's a big difference between you and him, Ben." Interrupted Rodney. "He don't kill for pleasure!"

"And I do?"

"You kill because ya can!" Said Billy. "Or did! . . . When did you become a thief?"

Childers' eyes softened then. "Five years ago, . . . not bad, Bill! . . . I was hired by a big spread in northern Montana, wanted me to stop a gang of rustlers from stealing his herd . . . . When I did, he wouldn't pay up! Instead, he had a dozen hands rough me up, and run me off . . . . Man stold a thousand dollars from me, by usin' force. I was easy pickings. That's when I changed my occupation."

"And wound up here!" Added Rodney.

"You're not bad yopurself, Marshal! . . . By th' way, thanks for not lettin' your horse go over that rim with ya, saved our lives."

"Wasn't doin' you no favor, Ben, . . . but you're welcome."

"When you gonna tell me who you really are, Bill, . . . or was?"

"When you gonna tell me why McCreedy's after us?"

Grinning, Childers sat down on his blanket laid down, and then covered his face with his hat.

Billy looked at Rodney and shrugged, who only nodded and walked away. Sighing, he pulled his watch to check the time. Almost noon, he thought wearily. They would have no choice, but to leave tomorrow, and the dread was already building on his mind. Considering what he thought to be true, that McCreedy had in fact circled around the mountain they were on, he was beginning to worry about their chances. Because if that was what happened, they would surely be ambushed . . . . And if they did keep the four men between them, McCreedy was said to be a Union Sniper. He would have possession of a large caliber rifle, making their preventive tactic much less appealing unless one of them used Childers as a shield. That, he thought, just might be the only way to keep Rodney alive, . . . he would make sure to put him next to Childers before reaching the bottom!

Regret was weighing heavily on his mind, as well, because, he thought, he should have dropped back and stopped then three days ago. He sighed then, thinking it too late for regrets. He looked down at Childers' prone form then and knew he was awake, . . . it was only mid-day!

"Ben," He said. "Pretending you're asleep only prolongs th' questions, and ignoring th' questions ain't gonna help . . . . Because your "Pard" will pay a high price to get you back, and if he does, I'll kill 'im for it!, . . . And then I'll kill you!" He turned away then as Long finished shaving and washing the razor and mug with water, and walked over to take them from him.

"Ready to pick some more berries, man?"

"When you are, Marshal/"

*   *   *

McCreedy replaced the watch and stared angrily at Haskell. "You sure about this, Joe, cause they damn sure ain't commin' off that mountain yet?"

"I'm sure," He nodded. "Their trail led to th' mountain, only other way, was th' way we came., . . . and there was no trail!"

"Then what th' hell are they doin' up there?"

"They know we're here, Ed!" Said Ellis. "That's the only thing it could be."

"How could they, Morgan, you tell me that!"

"Don't know, but one of 'em's got a lot a savvy."

"Bull shit, Morgan. They wouldn't a camped in th' road, they knew we was comin'!"

"Bull shit, or not, . . . it's hotter'n hell up here . . . . Sweat's runnin' down th' crack a my ass!"

"They got a be up there!"

"Hope they got supplies, if they are, cause we sure don't!"

"They're there, Mister, McCreedy." Assured Haskell. "You would have seen movement in the trees, if they were coming down."

"All right then! . . . This being our last chance at Childers, . . . and that bank money, . . . if we don't see some kind a movement up there by daylight tomorrow, we'll go up and get 'em!"

"That's crazy, Ed, we'll get our fuckin' ass shot off!" Exclaimed Ellis. "Them bastards up there ain't dumb-asses! . . . They know what they're doin', I'm tellin' ya!" He took his hat and bandana off to wipe his face and neck. "This ain't about th' money, anyway, you already told us that story about your self-esteem, . . . self-esteem won't do you a bit a good, if your dead!"

"God damn it, Morgan, that's right! . . . But killin' him will do that, and that's what I intend to do! But I want that money, too, it's ours, . . . and he stole it from us! What's wrong with you, anyway, Morgan, you never backed down on a fight before?"

"We always knew what we was doin' before, . . . you planned it, and we did it! . . . Your plans ain't fuckin' workin' here, . . . and this time we're gonna lose! . . . Come on, Ed, you ain't been yourself since he ran off with that money, . . . well, since we broke 'em out a jail, anyway. But he screwed all of us, and we let 'im do it! . . . It's time we cut our losses and ran."

McCreedy glared angrily at him for a time before finally nodding. "Tell ya what, Morgan, . . . if we don't spot 'em by morning, we'll do it your way."

"Now, you're talkin', Ed! . . . Hell, th' three of us can steal that much money in a week, what with you plannin' it, and us doin' it, . . . right, Joe?"

McCreedy watched him for another minute then raised the rifle again to peer through the scope at the mountain. 'We'll leave', he thought angrily. 'Like hell'!

*   *   *

He helped Rodney sit down against the tree again. "How's that?" He asked, standing up to look down at him.

"Feels pretty good, . . . kind a wore myself out."

"Ya think so, . . . hell, ya been pacing this rock for more'n a hour! . . . But, that fall took a lot out of ya, th' chills, too! Hell, I'm tired myself . . . . Think you're up to watchin' th' prisoners again?"

"Nothin' wrong with my gun arm, . . . why?"

"Thought I'd take Long, and get some more berries."

Nodding, Rodney pulled his pistol and checked the action and loads. Before laying it across his lap. "If you're waitin' on me, you're backin' up!"

"Good, be back in an hour." He walked across the clearing to stand at Childers' feet then.

"I'm takin' mister Long to get more berries, Gents." He eyed them all sternly. "Th' Marshal there is hurt, but he's alive and able, and th' best shot up here! . . . Try anything while I'm gone, and he'll plug ya . . . . You want a get up, get permission first, you do manage to run, I'll hunt ya down." He nodded at Long, and followed him out into the trees.

"How are ya feeling, Marshal?" Queried Childers from his bedroll. "You look all played out from all that walkin'?"

"Looks like shit to me!" Mouthed Wallace.

Rodney held up the pistol and cocked it. "Mister Wallace, I can trim your hair like a barber from here, or I can shoot your eyes out! . . . Likw Billy said, I ain't dead! . . . Now lay back, and shut up! . . . You, too, Ben."

Billy was back in less than an hour, and after sitting Long down again, came on to kneel by Rodney. "Any trouble?" He asked, opening the berry-stained bag.

"Not a bit!" He held his hand out while Billy filled his palm with berries agin. "Couldn't find a steak anywhere, Billy?"

"Fresh out, everywhere I looked." He said, turning to watch the prisoners. "Spread your bandana on your lap, Rod."

"My bandana, why?"

"To hold th' berries." He waited while he removed it then helped him spread it out before filling it with the juicy berries. He got up then and went to share them with the others.

"Berries don't do much for a man, Bill." Said Childers when he came back by him.

"Works for bears." He grinned, stopping to look down at him.

"You know McCreedy's up here somewhere, don't ya, Bill?"

"Yeah," He replied, and squatted down in front of him. "He's here somewhere."

"That don't worry you none?"

Billy shrugged. "Getting' up in th' mornin' worries me, Ben."

"He could be closing in on ya right now, does that worry ya?"

"If he does, he'll never find out where you hid that money."

"You'd shoot a chained-up, unarmed man?"

"I would!"

"Marshal said you wouldn't kill for pleasure."

"I'd get no pleasure from it, I just wouldn't give McCreedy any!"

"You're a strange man, Bill, I swear you are! . . . I don't know whether to like ya, or hate ya."

"Lot a men are limited that way!"

"Is Bill Upshur your whole name, or just th' one you're usin' now? . . . Tell me, why don't ya, see if I ever heard of ya?"

"You ain't . . . Same as you ain't got no money hid! . . . Why's he after us so hard?"

"I told ya, we're Pards, that's all, . . . there ain't no money!" As Billy nodded, and got to his feet. "What do ya think a that?"

"I think you shouldn't a changed professions." He went back to sit down whith Rodney.

"How's th' shoulder, Rod?"

"Even hurts when I move my fingers."

"Might be a broke bone in your shoulder somewhere."

"I figure, th' collarbone is, can't put a splint on that! . . . Gettin' late again, ain't it?"

"Two-thirty, quarter a three, I guess." He reached into the bag and ate a handful of berries.

"He tell ya where McCreedy is?"

"Said he was here, asked me if I knew it?"

"Where do you think he is?"

"Rod, . . . if I was a sniper with a big gun, one with a scope on it, . . . I'd be down below this mountain somewhere watchin' for us. Can't see us for th' trees, but he'll se us movin through 'em, once we start . . . . I ain't really went to the rim out there for a look down yet, but there's got a be another hill, or high point down there for them to hold up on. I'll go into th' trees over yonder later for a look."

"What kind a gun you think he's got?"

"Like I said before, likely a buffalo gun, Sharps, maybe. Or a Springfield, . . . that Kragg a yours would make a good one! . . . I don't know, Rod."

"Buffalo gun, . . . Damn things will shoot a mile!"

"He won't be no more than a thousand yards away, if that many! . . . Won't even hear th' shot that hits us."

"What'll we do?"

"Nothin' we can do, but try and make 'im miss . . . . When we get close to th' bottom, you loosen that tow-rope and move back beside Childers, knee to knee! I'll move up beside Long, bullet will have to go through them to hit us, and it won't be that easy anyway, we'll be at full gallop, and he'll be shootin through trees . . . . Take a lucky shot to hit us."

"Yeah, well I ain't been so lucky lately, either!"

"Sure ya have, you're still here, ain't ya?"

"Point taken."

"We ain't dead yet, Rod." He grinned. "We still got a job to do."

"Amen to that! . . . Help me up, will ya, I want a walk some more."

*   *   *

Haskell and Ellis both had their shirt and vests off, and were still wiping sweat from their face with bandanas. McCreedy, with bandana in hand, was still glued to the rifle's scope, moving the long gun from mountain top, all the way down the north slope, . . . and mouthing a soft curse each time he failed to see anything. He finally pulled the gun down and removed his hat to wipe his face before looking at them both.

"One a you take over, okay?" He moved aside to let Haskell by him then sat down on another of the dead logs. "My fuckin' eyes hurt!"

"Still think they're up there, Ed?"

"Beats hell out a me!" He growled. "Joe's an Indian, he seems to think so, . . . he ain't been wrong yet!"

"Always a first time."

"I got a feelin' they're up to somethin' up there . . . . I'd just like to know what?"

"Could be, they got one a them scopes, too, Ed . . . . Could be watchin' us right now."

"I thought a that, Morgan, but we're fairly well hidden down here, thick trees and all, . . . but they likely got a good, cool breeze, bein' that high up!" . . . And you're right, they could be just waitin' us out."

"That mean, you finally admit they might know we're here?"

"I admit it's possible, nothin' else!"

"They just might be able to wait us out, too, . . . because, right now, come tomorrow mornin', my gut's gonna be eatin' at my backbone!"

"We got any jerky left?"

"Couple a sticks, down on my horse."

"Put on your shirt, and go get 'em, why don't ya?"

"Yeah," He sighed. "Why don't I?"

McCreedy watched him until he dropped from sight then looked up through the trees at the mountain. 'What are they doing up there', he wondered? . . . And were they even there at all? Ellis was right, he thought then, he was out to restore his pride, and his vanity wouldn't allow him to give up. Until Ben Childers, no man had ever bested him at anything, and he would kill him for it! . . . 'After he takes us to the hidden money'. That, he thought, would be the bonus! . . . But, . . . Childers would have to believe that all was okay, that he was still in solid with them . . . . He smiled then, . . . not a problem!

He had been so sure of him, he remembered angrily, had even had long term plans for a partnership with him, Collins and Long. 'Childers made fools of us all, even Collins and Long was in on it with him', he thought. Hell, they even went their separate ways, too, like it was all on the up and up! . . . 'Worked, too', he thought, until he found out all three were in prison together. But even then, he hadn't been sure enough to suspect they all three had not been caught separately, . . . and just wound up there together.

'I know now, Ben'!, he thought selfishly. 'I know it all, . . . but it ain't gonna be your way anymore, old son, . . . it's all gonna be my way'! He watched Haskell then, as he intently peered through the scope, and thought it great that the Indian showed him the respect now, that he had been used to in the war. He had been called Mister then as well. He liked the Indian, he thought, and he spoke better English than Morgan Ellis! . . . He would keep Joe with him, when this was over.

Ellis came back then and gave him a stick of the rolled up jerky, which he cut in half, and shared with Haskell. "See anything, Joe?"

"Only a deer in that clearing, you talked about, but no sign of the Marshals . . . . But, they are still there!"

"How do you know?" Queried Ellis as he chewed.

"Only an Indian would take so many hours needed to fool his enemies, by going where they were not expected to go."

"Run that by me again, Joe!" Exclaimed Ellis.

"Okay, . . . We know, that they know we are here, they just don't know where . . . . An Indian would go down the west side a that mountain, and even farther before turning north again . . . . A white man would not take th' time, and he wouldn't veer away from his destination . . . . Even you, Morgan, would come down th' north side, because north goes to Fort Smith."

"By God, Morgan, I think he's right, time means nothing to an Indian, but everything to a white man! . . . Good Job, Joe, I'll try not to forget that!"

"You both lost me!" Said Ellis. "Makes white men out to be idiots! . . . Hell, we wiped out th' Indians, remember? Sent th' rest to reservations."

"How did you do it, Morgan?" Asked Haskell . . . . You outnumbered the Indian, that's how! . . . And I'm not putting you down, Morgan, don't get mad. Your way, is my way now, we're friends! . . . I only answered a question."

"I ain't mad, Joe, shit! . . . I just never thought about it."

"I know, . . . but just so you know, Quanah Parker's Comanche ain't surrendered yet. He's still kickin' white men's ass!" He went back to searching the mountain again.

"He's somethin' else, Ed."

"Yes, he is . . . . A good man to have around." He checked his watch again. "I'll take over again, Joe."

*   *   *

"Getting' any easier, Rod?" Asked Billy, coming to walk beside him.

"Yeah, it is! . . . just a twinge now and then . . . . Right now, it's my back that catches, when I move a little wrong . . . . But I'll work it out!"

"I know ya will. Just don't walk too close out there, they got a scope on that gun."

"Amen to that! . . . You get a look over the edge yet?"

"Some, . . . I think I might know where they are, can't be sure though . . . . I'll take another look in a bit."

"Well, let me lnow."

Grinning, he went back toward the horses, when he saw Wallace get to his knees. "No sudden moves, Wallace!"

"I got a fuckin' piss, okay? . . . Jesus!"

"Okay, Wallace, . . . rest of ya got a go, do it now." He stood and watched until they were all seated again.

"How long we stayin' here, Bill?" Queried Childers.

He walked over to squat at his feet again. "Decided to talk again, huh? . . . What's th' big hurry, you ain't sweatin', th' wind's cool? Couldn't ask for any more! . . . So why ask a dumb question, when you know th' answer?"

"Conversation, somethin' to do." He shrugged.

"All right, conversation it is, tell me about your Pard."

"McCreedy? . . . I only knew 'im for six weeks before he broke us out . . . . He's a damn good man when it comes to planning things out, weighing th' odds and such. Good with mathmatics, and has a pocket full a war medals, all for his service as a Union Sniper! . . . Oh, yeah, he has a large caliber rifle with scope, carries it in a special boot on his saddle . . . . He's also equipped with th' largest ego a man ever had!"

"Ego?"

"His love for self, Bill."

"Why does he want you so bad, and don't give me that Pard, shit?"

"That's all it is, Bill. He likes me, what can I say?"

"Dot a damn thing!" Said Billy, and got to his feet.

"Come on, Bill, I told you about Ed, want a know about me?"

"I know about you, Ben. You're a gunslinger with as big a one a them egos as McCreedy has . . . . But I will answer one a your questions, just so you'll know . . . . On th' best day you ever had, I'd kill ya!" He nodded and continued on to the horses then, leaving a frowning Ben Childers in his wake.

"Found somebody you can't fuck with, ain't ya, Ben?" Grinned Wallace.

"Shut th' fuck up, Lionel!"

"You ain't much in a position to make me, Ben! . . . Ha, ha, ha!" He laughed loudly. "Ben Childers met his match!"

"That's enough, Wallace!" Snapped Billy. "Unless you'd like to answer my questions?"

"Fuck you!"

"Then shut up!" He saw Rodney going back toward his blankets then and went to help him.

"I can do it, Billy!" He went to his knees, and sat down against the tree. "Getting' better all th' time."

"I'll say." He grinned, and sat down beside him. "We'll do th' hot rocks again tonight, and leave early."

"Amen to that! . . . Can't wait to get shot at, get th' blood flowing, know what I mean?"

"I weren't lookin' at it quite like that, Rod."

"Me, neither!" He breathed deeply then, and nodded toward Childers. "What was Wallace cacklin' about?"

"Just bein' Wallace! . . . Be glad to be rid a that bunch."

"Saw you talkin' with Childers again, learn anything?"

"Nothin' we don't know already . . . . Tried, I think, to say that McCreedy's ego was why he was so persistent in stoppin' us."

"And you don't believe 'im."

Billy looked at him with a frown. "Not unless ego is spelled, money! . . . I'm convinced there's a lot a money involved in this . . ."

"It's th' stuff most men die for, Billy, including us!"

"Don't write us off yet!"

"I won't! . . . Where do ya think that high point might be?"

"Where they're hidin'? . . . Like I said, I didn't get a good look. There's not much more than a million Pine Trees there, and about that many places to hide." He looked out at the treetops then. "See them taller trees yonder, Rod? . . . I think there's another hill down there, about five hundred yards out, and about three hundred down . . . . Man with a rifle scope would have a pretty good view of this whole mountain, and maybe even see th' north slope, . . . our way down!"

"Then he knows where we are!"

"Not likely, too much wind up here to see smoke from th' fire, might not think we're here at all . . . . What I do think, is that, that Choctaw Indian is what's keepin' 'em from goin' home."

"How?"

"I'd have to think like an Indian to know that, Rod. It's just a gu . . . ."

"Gut feeling!" He said quickly, causing Billy to grin."

"I guess it is." He looked back at the treetops again. "As long as we stay away from that rim, they won't see us."

"You said they could see th' north slope, . . . how far away would it be?"

"Like I told ya, under a thousand yards . . . . In range, if that'll make ya feel better? . . . But he'll have to shoot through gaps in a thousand tree trunks, . . . and a million branches to hit us, so stop worryin' about all that!"

"If he's as good a sniper, as he's made out to be, he could do it!"

"Even at a gallop, Rod? . . . Best he could do is hit one a th' horses, and pile us up. Be tricky as hell to hit one of us!"

"If we did pile up, and ir didn't break our necks, . . . we'd be easy pickings . . . . What's our odds, Billy?"

"At that distance, sixty-forty, in our favor."

"Like fallin' off a log!" Nodded Rodney. "Well, I ain't no gambler, but I have learned that, at poker, them ain't bad odds!"

"Where'd you hear that?"

"I'd rather not bring up bad memories, Billy."

"You heard it from Lang, right?"

"Not long after he hired me."

"That, . . . don't bother me anymore, Rod."

"I know that, but bad memories are best left alone . . . . What time's it getting' to be?"

He pulled the watch, wound it a bit then opened the lid. "Quarter of five! . . . Time flies when you're havin' fun!"

"Well, it ain't much fun to me." He said, pulling up his legs to get to his knees. "But I need to walk some more before we start them hot rocks again." Using the tree, and good arm, he pushed to his feet again and walked off toward the horses.

He watched him for a minute then scanned the silent faces of Childers, and the other men as they also watched him. Sighing, he then stared out at the waving tops of the tall Pines just off the rocky ledge of rock, finding himself wondering just how tall that hill might be below them. If it was tall enough, they might see into the clearing enough to tell they were here? . . . He discarded that, thinking there was total shadows where they were, that noon was the only time there was not!

Besides, with what Childers had said about McCreedy, and as hot as it had to be where they are, he was not so sure McCreedy would not have chanced a shot at them. No, he thought, he didn't believe they could know where they are, . . . and they didn't find the deer trail, or even know about it . . . . In fact, he thought, his first theory had to be right, . . . the Choctaw had led them around the mountain. They were definitely down there, and that hill was their only vantage point to watch the mountain from. 'That's where they are', he thought drearily, and he has that sniper rifle with him! . . . He pushed the cloudy thoughts from his mind, folded his arms around his drawn-up knees, and watched Rodney.

*   *   *

It was close to sundown when Wallace once again had a bladder problem, and as Billy got up and went to watch them, Rodney went back to sit down against the tree.

Once the prisoners were seated again, he went to add more wood to the small fire, and push the stones into place again, to heat up.

"Guess they did th' trick, huh, Bill" Asked Childers.

"Looks that way, Ben, . . . thanks."

"Any time, Bill."

Billy nodded. "Guess ya know, I got a tie ya down again tonight."

"Looked forward to it all day, Bill." Grinned Childers, and drawing up his legs as he leaned back on the tree. "All day long!"

*   *   *

"What now, Ed?" Queried Ellis as he brought down the gun, and propped it against a tree. "Can't see a thing in th' dark, have to wait for th' moon! Or wait till mornin'!"

"We don't see 'em then, we leave, right?"

"Yeah, . . . we'll leave, Morgan . . . . We'll give 'em till noon tomorrow, then go." He looked at Haskell's dark outline then.

"Guess they was more Indian than you thought, huh, Joe?"

"No, they're up there, Mister McCreedy."

"Well then, tell me how you fuckin' know that, Joe? . . . And don't give me any more a your Indian lore, or legends! . . . I'm about at the end a my Patience here!"

"I can see 'em!"

"What?" He gasped. "You see 'em, where?"

"Look up there, Mister McCreedy, at th' top . . . . See th' firelight on th' trees?"

Both of them stared up through the trees then, and finally, McCreedy slapped Haskell on the back.

"Ahaaa!, . . . God damn!" He exclaimed. "They got a fuckin' fire goin' up there, whole place is lit up!" He sat down and grabbed the rifle, pointing it upward to stare through the scope. "There's a rock outcropping up there, couldn't see it in th' daylight." He adjusted the scope for more clarity and continued to look. "I can see shadows on th' trees, somebody's moving back and forth . . . . That's okay, though, I can watch and wait. One of 'em's bound to come into my sights, and when he does, he's mine!" He looked at them then. "You boys just sit tight, this thing's about over!"

*   *   *

Billy was still sitting on his blanket, when Rodney started back, and was grinning widely when he dropped to his knees. "Had enough?"

"I'm wore out!" He nodded, sitting back on his legs. "It's getting' easier though, I'll be ready in th' mornin'."

"Th' rocks are about ready when you are. Won't take that swelling down, but it'll help your back a lot!"

"In a minute, Billy, right now, sitting like this feels pretty good!" He looked out past the rocky rim then. "What is it, eight, nine o'clock?"

"Don't matter, it's dark . . . . But you need to at least lean against that tree, your legs could cramp up."

"Yeah, you're right." He got to his knees again, and sat down to rest against the tree. "That's better, too."

"Well you rest a minute, Rod. I'll go let our bad guys empty their bladders before I tie 'em up for th' night."

"Sure, go on, this feels good. I'll lay down in a minute."

*   *   *

McCreedy adjusted the scope again and continued to look, seeing Rodney as he leaned back on the tree. "I see one of 'em!" He said excitedly. "Sittin' against a tree up there, one a th' Marshals, too! . . . Can't see nothin' but his head, and part of a shoulder, . . . but it's enough!"

"You ain't gonna try a shot now, are ya?" Queried Ellis. "It's too risky, Ed, you miss, they'll know we're here!"

"They already know, Morgan! . . . And we're about to have one less lawman to worry about!"

"Come on, Ed, . . . think about this! . . . Th' dark can play tricks on a man, . . . I'm tellin' ya, it's too risky. You ain't gonna hit nothin'!"

"I think I will, Morgan. But even if I don't, it'll flush 'em out a there. Make 'em head for that north slope."

CHAPTER FOURTEEN

"You feelin' okay, Rod?" Asked Billy as he squatted to pick up a blanket.

"Yeah, I'm okay, what are you doin'?"

"I'm gonna use this blanket to bring th' hot rocks over."

"Got th' prisoners tied down?"

"Not yet, thought I'd wait as long as I could . . . . You sure you're okay?"

"Yeah, . . . just dead tired, and sleepy as hell!" He grinned, and then leaned toward his blanket to lie down, and in that split second, that part of the tree, where his head had been, exploded outward as the bullet gouged a two inch wide deep furrow in the pine trunk, showering Billy with bark and sap, . . . and knocking him to his back on the gritty rock.

He was quickly on his feet, as the thunderous shot echoed through the trees, and with pistol in hand, ran to the rock ledge to fan all six loads down in the direction of the hill below. Doing so before the explosions echoed away. He quickly backed off the ledge and ducking, ran back to squat beside an ashen-faced Rodney.

"My God, Rod, you okay?"

Rodney looked up at the ragged furrow in the tree before looking at Billy. "That's where my head was, man!"

"I know, Rod, . . . you ain't hurt, are ya?"

"Pissed all over myself, is all!" He raised up on an elbow and looked at the prisoners. "Where's Childers, Billy?"

He whirled around to look at the vacant tree, then at Wallace, and the other two before getting up to confront them.

"Where's Childers?" He asked harshly. "Where is he, Wallace?"

"Fuck, I don't know, we was all watchin' you!"

"Collins, Long, you see 'im leave?"

"No, sir, Marshal." Returned Long." Like Lionel said, we was watchin' you th' whole time!"

"Son of a bitch!" He pulled his pistol and quickly reloaded it then looked at Rodney. "Watch 'em, Rod, . . . I'll see if I can find 'im." He went into the trees behind where Childers had been sitting, and disappeared.

*   *   *

"God damn it!" Yelled Ellis as the bullet creased his arm. They all ducked then as two more slugs struck the tree trunks around them, . . . and then there was nothing but the echoes of gunfire fading away.

"Son of a bitch damn near shot me!" Gasped Ellis as he checked his arm.

"You hit bad, Morgan?" Queried McCreedy.

"Just a scratch, burns like hell . . . . Damn sure could a been bad!"

"Man knows his way around a hand gun!" Breathed McCreedy. "Elevation and windage! . . . Not many would know that, and very few would automatically consider it when returning fire . . . . That's a dangerous man up there, boys!"

"Ya think, Ed, . . . I been tellin' ya that for days!"

"I know, Morgan . . . . But them was lucky shots, never th' less." He said, looking back at the clearing. "He was just guessin' at where we was."

"No, Mister McCreedy," Said Haskell. "He was not guessing . . . . Four rounds hit the trees out there, two came here."

"Why not use a rifle then, Joe?"

"He weren't expecting to be shot at, Mister McCreedy, . . . no time."

"Well, there's just one of 'em now! One less to worry about."

"You real sure you hit 'im, Ed?"

"Morgan, I can strike a match with this gun at that distance . . . . I got 'im!"

"Mister McCreedy," Said Haskell. "If he is dead, there ought a be blood on that tree up there, a lot of it!"

McCreedy hastily looked again then lowered the gun. "I don't fuckin' believe it! . . . I never missed a shot like that in my whole life."

"No blood, huh, Ed"

"No, God damn it, there ain't no blood!"

Then, all we got is a Mexican stand-off . . . . They know we're watchin' th' north slope now, too . . . . Know what that means, don't ya?"

"No, what does that mean, Morgan?"

"Means they'll be thinkin' like an Indian does, right, Joe?"

"They might, . . . maybe not, too. No one knows."

"They'll take th' back way down, Ed, . . . you can count on it!"

"We'll wait till mornin' anyway." Growled McCreedy. "Won't be th' first time we lost a bet . . . . Anyway, they ain't gone yet, wouldn't leave a fire burnin' like that."

"They are there." Agreed Haskell.

*   *   *

Billy was back in an hour, scratched, some bloody, and tired. Walking up to the fire where Rodney was standing to watch the prisoners, he shook his head to Rodney's unasked question. "He's gone, Rod! . . . I could hear 'im crashing through th' brush ahead a me somewhere, but I couldn't catch up." He looked at the remaining prisoners then.

"Wallace, Collins, you, too, Long. Move over by th' fire and sit, we got a talk . . . . I ain't askin', damn it!"

"All right!" Mouthed Wallace as all three got to their feet and came forward.

"Sid sown right there." And when they did. "Stretch your legs out in front a ya."

"What th' fuck you gonna do, man?" Asked Wallace. "We didn't see 'im leave."

"No, but you damn well know where he' goin'! Now sit still and listen . . . . Collins, you and Long were with 'im when he was caught, that means the three of you were partners, . . . it also means you know where he's going! . . . Now, . . . before I ask you, and you lie to me, consider this! . . . McCreedy's down there somewhere, and Childers is gone. They're gonna find each other before daylight, and then they're gonna leave together, and without a thought in their minds about you!"

"Collateral damage, I think is what they call it, and that's all you are to 'em. They'll be free, while you hang! . . . If that's okay with you, don't answer my questions, . . . but I think you know th' alternative!"

"I ain't got time for any games, here . . . . Mister Collins, Long, . . . what's McCreedy after? . . . Come on, you don't owe Ben Childers a damn thing now, he fed you both to th' wolves, what's he after?"

Collins looked at Long and nodded. "Fifty thousand dollars." Said Long.

"I figured that, . . . tell me about it."

"McCreedy came to us four months ago," Said Collins. "Had a plan to rob the Reserve Bank in Memphis, Tennessee. Said he needed six men to pull it off, and he only had three . . . . Ben liked the idea, and we joined up, got away with that much."

"We thought we got away clean, once we crossed into Arkansas." Added Long. "We was stopped, and countin' the money, when Lionel spotted the Cavalry on our tail. Ben put the money away, and we all ran . . . . We thought we'd shook 'em just north a Little Rock, but by then, a twenty man posse took in after us . . . . From Little Rock, I guess."

"We thought we'd lost 'em at Saint Jo!" Said Collins. "But they jumped us again, had to go up and over a mountain to save our necks . . . . They kept comin, though."

"What then?" Urged Billy.

"We took th' Van Buren road to just outside a Clarksville, where we stopped again, that's where Ben convinced us all, that if we was goin' to get away at all, we should split up and go separate ways . . . . Said he'd take th' money to Van Buren where he knew folks that would hide him. Said we could all meet there in a month and divide th' money."

"What then?"

"Well," Said Long. "Me and George been a long time with Ben, we knowed 'im well enough not to trust 'im, so we met up, doubled back and followed his trail to the old Van Buren road, . . . used to be the stage route. We followed it to just outside a Coal Hill to the old abandoned stage stop."

"Ben was already in custody when we got there." Said Collins. "But before we could run, another Marshal had us."

"You know th' rest, Marshal" Said Long. "There was no sign of th' money bag anywhere, so we're sure he had time to hide it."

"Coal Hill! . . . That where they'll go?"

"Got a be." Said Collins. "He wouldn't leave that much money to rot."

"Where is this, Coal Hill?"

"South a Clarksville's all we know." Added Collins.

"You goin' after 'im, Marshal?" Queried Long.

"Damn right, I am!"

"Good!" Nodded Long. "We used that old station a time or two to hide out in. That road crosses th' old Clarksville, Waldren road. We used to come to Waldren to hold up stages on that road down yonder."

"They'll be goin' up that Waldren road to Coal Hill, too!" Added Collins.

"Okay, . . . where's this Waldren?"

"Back down on that road, not more than five miles from Y-City."

"Thanks, men . . . . Got anything to add, Wallace?"

"Fuck you, I ain't no rat! . . . Go ahead, shoot my legs, I ain;t sayin' nothin'!"

"Rod?" Said Billy, turning to look at him. "I'd like you to do your best to set aside these two men's sentences. Time in jail ought a be enough."

"Thanks, Marshal." Said Long.

"No, . . . thank you! . . . Best get on back to your places now." He watched them go then looked at Rodney again. "Think you can take 'em th' rest a th' way?"

"You're gonna be facing four gunmen, Billy, you sure you can do this alone?"

They tried to kill ya, Rod, Childers tricked us, I can't let that stand! . . . That's th' way I am."

"But it ain't your way to go lookin' for trouble, . . . I know you that well!"

"Don't want your last job to end in failure, do ya?"

"No, . . . I don't! . . . But I don't want a get you killed, doing it! Connie would kill me twice a day, from now on!"

"Rod, you know I'm goin' after 'em, . . . like you know I have to! . . . Now, come on, let's move your blankets to another tree."

"But, Billy . . . ."

"Rod, Childers made a fool of us! . . . He expected McCreedy would do just what he did, and when he did, he ran! . . . I don't blame 'im for it at all, . . . but it don't sit well with me, so I'm gonna bring 'im back!" Crouching, he moved in to pull the blankets over to the next large tree and spread them.

"Them rocks ought a be good and hot by now, you want a lay down?"

"I'm just a little too shook up to lay down . . . . Why are you really doin' this, Billy, you know Childers is a gunslinger, maybe all of 'em are?"

"And you're afraif one of 'em might be th' one I talked about."

"Ain't it possible?"

"Rod," He breathed deeply. "If I ever do meet my match, and I might never meet 'im, . . . but when I do, I'll take him with me. I'm sure a that!"

"That don't make me feel any better, Billy."

"Me, neither, Rod . . . . Truth is, I'm scared to death, I might not be goin' back with ya. Not goin' home is th' worst thing could happen to a man. Nothin' in th' world means more to me."

"Then why?"

"Promise, I made to myself, and it's private!"

"Okay, Billy, . . . when ya leavin'?"

"Once we hit bottom."

"What about McCreedy?"

"Him and Childers will find each other by mornin', they'll light out to find that money . . . . That's all McCreedy wanted."

"HELLO, th' camp!" Came a loud voice from the darkness of the trees, causing Billy to whirl, gun in hand to see the man walk out into the firelight.

"Put your gun away, son, I'm not armed!"

The man was of medium height, a friendly face under a brimless cap, and a full mustache under a flaring nose. He wore a blue shirt, and cotton pants held up by red suspenders, the pant-legs were stuffed into the tops of high-topped workmen's shoes.

Billy holstered the gun as he appraised him.

"Name's Packard Sweeney, point man for a logging company working this area." He shook hands with Billy, and as he shook Rodney's, noticed the hurt arm. "I heard all the shooring up here, that's why I came to check on it . . . . Wouldn't have paid any attention, but the shots were so close together, I knew it wasn't a hunter."

"I'm United States Marshal, Rodney Taylor, Mister Sweeney, this is my deputy, Billy Upshur. What you heard, was men trying to take our prisoners from us."

"They shot at you, huh? . . . I heard that loud rifle shot, just before the pistol shots."

"What are you doin' up here, Mister Sweeney?" Asked Billy.

"I was marking trees to be cut, or rather thinned out . . . . Got a crew working down below us, or will be by tomorrow . . . . What happened to your arm, Marshal?"

"Fell off a cliff yesterday . . . . You say loggers will be workin' down there?"

"Have been for several months now, cleared a fair swath west, and a little north of here. My wagon is down there on the North slope."

"That mean, there's a road down there?" Asked Billy'

"Graded it ourselves." He nodded. "We haul logs on it all the way to Fort Smith every day."

"Your way's all laid out for ya, Rod!"

"Looks like it." He nodded.

"There an easy way to a town called Waldren?" Queried Billy.

"Road goes there, too, Waldren, all the way to Clarksville, and west, all the way to the Cherokee Nation . . . . If you men don't mind, I'd like to stay here tonight, too touchy up here in the dark. I left my back-pack out there a ways, didn't know who you might be, got some coffee in it, pot and all." He looked at the prisoners then. "Got a couple a sandwiches, not enough to go around though."

"Coffee's plenty for us, it's been a few days." Said Rodney. "We're out of everything, been eating berries."

"Well, I'll fix us all a bait when we get to th' wagon . . . . I was on my way back when I heard the shooting."

*   *   *

"What do ya think, Ed?" Asked Ellis.

"Think they're still up there?"

"Fire's still lit, they're up there, likely sleepin' like babies."

"Well, it's got a be midnight, or after."

"More like one or two . . . . Why don't you do like Joe, Morgan, get some sleep?"

"What about you?"

"Me, . . . I'm hopin' one of 'em gets brave enough to look over that rim again. I want another chance at th' fu . . . ."

"McCreeeedy!" Came the distant voice, barely audible in the forest of trees. "Edddd McCreeeeedy!" Came the voice again.

"Who th' hell is that, Ed?"

"Could it be?" Grinned McCreedy.

"Could it be what?"

"Wake Joe up, Morgan, we're goin' down to th' horses."

It took a half hour for them to descend the brush and tree covered hill, and when they got to the horses, he took both their arms in his hands.

"That was Ben Childers voice we heard, Ed . . . . Somehow, he managed to escape from th' lawmen up there, likely during all that shooting! . . . Now, when he gets here, we treat him like a long-lost brother, all th' way to that money! . . . Like nothin' ever happened, okay? . . . After all, he's gonna be history!"

"Eddd McCreeeedy!" Came the voice again, much closer this time.

"Who's out there?" Asked McCreedy loudly.

"It's me, Ed, Ben Childers, where th' hell are ya?"

"Just keep coming like you are, Ben, . . . How'd you get away?"

"Slipped away when th' shootin' started! . . . Where are ya, man, I can't see a damn thing?"

"You're almost here, Ben, we can see you . . . . Straight ahead now."

McCreedy came down to meet him then, and grabbed for his hand. "What th' fuck is all this, Ben?"

"Last I, . . . last I heard," He gasped, catching his breath. "It's called chains, Ed. I can't move my hands more than a few inches . . . . I'm bleedin' all over, too. I've been stabbed by dead wood, scraped by six inch thorns, legs gouged by, I don't know what?"

"Come on up and sit down, man, we cleared a spot up here."

Thanks for comin' after me, Ed, . . . and for firing that shot!"

He helped Childers up and into the area with the horses, and then helped him to sit down.

"When he returned your fire, I rolled back into th' trees and ran."

"Did I hit anything, Ben?"

"Does a tree count? . . . Naw, he laid down as you pulled the trigger."

"What about Wallace, and your boys?"

"Fuck 'em, Ed! . . . You and me, these boys here, we're gonna go get our money, and kiss this fuckin' state goodbye!"

"That's what I wanted to hear, Ben."

"But first." He panted. "We'll pay a visit to a blacksmith over in Waldren, get these fuckin' chains off! . . . Got any water, Ed?"

"Get 'im a canteen, Haskell."

"Haskell, . . . who's Haskell?"

"Another man, we picked up, he's an Indian, kept us on your trail all this time."

"Yeah? . . . Many thanks, Haskell."

"You really got any use for Wallace?"

"Name's Joe." He said, giving him the water.

"Thanks, Joe . . . . Ed, do ya mind, . . . I can't raise this thing."

McCreedy helped him drink then gave it back to Haskell. "You sure about leavin' Collins and Long behind?"

"You got any use for Wallace?"

"Point taken, . . . enough said! . . . They look for ya any, up there?"

"One of 'em did, gunslinger name a Bill Upshur, . . . wears a Marshal's badge now. That's all I know about 'im, but he's a dangerous man."

"Yeah, I'd say he is, he introduced his self to Morgan last night, fucker can use a hand gun, six rounds all around us, two where we was hiding, and from three hundred yards up!"

"You get hit, Morgan?"

"Brought a little blood, Ben, that's all."

"Tell me, Ben, . . . I know we went through this Waldren, but exactly where is it from here?"

"Straight East from us, no more than five miles! . . . We'll go northeast on that cross road there, all th' way to our money! . . . You saw th' road when we came through."

"We're from Tennessee, Remember. I wouldn't know Waldren from any other town." Chuckled McCreedy.

"No matter, Ed . . . . Tennessee's gonna have a new resident, once we get that money, cause I'm going back with ya, not to Memphis, though! . . . Anyway, Arkansas's too damn hot for me!"

"All right, Ben, . . . but how do you know that Marshal won't come all th' way down here lookin' for ya?"

"It was daylight, I think he would . . . . Naw, I heard 'im turn back."

"What about tomorrow, th' day after?"

"They'll be lookin' for me from now on, Ed . . . . But as far as these two, I doubt it! . . . Parker pulled 'em out a th' Nations to bring us back!"

"They might, Ben." Said Ellis. "If they know where we're goin."

"You're thinking George, Or Phil might talk, ain't ya? . . . They won't, them old boys will go to the gallows thinking; I'm gonna spring 'em at th' last minute! You gonna worry about somebody talking, My money's on Lionel, he's a loud-mouth."

"Lionel's a fuckin' pain in th' ass." SAaid McCreedy. "But he on't say anything . . . . Besides, he don't know anything! . . . We won't miss 'im."

"There ya go, Ed! . . . We'll have that money and gone before they ever get to Fort Smith with those boys, hell, it's forty miles from here!"

"Good enough, Ben! . . . Why don't you get some rest now, I'll wake you at dawn."

*   *   *

It took almost three hours to transcend the north slope, with Mister Sweeney riding Childers' horse behind Rodney. Being cautious, Rodney stopped the horses at an open area before reaching the bottom, and level ground again., automatically bracing himself for a bullet that didn't come, then urged the animals across it.

"You can see my wagon there in the trees." Said Sweeney.

Nodding, Rodney reined the horses toward it to stop in the shde and dismount.

"My home away from home!" Said Sweeney as he unloaded his backpack. "If one you can start a cook fire, I'll whip up some ham and eggs for everybody."

"Don't have to ask us twice." Said Billy. "Rod, you sit down somewhere while I untie th' boys' feet, they can tote in th' firewood, and you can watch 'em."

Twenty minutes later, they were wolfing down day old biscuits, fried eggs and thick slices of jerked ham, along with more fresh coffee.

"Mister Packard Sweeney." Sighed Billy. "I am damn glad to have met you!"

"You are very welcome, Marshal, but tell me, what happened to the men that were shooting at you, you never said?"

"Oh, they got what they came for." Said Rodney. "That man escaped during the shooting."

"Sorry to hear that." He said then looked at Billy. "And you are going after him?"

"Just as soon as I find that road to Waldren." Nodded Billy. "Will Rod have any trouble getting' to Fort Smith from here?"

"Straight shot from here. Only traffic you might see will be folks coming in from the Cherokee Nation. Other than that, nobody used it but th' loggers. Today is Wednesday, empty wagons be coming back today sometime, you;ll meet 'em."

"How far is that road, Packard?" Asked Billy.

"No more than two miles, our road starts in the trees behind us, a couple gundred yards . . . . Goes on South to where the trees are being harvested. Be cutting some off this mountain in a couple a weeks."

He looked at Rodney then. "Might I take a look at your shoulder before you go, Marshal, I'm also the M.D., and vet for the outfit."

"I'd sure appreciate that." Said Rodney, getting up to remove the sling, and almost crying out in pain as he lowered the aem to his side. Billy helped him off with the shirt, and had to step back. The entire shoulder, and upper arm was solid mixture of dark nlues, purples and red colors, . . . and it was swollen badly.

"Good Lord, Son, . . . how far did you fall?"

"Don't know, maybe fifteen feet . . . . A sapling stopped th' fall! . . . I hit on my back and shoulder."

"I'll say you did!" He said, walking around to look at his back. "What did you do for it?"

"He had hard chills that night." Said Billy. "I used hot rocks under his blanket till they passed."

"Any fever?"

"No fever."

"Worse thing you can do for swelling, is using heat, course with chills, you had no choice . . . . Afraid I can't feel for any broken bones, swollen that way. But what I can do, is give you some laudanum for the pain, take a swallow when you need it." He grabbed a large bottle from a shelf and poured a smaller one full from it. "A swallow now will help, put it in your pocket." He took another bottle down then, and opened it.

"Horse leniment?" Grimaced Rodney.

"Best thing for your sprains and sore limbs." He rubbed Rodney's back and shoulder first then the arm wit it. "You can put your shirt on now."

His arm back in the sling, and the prisoners in the saddle, they said their goodbyes and headed off into the trees, and the road beyond.

*　　　　　　*　　　　　　*

"All right!" Said McCreedy loudly, grunting to his feet. "Time to go, Morgan, Joe . . . . Come on, Ben!"

"Owww, shit, Ed! . . . I'm sore all over, man."

"You look like shit, too!"

"God damn, Ben!" Exclaimed Ellis. "What did that bobcat look like?"

"Is it that bad?" He asked, letting McCreedy help him to his feet.

"It's worse!" He said, and went to his horse to tighten the cinches. "Ben will be ridin' double with you, Morgan." He said, turning to look at him. "At least till we get to that blacksmith . . . . Joe, you lead out again, we're goin' East." He led his horse past them, and down off the higher ground, mounted and waited for them. "I'll take th' rear, Morgan, just follow Joe."

They filed back into the trees then, and began the arduous trip back toward the Fort Smith road, and the town of Waldren.

*   *   *

Rodney tried holding the horses to a trot along the grass-covered road, but could not because of the jarring pace, and slowed to a fast walk instead.

Billy followed them while trying to put himself in McCreedy's shoes. He had no doubt that Childers was now with them, would have likely made it down to that small hill by, maybe two o'clock, he thought. They would sleep till first light before heading for Waldren, which was maybe five miles away.

Childers had chains on him, his first stop would be a blacksmith, he decided. From here to waldren, he figured to be maybe five, six hours through the woods, another one to get the chains off. He pulled his watch to look at it. Nine o'clock, he thought, nine-thirty when they reach that Waldren road . . . . He would make Waldren around two o'clock, by riding at a gallop, . . . and McCreedy would have made it by Eleven, maybe twelve, and would be leaving by one o'clock . . . . He would be behind them by an hour, or less, . . . and that's where he wanted to be, close behind them.

Rodney stopped the horses at the crossroad to wait for him.

"You okay, Rod?"

"Yeah, soon as that liniment stops burning! Good thing is, that laudanum works great!" He peered at Billy then. "You don't have to do this, ya know."

"Yeah, I do, Rod. Wouldn't want me to break a promise, would ya?"

"Heaven forbid!"

"It's gonna take you a day or two, having to walk these horses, but you got biscuits and ham enough to get you there. They got a piss, make 'em stand in th' stirrups again . . . . You got a stay in th; saddle, Rod. Don't get off till you get to that courthouse, and get help! . . . . And get to a Doctor damn quick!"

"Billy, I know all that! Don't worry about me, I know my job."

"Yeah, I know ya do, Sorry, Pard . . . . Tell that Judge Parker, I'll be there in a few days with Ben Childers!" He reined his horse around that of Rodney's, and spurred it to a mile-consuming gallop.

*   *   *

'Ten after eleven o'clock', thought McCreedy as they finally rode out of the forest of Pines, and onto one of Waldren's side streets. "Hold up, Joe!" He yelled then rode beside Ellis and Childers. "Ben, you know where we're going, you and Morgan take the lead . . . . Here, he reached back and pulled a shirt from his saddlebag, and draped it across Childers' shackled hands. "You two go on in, . . . where's that blacksmith, Ben?"

"Go left there on Main street, Ed, . . . end a th' street."

"All right, I'll be about a minute or so behind ya, Joe behind me . . . . We're in a hurry, so don't take no lip from that hammer-swinger! . . . Move out."

Once inside the Livery, blacksmith shop, McCreedy dismounted to watch while the Smithy cut through the lock at Childers' waist, and then to finally forge a tool to unlock the spring-loaded wrist-irons.

Childers raised his arms and stretched. "You don't know how good this feels, Ed . . . . Many thanks, Smithy."

"Okay, Smithy." Said McCreedy. "Get over in one a th' stalls there."

"Wh, . . . what you gonna do?"

"Relax, man, we ain't gonna hurt ya none, go on . . . . Morgan, tie and gag him!"

Childers was already putting a saddle on one of the stable horses, when Haskell called out from the doorway. "Rider comin' in."

"Let 'im come in, Joe, . . . stop 'im, and get 'im down."

"Hold it, Mister!" Said Haskell, once the cowboy entered the barn. "Get off th' horse, and nove over to th' stalls."

"What's goin' on here?" He asked, and dismounted. "Where's Swede?"

"Shut up!" Said Childers, coming to unbuckle the man's gunbelt, and buckle it around his own hips. "Come on, man, move to that stall there, . . . got another one for ya, Morgan!"

"And hurry up!" Said McCreedy. "Joe, come help 'im."

"Wait up, Joe!" Said Childers, coming into the stall after them to turn the cowboy around. "Take off your clothes, man!"

"What?" He gasped. "Yo . . . ."

Childers whisked the pistol out in a blur, and had the barrel of it in the cowboy's open mouth. "Got no time to argue, jackass, shed 'em!"

Wide-eyed, the man quickly removed his vest and sweat stained shirt, giving them to Haskell, as Childers pulled the gun away and holstered it.

"Pants, too, come onQ!" He said, and quickly began to undress, while the cowboy sat down on the hay of the stall and removed his boots.

Childers was dressed, and buckling on the gunbelt in a matter of minutes.

"Except for the cat scratches on your face, Ben." Said McCreedy. "You look like your old self again."

Ellis placed the gag in the cowboy's mouth and stood up. "Let's get th' hell out a here, Ed, . . . before more company shows up."

"Joe, Ben." He nodded. "Let's go!"

"Not before I eat somethin'!" Voiced Childers. "Ain't had nothin' but wild berries in three days, I'm starving!"

"We ain't got time for that, Ben!" Argued McCreedy.

"Then we take time, Ed, I'm hungry."

"Somebody's liable to find these men."

"Don't see how, we'll lock th' doors! . . . He's closed for th' day, right?" He grinned then. "Come on, little café just down th' street!"

"Ohhh, God damn it!" Exclaimed McCreedy. "Talk about brazen, . . . But a good steak does sound good! . . . You're on, Ben, come on!"

*   *   *

Billy slowed the heavily breathing horse to a fast walk, and after a look around, checked his watch before reaching down to pat the animal's sweaty neck. "I know it's hot, old girl," He sighed. "But hang with me, I need ya!" High noon, he thought, watching the horse's bobbing head. He knew McCreedy and Childers were close, if not in Waldren already, and could already be on their way. He reached and touched the horse's neck again, still finding it wet, but it's breathing was normal.

He urged the animal back to a fast gallop again, and pulled his hat down on his head, as the hot wind dried his shirt. He let the horse run for the better part of the next hour, only slowing when he saw the buildings of town, . . . and was soon walking the winded animal down the street of Waldren, thinking he had to know for sure they had been here before heading for Coal Hill. The town was some busy, he noticed, and then saw the crowd of men gathered around the Livery doors.

He urged the horse to a trot and stopped beside them. "What's th' ruckus about?" He asked, causing a cowboy to look up at him.

"Don't know, th' doors are locked! . . . Got a man lookin' for Swede to open up."

"He of a habit a doin' this?"

"Hell, no! . . . Never done it before!

"Then ya better get it open!" He said, taking the badge from his shirt pocket and holding it up. "I'm a Federal U. S. Marshal! . . . I'm lookin' for four men, one in chains . . . . If your Mister Swede is th' blacksmith, ya better get it open."

"He's the only one we got!" Said another man. "Think they might a done 'im in?"

"Could be, maybe not, . . . but ya best see about it."

"Yeah." Said the cowboy. "One a you men go for th' Sheriff, Charlie, grab us a crow-bar!"

They had the doors open in short order, and Billy dismounted to follow them inside the strong-smelling structure.

"Over here in th' stall!" Yelled one of the men, and all pushed their way in to untie the two men.

The cowboy was released first, and in nothing but long underwear bottoms, quickly got up to grab Childers' discarded, blood-stained pants and pulled them on while Swede was being released.

Billy watched for a time then spotted the chains in the hay, and picked them up. They were here, he thought, but how long ago? He turned then, as the cowboy came rushing by, and grabbed his arm.

"Hold up a minute!"

"Leave me alone, God damn it!" He tried to jerk away until Billy showed him his badge. "You th' law?"

"Marshal . . . . What happened here?"

"They took everything I had, that's what happened!! . . . Clothes, gun, boots, all but my horse." He nodded at the saddled pony. "Bastard stuck my own gun in my mouth, I had no choice!"

"How long ago?"

"Hell, man, I don't know, . . . hour, maybe two . . . It was a long time! . . . Now, if you're done, I want a go home." He released his arm and watched as he led his horse outside, mount, and leave before turning to look at the four men talk with a burly man in a leather apron. Mister Swede, he thought, then went on out to his horse where he stopped to watch the approach of several fast-walking men as they went inside then mounted to look at his watch again.

Almost two o'clock, he thought, and was putting it away when a man came out of the stable along with the one called Swede.

"He ain't one of 'em, is he?" He asked, looking up at Billy.

"I told you they was gone, been gone two hours now!"

"All right, Swede, okay! . . . Who are you?" He asked, looking up at Billy.

"Federal Marshal." He said, showing the badge. "I trailed four men here, Sheriff, one in chains . . . . Found th' chains on th' floor in there."

"Could be th' same four!" He said, in thought.

"Same four, Sheriff?"

"Huh? . . . Oh, yeah. About an hour ago, a little less, four rough-lookin' men had a meal at th' café, and left without payin' for it!"

"Sounds like 'em."

"I'm Sheriff Raven, Carl Raven." He reached up to shake Billy's hand. "Who are they anyway?"

"Ben Childers, Ed McCreedy, Morgan Ellis, and an Indian."

"It was them, all right. One of 'em was an Indian . . . . I remember getting' a wire on 'em, I think, too!"

Nodding, He reined the horse around, and galloped back to the Clarksville road, and turned up it at a run.

*   *   *

The horses were beginning to lather up when McCreedy looked back to see that Haskell had stopped, and was walking his, and yelled for Childers to stop. He pulled alongside of him then.

"What is it, Ed, we got a move?"

"Won't go far without a horse, Ben."

"What th' fuck sre you talkin' about!"

"One thing I learned riding with Joe, back there, is that when a horse lathers up this way, we rest 'em, or we'll be walkin' pretty damn quick!"

Childers looked down at his horse's neck then heard it's hard breathing, . . . and nodded. "Okay, . . . we cook 'em off a bit."

"You was flogging this animal like th' Devil was after us, Ben!"

"You could be right, Ed, . . . I ain't discounting th' fact that deputy weren't a Marshal at all, maybe just lending a hand to a friend, or something . . . . But he is a gunslinger, good one, too, I think."

"And you think he'll be comin' after us, that it?"

"I think he already is, Ed . . . . I bested 'im, by getting' away from 'em! . . . That won't set well with a man like him . . . . Wouldn't with me, neither."

"I wouldn't worry about 'im, we're twenty miles ahead of 'im now. Relax, there's four of us, and besides." He said, reaching down to pat the gun scabbard. "I'm a damn good shot with this thing, spot 'im a mile away with that long scope."

"You missed last night, Ed."

"None a my doin', he ducked, won't happen again! . . . And stop trying to make me mad, we did what we set out to do, and so did you. You got away and in essence, we saved you from the hangman."

"I'm damn grateful, too, Ed, believe me."

"Hell, I know that, Ben . . . . How far is it to where we're goin'?"

"Don't know, . . . but it's got a be eighty, ninety miles tp Coal Hill."

"Coal Hill? . . . That where you hid th' money?"

Childers looked at him and grinned. "There abouts, yeah."

"There abouts?" . . . It's our money, too, Ben, we all stole it, remember? . . . So why th' secrecy?"

"Come on, Ed . . . . Think I don't know, you thought I was keepin' th' money for myself? . . . I was a wanted man here, it was only a matter of time . . . . We couldn't shake that posse by staying together, and I knew a good hiding place! . . . It was just bad luck, my running into those Marshals! He grinned at McCreedy then.

"Surprised hell out a me, seeing you show up at that prison to see me. No way, I thought your plan would work! . . . Didn't think you'd break all three of us out, when it did! . . . Never seen a man could plan a job, like you do, Ed . . . . The money's still there, all of it!"

"I'm speechless, Ben, you flatter me."

"Yeah, but don't forget, I know you're also a thief with an enormous ego! . . . I know you, Ed . . . . We're gonna be partners for a long time, so don't try to con me anymore, okay?"

"My apologies, Ben."

"Accepted . . . . Now, let's go!" He spurred his horse to a gallop again.

McCreedy waved Ellis and Haskell on then followed Childers at a run.

CHAPTER FIFTEEN

Isaac Parker opened the door to his office as he removed his robe, and used a hangar before hanging it on the rack, and going to his desk to pick up the two wires, walked to the window to peer out at the mid-afternoon street traffic, . . . another every day sight for him as he had not yet gotten over the failure of losing the condemned prisoners.

He reread the wire from Shreveport then the one from DeQueen, and once again, his brow wrinkled with worry. In all his tenure as Judge, it had never happened before and in his mind, was a black mark that would always accompany his name. One of the men on the long porch saw him and waved a hello. He nodded, and straightened just as the office door opened.

"Mome in, Marshal."

"You need to come outside, sir, . . . something you need to see."

Curious, he followed him out, and then to the porch to watch the approaching horse and riders, . . . and when they got closer, he recognized Rodney's slumped-over figure and quickly jumped the three feet to the ground, and ran to meet him. He reached up as Rodney slumped even further, and caught him as he fell from the saddle.

"Give me a hand, you people!" He yelled, and as they rushed in to take his limp body from him. "Take him to the hospital! . . . Marshal," He said, turning back. "Get some help, get them prisoners down and get them looked at!" He followed the men who were carrying Rodney then looked back. "And see to them animals!" He yelled.

He pushed through the throng of onlookers, and entered the hospital corridor in time to see interns rushing Rodney into the examination room, and when the door was slammed shut, turned back in time to see several men ushering in the prisoners where another Doctor took charge.

"He work for ya, Judge?" Asked the Marshal as he came to stand with him.

"I don't think I know 'im."

"He works for us, Jason, not me!" He said, looking back at the door. "Marshal Taylor works the Indian Territory."

"Oh, yeah, . . . the one bringin' in Ben Childers?"

"That's him."

"Well, Ben Childers ain't with 'em, Judge . . . . Got the other two, but no Childers . . . . Don't know th' third man."

"That's Lionel Wallace." He said. "One of the men that abetted Childers' escape."

"From the looks of 'im, he must a had a hell of a time out there!"

"No doubt, Jason, . . . but he brought three of them in, and almost died doing it!"

"Yes, sir, over tqo hundred miles by horseback . . . . I'd sure like to know what happened in between?" The door opened then, and a nurse came out in a hurry. "Tell me something, Ruby!" He said, stopping her. "How is he?"

"He's only been in there five minutes, Judge. He's being cleaned up and undressed now. The Doctor will be out when he examines him, . . . now excuse me, I have to send for some ice."

"Ice?" He watched her leave. "Jason, . . . go tell the Bailiff to cancel court for this afternoon. When you get back, you can stand by and take charge of the prisoners."

"Yes, sir! . . . But where'll you be, Judge?"

"Right here!"

*   *   *

"This is the third day without any rest, Ben." Said an exhausted McCreedy as they walked the animals again. "Where th' hell is this Coal Hill, anyway?"

"We've come close to eighty miles, Ed." He said tiredly. "Can't be more than ten or twelve more . . . . it's on this road, I know that!"

"We can't go any farther without a little sleep, Ben . . . . Any more and we won't be able to function, especially if we run into any trouble."

"I guess you're right, Ed, . . . I'm falling asleep in th' saddle myself . . . . We can pull off in them trees over there, sleep a couple hours." He reined his horse off the road and into the trees.

*   *   *

Having developed a knack, of sorts, for sleeping in the saddle, Billy was jarred awake again when the horse snorted, and looking at his watch, determined he had been dozing for about fifteen minutes this time, and put it away as he spurred the horse to a gallop again along the seldom used road.

Not knowing how far ahead of him they were, was beginning to wear on his nerves. He knew, that if they were too far ahead, they would have the money and be gone by the time he got there, . . . and he'd likely never find them again! No, he thought, he would find them, he had to, . . . and that thought alone made him more determined than ever to find, and return Childers to Fort Smith. He would finish the job assigned to Rodney . . . . His last job as Marshal could not end in failure. Both Ben Childers, and Ed McCreedy took that honor away from them both and then rubbed their noses in it. He could not let that go unaccounted for . . . . It just was not in him!

Just how far was this Coal Hill, he wondered? Two nights, and almost three days of napping in the saddle, and he had not met another soul on this road. All he knew for certain, was their destination and as yet, had not seen a marker with Coal Hill on it. He could only assume they had not stopped to rest either, and unless they had learned to sleep in the saddle, had to be about ready to drop from exhaustion. He reached down to pat the horse's sweaty neck in reassurance.

Rodney was sure to be in Fort Smith by now, he thought, but he was worried that he might be hurt more than he let on, and that being the case, he may not be there. If he fell from the saddle for any reason, Wallace, and the other men would eventually find a way to get free, . . . and Rodney had the key to their chains. His entire last job would end in total failure, . . . and all because he didn't stay with him! . . . Hell of a time to think about that, he thought drearily. No, he decided, he knew Rodney well enough to know he would make it to Fort Smith. One way or another, he would get there!

*   *   *

Childers woke with a start to rub at his badly matted eyes then looked at McCreedy, thinking that the last thing he wanted to do was share that money with them. But, he knew he had no choice now, so he shook his head and slapped at him with his hat, to wake him.

"Time to go, Ed, wake th' boys." He got up, tightened his horse's cinches, and mounted as they got to their feet. He sat and studied the surrounding trees while they made their animals ready and mounted up, and then headed out to the road again with them on his heels, . . . and had one of them bothered to look behind them, they'd have seen the lone horse and rider almost a mile away.

Coal Hill, once a thriving town on the old Van Buren stage route, was now only a community of close to fifty residents. Childers slowed to a walk again as they neared the crossroad, and then turned west to gallop the animals again for yet another half-mile before he stopped to look the old way-station over.

"That it, Ben?" Asked McCreedy at his side.

"That's it." He nodded. "Me, and th' boys hid out here a few times."

"Why are we stopped?"

"I didn'y, th' last time, and got caught! . . . This time, I'm gonna be sure . . . . Why don't you send your Indian off to the knoll on th' North there, . . . he can keep watch!"

McCreedy reined his horse back to give the order then came back as Haskell galloped off into the brush.

Childers watched him until he dismounted and climbed up the slight rise, and then walked his horse the last hundred yards to the abandoned building, where they all dismounted.

"What now, Ben, . . . where is it?"

"Under a loose floorboard, stay here and I'll get it! . . . And keep your eyes open!" He was back in a few minutes with the bank-bag of monery, only to stop short at sight of the gun in Ellis's hand.

He peered at McCreedy then, and shrugged. "Guess I should have expected this, Ed, . . . but I didn't, my mistake! . . . You gonna kill me right here, sound will carry a long way?"

"Drop th' bag on th' porch, Ben, gunbelt, too." He pulled his own gun then and cocked it. "Be careful doing it, Ben, I know how fast you are." Childers did as he was told, and then was ordered to sit down against the wall.

McCreedy sat down on the porch and opened the bag.

"Watch 'im, Morgan, while I count out th' money."

"You gonna divide it here, Ed?" Asked Childers. "Bein' sort a gutsy, ain't it, never know who's close by to see ya."

"Joe'll tell us, if they are, shut up, Ben!" He placed the paper bills in eight large stacks on the porch before standing up and taking two of them to his saddlebags and putting the money inside. He pulled his gun and came back. "Your turn, Morgan, two stacks."

"Leave it alone!" Said Billy, stepping out from behind a nearby Pine, his voice causing McCreedy to freeze, his gun already cocked to fire, and Ellis, already half-squatting, gun in holster as he was about to pick up his money.

"Mister McCreedy!" You move that pistol another inch, I'll blow your arm off! . . . And you!" He said to Ellis. "If you ain't takin' a shit, get up and grab your hat-brim with both hands." And once he complied. "Move out away from th' porch."

"Hi, ya, Bill!" Grinned Childers. "Where th' hell did you come from?"

"You knew I'd come for ya, Ben." He looked at McCreedy then. "Put that gun in th' holster!" He said, and motioned with the pistol as McCreedy did as he was told. "Now, grab that hat-brim, and hold on to it! . . . Both of ya back out into th' yard a ways." He watched as they moved aside then nodded. "That ought a do it."

"Put th' money back in that bag, Ben." When Childers scooted forward, he encountered his fallen pistol, and stared down at it.

"Don't even think about th' gun, Ben!"

"I ain't no fool, Bill." He grinned, and then put the money back into the bag. "What now?"

"Get the money from McCreedy's horse, and put it back."

"What are you gonna do here, Marshal?" Queried McCreedy. "You let us keep our guns, so what's on your mind here?"

He watched as Childers replaced the money and then stood up again. "Okay, Mister Ben Calico Childers, . . . pick up your gun and holster it, . . . slowly."

"Bill, if you're out to do what I think you are, you're about to shatter my high esteem of you."

"Well, Ben, . . . th' Marshal and me went through a lot bringin' you in, . . . all that wasted time, and effort tryin' to keep Mister McCreedy there from catchin' up to us . . . . Th' loss of sleep, goin' hungry! . . . And then to have you slip away like a thief in th' dark! . . . It all comes down to this! . . . You stole something from th' Marshal and me, what, I don't exactly know, or maybe I just don't know how to put it in words, whatever! . . . I do know that you all were laughing at us, because you put one over on us, or thought you had . . . . But, to sum it up, you took somethin' of ours, . . . and one a my rules is, that nobody does that. I won't allow it! . . . Grab your hat-brim, Ben."

"You told Rodney, you could beat me with a gun, Ben." He looked at McCreedy then. "You, sir, tried to murder my friend, like a coward would, from a safe distance." He shook his head. "You'll have to pay for that! . . . And you, Mister Ellis, are just guilty by association . . . . I have no idea where your Indian friend is, and I know you won't tell me, so, . . . I'll have to attend to him later." He holstered his pistol then, and dropped his hand at his side.

"Money's on th' porch, gents . . . . It's all yours, if you can keep it!

All three of them went for their guns at once, and the stillness erupted in thunderous gunfire, as Billy drew and fired. Childers had only cleared the holster when his gun arm was shattered, knocking him to his back in the dirt. McCreedy's gun was coming up when Billy's bullet struck his shoulder, causing the gun to fly from his hand as he also was thrown backward'

Fanning the pistol quickly, He shot Ellis in the gun arm before he could pull the trigger, sprawling him in a heap atop the cursing McCreedy. They all three sat up in the dirt and grabbed their bleeding wounds as they glared hatefully at him in their pain. He holstered the gun, and went to squat in front of them.

"Guess all that money belongs to me now." He grinned.

"You fucking Bastard!" Growled McCreedy.

"Watch it now!" He grinned. "I had a mother and Father! . . . But while we're talkin', where's that Indian that's been readin' our trail?"

"He's got a bead on your ass right now, Gunfighter!"

"Don't worry about this one!" Came a sudden, loud voice from the trees.

Sudden fear, and panic overwhelmed him on hearing the strange voice, his gun came out in a blur as he twisted his body in position to fire, . . . but sight of the horseman's raised hands caused him to hold his fire

"Is this th' man you're lookin' for?" He spurred his horse forward, forcing Haskell to move out into the yard with his hands raised. "I found him on that knoll behind th' house." He said loudly. "Figured he was th' lookout." He moved his hands farther away from his body as he spoke.

"You can put th' gun away, friend." He said then. "If I was gonna kill ya, I could a done it already, we watched th' whole thing from th' trees back there . . . . I'm not an outlaw, thief neither, so please, lower that hammer, it makes me nervous?"

"Then, why th' mask?" Queried Billy, getting to his feet.

He shrugged. "Thought, by chance, you might know me, . . . it's sort of a trademark!"

"Why are you here, what brought ya?"

"Few weeks back, I saw six men, and a posse come over Wakefield Mountain. Them three there, was part a th' six . . . . I was curious, so I followed them, when they split up, that one by th' porch came here."

"You see 'im caught?"

"Too far away, I went back! . . . It's a long story, and not very relevant." He used a raised hand to motion with his finger. "Th' gun, please . . . . I ain't about to draw on ya, friend, I watched you handle that thing."

Billy holstered the pistol, and watched as the man lowered his arms. "Thanks for bringin' 'im in."

"Por nada." He said, folding his hands on the saddle horn. "Are you th' law, or just another gunman lookin' for loot?" And when Billy stiffened. "I'm only askin', my friend, . . . meant nothing buy it."

"Deputy U. S. Marshal, from out a th' Nations . . . . I'm takin' these men back to Fort Smith . . . . Now, who are you?"

"Folks in the Ozarks call me, Guardian." He straightened in the saddle then. "I'm gonna toss you this man's gun." He arced it through the air, to land almost at Billy's feet. "And now, if you don't mind, I'm a long way from home." He nodded, and then reined the gray horse out of the trees and into the road, . . . and just as quickly rode off in the direction of Coal Hill

He watched him leave, and was still wondering what his motives were. He was a gunman, he felt that the second he saw him. Whoever he was, he was a strange man, he thought, then looked at Haskell's unkempt appearance. 'Definitely a Choctaw Indian', he thought. "You th' tracker for this bunch?"

"Yeah," He nodded. "I followed you."

"Your name Joe Haskell?" And when he nodded. "Come on over here, Mister Haskell, you got some wounds to dress." He looked at the wounded then. "And you three sit still while he does it!" . . . Come on, Haskell, move it, bullets all went clean through! . . . That your horse, that fella led in?"

"It's my horse." He said, going to his knees in the dirt beside McCreedy. "I need to use my knife." He touched McCreedy's shirt. "I have to cut away the sleeve."

"Make sure that's all you do!" He watched Haskell as he worked to slit the sleeve up almost to the neck, revealing the shoulder wound. "Go ahead and cut the other sleeves, Mister Haskell, then build a fire, you can use that knife to seal th' wounds."

He looked at Childers then as he went to the porch and sat down. "Got anything to say, Ben?"

"You should a killed me, Bill, . . . I don't like hangings."

"Then what you should a done, was not commit a crime! . . . I ain't much on killin' a man, Ben, . . . robs 'im of his life!. Besides, th' warrant said alive . . . . Wouldn't want a cheat th' hangman."

"It ain't natural th' way you handle a gun . . . . Thought you was bragging when ya told me."

"You ain't th' first, to think that!"

"So th' Marshal said, . . . I didn't believe him, neither!"

"Hold still, Ben." Said Haskell as he slit the sleeve, and then looked up at Billy. "I start th' fire now?"

"Go ahead." He nodded then looked back at Childers. "You ever see that masked man before?"

"No, not up close! . . . Saw that gray horse in th' mountains, though. He was a long ways off, just sittin' and watchin' . . . . Why, you ever seen 'im?"

"Nope, . . . sure knows how to sneak up on a man, though."

"Who th' hell, are you, Bill, . . . what's your whole name?"

"William Otis Upshur, Mister Childers . . . . And you never heard of me!"

"No, . . . I guess not! . . . Should have, man with your speed." He peered at him then. "How'd you know where we went, who told ya, Collins, or Long?"

"Both! . . . They knew you fed 'em to th' wolves."

"You'd think a man would know them he rides with!"

"They knew you well enough!" He looked at Ellis then, who had been glaring at him since the time he was shot. "You got somethin' to say, Slim?"

"I'm gonna fuckin' kill you, I ever get out a this!"

"If looks could kill, I'd already be dead . . . . You had a fair shot at me, Mister Ellis, the only one you'll ever get, so save your strength, got a long ride ahead of us."

"Fire's ready." Said Haskell.

"You're an Indian, Mister Haskell, you know what to do now."

Nodding, Haskell inserted the knife in the fire, and waited while the blade became red hot.

"All right, Gents." Said Billy, getting to his feet. "He's gonna close them wounds for ya, and then we're leavin'. Got a long ride ahead, and I don't want you bleeding to death on th' way, so hold still for it."

Less than an hour later, Haskell had the three men bandaged and roped to their saddles per Billy's instructions, and after retrieving his horse, took the tow rope in hand and walked with Billy into the trees to retrieve his before returning to the road.

"Mount up, Haskell." He watched him mount up and settled, then went to mount his own and pull up beside him. "Got one question for ya, man . . . . Before tyin' up with these men, you ever rob any banks, or kill anybody?"

"Many years ago, I killed, but not since, . . . no banks either."

"Then tie that rope on your saddle and lead out, I'll bring up th' rear."

"You ain't gonna tie me up?"

"You ain't on my warrant, Mister Haskell . . . . Far as I know, you're only guilty of trackin' for 'em. You'll likely just get a fine, or a few days in jail, and released . . . . But, you think ya need it, I will tie you up?"

"No, sir, . . . I won't give you any trouble."

"What about their rifles, and mine, you gonna take 'em?"

"They can't get to 'em, and I don't think you want to. Go on, lead out, and we want a save horseflesh, so a good lope is good enough!" Nodding, Haskell led them off at a steady lope, as Billy took his place behind them.

*   *   *

Isaac Parker got up from the bench, as the Doctor shook him. "How is he, Lester?"

"Have you been here all this time, Isaac?"

"That's my Marshal in there, Lester, one of the best I have . . . . Where else would I be? . . . How is he?"

"He'll recover just fine, Isaac. The ice brought down the swelling in his shoulder and arm. Never seen a man bruised that bad before. Anyway, I couldn't find any broken bones, and there's no way to tell if any are fractured. But if there are, they'll heal in time . . . . Other than that, he's fighting infection, from going too long without treatment, and without rest! . . . Probably hasn't slept in a few days either. He's malnourished, too, so I'm giving him a weakened honey derivative in his veins while he sleeps . . . . Now, you know as much as I do!"

"That's a relief, Lester, thank you."

"Any time, Isaac, now go get some sleep, it's past ten o'clock. You can see him tomorrow afternoon."

*　　　*　　　*

Billy found him-self falling asleep in the saddle and decided it best to stop for the night, lest he should lose his prisoners, and urged the horse up beside Haskell.

"Pull into them trees yonder, we'll stop for th' night . . . . Find a place for a fire."

Nodding, Haskell slowed the animals to a walk, as Billy fell into line, and was soon leaving the road and into a grove of Wild Pecan Trees.

"This good enough?" Asked Haskell when he stopped.

"It'll work." He said, and dismounted. "Clear a spot for a fire, I'll get some wood."

Once the fire was going, they both untied the three and helped them from their horse, and then sat them down against the nearby trees.

"There's six, or eight old biscuits and jerked ham in my saddlebags, get it and pass 'em around . . . . Leave th' guns alone, Joe!"

"You don't have to worry about me." He said, going toward Billy's horse.

He didn't know what it was about the Indian, but there was something that made him like him. He also knew that he most likely lied about not killing anyone in a long time, . . . but he could understand that, his life was on the line. He made the mistake of joining forces with McCreedy and now, couldn't find a way out! All of this, he could understand . . . . He also knew that Haskell had, for the most part, given up on the idea of getting out of the situation, and had begun to accept it,

He watched him give out the meager rations, take a sandwich for himself, and then brought the cloth sack to him. Haskell left without a word and went back to sit with the others to eat and stare back at him.

The meal finished, he grunted to his feet and went to retrieve ropes from the horses. Walking over to Haskell, he dropped one in front of him. "Help me tie 'em to these trees, don't leave a knot where they can get to 'em."

They were finishing up when Billy peered at him. "You been lookin' at me kind a funny=like, Joe . . . . Want a tell me why?"

Haskell shrugged then shook his head. "It's just that I think I know you, or maybe I've seen you before . . . . You been to the Choctaw Nation?"

"Been there, live there, Joe."

"Then that's it!" He grinned. "Sure, . . . you're th' Man-with-glass-eyes! . . . That's what them Ghost Indians called you, right?"

"What are you talkin', Joe?" Said Childers. "Ghost Indians?"

Haskell looked down at him and nodded. "Choctaw Indians, from long ago, . . . Ghosts! . . . He was their friend."

"Ghost Indians?" Growled McCreedy. "That's bull shit, Joe! . . . Thought you with better sense."

"Mister McCreedy, you know nothing about this world." Said Haskell. "But, they were real, lived in Devil Mountain!"

"Joe, you're crazy as hell!" Muttered Ellis.

Haskell turned to face Billy then. "Am I crazy, Marshal, . . . you him?"

"I've been called a lot a things, Joe! . . . Now, come on, I have to tie you up, too . . . . And get some sleep, all of ya, we won't be stoppin' again."

CHAPTER SIXTEEN

"Come on in, it's open!" Said Rodney as he ate the steak, and when the door opened, quickly put down the fork. "Come in, Judge." He said, swallowing the half-chewed meat.

"They finally let me in to see you, my man!" He smiled, and came on to sit in the chair by the bed. "How are you, Marshal?"

"Well, other than, I don't remember getting' here, I'm fine! . . . This is my first meal in, I guess three days."

"Fourth day, today, . . . how's the arm, and shoulder? . . . Lester said he had never seen one quite like it."

"He said it would be okay, course, I can't feel th' pain right now, thanks to laudanum . . . . Ahh, Judge, I lost Ben Childers, at least for a few days."

"I know, I saw the extra horse." He nodded. "But, . . . you said, at least for a few days, . . . what does that mean?"

"Means, Billy's bringin' 'im back."

"Well, . . . I was under the impression Childers was dead, the spare horse, and all . . . Does that mean, he escaped?"

"Yes, sir, it does . . . . I'll have a full report for you by tomorrow, if I can get them to bring me pencil and paper?"

"No, no, let's talk about this right now . . . . Who is this, Billy, . . . and please, Marshal, start from the beginning."

For the next fifteen minutes, Parker listened intently to Rodney's rendition of the past ten days, only reaching up to scratch his chin from time to time, and grimacing when told of his near-death fall into the crevice, . . . and when he was done.

"He went after three gunmen, alone, that what you're telling me?"

"Four men, Judge, . . . they had an Indian tracker with 'em."

"Why did he do that, why did you allow him to do that, Marshal, . . . he's a civilian.

241

"No, sir . . . . He's a deputy U. S. Marshal, Judge, I deputized 'im! . . . He's also my best friend in th' world, who refused to let me do this on my own! . . . I told you about Billy Upshur before."

"Yes, I remember, but something like this, . . . he could be killed, he doesn't have the experience! . . . I don't know why he would even consider it on his own?"

"It's his way, Judge! . . . Believe me, you have no idea what's be's capable of, I do! . . . He'll be here in a day or two."

"With Childers?"

"Maybe all of 'em . . . . And Judge, while you're here, I might as well tell you . . . . I'm resigning from bein' Marshal, effective when I leave th' hospital. Somethin' else, too, . . . I'd like your approval to give my badge to Peter Birdsong when I get home. He's better at this job than I am anyway, even Bass Reeves comes to him for help."

"Well, . . . this is a bit much for me to ingest at the moment, Marshal. I'll have to think on it some, . . . I'm sure you understand."

"I do, Judge, I really do! . . . And Judge, in my satchel, on th' floor there, is a letter from Sheriff Lake in Shreveport, and be sure, Sir, I'm here to tell ya, it's all true!" He watched as the Judge found the letter, and put it inside his coat.

"I will read it later."

Could you also do me a favor, sir?"

"You have certainly earned one, what is it?"

"Send a wire to Paris, care a Jim Stockwell. Tell 'im we are fine, and to please get word to our families to that effect. He knows where . . . . I'd rather you didn't mention my bein' hurt, or any of this."

"I will do that today." He nodded and got up. "I will still need that written report, Marshal . . . . And I'll be back to see you tomorrow! Now, finish your cold meal." He grinned and started for the door, then looked back.

"You sure you want to send that wire today, son, or wait until Mister Upshur returns . . . . You know, in case?"

"Send it today, Judge, and thanks."

*   *   *

Billy relieved him-self and remounted to watch as Haskell released Childers and the other two, one at a time, allowing them to do the same, and once they were in the saddle again and secured, nodded at Haskell and watched him mount up again to lead off.

He checked his watch as they galloped away, then put it away, pulled the bandana up over his lower face and followed them. Late afternoon already, he thought, as he caught up. He had once again, been riding drag behind wanted prisoners for longer than he wanted, with nothing but the sounds of shod horses on the dry, hard road, and the groans of abused saddle leather to keep him company, that, and the insistent cawing of the ever-circling crows overhead.

His thoughts had been on Haskell off and on during the day, and even though, he knew the man was far from being an innocent bystander in all this, . . . was likely guilty of far worse crimes than this. Yet, he did not believe that his participation in all this would require that he be hung, . . . not just by association.

Making up his mind, he was thankful when the Indian finally slowed again to rest the animals, . . . and almost sure that Isaac Parker would not hesitate to hang the Choctaw along with the rest of them, he pulled the bandana down and galloped up to walk his horse alongside him. Looking back at McCreedy, just behind Haskell, saw that he was almost asleep in the saddle then studied Haskell's silent profile for a moment.

"What do you think about all this, Joe?"

"All this?" He replied, turning to shrug at him. "Feels like I'm ridin' into th' fires of hell, and can't do nothing about it . . . . Been thinkin' about all the things I done, people I hurt, you know, . . . my family! . . . I ain't never been in a jail more than one night, for bein' drunk! . . . Now, . . . I'm lookin' at prison time, or a hangman's rope! . . . I'm thinkin' I messed up real bad this time, Marshal. I shouldn't have listened to Mister McCreedy."

"You got family here, a wife?"

"I have a woman, in the swamp at Shreveport, but she won't be there now . . . . I took her from her family! . . . She's gone by now."

"What did McCreedy offer ya?"

"A share in that money, more money than I ever heard of . . . . All I had to do, was help them get Childers loose, sounded easy enough!"

"Yeah, but if it sounds easy, Joe, it most times ain't . . . . Joe." He said, shifting his weight in the groaning saddle. "I think there's a lot a things you're guilty of, maybe things you ought a be hung for . . . . But in this, I think you might be a victim of what they call, association! . . . Tell me, Joe." He said quickly. "Can you make out that road marker?"

"It says, Fort Smith, thirty miles."

"Good! . . . You kill anybody in all this?" He asked, looking around at the trees.

"No, never! . . . Marshal, what is this, association? . . . What's it mean?"

"Don't know th' lawful explanation, but, . . . if you're with somebody, and that somebody commits a crime, it makes you as guilty as he is."

"Means I'm a dead man! . . . Damn, I was stupid!"

"Joe, I ain't got a warrant on you, neither does th' Marshal. Your only sin is bein' a victim in all this, and stupid, I guess!" He reached back in the saddlebag for one of the pistols and brought it out.

"We'll be ridin' all night tonight, Joe, and that ought a put us within five miles a Fort Smith come daylight . . . . At first light, I want you to walk th' horses again, and when I come up to join you, like now, . . . I want you to get th' hell out a here! . . . Don't say a word, don't even look at me, just run like hell and don't look back! . . . Because I ain't real sure it's th' right thing to do!"

"What are you sayin', Marshal, that I can go?"

"Unless you don't want to?"

"You just don't know how I want to!"

"Then you'll need this." He slipped him the gun. "When that sun comes up, I never want a see you again, Joe."

"You won't, Marshal, and thank you." He took the gun and stuck it in his belt.

*   *   *

His two day stay in the hospital had him up, and pacing the floor of the small room, which is what he was doing when the Doctor came in.

"Up again, are you?" Queried the smiling Medic,

"I'm ready to get out a here, Doc, I know that!"

"I think so, too. How's that shoulder feel?"

"Hard to tell, ya got it wrapped up so tight, arm against my belly and all, . . . is that necessary?"

"I'm afraid so, for the next few weeks, at least! . . . I'm almost sure you have a few fractured bones in that shoulder area, including your collar bone. They take time to heal . . . . After you've had your lunch, you can go, how's that?"

"Best news I've had in two days, is all!"

"Good, get dressed, but leave that arm under your shirt! . . . I'll be back at twelve-thirty."

Isaac Parker was once again in his office when Doctor, Lester Bigham was shown in by the Court's Marshal on duty.

"Come in, Lester." He said, getting up to shake his hand. "I was just thinking of calling on my Marshal again."

"No need, Isaac, I'm releasing him after lunch. I thought you would like a report on him, in person."

"Of course, Lester, please sit."

Bigham sat down, as did he. "Isaac, your Marshal is in perfect health, except, I'm much afraid for his use of that left arm! . . . I'm not one hundred percent certain, mind you, but I believe major tendons have been damaged, if not severed in that upper arm area, and shoulder. I'm a surgeon, but I have to know what I'm doing when I operate, and I lack the expertise needed to repair that sort of damage, and I can't think of anyone that does, this side of Chicago, Illinois . . . . It's also possible he has hairline fractures of the collar bone, and at least three ribs on the left side."

"He will mend fine! . . . But I'm afraid he will lack full mobility of that arm, unable to raise it as high without pain. He won't be able to lift as much with it, that'll put stress on the damaged tendons, and muscles. He will be in pain from the injury off and on, from now on! . . . And by your standards required for a man to be a U. S. Marshal, Isaac, . . . he no longer qualifies . . . . I'm sorry, Isaac."

"Okay, Lester, thank you. Will you tell him what to expect?"

"Before I release him, yes." He got up then, and left.

'Well', he thought, 'that solved my problem', having had toyed with reasons he could use to keep Rodney from resigning. Now, he wouldn't bother . . . . But he was certain, he would regret losing him! He looked at his pocket watch then, his mind on Billy Upshur, and the man he was expected to bring in, rather, that Taylor expected! . . . He looked up then as Jason opened the door.

"Another Marshal comin' in, Judge, I think! . . . Anyway, he's got three wounded men."

He got up to follow Jason out onto the porch again, and quickly jumped to the ground as Billy stopped at the hitch-rail.

"Billy Upshur?" Asked Parker, looking up at him.

"That's me, if you'd be Judge Parker?"

"I'm Isaac Parker."

"Then, your Ben Childers is behind Mister McCreedy here. Morgan Ellis is behind him . . . . Takes care of your warrant, don't it?"

"And then some, Mister Upshur, . . . and you have my disbelieving thanks, Sir!" He reached up and shook Billy's hand.

"Disbelievin'?" . . . Didn't Rod tell you I'd be here, Judge? . . . He is here, ain't he?"

"He is, and he did tell me! . . . Get down, Billy, you must be dead tired." He turned to his Marshal then. "Jason, see the prisoners to the hospital." He stepped back as Billy dismounted, taking the towrope from his hand, and giving it to Jason.

"Let me take you to the hotel, Billy, . . . get you a hot bath and a good meal?"

"I'll take you up on that, Judge, but I want a see about Rod, first, where is he?"

"The hospital, he'll be released in an hour. Come, I'll walk you over." He ushered Billy across the large, wide and crowded street. "Taylor said you were bringing in four men, an Indian?"

"Joe Haskell, yeah, I was . . . . He managed to escape durin' th' night, last night. I couldn't very well go after 'im, with three wounded men on my hands, so I didn't! . . . He weren't on your warrant anyway, and all he did was track us for McCreedy, . . . had no part in th' rest of it. So, I let 'im go. That gonna be a problem?"

"Not today, Billy Upshur!" They shouldered their way to the hospital and went inside. "His room is there." He said, knocking on the door.

"Come on in!" He looked to see Billy, and the Judge come in, and went to meet them, shaking Billy's hand vigorously. "You're damn near late, what kept ya?"

"They didn't want a come!" He grinned, and turned to the Judge then.

"All six of 'em pulled that Reserve Bank job in Memphis, a few months back, Judge, th' money's on my horse, stuffed th' bag in my satchel!"

"Jason will take care of that! . . . Is that what all this was about?"

"Fifty thousand dollars, I'd say that's enough! . . . Childers, McCreedy, and th' rest pulled th' job, and Childers hid it!"

"That reminds me, Sir." Said Rodney. "Collins, and Long were very cooperative the whole way, no trouble at all. Even told Billy where to find them. Anyway, we told them we'd talk to you about changing their conviction to jail time, instead of hanging."

"I'll consider it, no promises, though."

"I forgot to give you this earlier, too." He gave him the requisition.

"Six horses, and rigs? . . . And signed by Colonel Ford."

"You now have all six of 'em, Judge." Said Billy.

"Okay, I'll handle it! . . . Unless you plan on riding them back?"

"No, thanks," Said Billy. "My eye's are on a stage coach, all th' way!"

"That's a big, Amen!" Laughed Rodney.

"Ever hear of a masked man, calls his self, Guardian, Judge?"

"Yes, I have," He nodded. "For several years now. According to my area Marshals, the man has been an asset of sorts, from time to time . . . . He's committed no crime, that anyone has heard of, . . . but no one knows who he is? . . . Where did you see him?"

"Didn't, I met 'im! . . . Brought our Mister Haskell in to me, guess he'd been placed on lookout somewhere. Couldn't see th' man's face, for th' mask, but he seemed a likeable sort."

"And you say, this Mister Haskell escaped last night?"

"Yes, sir, . . . must a had a knife hid on 'im. He was gone this mornin'."

"Okay, . . . Grab your things, Marshal." He said, just as the nurse came in with his food tray. "All right, you stay and eat, the Doctor will need to talk with you before you leave. I'll take Billy to the hotel . . . . You'll both be my guest for one more night."

"Amen to that!"